Also by Barb Han

Marshals of Mesa Point
Ranch Ambush
Bounty Hunted
Captured in West Texas
Escape: Big Bend Canyon

The Cowboys of Cider Creek
Trapped in Texas
Texas Scandal
Trouble in Texas
Murder in Texas

Also by Karen Whiddon

Texas Sheriff's Deadly Mission
Texas Rancher's Hidden Danger
Finding the Rancher's Son
The Spy Switch
Protected by the Texas Rancher
Secret Alaskan Hideaway
Saved by the Texas Cowboy
Missing in Texas
Murder at the Alaskan Lodge

Discover more at millsandboon.co.uk

LONE STAR COUNTRY PROTECTOR

BARB HAN

COLTON ON GUARD

KAREN WHIDDON

MILLS & BOON

First Published in Great Britain 2025
by Mills & Boon, an imprint of HarperCollins*Publishers* Ltd
1 London Bridge Street, London, SE1 9GF

www.harpercollins.co.uk

HarperCollins*Publishers*
Macken House, 39/40 Mayor Street Upper,
Dublin 1, D01 C9W8, Ireland

Special thanks and acknowledgment are given to Karen Whiddon for her contribution to *The Coltons of Alaska* series.

ISBN: 978-0-263-39732-1

1025

MIX
Paper | Supporting
responsible forestry
FSC™ C007454

LONE STAR COUNTRY PROTECTOR

BARB HAN

All my love to Brandon, Jacob and Tori,
my three greatest loves.

To Babe, my hero, for being my best friend,
greatest love and my place to call home.
I love you with everything that I am.

Chapter One

"Good game tonight, buddy," Blakely Adamson said with a smile. Her seven-year-old nephew beamed back at her from the back seat, his excitement barely contained.

"I never did that before," he said of his first goal. He'd been kicking the back of her seat for ten minutes, reenacting the game-winning score. Out of nowhere, his mood shifted, the moment of jubilee darkened and his shoulders rounded as he exhaled.

"What's wrong?" Blakely asked, checking on him through the rearview mirror.

"It didn't feel so good when it made the goalie cry," Chase explained, shaking his head with the most somber expression. He had a sensitive side that restored her hope in humanity. The world needed more Chases.

"Remember how you gave him a hug?" she gently reminded. "And asked him over for a playdate after telling him it's just a game?"

Chase's smile came back. Kids' emotions were a roller coaster, but they were also pure. "That made him happy again."

"Yes, it did," she agreed. To be seven years old again and so innocent, unlike the grownups she sentenced to prison terms because they didn't know how to play nice anymore.

"Games are s'posed to be fun," Chase pointed out as she pulled into her neighborhood. It was dark outside; the season was over now that the final playoff game had been decided.

"I know, buddy," Blakely said. He wasn't wrong.

"I don't want to play soccer again," Chase decided.

"Your mom and dad said it's your decision now that you finished the season," she said as she pulled onto her quiet street in the sleepy suburb just outside of the hustle and bustle of Houston. The peace was one of the things she loved most about this neighborhood. That, and the large shrub-lined front yards.

This was a quiet area. Dog walkers were out in the early mornings, always quick with a wave and a smile as she passed by on her drive to work. She didn't know her neighbors well, but someone always hosted a gathering around the holidays. The moms usually hung together, discussing the local school and teachers while arranging carpools and playdates. The few singles in attendance normally kept close to the food spread or bar setup. Blakely's fraternal twin sister, who also happened to be Chase's mom, would fit right in with the former.

Blakely, on the other hand, would rather nurse a drink while trying to blend in with the wallpaper. She wasn't the social twin. After a long, busy workweek, she much preferred a warm bath, a good book and an even better glass of wine. Unless Chase was sleeping over, like tonight. Then, it was tent forts, Nerf wars and a bone-tired level of exhaustion by the time he finally passed out. As much as she loved having her nephew sleep over, she didn't once dream of becoming a mother. If that made her broken, it was too bad. She had a four-inch scar at her hairline on her forehead to remind her that she didn't do long-term relationships either.

Chase sighed like he'd just been asked to solve the climate crisis. "I know." He sat up even straighter. He'd clearly been contemplating her last statement. "My team needs me."

"I'm sure your friends will understand if you decide not to return," she noted. Her experience with first graders might be limited, but most had the attention span of a gnat, off to the next shiny object in a second without looking back. If they were sad, you knew it. If they were happy, you knew it. She highly doubted any one of them lay awake at night, churning over whether they gave the right answer on a test or the right advice to a buddy, let alone whether their friend stayed on the soccer team.

What would it be like to live in the moment again like kids did so effortlessly?

Blakely couldn't imagine.

A bag of leaves that the landscaper had set out for bulky trash pickup blocked her driveway entrance. Another had been knocked over by the wind, its contents spilled onto the drive. Blakely kept her lights trained on the driveway as she put the gearshift in Park, leaving the engine idling. She'd only be ducking out for a second, so she wasn't worried. Force of habit had her surveying the area anyway.

No movement caught her eye, so she hopped out of the driver's seat, leaving the door wide open in the event she needed to reclaim her seat in a hurry. "Stay here, buddy. I'll be back in a second."

Chase nodded before picking up his Switch and turning his attention to the screen and the Super Mario game whose music she could hum from memory. Needless to say, it was his favorite.

Leaves were strewn in a thick blanket in front of her, but she could deal with that later. Tall trees were one of many things she loved about living here. The HOA rules stated leaves had to be picked up in a timely manner, though her neighbors had never complained about hers to her knowledge.

Blakely bent over to set the bag upright when she glanced back to check on Chase and, once again, scan the area. Her Krav Maga training had taught her to always be observant of her surroundings. But then, so had the reason behind the scar on her forehead.

A split second was all it took for Blakely to pick up the bag to use as a landing for the sharp blade coming at her. A ski-mask-wearing male flew through the air, causing her to scramble backward.

Blakely pushed the bag toward Ski Mask as he slammed into it, thrusting the knife deep into the brown paper. Her headlights practically blinded her as she attempted to twist the heavy bag in order to flip Ski Mask sideways.

The move knocked her off-balance instead as he turned with momentum, pulling her with him. Panic ripped through her. Screaming would only alert Chase, who'd been glued to the screen in the back seat. She could hear the music from his Switch as she landed on her side, her head bouncing on the pavement.

Would Ski Mask run toward Chase if he realized the kid was in the car? Take him?

"What do you want?" Blakely managed to grind out. She couldn't get a good visual on his facial features. With him wearing all black along with a hoodie, she couldn't get a decent physical description either. Could she rip the mask off?

"You!" The voice wasn't familiar, but then it was practically a feral growl. Nothing about it sounded human. That one word spoken directly into her ear sent ripples of fear through her. All hope this was going to be a random mugging vanished. As strange as that may sound, it was better than the alternatives.

Fear that she was about to be killed in front of her nephew—and then what would happen to him?—was a punch to the solar plexus. Like prey in the jaws of an alligator, Blakely drew on all her strength to spin out of Ski Mask's grip.

The move worked, temporarily at least. But Ski Mask reacted with the speed of a cobra strike. In the next second, she was flipped on her back. Ski Mask was on top of her, his thighs pinning her arms to her sides, crushing into her ribs.

In case she lived, she started memorizing details about her assailant. He had to be just shy of six feet tall. Built like an athlete with wide shoulders, straight hips and a slim, muscular figure. Not exactly a body builder, but Ski Mask lifted weights.

The description might not be much, but it was better than nothing.

Blakely bucked her hips, or at least she tried. But Ski Mask was too strong. He drew his arm up. The metal blade glinted in the light from the headlamps. Stabbing someone with a knife was a personal way to kill them. It reeked of hatred and revenge.

With every ounce of strength in her five-foot-seven-inch body, Blakely fought back, convulsing. The move was the equivalent of attempting to break free from a straitjacket. Ski Mask had her locked down and was about to deliver a fatal blow.

"Auntie!" shouted the frightened voice of her nephew.

Ski Mask flinched. He immediately turned toward the noise.

"Run!" Blakely shouted, her heart cracking in half that Chase had to witness his aunt's murder. "Go!"

Except the distraction caused Ski Mask to loosen his grip momentarily. And Blakely seized on the moment.

She bucked and twisted. This time, he flew off. The sound of metal skidding across the pavement meant he'd been disarmed, temporarily at least. The next noise was a guttural groan as she connected her knee to the tender flesh of his inner thigh. Blakely was free from being pinned down.

Popping onto all fours, she scrambled to get out of the attacker's reach a second too late. A hand gripped her ankle with the force of a vise. Blakely bit back a curse as she attempted to kick free.

Another hand came around, squeezing so hard she was shocked her bones didn't shatter. Risking a glance toward the car, a moment of relief washed over her at the sight. It was empty. Chase was gone.

Chase was gone! The reality of her nephew disappearing and the possibility of something else bad happening to him sent white-hot anger roaring through her.

Fighting for her life, she drew all her energy and kicked one of her attacker's hands with her free foot. His grip loosened. But only for a split second. Blakely reached toward the fence, struggling to gain purchase.

Trying to claw away from Ski Mask was futile. His grip wasn't allowing her to go anywhere. She needed to come up with a new plan. *Now.* Before he recovered the knife he was reaching for.

Blakely's leg was like an overstretched rubber band at this point. Rather than resist, she curled her body in a ball the second Ski Mask's attention shifted toward the knife that was inches from his long, outstretched fingers.

Body in a tight circle, she reached for his arm and then dug her fingernails into his wrist. The man hardly flinched, but she wasn't expecting to break free from his grasp. His hands were gloved, and the material from his hoodie kept her from reaching skin. *Or obtaining DNA evidence.* At least the material fibers that were now underneath her fingernails could give investigators something to go on.

Ski Mask's fingers were almost to the knife. Blakely tightened her grasp and then exploded, twisting around once again, scraping the side of her cheek on the pavement.

His grip broke. For a split second, she froze, unable to believe what had just happened. Reality smacked hard. She had to get the hell out of there. After popping up to her feet, she ran as fast as her legs would carry her while screaming one word over and over again…*"Fire!"*

If you wanted help, you had to yell *fire* instead. People were afraid when they heard the word *help*. They hid behind the miniblinds, praying whatever was outside couldn't get them too. They instantly reacted to the word *fire*. They practically ran outside to make sure none of their belongings were in the path. *Help* was useless when you needed it most. The reality of people's survival instincts needing them to stay safe was coded into their DNA.

Half expecting to hear Ski Mask's heavy breathing and footsteps coming up from behind, Blakely pushed her legs until her thighs burned. All those Krav Maga lessons she'd taken over the years had just paid off. The Israel Defense Forces self-defense method was created for dealing with real-life situations, like this. She didn't dare risk glancing backward. A second could give an opponent the advantage.

Porch lights came on one by one as dogs barked over her screams. From the corner of her eye, she saw a front door open.

Blakely cut a sharp left and made a beeline for the opened door, yelling the word repeatedly until she reached the front porch.

Mr. Bowman, a widower, stood there in his slacks and

sweater with his forehead wrinkled in concern. His hands were balled into fists on his hips as he studied her. The fact he didn't look behind her said Ski Mask didn't follow her.

She expected to hear the squeal of tires as the perp stole her car, but that didn't happen either.

"Call 911," she managed to say through heaves to Mr. Bowman as she hopped onto his porch, skipping the stairs altogether. "Tell them Judge Adamson was attacked outside her home and her seven-year-old nephew is missing. I need help *now*."

Without questioning, Mr. Bowman did as instructed, leaving his door open as he disappeared into his house. Blakely turned around once she made it to his door and could slip inside, close the door and lock it behind her at a moment's notice. The yard was large and boxed in by hedges that replaced fencing. With the porch light on, she would be able to see anyone coming before they could get to her. And she couldn't go inside without knowing what happened to Chase.

Heart pounding the inside of her ribcage, she struggled to breathe as she continued scanning the yard. There was no sign of her nephew or the perp. Was Chase hiding? Running? The thought of him alone in the dark, scared, was a knife through her chest. Her doors were always locked, so he couldn't have gone inside her home.

Where did you run off to, buddy?

Sirens split the air before she caught her breath. Help was on the way, but no real relief came. With Chase missing, there was no way she could relax. She had to find her nephew before Ski Mask did, if he hadn't already.

Don't go there. Not even hypothetically. It will literally unhinge you.

Mr. Bowman came up behind her, cutting into her little pep talk.

"Do you have a weapon?" she asked the older gentleman. "Hunting rifle? I'd take anything."

"I'm afraid not," he said as he came up beside her. "The wife, rest her soul, wasn't comfortable keeping one around since the grandkids." He stood next to her. "Is that your car running?"

"Yes," she answered, grabbing at her side in an attempt to soothe the ache. "It is."

"I can walk over there with you, if you'd like," Mr. Bowman offered. "Hold on a second."

He disappeared and then returned a few moments later with a fireplace poker, a baseball bat and a flashlight. He showed her the offerings. Mr. Bowman was a former runner who was in his early seventies. His build was slight, but she'd seen him out in his yard helping the landscaping crew spread mulch in his wife's flower beds—beds that he'd kept going since losing her last year. The thirty-plus-pound bags were no joke to carry. Mr. Bowman would have one in each hand. Meaning, he was strong as an ox. She knew a few details of his life since he'd joined her at the food spread during last year's holiday party.

"I'll take the fireplace poker," she said. "Thank you."

He locked up behind them and pocketed his keys, and then she backtracked toward the car with Mr. Bowman a step behind.

Blakely needed to get to her phone. She had to call her sister immediately to inform her of the situation. *If* Ski Mask left her purse, which she doubted.

She couldn't remember the last time she'd said a prayer… elementary school? But that was exactly what she did as she neared her vehicle. She prayed her nephew would return to the scene unharmed too, figuring it couldn't hurt.

Because kidnapping Chase was another reason Ski Mask might have taken off without pursuing her on foot.

An icy chill gripped her spine.

A marked SUV came roaring up, sirens blaring, along with a fleet vehicle from the Marshals Service. Would her nephew realize it was safe to come out of hiding? If that was the case, and she could only hope it was because the thought of Ski Mask taking Chase…

Blakely involuntarily shivered at the thought.

Chase, buddy, where are you?

Chapter Two

Dalton Remington, US marshal, parked on the tree-lined residential street and shut off his vehicle. He'd recognized Adamson's name the second the assignment to protect the judge came down. He'd almost beat the local cop cruiser to the scene since he'd been outside of her neighborhood having dinner alone on his way home from court.

Houston PD exited his vehicle first. Dalton was only a couple steps behind.

Blakely Adamson was a dead ringer for a young Jessica Biel, bangs included. Except that Blakely was even more beautiful, in his opinion. Seeing her again was a jolt. The last time, they'd been arms and legs in a tangle in the sheets during the best weekend of his life. Until they broke the rule they'd agreed on at the outset: no discussion of personal lives. On Sunday morning, before checkout time at the Galveston house rental, she'd asked what he did for a living over breakfast in bed. She'd joked that he had law-enforcement swagger and then followed up by asking if he was Dallas PD because she thought she saw something of his with the logo in the back seat of his car.

His response had sent the covers flying. He'd never seen someone get out of bed and dress so damn fast a firefighter would be jealous.

Blakely had sped off, and that was it. They hadn't exchanged numbers, so he'd left it at that. Disappointed didn't begin to describe his mood after she'd made a beeline for the door. There were a lot of people who refused to date anyone in law enforcement due to the dangerous nature of the job.

Now, he suspected he knew the reason she'd bolted. It wouldn't be considered professional for a judge to date someone from the US Marshals Service, considering he could be assigned to protect her. Though, she didn't look much like a stuffy judge while wearing form-hugging athletic wear. The purple sports shirt that fit like a second skin and coordinated leggings highlighted a body meant for making love slowly on Sundays and breakfasts in bed. He shelved the thought, considering the feeling wasn't mutual.

The temptation to write down her plate number had been strong as she'd driven away weeks ago. Not now. Dalton had never chased anyone. His pride wouldn't allow him to start anytime soon no matter how deep their connection had been.

So deep she couldn't get away from you fast enough, dude!

Blakely's gaze widened as it settled on his face, but panic seemed to win out.

Scanning the area, Dalton didn't like the judge standing on the sidewalk, exposed. There were too many places for a perp to hide, get off a shot with a rifle.

"Let's move this inside," Dalton said to her. No need for introductions, and there was no time for courtesies while she was in danger.

"No," Blakely quickly countered. "I need to call my sister and search for my nephew."

"That's not a good idea," Dalton stated. "Someone assaulted you, and it's my job to keep you safe, Your Honor."

"Blakely," she said, standing her ground. "But you already knew that, Dalton."

After a brief rundown of the situation, Blakely moved to the driver's side of her vehicle and retrieved her cell. She held it up toward Dalton and the officer who identified himself as Roger Nordegren. Normally, Dalton might ask if the man was related to Tiger Woods's ex-wife, but there was a time and place for a sense of humor. This was neither the time nor place.

"There's been a situation, Bethany," Blakely started. He remembered mention of a twin, but something about not identical. "When you get this message, come to my home, okay? Just come here, and I'll explain everything."

She ended the call and turned toward Dalton. "Voice mail," she said as though that explained everything.

He wasn't a parent, but a missing child was unimaginable. His heart went out to the parents and to Blakely, who looked so tense her muscles might snap. Understandable, under the circumstances. He thought about what he'd asked her to do a couple of minutes ago. Bad move. All he had to do was put himself in her situation to realize he'd wasted his breath. He wouldn't go inside either if he had a missing nephew out there, not to mention if that child had been in his care.

"What's your nephew's name?" he asked.

"Chase," she supplied and then gave a quick description as she pulled up a recent photo on her phone. The look of horror on her face along with the pleading in those honey-brown eyes of hers made it impossible to stay frustrated with her for the disappearing act in Galveston a month and a half ago. If he'd known she was a judge back then, he would have taken a hard pass on the fling. First of all, she looked way too young and hot to be a judge in the first place. Since they hadn't exchanged personal information other than their real names, he had no idea how old she was or where she lived. Wasn't that the point of a weekend fling?

But Dalton didn't typically engage in sex-for-sex's-sake encounters. Meeting Blakely had made him believe in twin flames.

Dalton cleared his throat before he tripped down Sentimental Lane. He needed to get over himself and the sting that had come with her rejection to find the missing boy.

"You go east, and I'll take west," Blakely said, pointing in opposite directions.

"No, ma'am," Dalton disagreed. "Until the perp is caught, I'm your shadow."

"I've wasted enough time standing here," she said, grabbing her handbag out of her vehicle.

"Wallet still intact?" he asked, motioning toward the bag.

On a frustrated sigh, she opened it and checked credit cards, ID and cash. "All here."

He had to rule out attempted robbery so they could move on. He glanced over at the beat cop. "You got that, right?"

"Yes, sir," the cop immediately responded before calling in the search for the missing kid and alerting his supervising officer of a perp on the loose.

With not much of a description to go on, locating the perp, let alone identifying him, would be the equivalent of finding a needle in a haystack.

"Your nephew might not be far," he said to Blakely. "He might be too scared to come out of a hiding place."

She nodded as her pulse pounded at the base of her neck. Her dilated pupils and quick, uneven breathing told him an adrenaline rush thumped through her.

"Start looking in the shrubs, okay?" he said to her.

"Got it," she confirmed, immediately moving to the nearest greenery.

"Okay if I stay out here and search?" the older gentleman who'd introduced himself as John Bowman asked.

"We can use all the help we can get," Dalton confirmed. "Why don't you start across the street?"

"Yes, sir," Mr. Bowman said with a salute. Other neighbors came out to see what the commotion was all about. Dalton enlisted them to check their shrubs first, then any other possible hiding place a seven-year-old could squeeze into, including unlocked vehicles or boat tarps.

All told, there were a dozen folks out searching for Chase, who was likely to be scared out of his young mind at this point. He might only respond to his aunt's voice, or not even hers depending on how traumatized he was from witnessing the attack.

Taking a moment to examine the scene while it was fresh, he noted the hole in the lawn-and-leaf bag where a knife had been drilled in. Much of the contents were now strewn all over the driveway. He searched for the knife, but the perp must have been clear-minded enough to pick it up before he disappeared.

The scene itself fit the description of what went down according to Blakely. Setting aside his personal feelings about the judge was something Dalton was good at doing. He shoved them down deep, then locked them there. No need to let those rise to the surface again.

Dalton would handle the protection detail and then move on, no matter how much he wanted to ask what he'd done so wrong that Blakely couldn't get out of his Galveston rental fast enough.

BLAKELY TRIED TO steady her voice as she called out for Chase. Maybe he would feel safe enough to come out if she could manage a calm, soothing tone. The thought of telling Bethany that her son was missing knocked the wind out of Blakely. It was horrific enough that he'd had to witness the attack.

What if Ski Mask got to Chase?

Hot, burning tears welled in her eyes. *No. That didn't happen. Chase ran. He got away in time.*

Panic gripped her with fingers that squeezed so hard her ribs might crack. The simple act of breathing hurt as she dropped down on all fours and crawled along the sidewalk in front of her neighbor's house.

She needed to think like a seven-year-old. And fast.

What did Chase like to do the most? The answer came immediately. *Tents.* He loved to climb in tents or find the smallest hiding places.

The trunk of her sedan? Could he have climbed in from the back seat? Would he know it was possible? Would he figure out how?

She popped to her feet and ran toward her vehicle while jamming her hand inside her handbag in search of the key. Her fingers closed around the key fob. She pressed the third button down, the trunk release. It automatically opened by the time she reached it.

Heart in her throat, she looked inside with a prayer Chase would be curled up playing his Switch—which was missing from the back seat—with the sound on mute.

Nothing.

How was she going to tell her sister that the light of her life was gone? Missing? *Abducted?*

To what end? Revenge?

Ski Mask wanted *her.* Would he kidnap Chase to get back at her?

Bethany, call me back.

Her sister's trust ran so deep that she turned off her phone during date nights. She insisted her husband do the same. International businesses ran twenty-four-seven. Even though her brother-in-law, Greg, had a capable junior manager, Greg felt a responsibility to take calls personally to give the kind of individual service that ensured their customers stayed on with the company. Being the sole breadwinner came at a price, and that cost was long hours and missed time with his wife and child. Greg was a good person, devoted husband and loving father. He was a damn fine brother-in-law too. Greg and Bethany Vendenburg were marriage goals because they made decisions together and worked as a team.

It was a great life for Bethany. At least, it had been.

Stress seemed to be getting to Greg, and he hadn't been himself in recent months. He'd obsessed over making plans for Chase in case something bad happened to either of them. He'd even brought up Blakely and Bethany's parents' unexpected deaths as a reason to get paperwork and finances in order. Cracks had been showing in the marriage for a while now too. A year? Ever since Blakely took the bench?

Bethany chalked it up to having a normal marriage. Said it was common to have ups and downs. That she and Greg were on a "down" cycle, but that it would get better. It was logical. Relationships were tricky, full of potholes and landmines.

Blakely, on the other hand, couldn't see herself being happy in so-called domestic bliss, not even when the relationship was on an upswing. She needed her work and had kept her head down for too many years, sacrificing everything, including a personal life, to give up what she loved doing. Besides, what Bethany and Greg had wasn't realistic for most people. Especially not Blakely. Not with her history.

A noise to her left caught her off guard, startling her. She jumped into a defensive position, ready to defend herself or strike anything that came her way. Realized it was just a rabbit.

She checked her watch. An hour and a half had passed since the attack. *Where are you, buddy? Please come out of hiding. Please.*

Out of the corner of her eye, she noted Dalton kept watch over her no matter where he was. Having someone around who had her back was a foreign feeling at best. Since her parents died in a highway pileup on icy roads, she'd been the one to step into the adulting role. Even while attending college in Arlington at the UT branch there, Blakely had looked after her sister, who attended Texas Tech in Lubbock, where she'd met her future husband.

While Dalton had her back, she could focus her full attention on finding Chase.

But where should she look next?

Other vehicles in driveways?

Backyards?

Dog houses?

Didn't her neighbors have kids and grandkids? Would they have forts outside? Tree houses? Jungle gyms?

Since there were a dozen neighbors or more searching the street, this area was more than covered. She glanced over at Dalton, who immediately picked up on the fact she was about to make a move. His offhand remark six-ish weeks ago about having found his twin flame had scared her then because there'd been some truth to it. Once he told her what he did for a living, she'd bolted. The last thing she needed was a fling showing up in court to protect her. Like now. This was exactly what she'd been trying to avoid. She prized her professional relationships and had no intention of damaging her reputation.

The whole fling caught her off guard anyway because she wasn't into casual sex with someone she barely knew.

Twin flame?

Something had caused her to break all her rules and give in to the overwhelming desire to spend time with this man she'd met. She'd believed him to be law enforcement because of his swagger and the Dallas PD baseball cap in the back seat of his vehicle, so trust came easily. Too easily?

When he'd confirmed his job, she'd run just as fast.

Was she letting her guard down? Because she had a four-inch scar at her hairline and another one under her right arm to remind her relaxing with anyone was a bad idea. Her ex had also taught her that it was impossible to really know anyone. People changed. Sometimes, right in front of your eyes.

Blakely made a beeline for her next door neighbor's driveway. In this area, backyards were protected by eight-foot wood board-on-board privacy fences. The community was known for it, and it was largely the reason she'd decided to buy her first home here. The neighborhood also had a metal gate with a box code needed to enter. The gate kept out solicitors easily enough. A determined criminal?

Clearly no.

The sense of security of the community had been shattered this evening. Blakely realized how false that sense had been.

Dalton saying she'd picked up a shadow was no joke. The man was a half step behind her almost the second she changed course. He kept a distance, though, allowing her the freedom to search everywhere, including underneath her neighbor's car.

Coming up empty, she moved to the backyard. A jungle gym immediately caught her attention. She bolted toward it, resisting the urge to call out to Chase in case Ski Mask was hiding inside instead. Or had Chase in there with a knife to her nephew's throat.

This outdoor swing set was built log-cabin style with a two-story fort that led to a green slide. A pair of swings were next to the fort.

Blakely's heart skipped a beat at the realization this was exactly the kind of place her nephew would hide.

Movement behind the window on the second story of the fort stopped her cold.

Chase?

Or someone else?

Chapter Three

Dalton drew his weapon as he moved beside Blakely. With a nod, he took the lead. Moving a few steps in front of her and then around to the side, he gave the fort a wide berth. Someone was inside. The last thing he wanted to do was further traumatize the little boy if this was Chase.

However, it was impossible to tell who was hiding inside the second story of the jungle gym. Dalton didn't take chances, and he didn't take anything for granted. Until he knew for certain the person in the fort was a child, he would treat the situation with caution.

Slowly, carefully, he scanned the backyard. There was an eight-foot privacy fence around the wooded area. The tree trunks were thick enough for a person to hide behind. Rather than risk being jumped from behind, Dalton moved from tree to tree with the stealth of a panther hunting prey. There was a dozen, give or take, and he checked each one as well as the canopy to ensure no one had found a way to climb up.

Blakely stayed rooted to her spot while he moved in from the back. She stood to the side of a tree, which would give her cover in the event a knife was thrown her way or the perp she'd dubbed Ski Mask had a gun. A knife, Blakely had noted, was an intimate way of killing someone. You had to get up close and personal, look someone in the eyes as you thrust the blade inside them. Ski Mask had responded to her question, asking what he wanted, with one word. *You.*

The fact she didn't recognize the voice wasn't surprising since Ski Mask had spoken the word in a growl.

As Dalton made it close enough to get a visual of the fort occupant, he noted the shape was that of a boy. He turned his attention toward Blakely, who had been studying his every move, and waved her toward the fort.

She caught on immediately and bolted toward the stairs. "Chase, buddy, it's me. I'm coming up."

The image of Blakely reuniting with the scared-to-death seven-year-old seared into Dalton's heart. The kid launched himself at his aunt, throwing his small arms around her neck before burying his face in her hair. His sobs echoed as Dalton informed the officer the search for Chase could be called off and that he'd been found safe. There was, however, still a perp on the loose in the neighborhood. He urged the officer to tell folks to go back inside and keep their doors locked. He further instructed the officer to tell them to exercise caution as they left their homes and report any suspicious activity immediately.

The officer confirmed the instructions. Then, Dalton reported to his supervisor as he scanned the perimeter, giving Blakely and Chase a few moments of safety and privacy. Watching the two of them stirred feelings inside his chest that he had no idea lurked there. Not yet thirty, he was too young to want a family of his own, in his opinion. He'd never had that pull to get married or have kids. His own father, who'd been a good man by all accounts, died not long after Dalton was born. His mother left the family high and dry. The woman took off after Dalton and his siblings had been dropped off to spend a weekend with their grandparents, and she never looked back. Rumor had it that the "Mother of the Year" was remarried with a teenage son. Why the woman who'd walked away from three young children had decided to give motherhood another go-round was beyond his comprehension.

To avoid passing on those genes, Dalton figured the messy bloodline stopped with him. He had siblings who used to feel the same, until his sister, Julie aka Jules, met Toby anyway. Those two were loved up now, planning a wedding. *A wedding.*

Sounded like the equivalent of being sentenced to life, if you asked Dalton.

He had no idea if Jules's future plans had changed. Now that all three of his cousins had found the loves of their lives—his cousin Abi had also become a stepmother—he figured it was just him and Camden left holding the bag. His brother was the oldest on both sides of the family at thirty-five years old. His cousin Crystal was second oldest at thirty-three. Then came sister Jules at thirty-two, followed by his cousin Duke, who was thirty. Both he and Abi were twenty-eight, pushing twenty-nine. All six of the Remington grandkids had followed their grandfather's footsteps into the US Marshals Service.

All six were devoted to their careers and their family. Each were taking turns holding vigil at the hospital after their grandparents were seriously injured in an accident on the farm road where they lived. Their paint horse ranch was being well tended while they were each in a coma, each fighting for their life. Dalton would take his turn next but kept close tabs on the situation, which could go either way at any moment. He couldn't imagine life without his grandparents after they'd taken him, his siblings and their cousins to raise.

Guilt was a gut punch at not being able to be there for them now. But it was Jules's turn. She'd wrapped a case and had taken leave. Everyone was taking a turn. Though, no one expected the hospital stay to last this long. Camden could take leave after Dalton's turn.

Blakely climbed down the ladder with her nephew glued to her and joined Dalton. "I need to call my sister but—"

It would be impossible to find her phone let alone manage a call without some help.

"Inside your purse?" he asked. His sister and female cousins had trained him never to touch a woman's handbag without express permission, potentially in writing. Once granted, he was never to dig around for more than what they'd asked for. Under different circumstances, he would crack a smile at the memory. This situation was way too heavy for any levity.

"Yes, please," she said, swiveling her hip so that he could gain access to her personal belongings.

He reached a hand inside, felt around for anything that felt like a phone and clasped his fingers around it to be sure. "Do you need me to make the call and hold it to your ear?"

"Would you mind?" she asked. Even now, her voice was like silk.

He tapped the screen and then held the phone toward her face for ID. A moment later, the screen came to life. "Sister's name?"

"Look at call history," she instructed. "She should be at the top of the list." She paused and waited as he tapped again. "Did she call back?"

"Not yet," he stated before holding the phone to her ear.

Being this close, he heard the call roll into voice mail. He could also smell the floral-citrusy scent that had stayed on the bedsheets and imprinted on his soul that special weekend.

Dalton cleared his throat. Another time. Another place. He might ask her what the hell he'd done wrong. Now wasn't the time.

"First of all, everything is okay," Blakely started. "Whenever you get this message, call me back or head over to my house. I'm fine. Chase is fine." She paused. "I'll explain everything once you get here."

Blakely turned her attention to Dalton. This close, he could see emotion flash in those honey-browns that said she remembered him and that weekend very well. Thick black lashes hid those intense spun-gold babies as she dropped her gaze.

"Thank you," she said, emotion thick in her tone as she held on to her nephew like they were on the Titanic as it was going down. "I don't know what I would have done if anything…"

Her voice trailed off as Dalton scanned the perimeter once more. "You said in your statement that you grabbed hold of the perp's wrists."

She nodded. "That's right."

"Let's get you home so we can collect evidence," he urged. He didn't like her being out in the open like this even though Ski Mask should be long gone at this point. A smart perp would get out of Dodge to save his own hide. A determined perp would bide his time before returning to finish the job. A deadly perp would come back even more prepared.

The threat might be at bay for now, but professional instinct honed by years of field experience said it wasn't over.

BLAKELY WALKED NEXT door to her home and finished giving her statement while sitting on the couch in her living room. In the meantime, Dalton walked the house, closing blinds and ensuring all windows and doors maintained their integrity and remained locked. The medical examiner paid a visit to collect evidence and swab her nails. She managed to take off her jacket while Chase stayed plastered to her body like a baby gorilla to its mother in the wild.

By the time Dalton joined them, he'd inspected the home inside and out. He'd checked the perimeter and set up surveillance cameras at critical points. What could she say? The marshal came prepared.

They probably needed to have a conversation about what happened in Galveston, but that had to wait until grown-ups could talk without young ears tuned in to every word. At this rate, though, Chase might just have to fall asleep for that to occur. Even then, he might wake up the second she put him down, much like he'd done as a colicky baby years ago. Blakely remembered well the nights her sister had called bawling, unsure of what to do as she paced the floors. Outside of those weeks of colic, Chase had been an easy baby.

The fact she and Dalton had a fling didn't need to be common knowledge. She would ask for his discretion even though he came across as the kind of person who could take a secret to the grave. The man was honorable, intelligent and drop-dead gorgeous. The term *easy on the eyes* applied in spades. It was followed by *hard on the heart* because a man this tall, dark and ridiculously handsome was no doubt a heartbreaker. Had to be, even though her heart wanted to argue against the idea.

Hearts had a mind of their own. Logic kept her from making the same mistake twice—one that could have cost her life at fifteen. Blakely didn't survive that horrific incident just to dive right back in and make a similar mistake—one that could end differently this time—no matter how many years had passed.

Chase snored against her chest, hugging his Switch to his chest. She didn't have the heart to move him when he looked so comfortable. What he'd witnessed might leave mental scars. Blakely knew all about those. She had physical ones, too, as reminders. But the emotional scars ran the deepest.

"I hope he's young enough to forget all about this night," she said to Dalton as he took a seat in the chair near the couch.

"Kids are resilient," he said. Was he speaking from personal experience? She had no idea. He wasn't married. She knew that much. Which didn't mean that he wasn't a dad.

Considering they'd spent time intimately with each other, Blakely figured they ought to know something about each other now.

"Have you been assigned to me?" she asked, starting there first.

"Yes," he confirmed before diving into what he'd been up to in order to secure her home. "I set up security cameras with sensors on the perimeter. They'll send an alarm to my phone if something with enough body heat and size to be human enters the property."

"I probably should have done that years ago," she said, wishing she'd thought of it.

"You didn't have a reason until now," he pointed out. "Plus, this neighborhood is quiet. You had no reason to suspect a perp would slip past the gate." His forehead wrinkled as he studied her. Under different circumstances, his expression would have been part adorable, part sexy. Right now, all she could focus on was the close call she'd just had and the fact she'd unknowingly put Chase in danger. "How did you fight him off?"

"Krav Maga training," she admitted with more than a hint of pride.

"That's good training right there," he said with a nod of appreciation. She didn't need it, but the approval was nice anyway. "And most likely the reason you survived the attack."

An involuntary shiver rocked her body at the last word. Chase stirred but immediately fell back to sleep. Between running around on the soccer field, the chicken nugget dinner the medical examiner had brought for Chase—she made a mental note to thank him for it later—and stress, Chase was out like a light not long after his belly was full. He smelled like grass, dirt and little boy, and she wouldn't have it any other way. Plus, there was no way she would have been able to pry Chase off her long enough for him to take a shower.

As long as he was in her house, though, he was potentially in as much danger as she was. For once, she wished Bethany would break the no-cell-phone-on-date-night rule and check her voice mail.

Sending an officer to her sister's home would freak Bethany out, causing undue stress. Plus, she planned elaborate outings involving tents, camping or hotel rooms sometimes. Blakely wished she'd taken more interest and asked more questions about where Bethany would be tonight. Since Blakely had emergency authorization to make medical decisions for Chase, a precaution no one ever expected to need, her sister had the freedom to do whatever she wanted.

Blakely shifted her gaze to the sex-on-a-stick marshal.

"Should we get to know each other a little better, considering…" Her voice trailed off as heat flushed her cheeks.

"I'm assigned to keep you safe, Your Honor," he started.

"We're well past being formal when there's no one around, don't you think?" she asked, trying to let some of her embarrassment roll off. The man still affected her. His voice alone was the equivalent of whiskey poured over crackling ice.

Dalton was tall, six feet three inches if she had to guess. His hair was just long enough on top to curl. The sides were tighter clipped. Small waves of the blond tips contrasted against dark roots that were almost black. He had a dimpled chin covered by a day's worth of scruff and the most piercing set of intense dark eyes hooded by thick black lashes.

For someone so tall, he was built like a brick house. His biceps were stacked. Greek tragedies could be written in honor of his God-like bod and the carnage left behind when he was done with a relationship.

If he wasn't so damned intelligent, he'd be written off as arm candy. But he *was* smart, so that was out.

The way he'd looked at her when she was reunited with Chase earlier said he had a soft spot and was kind underneath all those intimidating good looks.

"Point taken," Dalton finally said with a half smile that warmed places in her that didn't need to be focused on.

The phone alarm caused both of them to jump. Dalton stared at the screen. "There's a woman walking up to the front door who looks similar to you." He glanced over at Blakely and tilted the phone so she could see the screen.

"That's my sister," she said, immediately standing up and making a beeline for the front door.

The marshal was half a step behind. A trill of awareness skittered across her skin at his closeness.

But she was about to face her sister, so she dismissed it.

Even after the fact, she struggled to find the words to tell her sister that Chase had gone missing for a couple of hours. Those were words no parent wanted to hear and no sister wanted to deliver.

Based on the look on Bethany's face, all hell was about to break loose.

Chapter Four

"Keep your voice down or you'll wake him," Blakely whispered to her sister. She gave a quick rundown of the situation.

Bethany pushed through the door and then marched straight into the family room. Wild brown eyes scanned the space before landing on the sleeping boy.

Bethany couldn't get to her son fast enough. She scooped him up, waking the sleepy boy.

"Mama," Chase said as he wrapped his arms around his mother's neck and buried his face in her hair.

"Where's Greg?" Blakely asked as Dalton leaned against the wall.

"We had a fight," Bethany explained as she clung on to her son like he was a life preserver, and her head was dipping underwater.

"Makes sense why you checked your phone," Blakely reasoned as Dalton watched from the sidelines.

Bethany turned toward the front door and then startled when her gaze landed on Dalton. "Who is this?"

"My name is Dalton Remington," he said before Blakely could. "I work for the US Marshals Service," he added when her forehead wrinkled. "And I'd offer a handshake if yours weren't already full."

Blakely's twin offered a pinched smile before she turned to her sister. "I'm taking Chase home. I'll call you later."

"Why not let him sleep here tonight?" Blakely asked, surprising her sister with the question.

"Is it safe?" Bethany asked.

"Safer than you getting back on the road this late," Blakely pointed out. "Plus, I have new security cameras and a personal bodyguard." She walked over and rubbed Chase's back. "He's already asleep. Why risk waking him when you can put him to bed here?"

"Greg will worry," Bethany countered. And then a spark passed behind her eyes. "Maybe that's not such a bad thing tonight."

"What happened between the two of you?" Blakely asked.

"Nothing," Bethany said, her body stiffening like she was tensing up to protect herself from a physical blow.

Blakely bit down on her bottom lip. "It doesn't sound like nothing."

"We had a fight," Bethany said. "Married couples argue." Her gaze shot toward Dalton. "Are you married?"

"No, ma'am," he said.

Bethany shook her head. "Call me ma'am and I look over my shoulder for my mother."

"She's dead," Blakely said with a hollow cast to her voice that sent a nail through the center of his chest. He was starting to regret the pact they'd made in Galveston not to discuss their personal lives. Now more than ever, he wanted to know more about the off-limits judge.

"Doesn't matter," Bethany said. "You know what I mean."

"Right," Blakely conceded. "It wasn't my intention to be defensive about our parents. Tonight has been hell."

Bethany sighed. "Every worst-case scenario possible slammed into me after I heard your first message. All my thoughts went to something happening to Chase. It never once occurred to me that something might have happened to my big sister." Bethany's tense expression softened. "What happened to your face?"

"Put Chase to bed," Blakely said. "I'll open a bottle of wine."

"Are you sure it's safe to stay here?" Bethany asked before another glance at Dalton, searching for confirmation from a second source. He gave a slight nod as her sister reassured her the home was safer than Fort Knox. Bethany nodded before another glance in Dalton's direction. "I could use a drink." Then, she disappeared up the back stairwell in the kitchen.

He had questions but didn't figure it was his place to ask. So he joined Blakely in the kitchen as she pulled out a bottle of white wine from the fridge. "Can I help?"

"Sure," she conceded like she'd just asked to borrow a thousand dollars, and he'd agreed to be her lender. "Corkscrew is in that drawer over there." She motioned toward the granite island and the row of drawers closest to him. The all-white kitchen somehow managed to come off as modern and welcoming with the touches of green plants instead of sterile. The decor fit Blakely to a T.

Dalton moved over to the drawer and then located the metal opener. Joining Blakely on the other side of the counter, he stood close enough to smell her clean citrus and flowery scent—a scent like none other. But he didn't want to think about her unique traits despite seeing her pulse rise at the base of her throat when their fingers grazed as she handed over the chilled bottle.

"Do you want a glass?" she asked after clearing her throat.

He gave a small headshake, needing to be clear-minded

in case the perp returned tonight. Plus, he didn't need to relax and let his guard down again around Blakely. There was no logical reason to touch that hot stove twice.

Dalton removed the packaging on the wine bottle, revealing the cork.

This close, he was reminded of the four-inch scar hidden behind bangs. Was that part of the reason she'd bolted? There were other scars too. One just under her third rib. He'd smoothed his fingertips along all the markings on her body. But ran into a hard wall when he'd asked how she'd accumulated so many.

Dalton stabbed the pointed end of the corkscrew into the plug and twisted.

She'd muttered something about Krav Maga training, but unless she'd actually served time in the Israeli military, there was no reasonable explanation for her to have this many scars.

His ego tried to convince him that the marks were somehow related to why she'd bolted out the door. Were they?

Or had he done something wrong?

With effort, Dalton freed the cork from the bottle with a *thmp* sound.

"I should probably know what you prefer to drink after..."

"We weren't there to talk about personal habits, remember?" he quipped, wishing he could reel those words back in after seeing the blow they landed. "Hey, sorry. I didn't mean to—"

Blakely stared at him. Her expression stopped him mid-sentence. "You're right, though. We had an agenda that weekend that had nothing to do with getting to know each other. No use getting twisted up about the past."

"Fresh start?" he asked, hoping she'd accept the verbal peace offering.

Blakely studied him. Those eyes piercing right through him. It took a helluva lot to unnerve Dalton. The judge's accomplishment didn't go unnoticed.

"Okay," she said with reluctance in her voice as she set two wine glasses down in front of him. "Do you mind pouring?" She held up shaky hands. "I have serious doubts about my ability to steady my hands enough to get the wine in the glasses." The moment of vulnerability that flashed behind her eyes shouldn't warm his heart. What the hell did it know? It had him itching to reach out and take her hands in his, offer comfort that wasn't part of this assignment. His mission was to keep the judge safe and alive until the perp was caught.

"Not a problem," he answered. After the glasses were filled, she offered water or juice.

"Water's good," he said, thinking a cold beer would be better. Not an option under the circumstances, but better nonetheless. This also seemed like a good time to pepper her with questions while her sister was upstairs putting Chase to bed.

Blakely nodded as she moved to the cabinet to retrieve a glass. Her hip bumped into him as she passed by. Again, he had to ignore his body's reaction to the beautiful and intelligent judge. "Do you have any idea who might want to harm you?"

"A better question might be who doesn't," she said with a frustrated sigh.

"Are you in a relationship?" he asked. He'd glanced at her ring finger the second he'd seen her again. At one point, he'd half convinced himself she must be married, but that was just his ego coming up with more excuses as to why she couldn't get away from him fast enough.

"No."

"Ended one recently?" he continued as he did his level best to convince himself this line of questioning was for professional purposes only.

Blakely stood at the fridge with her back to him, filling his glass with the waterspout on the door. The water stopped mid-fill. "No." Her voice was low and a little too calm. "Unless you count that weekend."

"Nope," he said a little too quickly. "I don't think it qualifies as more than damn good—"

"He's asleep," Bethany said as she hit the last couple of stairs leading into the kitchen.

Dalton had no idea why Blakely would want to live in a house of this size alone. *Leave it alone, Dalt.* Her reason was her own business. Maybe she intended to start a family soon. Dalton involuntarily shivered at the thought as he joined Blakely at the fridge, fighting the urge to loosen his collar. She handed over the water glass three-quarters of the way full.

For a split second, he thought having a family with someone like her might not be a death sentence.

Hold on there, Dalt. He banished the thought. Not yet thirty years old, he had plenty of time to think about tying the knot in the future. No reason to rush it now, especially because he still lived with the mental scars from his parents.

Had his mother's disappearing act not long after his birth given him mommy issues? He didn't need a psychologist to confirm what he already knew. Yes. Being rejected by your mother not long after you were born did that to a person. Not to mention the fact she never once looked back. The woman could be dead for all he knew. One thing was certain. There was no reason to continue those bad genes or dump them on some unsuspecting kiddo. Dalton's father might have been a good person. Hell, Dalton had been too young to make the determination himself, so he relied on his siblings and cousins. They were convinced the man was close to sainthood. Dalton hoped it was true for their sakes. As for him? He'd learned to depend on himself so he didn't and wouldn't need anyone else.

"Good," Blakely said, clearing her throat. It was then he realized she'd been watching him while he'd been lost in thought. "He's been through a lot tonight. I hope the whole thing doesn't leave too many scars."

Dalton knew about those. Too well?

BLAKELY COULD FEEL her cheeks turn crimson as she looked at Dalton, so she forced her gaze from the gorgeous lawman standing in her kitchen and refocused on her sister.

"I know whatever happened isn't your fault," her sister said, cutting into her thoughts. "So please, start from the beginning and tell me exactly what I'm dealing with here."

Blakely gave the elevator version of the attack.

"Ohmygod, Blakely." Her sister cut across the kitchen and wrapped her arms around her. "I'm so sorry. All I thought about was Chase. I didn't even consider how awful this whole attack must have been for you."

Bethany's body was shaking.

"You must have been terrified," her sister continued. "Especially after all you've been through."

Blakely cleared her throat a little louder this time as she hugged her sister. "The past is the past. We don't need to get into any of that now." But it was too late. The hunk of a marshal stood halfway across the room, his gaze fixed on her, questions dancing in his eyes. "Besides, I'm much more worried about the impact this might have on Chase."

"Kids are more resilient than we give them credit for sometimes," Bethany said in a moment of wisdom beyond her years. Her sister could come across as borderline ditzy at times, but then she would say something profound, revealing a deeper side to her.

"That might be true," Blakely conceded, not ready to let herself off the hook for the whole ordeal. "But I hate the fact I couldn't protect him." She couldn't go there with questions about what might have happened to Chase if she hadn't fought off her attacker.

"Both of you are safe, and that's all that matters," Bethany said before taking a pull of wine. She studied the rim. "Family is the most important thing." There was a depth to those words too, along with a hint of desperation.

What was that about?

Blakely remembered the fight her sister said she'd had with her husband, Greg. "Is everything okay on the home front?"

Another long pull instead of a verbal response told Blakely everything she needed to know.

"Tell me what happened," she said to Bethany.

Her sister's gaze shifted from Blakely to Dalton and back.

Bethany motioned toward the small four-top table in the kitchen next to a window. It was one of Blakely's favorite spots for drinking coffee on the weekend. She liked to look out at the tall trees and think. "Mind if we sit down first?"

Blakely picked up the still-full wine glass and headed over to the table. A glance out into the darkness of the backyard caused a chill to race down her spine.

"I can turn on the porch light," Dalton offered, like he could read her mind. Then again, the man was experienced at reading body language, so she shouldn't be all that surprised he'd picked up on her apprehension. Especially considering she was pretty sure she'd involuntarily shivered at the cold front making its way down her spine. Then there was the tension in her muscles that made her shoulders feel bunched up as a headache formed at her temples. So, yeah, she wasn't exactly giving off any relaxed vibes.

"Sounds good," she said before thanking him.

Dalton popped his chin up in a quick nod before heading to the back door. He flipped on the light, which helped ease some of Blakely's nerves. Despite all the Krav Maga training over the years, being attacked had still thrown her off-balance emotionally. Frustration nipped that anyone could make her feel helpless or scared or both again.

A small voice in the back of her mind reminded her that the situation would have been so much worse without all the training she had. Where would Chase be now if she hadn't been prepared? She'd responded to the threat quickly and dispatched the enemy. She'd done her job, which was to defend herself.

And yet, a different nagging voice reminded her that Chase had been in danger. He might be scarred for the rest of his life despite the reassurance from Bethany. Kids were resilient. Except she should never have put Chase in the position to be resilient in the first place. For that, she would never forgive herself.

"Earth to Blakely." Bethany snapped her fingers roughly two inches in front of Blakely's face.

"Sorry," she mumbled, tuning back into the present.

"Where did you go just now?"

"To a bad place where I wasn't able to fight off the sonofa—"

"But you were," Bethany soothed. "That's the important thing. Chase is safe. You're safe. There's no use torturing yourself with what might have happened." As much sense as Bethany made, Blakely still couldn't let herself off the hook.

"Hey," her sister continued. "Talk to me."

"I'd rather hear what happened between you and Greg tonight," Blakely said, turning the tables.

The look on Bethany's face said she was about to lie.

Chapter Five

Dalton borrowed a spare key from a hook on the side of the kitchen cabinet, walked outside and locked the door behind him. He made a trip around the perimeter in search of traces that Blakely's attacker had returned now that the crime scene had cooled down. So far, no sign of the twisted individual.

A list was forming in Dalton's mind. He knew that she hadn't broken up with anyone recently or been in fights with friends. The way she'd said the word *friends* made him think she kept a close circle. She didn't strike him as the outgoing type, which was confirmed through her answers. Basically, she worked and spent time with her sister's family.

His mind went over the details of everything he'd heard so far, stopping at the fight that took place between Bethany and her husband. Since the two were together, there was no way the husband could have attacked Blakely. Plus, she very likely would have recognized her brother-in-law. Curiosity had him wanting to know what Bethany and her husband had been fighting about earlier in the evening. The investigator in him wanted to put together a timeline of events. Was it necessary?

That was always the question, wasn't it?

These types of investigations commonly had a couple

dozen offshoots. Taking a wrong turn early on could let the trail go cold. Cold cases were the most difficult to close. There was a reason. A cold trail, lack of resources, not to mention lack of evidence meant perps walked around free to relocate, repeat their crimes or move on to bigger ones.

In this case, the perp told Blakely he wanted *her*. He left her handbag alone. No money was missing. He hadn't tried to steal her vehicle—thankfully, because Chase had been in the back seat. Carjackers had made off with children in similar circumstances. Most were recovered healthy and in one piece, deemed an inconvenience and dropped off at the perp's first opportunity. A small few weren't so lucky. He mentally shook his head at the senseless losses.

His cell buzzed, pulling him back to the situation at hand. After fishing the device out of his pocket, he checked the screen.

His heart skipped a couple of beats the second he realized the message came through on the family group chat. This was, no doubt, an update on their grandparents. Too much time had passed since both his grandparents landed in a coma after an automobile crash for him to expect good news. A tiny sliver of hope was all he had left, and he intended to hang on to it despite the odds of either of them making a meaningful recovery.

Once again, time was the enemy.

After tapping his thumb on the notification and then verifying his identity with the facial recognition software, the long update filled the screen. His sister, Jules, was at the hospital.

According to the message, Grandpa Lor—short for Grandpa Lorenzo—had coded—again!—but was now in stable condition. A fresh wave of guilt for not being in the hospital at Grandpa Lor's side struck like a prize fighter, cracking ribs in the center of Dalton's chest.

A quick mental calculation weighing how miserable he would be if he took immediate leave, leaving Blakely to fend for herself should her attacker return, versus how miserable he was currently by not being at the hospital, added perspective.

Who did Blakely have to protect her?

A quick thought that she could possibly move in with her sister temporarily until law enforcement could **be certain** she'd be safe whipped through his mind like a **breeze** on a spring morning. Leaving her wasn't an option. Bethany and her husband had had a fight. Marriage could be hard. Apparently, so difficult that a woman could leave her children less than a year after giving birth to her third. And then the loss of a wife could break a man to the point he died.

Was that being fair about his parents' situation? Who the hell knew. No one ever talked about his parents. Or, to his knowledge, ever tried to reach out to his mother for her side of the story. *Anyone who could walk out on three young children without looking back already made her statement.*

Fair point.

Dalton shoved the thought deep down inside, into the darkest reaches of his soul, before responding to the text. Do you need me to come?

Those tiny three dots indicating someone else was typing hit the screen.

Not now. Will keep you posted. K?

He typed a response that he would wait until called. Besides, he was up next once this assignment was over.

For now, he would leave the situation with his grandparents alone and deal with his own heavy heart.

K.

Out of the corner of his eye, he caught movement to the left. For a split second, he thought about this being a decoy. However, the initial attack was alone. Signs pointed to the perp being someone who had a grudge against Blakely, an individual. It wasn't likely he would have someone in the wings.

The moment of hesitation shoved aside, Dalton pulled his weapon from his shoulder holster and headed south in the direction of the stirring. Winds kicked up, causing him to question what he saw. Could have been leaves or a piece of debris floating past a tree trunk. Was he chasing thin air?

The snap of branches in the darkness said he was on the right track. Something was out here. What? A stray dog? Could be a coyote. Raccoons were nuisances out here, as were skunks. The last thing he needed was to be sprayed, causing him to stink to high heaven. Bobcats were a danger in these parts despite being in the city.

With the stealth and precision of movement of a jaguar, Dalton made it to the tree line and back fence of Blakely's small property in less than a minute. Whatever had been in her yard—and he was now certain some living creature had been here—was gone. Giving chase meant moving farther away from the residence.

On balance, it was a risk he couldn't take tonight. Not in the dark. Not when the perp might have visited this site multiple times when planning an attack. Rather than continue, he doubled back instead, pulse racing not from exertion but from stress and fear that he'd left the door open for the perp to attack once again.

The fear wasn't rational. But then, fear never was. He knew, on some level, that he hadn't gone far enough for the perp to double back, beat him to the house, break in and still catch Blakely off guard.

Besides, the perp had learned another point tonight. Blakely knew how to defend herself. She might have taken a few hard scrapes and will wake with a sore body and bruises tomorrow, but she'd fought the guy off. She'd escaped.

Would he use a different method now?

A long-distance shot? The thought of her sitting next to the window—a sitting duck—pushed his legs a little faster. By the time he reached the back door, he was breathing hard and his thighs burned.

As suspected, he saw her sitting at the table near the window as he neared the home. At the back door, he quickly entered and then relocked the door behind him.

"You might want to close those blinds," he said as he joined Blakely and her twin.

A look of panic crossed Blakely's features as her skin momentarily paled. "I close those and someone could be standing on the other side without my knowledge." She straightened her back and shoulders, giving her a royal bearing that shouldn't form the word *princess* in his mind. She had an elegant beauty to her when her chin came up in defiance of whatever or whomever stalked her.

Could Dalton keep her safe?

BLAKELY HAD KNOWN Dalton was heading outside to walk the perimeter. She didn't want to cause unnecessary panic. Bethany had drained her wine glass and asked for a refill while explaining that marriages go through ups and downs.

However, her eyes told a different story. Bethany might be able to convince others that she wasn't concerned about her relationship, but Blakely could read her sister like the back of her hand. They might not share exact DNA, but they'd lived in the same womb together, and it was clear that her sister had concerns about her husband. Bethany was holding back.

Chase hadn't mentioned anything or seemed different in any way, which was a good sign that he had no idea what was really going on at home. At his age and with his innocence, he would likely blurt out any secrets. Which only proved he didn't know any.

That had to be a good sign. Right?

"They can stay open," Dalton said after a thoughtful pause.

Bethany bit back her third yawn in a matter of a minute.

"Why don't you sleep with me in the main bedroom?" Blakely asked. "When Chase wakes up, it's the first place he'll head anyway."

Bethany drained the rest of her second glass without noticing Blakely still hadn't touched hers. "That's probably a good idea."

"Should I let Greg know you're staying over?" Blakely asked when Bethany stood up and stepped away from her handbag without a second thought.

"Let him worry," she said before heading up the back staircase.

"That doesn't sound good," Dalton said under his breath.

"They had a fight," she said.

"Did she say what about?"

"Well, no," Blakely responded before adding, "but it's not uncommon for a married couple to disagree."

"Exactly the reason I have no intention of ever willingly falling into that trap," he muttered.

"Same," she said quietly. He tilted his head and half smirked. Meaning, he must have heard her. Not that it mattered. Blakely's marital status and views toward the institution had no bearing on the man. They'd had a fling, nothing more.

A little voice in the back of her mind argued against the idea of "nothing more." Because the sex had been the best of her life, and she'd gone to sleep many nights since only to wake up thinking about how incredible he'd been. How intelligent and funny he'd been. And how easy it had been to let her guard down in a few short hours with the stranger. The term "stranger danger" applied to everyone outside of her inner circle—a circle that had precious few inside. Three, to be exact.

"We should probably get some sleep too," Dalton said, cutting into her thoughts.

She started toward the front door. "I'll see you out."

He didn't follow.

When she turned around to check, her heart gave a little flip at the sight of him. Dalton Remington stood there, leaning against the wall with thick, muscled arms folded across a broad chest. "Good try, Your Honor."

"What are you thinking? That you'll stay the night?" She shook her head. "I thought you were kidding about that."

"No, ma'am."

"I think we're well beyond formalities, Dalton," she snapped, not liking the change in tone.

"That may well be… Blakely," he quipped, not budging from his spot. "But you have a shadow until this ordeal is over." Before she could argue, he shook his head. "Let me do my job. This isn't personal."

Why were those words the equivalent of pinholes in a balloon? Pinholes that let all the air seep out, deflating the party favor.

Shoulders deflated like said balloon, Blakely conceded.

"Try not to look so disappointed that I'll be sleeping under the same roof," he stated, all cavalier. "You might hurt my feelings."

Despite the horrific evening, Blakely laughed.

"That's better," he said with a self-satisfied smile that she wanted to wipe off his face. "See, that doesn't hurt."

"You're not funny," Blakely countered even though she found herself laughing even harder.

Dalton laughed too, and it shouldn't be the sexiest sound she'd heard even though it was just that. Sexy. Dalton was sex in a bucket. He was also dangerous. As it was, her traitorous heart seemed to need the reminder.

A man like Dalton could smash down all the protective walls she'd built over the years. Walls that kept her heart from being shattered. Walls that kept her from having her head beat in. Again. Walls that kept the world out.

Blakely couldn't risk it even though Dalton didn't seem like the kind of person who would raise a hand toward anyone smaller or more vulnerable than him. Somewhere deep inside, her conscious mind registered the fact she'd brought her hand up to her forehead, where her index finger traced the raised skin at her hairline.

No one ever got to make her feel weak and afraid again. But she would be smart and accept Dalton's help. She wasn't handing over her power so much as using all available resources at hand.

The bastard who'd sent her back to that place—even for a few seconds—of being scared and alone wouldn't get away with it.

"Thank you for the offer of help, by the way," she said to Dalton. "There's a blanket and extra pillow in the ottoman. Hope you don't mind sleeping on the couch since my third bedroom has been turned into my home office."

"Fine by me," he said. "Doubt I'll get much sleep anyway."

"Okay," she said before getting out of the room, up the stairs, and as far away from the man as possible. Being in the same room with him alone made her fingers crave the way his hard muscles under silky skin felt.

Blakely cleared the sudden dryness in her throat. By tomorrow, the perp would be long gone or caught, and Dalton would walk out of her life forever.

Why was the thought no different than a stab wound in the heart?

Chapter Six

Dalton slept in fits and starts over the next four hours until sun streamed in through the windows. He rolled out of bed, fired off a couple dozen push-ups, and then headed to the shower after making a quick trip to his truck to retrieve his emergency supply backpack. In it, he kept a change of clothes and a travel kit with toothpaste and a toothbrush, a comb, deodorant. Pretty much all the basic supplies to get him through a night or two on the road if he couldn't get back home. There was a backup weapon inside, just in case.

On the ground floor of Blakely's home sat the living room, kitchen and dining area. A short hallway to the right of the front door led to a full bathroom and a bedroom that, true to her word, had been converted to a home office. The whole downstairs had a comfortable but minimal feel to it. The place was filled with cream-colored furniture with just the right amount of color worked in. He was no decorator and would never claim to be one. But this space felt welcoming. Like it invited you to sit down and get comfortable so you could stay for a while. Unlike its owner, who seemed like she couldn't get him out of her home fast enough. Blakely was a study in contrasts.

Dalton had no patience for someone who spent most of their time pushing him away despite needing him more than ever. Of course, she wouldn't see it that way. The determined set to her chin said she'd rather eat nails than admit she needed a bodyguard. She was also intelligent enough to accept his help, which he appreciated about the good judge. And a growing part of him wanted to know more about her. Where did she grow up? What happened to her parents? Did she have any other living relatives other than her sister and nephew?

Of course, all those questions were off-limits since they didn't help solve who attacked her last night. On the other hand, they weren't totally out of bounds considering this was an investigation. His job might be to act as bodyguard to the judge, but that didn't mean he couldn't put his investigator hat on. Working with Houston PD was out. They wouldn't share information unless they deemed it relevant to protecting Blakely.

A shower and fresh clothes were the best attitude adjustment he could think of after sleeping on the couch. Since Blakely and her sister were upstairs, he didn't figure a little noise in the kitchen would wake them. His stomach growled, reminding him that he'd skipped supper last night, and he needed caffeine to think clearly.

As he moved into the kitchen and flipped on the light, he heard the creak of a floorboard at the top of the staircase. It was windy outside. Might be the wind. Older homes had a language of their own, creaking and groaning with the weather. Then again, this house wasn't too old. Was someone coming down? Blakely?

He checked cabinets until he found a coffee mug. Then moved to the general area of the coffee maker. She had one of those machines that took pods. Wa-la! A colorful carousel filled with pods sat on the opposite side of the black-and-chrome machine. He grabbed a purple pod, popped it into the machine and set the mug underneath the spout. All these pod machines worked pretty much the same. The noise was worse than he anticipated, drowning out the floorboard creaks, the machine hissing as it spit out coffee. He figured this was meant to replicate the coffee shop experience. As long as the coffee didn't taste burnt, he could care less what kind of noise the machine made. His only hope was that he wasn't waking anyone up.

"Hello," a female voice he recognized as Bethany's said.

"Hey," he answered without turning around. "Do you want a cup of coffee?"

"No," she said, sounding half asleep. "Thanks, though. I just came down for water."

"I can make that happen for you," he said, retrieving a glass and filling it with water from the fridge door before she could plop onto a bar chair pushed up to the granite island.

"Thank you," she said after taking the offering.

"I'm a regular barista," he quipped, laughing at his own joke.

Bethany laughed too. Dark circles cradled her eyes. Stress lines were etched into her forehead. She and Blakely looked like sisters. The family resemblance was strong. To his liking, Blakely was the more beautiful twin, but he admitted that he was biased because there was something about her smile—the few times he'd gotten to see it—that sent a tornado whirling around inside his chest.

"Should I know who you are?" Bethany asked, and he realized she'd been studying him as he retrieved his mug and then joined her, standing across the island.

"What makes you ask that question?"

"You seem at home here," she said on a yawn.

"First time," he said before she could spin a yarn in her

mind that had him shacking up with her sister. Not that he'd mind all that much. But he couldn't offer anything more than temporary, and Blakely Adamson was not the temporary kind.

"Really?"

"Don't seem so shocked," he teased. "Kitchens all pretty much work the same. It's not hard to figure out where coffee supplies are, or a glass for that matter. Most folks keep them in similar places. Glasses near the dishwasher and coffee supplies on the counter."

"True," she said with a raised eyebrow. "Do you go into a lot of homes in your line of work?"

"I do," he said a little too enthusiastically. If he wanted to convince her that he didn't know Blakely intimately, he needed to calm down. "It's my job to protect judges like your sister when there's a threat present."

Bethany covered a gasp with her hand. "My sister is in real danger, isn't she?"

He gave her a second to let those words sink in because the question was rhetorical. Besides, there was an obvious threat to Blakely. Had she told her sister the perp was specifically after her? He didn't think so because Blakely wouldn't want to worry her sister more than she had to.

"She's been through so much already," Bethany said. "She's a good person too. She doesn't deserve any of what's happened to her."

"The horse-riding incident that left the scar?" he asked, knowing in his heart the explanation had been flimsy at best. He hadn't asked follow-up questions or quizzed her. He'd been in the brain fog that always accompanied being lost in desire. Being with Blakely had felt a whole lot like what he imagined being in love would be like. Couldn't say he would ever let himself go down that road with anyone.

Not with his genetic disaster waiting to happen. For a time, he considered only dating single mothers because the pressure to have a kid wouldn't be a constant undercurrent as he approached thirty. Biology took over with many of his dates, and he found himself being assessed as a potential life partner and father material over dinner when he'd barely eaten the first course.

Bethany stared at Dalton. "Is that where she told you the scar came from?"

"Yes," he confirmed.

She clamped her mouth shut as she shook her head. "Then I sure don't want to be the one to tell you any different."

"She's guarded with me," he explained, hoping to gain a better understanding of the reason while he had her sister alone.

"Not just with you," Bethany said without hesitation. "Although, to be honest, she's more relaxed around you than anyone else I've seen." Bethany's face twisted. "In fact, I thought there might be more between the two of you than an assignment."

"No," he said quickly. Too quickly? It would be unprofessional as hell for him to be in a relationship with someone from work. The consequences of a fling with a judge ending badly were...

Already crossed that bridge, dude. Not on purpose. Looking back, the secrecy had been a mistake—a mistake he couldn't bring himself to regret.

Bethany's eyebrow shot up. "You sure about that? Cuz I could have sworn..." She swatted like there was a fly in front of her face. "Never mind. You don't have to answer that. I'm sticking my nose where it doesn't belong, and I'm probably off base anyway. Of course, my sister would be more relaxed with extra security in the house. Makes sense."

She heaved a sigh. "It's just that…she deserves a break. You know? Not some random creep attacking her in her driveway." She caught herself again. "This was random, right?"

"It's too early to tell," he said. "Blakely didn't recognize her attacker, which rules out anyone close to her." *Unless… there were others involved.*

"She sends people to prison in her job," Bethany continued. "That has to count for something."

"We're looking into that angle," he confirmed.

"I knew it," Bethany said on another sharp sigh. "She has gone to great lengths to be ready for the next…" Bethany flashed eyes at him. "You know…to be ready." She chose her words carefully, which meant there was a whole lot more to the story with Blakely's forehead scar.

Dalton had a feeling he wasn't going to like the reason any more than he liked the judge being attacked so close to her home. Given this was personal, someone had to have been monitoring her activities. Waiting for the right time to strike.

His ego wanted to blame the source of the scar for the way she'd treated him. An abusive relationship would make her far less trusting of the opposite sex.

Less trusting of him.

BLAKELY HEARD VOICES in the kitchen as she got up for an early morning bathroom break. Considering her sister wasn't in bed next to Blakely, she assumed the low hum was Bethany and Dalton. Should she be worried the two of them were talking? *Yes.* She should get downstairs before Bethany gave Dalton all the details of Blakely's past.

Her sister wouldn't. Would she?

The older twin by a few minutes, Blakely had always been told she was an old soul. She'd always looked out for her sister and thought of her as much younger despite Bethany getting married first and becoming a mother at a young age.

After finishing up in the restroom, Blakely turned toward the stairs and then headed down. She doubted she could go back to sleep now that her mind was spinning.

Downstairs, she joined Bethany and Dalton in the kitchen.

"Coffee?" Dalton asked, looking a little too good standing in her kitchen in jeans and a black long-sleeve T-shirt.

"Yes, please," she said, joining her sister at the granite island.

"How did you sleep?" Bethany asked.

"I heard you snoring," Blakely said with a smile.

"What?" Bethany feigned being offended. "I already told you that I don't snore."

A cell buzzed. Dalton reached for his and fished it out of his jeans pocket. He studied the screen and frowned. "A distressed-looking man who looks to be in his early thirties is about to hit the doorbell."

"Greg?" Bethany asked, but it was more statement than question.

Dalton crossed the room and held his screen toward them. "Is this him?"

Bethany pushed to standing as the doorbell rang. "He better not wake Chase." She gave her sister a look that could freeze a wildfire before stomping into the living room.

"Think we should go with her?" he asked Blakely, who shook her head in response.

Heated arguments between couples were a landmine for any law enforcement officer to walk into. Dalton would keep an ear toward the front door since Bethany admitted to having an argument with her spouse last night.

"Come home with me," the male identified as Greg said in a hushed but urgent tone.

"No," Bethany stated with more than a hint of defiance in her voice. Whatever the two fought about would most likely be considered a major roadblock in their relationship based on the cold freeze in her tone. "Absolutely not, Greg."

"Should we be listening?" Blakely asked in a hushed tone.

"It's a habit from the job," he admitted. "I need to know that your brother-in-law won't do anything to hurt Bethany."

"I highly doubt that G—"

Blakely held up a hand. She checked her phone, ignored a text from her former law professor.

"Actually, I can't afford to take that tact," she said. "I see it too many times in my courtroom as well as my colleagues'. You think you're safe with someone and that you know them inside and out. But you can never truly know someone, can you?" Blakely caught herself before she gave up too much about her past.

"I said no," Bethany said a little more sternly this time. "My sister's awake in the kitchen, and a US marshal is standing with her. I'll get them both if you don't leave right now, Greg."

"We need to talk," he pleaded.

From the corner of her eye, she saw Dalton reach for his weapon.

"That shouldn't be necessary," Blakely said, pushing to standing. She held up a hand, indicating Dalton should wait in the kitchen. The look in his eyes said he was reluctant. His quick nod said he would listen to her.

Good. The last thing this situation needed was more heat. If Dalton came around the corner with his hand on his weapon, the situation could explode. Not that she'd ever seen Greg completely lose his temper, but he had been buried under work and spending a lot of late nights at the office. He'd remarked that having his own company meant he worked all hours and that, at times, he missed his former corporate job that allowed him vacations and weekends off. The dark circles underneath his eyes were punctuation to that sentence. Her heart went out to him. The pregnancy had been unexpected and had blown apart their long-term plan. Bethany was supposed to finish her college degree and work for five to ten years before the two of them started a family. Chase was perfect and definitely worth a change in plans. But Bethany wanted to stay home with her baby, so Greg doubled up on work. Not only did he work a full-time corporate job, but he also started a side business that grew enough for him to quit his day job and focus on his business. The new plan was supposed to reduce his stress and give him more time to be with the family, but owning and running a business meant working more hours. Lesson learned.

Were they fighting about money?

Bethany had a spending habit, drove an expensive luxury sport utility like all the other soccer moms. She'd had her heart set on a big home in the best school district for Chase.

"Hi, Greg." Blakely stepped into view, using a neutral voice.

"Blakely, please, let me come in and talk to my wife," Greg said. He stood just shy of six feet tall with a runner's build. He had sandy-blond hair and cobalt blue eyes. He wasn't Blakely's type, but most would consider him to be good-looking. But right now, his tie was loose around his neck, and he was wearing the same suit from last night.

"That's not a good idea right now, Greg, but I promise Bethany will be ready to talk soon," Blakely soothed. She quickly assessed that Greg was sober despite bloodshot eyes.

They were red from distress and being rubbed, and most likely dry from staying up all night worrying.

Greg had never been *GQ* ready, but he put himself together well under normal circumstances.

"Leave or I'll tell my sister the real reason we're fighting," Bethany said as Blakely slipped her hand in her sister's and squeezed for reassurance. She had no idea what the fight was about, figured it wasn't her business. Her sister and brother-in-law deserved privacy. Plus, Bethany hadn't let on that anything devastating was going on between her and Greg.

Greg looked devastated. "Fine." He raked his fingers through his hair. "Promise you'll hear me out once the initial shock wears off."

Blakely had a bad feeling in the pit of her stomach. This scenario only proved that you never really knew the person you let in your heart. A piece of hers wanted to argue that Dalton would have been different.

Could she trust it?

The short answer…no. And she'd be a fool to let him in.

Chapter Seven

Dalton fixed a cup of coffee for Blakely, keeping close tabs on the conversation going on in the next room in case emotions escalated and he needed to intervene. Blakely was doing a stellar job of bringing calm to the situation. And he learned something else this morning. For reasons he might never know or understand, Blakely Adamson would never trust him.

The reality shouldn't cause a knot to form in his chest or a sense of dread to tighten around him like a vise. What the hell? The weekend he'd spent with her had been filled with great conversation, humor and the best sex of his life. He needed to let it go and move on because she was all business now. Her normal mode?

Easier said than done, buddy. Especially while he was standing in her kitchen, wanting to dig deeper to find out her secrets.

"Please think about what I said last night," Greg said.

"It's time to go," Blakely stated as Bethany returned to the kitchen, looking like she'd just lost her best friend.

Had she?

"You think you know what your life is, and then someone pulls the rug out from underneath your feet," she said, returning to her spot at the granite island. She looked over at Dalton as he set Blakely's coffee mug down where she'd been sitting moments ago.

"Life can throw curveballs," he agreed.

"People!" Bethany smacked the flat of her palm against the hard surface. "People can throw curveballs!"

"Yes, they can," he agreed as she took in a couple of slow, deep breaths. He'd seen her sister do the same thing to calm fried nerves. *Family trait?* A change of subject was in order. "What about your father?"

"What about him?" she asked.

"Are you close?"

"He's gone," Bethany admitted. She went from white-hot anger to normal on her next exhale. "He and my mother have been gone a long time. Car crash." Those words resonated. Too many lives were lost on Texas roadways. I-45, the road connecting Galveston to Houston and on up to Dallas, takes more than its fair share of lives every year.

"I'm sorry to hear that," he said, drawing on as much compassion as he could muster.

Bethany tilted her head to one side. "Looks like you have personal experience. Have you lost someone you loved too?"

"Grandparents," he stated with shame. He'd been in Galveston for work, not play, when he'd spent the weekend with Blakely. He'd been waiting for word because a felon he was tracking was supposed to show up there. Never did. But he couldn't bill the weekend as a total loss. Not when he'd met Blakely instead. Still, shame was a heavy cloud—he'd been having the best time of his life while his grandparents were in comas. Had Blakely provided a much-needed escape from his life? It had been the first time he'd felt anything but numb since hearing about the crash that nearly claimed his beloved grandparents' lives. Still might. "They were driving home and ended up in a single-vehicle accident that left them both in comas."

"Now I'm the one who is sorry," Bethany said with a frown. "Life is unpredictable. I mean, you think you know where it's headed and that you have a handle on it all. Then, boom! Everything you know changes, and you have to decide what steps to take next."

Dalton nodded.

"Forgive the directness of this question, but shouldn't you be with your grandparents right now instead of here?" Bethany asked, then bit down on her bottom lip.

"I have a couple of siblings and three cousins to share the responsibility with," he explained. "We set up a rotation based on who could take leave the fastest. My turn's next."

Bethany studied him. "How many of the five others have taken a turn?"

"Four," he stated.

"And when you take leave, I'm guessing it's at least a few days to a week," she said. "Which means this has been going on for a long time."

"Yes, it has." Too long in his estimation. And then he tuned in to the sound of the door closing in the next room. A couple of beats later, Blakely reappeared in the kitchen and reclaimed her seat next to her sister.

"Tell me about the fight you two had," Blakely said as she studied Dalton first and her sister second. It seemed to dawn on her that she might have interrupted them. "Everything okay in here?"

"Yes, of course," Bethany said. "Dalton here was nice enough to offer to make me a cup of coffee."

"That's right," Dalton said, appreciating the cover. He didn't want to get into his personal life with Blakely right now. There was no need to get personal with her at all now that all her walls had come back up.

Besides, what did he have to offer Blakely other than great sex?

Not much.

A person like her deserved more than he could give. So he wouldn't push the issue or attempt to break down those walls around her heart again.

He finished making the coffee, which wasn't much more than setting a clean cup under the spout, loading a pod and pushing a button. He had a French press at his apartment that he used on his days off. There was something about the routine of loading fresh beans into his hand grinder, heating water and going through the rest of the steps that relaxed him. On workdays, he grabbed a cup from the small coffee shop on the corner on his way into work. On days he was traveling for an assignment, he did the same. It was important to have a day-off ritual that signaled a change in the lineup. Otherwise, the days ran together in a sea of sameness.

Damn. Wasn't he getting philosophical?

"Here you go," he said to Bethany, serving her a fresh cup of coffee. At this rate, he might change his job description to barista.

"What?" Blakely asked, studying him.

He shot a look to indicate he needed more information if he was going to answer her question.

"You just smiled," she said. "And I wanted to know what put it there."

"Internal joke," he said.

"I could use a good laugh," she continued.

"I doubt it would translate," he said.

"Okay," she said with a hint of disappointment in her tone. He should probably feel bad except that she wasn't the only one who could keep things to herself. "How about food. Is anyone hungry?"

"I doubt I could eat," Bethany said with a frown.

"What about something calm, like yogurt?" Blakely asked her sister, ever the protective one. The fact they were twins struck Dalton as odd since Blakely took on the role of older sister, and Bethany seemed content to be taken care of as the baby of the family.

"I'll try," Bethany conceded.

Blakely served her sister before turning to Dalton. "How about an omelet?"

He remembered the one she'd made for him in Galveston. His mouth watered at the thought of another. "Only if you'll allow me to help."

"You've been serving up coffee," she quipped. "Your job is done." She motioned toward the spot where she'd been sitting moments ago. "Take a load off."

"I'll take a walk around the perimeter instead," he said, thinking whatever he'd chased last night might have returned.

The reminder of them being in danger struck Blakely like a jab. She straightened her back and moved toward the fridge.

He had a few minutes before breakfast would be ready, so he headed out the back way to investigate the commotion from last night more thoroughly. The sun was shining. Wind had enough of a chill to make him wish he'd worn a jacket. He'd be fine. It would take more than cold temperatures to make him turn around. Jogging helped get his blood moving.

Deer tracks didn't surprise him. He backtracked as best as he could.

Found human prints. Large. Men's.

BLAKELY PLATED HALF of the omelet, placing it next to sliced tomato, then walked toward the back door. As she neared, it opened, and Dalton filled its frame. Her heart gave a traitorous flip at seeing him. The wild look in his eyes sent her pulse racing. "What's out there?"

"Footprints," he said. "It was too dark last night to easily pick them up, and I stomped all over a couple when I chased what I thought was a wild animal away from your backyard."

Blakely brought her hand up to cover a gasp. "You didn't mention it last night."

"Didn't see the need," he said.

"Why wouldn't investigators use their flashlights to check the area?"

"My guess is the attack was initially believed to be random," he said. She'd sat on the bench through too many cases where a beat cop missed important evidence to dispute Dalton's reasoning. Instead, she gave a slight nod.

"Come eat before the food gets cold." Blakely never considered herself much of a cook. She could follow a recipe okay. But she wasn't exactly someone who "created" in the kitchen. Most of the time, she ordered prepackaged meals from a service. That way, all she had to do was toss it in the microwave, hit a button and, wa-la, dinner. Omelets on the weekend were a good way to change things up. Most of the time, she cooked them for brunch before curling up with a good book or hitting her playlist. Unless, of course, Chase was sleeping over. Then, the tent forts came out.

Speaking of Chase, she should probably go upstairs and check on him after breakfast.

Dalton sat down and picked up a fork. He stabbed the egg as he took a chunk out of the omelet and then ate it. Was he frustrated?

The man took his job seriously. Was that the only reason protecting her meant so much to him? Her heart wanted their weekend to mean more than casual sex, especially considering she didn't normally go there, and a place down deep said that Dalton was special.

Blakely stood at the island as she ate, far too wound up to sit down. She paced in between bites, considering how someone could have been lurking behind her home without her having the first clue. She'd kept the blinds open so no one could sneak up on her. She hadn't considered how easy it would be to watch her from afar.

Last bite down, she checked her sister's yogurt cup. At least Bethany was able to finish it. Thank heaven for small miracles. Blakely grabbed a banana and peeled it for her sister next as Chase bounded down the stairs. Tufts of his hair stuck up at odd angles in the most adorable way. That kid had her heart in his seven-year-old hands.

"Hey, buddy," Blakely said as Bethany seemed momentarily lost in her own world. Marital trouble had to be the worst.

He made a beeline to his mother after locking on, mumbling something that sounded like, "I'm hungry."

"Do you want eggs or waffles?" Blakely asked.

"Waffles," he said, perking up considerably at the thought of a sugar rush.

"You got it, kiddo," Blakely said before pulling his favorite brand out of the freezer and then popping a pair into the toaster next to the fridge.

Within minutes, Chase was happily perched in his mother's lap while gobbling down the syrup-soaked treat. Blakely poured a glass of milk then set it next to his plate.

Bethany held on to Chase like he was about to disappear into thin air. Her marriage must be in serious trouble. Not once had her sister bailed on a date night with Greg. The man had shown up looking like he needed a shower and a good shave. And the dark circles underneath his eyes said he was either working too hard or worrying too much. This wasn't the time to pry into her sister's marriage. Not with Chase in the room.

But Blakely was curious about what a marriage that looked perfect on the outside could possibly be facing. Whatever it was, it had to be bad to keep Bethany here. She hadn't made a move to go home or even mentioned the possibility.

"Do you want me to pick up a few of your things from home so you can stay over a couple of nights?" Blakely asked, and then received a warning glare from Dalton. She shot him a look right back.

"I can do it," he offered.

"No," Bethany said. "I can borrow anything I need from Blakely." Something between Bethany and Dalton had shifted this morning. A bond?

As strange as it sounded, even to her, they seemed a whole lot more comfortable around each other in a short amount of time. When she really thought about it, the change happened this morning, while she was at the front door with Greg.

"That a real gun?" Chase asked once he'd devoured breakfast. He was all big eyes and smiles now.

"Yes," Dalton responded. "But it comes with great responsibility and isn't meant for small hands."

Chase sighed. "My hands have always been too small. That's why I play soccer. Because I can never catch a football with these." He held up his hands with a look of disappointment that would melt the most ice-encased heart.

"Hands grow just like every other body part," Dalton reassured. His words resonated with her nephew, turning the frown into a contemplative nod.

A growing part of her liked the ease Dalton seemed to feel around the two most important people in Blakely's life. She gave herself a mental headshake before heading down that no-future trail. She would never trust anyone of the opposite sex. That had been stripped from her a long time ago along with her naïve belief that all humans had good in them. During that time in her life, she'd dreamed of becoming a social worker so she could roll up her sleeves and help people with their transformation.

Imagine the disappointment when she learned not everyone had redeeming qualities or wanted to be reformed. Blakely shook off the reverie.

Everyone she cared about was under one roof. Safe.

For now. Those two words haunted her.

Chapter Eight

Breakfast dishes were a team effort, reminding Dalton what it was like to have family around. He'd gotten used to living alone. Too used to it?

After documenting the shoe imprint and filing it with his office, he read the crime scene report from Houston PD looking for nuggets of useful information. The officer on the report had been wet behind the ears, barely in his twenties. Not that Dalton was old at twenty-eight, but the officer had seemed younger than his years. Besides, Dalton had grown up fast and never looked back. Did it have to do with coming from a big family? Probably. That, and growing up on a paint horse ranch where there was no shortage of work. Everyone pitched in. Chores were a way of life growing up in a ranching community.

Dalton had been as wild as a young buck too. His feet rarely saw shoes in the summer unless he was far out on ranch property. When he was bareback on a horse, he didn't see a need for shoes.

Looking back, it was a magical childhood even though he might not have realized it at the time. No. He'd taken it for granted. Like breathing. Walking. Getting out of bed every morning.

His grandparents' conditions reminded him to slow down and take a look around. Was he afraid of what he'd see?

"Can we play?" Chase asked, bringing over a plastic horse that was sized for a Barbie doll.

"I'm afraid I can't right now," Dalton said. He regretted the words the second Chase's shoulders rounded in defeat.

"I get it," the boy said. "You're too busy, just like my dad always says." He turned to walk away.

"Do you have a baseball?" Dalton asked.

Chase spun around, his face lit like a tree on Christmas morning. "Do I?" He bolted upstairs to what was probably his room. Despite his small size, he made quite a racket on the stairs as he ran up then down.

"Outside with that," Blakely warned, pointing out the back door. A second later, she realized that she'd just asked them to stay outside where Chase would be exposed in the open. "Or, maybe just go to your room to play."

Chase let out a disappointed sigh.

"I just don't want anything to get broken in the living room," Blakely explained.

"We should probably listen to your aunt," Dalton said.

"Will you go upstairs with me?" Chase asked, expecting Dalton to bail based on the kid's expression.

"Why not?" Dalton reasoned. "Let's go."

"Yay," Chase said, then chanted all the way up the staircase.

The little boy had a way of wiggling into even the coldest heart.

"Are you going to tell me what happened between you and Greg?" Blakely asked her sister as the two moved to the couch and then sat side by side.

"You go first," Bethany countered.

"Not sure I have anything to discuss."

"What really happened last night?" Bethany asked. "Who is he?"

"That's a question for law enforcement on the case," Blakely said. "Believe me, I wish I had an answer."

"Are you going in to work tomorrow?" Bethany asked.

"Why wouldn't I?"

Bethany made eyes at her. "Oh, I don't know. Because you were attacked in your driveway and could have been killed." Her sister's lips formed a thin line. Brackets formed around her mouth. Worry lines etched her forehead.

"I have twenty-four-hour protection," Blakely pointed out. "The chances of the bastard returning, let alone getting to me, are almost nonexistent." It was the crack in the sidewalk that allowed weeds to grow.

"Dalton will be staying over again?"

"Yes," she confirmed. "It's his job, and he pulled the 'lucky' card to protect me." She made air quotes with her fingers when she said the word *lucky*.

"That must be how you guys know each other," Bethany surmised. "I should have guessed. The two of you probably run into each other at the courthouse."

Not really. But Blakely had no plans to tell her sister the two of them hadn't seen each other before the Galveston weekend. Clearly. What were the odds he would pull this assignment?

When you considered her luck, they were high, actually.

"I'm guessing there's no word on a suspect yet," Bethany continued.

"I would have heard something if an arrest had been made," Blakely reassured. Which didn't mean she would necessarily know if the officers had a suspect.

"It's awful to think there's a possibility that I might lose you too," Bethany said.

Blakely put an arm around her younger sister. "I'm not planning on going anywhere." A tear fell, leaving a stain on Blakely's pajama bottoms. "Hey. I'm serious. I'm here, and I don't want you to worry. Okay?"

"You and Chase are all I've got left," Bethany said under her breath.

"Are you and Greg getting a divorce?"

Bethany exhaled a long, slow breath. Didn't speak.

"Okay, you have to tell me what happened with him," Blakely urged.

"He had an affair," she stated before giving in to quiet sobs.

The fact Blakely had just been nice to Greg, comforting him, caused bile to rise in her throat. She should have given him a piece of her mind instead. Once again, she was reminded those closest to you would only end up hurting you in the end.

"I'm so sorry, sweetie," she whispered to her sister as she stroked her hair.

"Someone from work," Bethany said.

"He confessed this to you last night?"

"That would have been better," she said. "But, no, I found out because she texted him while he was in the bathroom." A few sniffles quieted Bethany for several beats. "She was *sexting* him while he was on a date night with his *wife*. How cliché am I now? Married young. Had a child young. Husband cheated. Divorced before thirty-one."

"You two seemed to have it all," Blakely said. "There's nothing wrong with you wanting to believe the fairy tale."

"Except for the fact the traditional fairy tale is as outdated as I feel," Bethany said. "I didn't finish my degree.

What kind of job am I going to be able to get to support myself and Chase?"

"Greg will pay child support," Blakely reminded. "He might not have been around for Chase, but Greg loves his son and trusted that you were taking care of Chase's needs. There's no way he'll leave you in a bad situation. Besides, the last time I spoke to him business was thriving."

"Can I trust anything the man says?"

Good question. One Blakely didn't want to touch. "The love you shared with Greg was real. And he obviously doesn't want to lose you. I'm not saying you should forgive him or go back. Those are your decisions, and I'll support you no matter what. But he'll take care of you either way."

"Yeah?" Bethany asked with no sign of hope in her voice. Then, she added, "Who takes care of you?"

Blakely didn't have a good answer to her sister's question. Until recently, she hadn't given it a thought. Milestone birthdays had a way of sneaking up on you. Turning thirty had caused her to assess her life. Career was on track. Actually, she was doing better than she'd expected there. Personal life?

No one had it all. Right?

Except maybe someone like Dalton. The man was sharp, had a sense of humor and looks that could kill.

Thinking about last night, she regretted the last word.

"It doesn't sound like Greg to cheat," Blakely said. How well did she know her brother-in-law?

Bethany shrugged. "People change, I guess." She blew out a breath. "I should have seen it coming. All those late nights at the office, 'working.'" She hooked her fingers in air quotes.

"Did he offer an explanation?" Blakely asked. As awful as this was, it was taking her mind off her own trouble.

"For cheating or working late?"

"Working late," she confirmed.

"There was always an excuse." Bethany leaned her head to one side, resting it on her fist as she propped her elbow up on the back of the sofa.

"I thought he hired someone to be his right-hand person last year," Blakely continued.

"He did," her sister said. "Except that Greg said he had to be the one to deal with customers to ensure they had a good experience, or they'd take their business elsewhere." Bethany sank into the sofa. "It's probably my fault too. I mean, I kept asking for a bigger house and nicer cars." She tapped her wrist, which held several expensive bracelets. "I loved when he gave me presents." She gasped. "I think I started loving the gifts more than Greg." Another deep breath. "What if I walked him straight into the arms of someone else who would put less pressure on him?"

"You didn't."

"We don't know that," she said, shaking her head for emphasis. "It could be my fault too."

"First of all, I don't like hearing you blame yourself," Blakely said calmly. Relationships were complicated, and she didn't have a leg to stand on personally. But she'd witnessed the deterioration of many once-blissful unions. At least from the outside, the couples seemed happy. "You aren't the one who violated your marriage. Don't let Greg off the hook so easily. He could have talked to you first. Told you how he was feeling. Brought you into the workplace more. I'm sure you would have rolled up your sleeves and pitched in."

"What if I told him that I was too tired when Chase was a baby, so he never asked me again?"

"Again, not exactly your fault," Blakely pointed out.

"When Chase had colic, you didn't sleep for what felt like months. You could barely keep your eyes open while we were in the middle of a conversation."

"Funny how Father Time steals your memories," she said.

Some memories stuck with you forever, etched in the scars on your body as much as the ones in your mind.

"Don't tell me you forgot," Blakely teased.

"Honestly, that whole time was a blur," Bethany admitted. "If I didn't have pictures and videos, I wouldn't even remember Chase as an infant."

"Even that fresh-from-the-bath smell?"

"I could never forget that," Bethany said with a rare smile.

"Don't make any decisions about your life or your marriage while you're this tired, okay?"

"That's probably good advice." Bethany bit down on her bottom lip like she used to when they were teenagers and she couldn't decide what to do next. "It's just that I never see going back home and pretending nothing happened."

"I'm not telling you what to do, so don't take this the wrong way," Blakely said. She wasn't sticking up for Greg so much as making sure her sister played this smart. "But couples do work through infidelity."

"I never thought we were just like other couples, though."

If something like this could happen to Bethany and Greg, no one would be immune.

The crack of a bullet split the air. For a half second, she worried Chase had gotten hold of Dalton's gun. *Impossible.* Dalton would not be that careless.

Blakely shoved her sister to the floor and followed, crouching low. She risked a glance. The family room window leading out to the backyard was cracked and had a bullet hole dangerously close to where Blakely's head had been while seated on the couch. Wild shot?

Not a chance.

Blood pressure through the roof, she didn't hear Dalton until the lock snicked in the front door and then again when he locked it after leaving.

The thought of anything happening to him caused her chest to squeeze as she reached for her cell to call 911.

Blood on her arm sent waves of panic through her as she checked her body to see where she'd been shot.

But it wasn't her.

Bethany.

"Oh no," Blakely said as her sister's body went limp. "Bethany. Stay with me. You're going to be okay." She could scarcely get out the words through blinding tears and the frog in her throat. "Wake up. *Please.*"

Chapter Nine

Dalton couldn't get out of the house fast enough after the gunshot that shocked the hell out of him. *"Hide in the closet until I come back for you,"* he'd said to Chase, tucking him deep into the walk-in. Older homes in Texas were known for their closet space. The fact came in handy when Dalton convinced the boy to find a spot in the very back where no one would find him.

Dalton dismissed the fear that he would be shot and the kid would starve to death before anyone found him. Besides, Blakely knew Chase was upstairs. She would give her life before anything happened to that child.

Right now, Dalton needed to focus all his energy and attention on capturing the shooter. He ran toward the neighbor's house on the left to circle around and, hopefully, not be seen by the perp. Whoever it was, he was determined. Striking again this soon was a sign of his desperation. Bringing the fight to her doorstep sent a strong message… *I can get to you anywhere you are. No place is safe. Not even your home in your gated community.*

That was the problem with gates. They might keep vehicles out, but a determined individual would walk into the community. Probably scale a wall or fence if there was one.

So, no, they didn't work. He imagined they kept out folks who handed out flyers, but they weren't the danger.

As he rounded the neighbor's home, a dog barked. Dalton cursed. The noise would draw attention, giving away his location. Worse yet, the killer could be closing in on Blakely's home right now.

Dalton's training kept him from going to a possibly injured person instead of going after a perp. A quick glance into the family room had revealed Blakely and her sister hunkering down. The fact she hadn't called out for help most likely meant they were both fine.

Blakely would also know to immediately call 911.

As he doubled back, deciding to go round the other side of her residence, he heard the first emergency sirens. *That was fast.* Then again, folks didn't spend all this money to live in a protected neighborhood without law enforcement nearby.

A private-security vehicle came blaring up in front of the house as Dalton crossed the front lawn. He didn't have time to reach for his badge without possibly being shot as the for-hire armed security guard hopped out of his vehicle, wedged in the door and yelled, "Stop or I'll shoot!"

"My name is Marshal Remington," Dalton said, both hands high in the air.

"Toss your weapon," the rent-a-cop ordered.

"I'm a US marshal," Dalton continued as the front door swung open.

"He's okay," Blakely shouted. "You got the wrong man."

The security guy offered a quick apology before heading in the direction Blakely urged.

Then Dalton got a good look at her. Saw blood. "Where are you shot?"

"It's Bethany," she said with a vulnerability in her voice

that brought out all his protective instincts. "She's unconscious. Help. Please."

"Let's get some pressure on the wound," he said as he bolted toward the front door. The moment of relief that Blakely wasn't hurt was quickly replaced with the fear a seven-year-old was about to lose his mother.

The vise tightened around Dalton's chest as he ran inside and to Bethany. A dishrag was soaked with blood as it pulsed from the base of her neck on the right side of her body.

"Her pulse is weak," Blakely said as she dropped down beside her sister, who was lying on the carpet, limp.

"Let's get the bleeding under control before we do anything else," he said, taking a spot on the opposite side of Bethany. He put pressure on the wound using the dishcloth.

"I can't lose her." Blakely's voice was low, and there was a quiet desperation that ripped his heart out. "Or Chase." She paused. *"Chase!"* She gasped. "Where is he?"

"Hiding in the back of his closet," Dalton said, hoping the explanation was enough to reassure her that Chase was fine. Just in case, he added, "He'll wait there until I come for him."

"He can't see her like this," she said. "It'll devastate him."

"The bleeding is under control for now," he said to Blakely, who was clearly in a mild state of shock.

A knock at the door followed by the words "Emergency personnel coming inside" was the equivalent of Christmas morning back at the ranch.

"In the family room," Dalton shouted as Blakely practically jumped to her feet before bolting toward the front door.

In the next few seconds, the cavalry arrived. As Bethany was attended to by a pair of EMTs, Dalton disappeared upstairs to check on Chase.

The little boy was hiding, as he was told to, in the far reaches of the closet. He'd stacked a pile of dirty clothes on top of himself for further camouflage. The kiddo was smart and had good survival instincts.

Dalton had been surviving on his own ever since his mother walked out. Would Chase feel those same feelings of shame and abandonment? Wonder what the hell he'd done so wrong that his own mother would turn her back on him?

The vise tightened once again.

"Hey, buddy," Dalton began when Blakely showed up on his heels. "It's safe to come out now."

A shirt flew across the closet as the mound of clothes erupted and the little boy emerged.

"That was fun," Chase stated, chest puffed out, completely unaware of the danger they'd all been in. "Can we do it again?"

"Not right now," Blakely said. "But I promise we'll have more fun later."

Chase brushed himself off and ran into his aunt's arms.

"I have something to tell you," Blakely said. The sight of the two of them was enough to melt the coldest glacier.

"Are we playing another game?" Chase asked, hope in his big eyes.

"No," Blakely hedged. "This is serious, but I want you to know that everything is going to be okay."

Chase's smile faded.

"Your mommy has been in an accident," Blakely said before quickly adding, "She's going to the hospital, where doctors will take good care of her. I don't want you to worry one bit. Okay?" To an adult, those words would be a sign of just how bad the situation was. To a kid, they offered reassurance.

"What happened to Mommy?"

"She got hurt and started bleeding," Blakely explained in terms a child could understand. She was good with Chase. For a split second, Dalton saw her with their kids.

Hold on there, dude. Getting ahead of yourself. You have never wanted children.

What the hell was up with the vision?

It had to be the thought of losing his grandparents weighing on his mind more than he wanted to admit. Dalton reassured himself daily that they were strong and would pull through this. With each passing day, his resolve faded a little more. Facing losing them wasn't something Dalton was ready to do. Was this his brain's way to force him to face facts?

His grandparents might not make it, which brought up a whole host of feelings.

Cell in hand, he searched for good news from the home front. While he was wishing, he hoped the officers outside would catch the perp. More than anything, he wanted to be able to tell Blakely that she was safe. Chase had already burrowed himself deep inside Dalton's chest. He wanted to deliver the good news that the little boy was out of danger too. As well as Bethany.

Instead, his world was collapsing around him.

DISAPPOINTMENT AND SHAME shrouded Blakely at the fact she hadn't been able to keep her sister safe. At least Chase was safe. *For now.* She hated those two words.

"Can we go see Mommy?" Chase asked.

At a loss for words, Blakely stuttered. "I—um—"

"Think it might be best to let her get some rest so she'll be good and awake when we stop by later," Dalton said, saving the day.

Blakely wasn't normally at a loss for words. She appreciated the save and shot a quick thank-you with her eyes.

The smile he gave her in return caused her stomach to perform a somersault routine. Dalton had a surprisingly calming effect on her despite the electricity charging the air between them. Their chemistry was undeniable.

But chemistry wasn't everything. Bethany and Greg's had been obvious when they were in school. But she hadn't witnessed it for a long time, now that she really thought about it. They'd shifted into parent and business-owner roles, and all the heat was sucked out of their relationship. The thoughts were random at a time like this, but the brain had ideas of its own, bouncing around to different topics. It seemed to be she'd find solutions when she least thought about a situation. Always, the back of her mind was fitting together information bits to explain things she didn't immediately understand.

"Okay," Chase said, his spindly arms wrapped around Blakely's neck as he held on. She patted his back.

"What do you think about going somewhere else to play for a little while?" Dalton asked.

"Where?" A little of Chase's normal spunk laced the question.

"How about we pretend to be policemen?" Dalton said. She saw where he was going with this. They would have to go to the substation to make reports. Plus, it was probably best to get Chase out of the house before he saw the blood on the carpet. Her window was in need of repair before anyone could stay here again.

The thought of someone targeting her…*her home*…sat heavy in her thoughts. The perp wanted to take her out pretty badly if he was willing to come back so soon. Or did he have places set up in and around her home in case the attack didn't go as planned out front? Less than twenty-four hours had passed since the attack in her driveway. The perp had been clear about what he wanted: *"You!"*

Blakely involuntarily shivered at the thought someone could hate her so much they wanted her dead. Facing facts, she realized that being a judge meant locking criminals behind bars. She presided over jury cases. Technically, a jury made the call. However, she was responsible for sentencing. Figuring out who she upset to this degree was her first priority. Could Dalton take her to her chambers so she could look at case history?

The perp must have recently been released. His voice didn't ring any bells, but maybe if her memory was jogged, her brain might be able to fit those pieces together and give her a name. If she was going to die by someone's hands, she deserved to know who the bastard determined to kill her was.

Without another word, Blakely stood at the same time as Dalton. Chase was too old and too proud to be carried around like a baby. He reminded Blakely of the fact often.

Rather than take the back staircase, Blakely headed toward the front of the house to avoid the bloody scene.

"I'll talk to whoever is in charge," Dalton offered. "Do you want to hang out up here or wait for me by the front door?"

"Front door," she decided, wanting to get out of her house as soon as humanly possible. A shot of rage nailed her for feeling unsafe in her own home. She'd made a promise to herself no one ever got to make her feel that way again. *Not for long.*

The bastard might have won this round, but she'd be ready moving forward. First and foremost, she had to figure out what to do with Chase.

Greg.

In all the chaos, she'd forgotten to call Bethany's husband to let him know what happened. With Chase in her arms, there was no way she'd make the call now. Houston PD would deliver the news if she didn't. Could she make the call without alarming Chase or alerting him to the severity of the situation?

One thing was certain, Chase couldn't be around her until the perp was locked behind bars. It was too dangerous. The thought a stray bullet could have struck him instead was another shot to the heart.

Keeping calm was her best defense. So she tucked those thoughts away as she walked down the stairs, holding her nephew's hand. Dalton had gone ahead.

"Thought you might need this," he said, holding out her handbag. "Phone's inside."

"Thank you," she said. "Mind if I take a bathroom break before we head out?" She could explain what she was really doing once they got on the road.

"Not at all," he said. In a surprise move, Chase let go of her hand and grabbed Dalton's instead. The move choked her up a little bit.

"I'll meet you in the truck," she said.

"All right then," Dalton said, acting cool. The catch in his throat said he was affected by the move too.

Blakely excused herself before heading down the hallway to the bathroom. Once inside, she dug her cell out and studied the screen. Tapped her thumb on the side of the device. With any luck, Greg would pick up. If the call rolled into voice mail, she might lose her nerve to deliver the news.

With a deep breath, she located his contact information and made the call.

Greg picked up on the first ring. "Hello?"

"Hey, Greg."

"Bethany isn't returning any of my texts or calls," he said, sounding frazzled. "Is she there?"

"Are you sitting down?" she asked.

"No," he said. "Why? Is it that bad?" Before she could respond, he asked, "Is she leaving me? Because I messed up royally, and I—"

"Slow down, Greg," Blakely said as calmly as she could. How did she tell the man his wife had been shot at her house—a house where his son also spent the night? "I have something important to tell you, and I need you to sit down."

The phone went silent for a moment.

Then came, "Okay, I'm sitting. What is it?"

How did she get him up to speed with everything that had happened in the last twenty-four hours?

Maybe she didn't. Maybe she stuck to the facts about what had just happened.

"Bethany is being taken to the hospital right now," she began.

"What?" The question was rhetorical.

"My life is in danger, and I'm afraid Bethany was caught in the cross fire," she continued in as calm a tone as she could muster. Hearing those words come out of her own mouth was surreal. Was this really happening? "Bethany was shot, Greg."

"Oh dear G—"

"We were able to stem the bleeding until EMTs arrived," she explained. "I can't tell you what her current condition is. Only that she is being taken to Houston General in an ambulance."

"Alone?"

"Yes, for now." Blakely had to stop by the local substation before she could head to the hospital.

"You were there," Greg said, his voice filled with disbelief. "You have to have some idea as to whether or not she's going to make it."

"I'm hoping and praying just as much as you are," Blakely said. "And don't worry about Chase. He's with me."

"All due respect, Blakely, so was my wife." This wasn't the time for Greg to be indignant, but she understood him needing to take his frustration out on someone. "Sorry. I didn't mean that."

"An apology isn't necessary," Blakely reassured. "I know you didn't mean it."

"Still," he said on a sharp sigh. "Are you heading to the hospital?"

"After I stop by the police substation," she said. "What do you want me to do with Chase? Can you take him?" She paused a beat. "I think he'll be safer with his father."

"Yeah, I guess," Greg hedged. Not exactly the response she was hoping for. "The hospital isn't a good place for him, though. I thought maybe he could stay with you or—"

"Never mind," she cut him off, offended that he wouldn't want to comfort his son while the kid's mother was in the hospital. "I'll make arrangements for him." She needed to think because there was no way she could keep him with her and ensure his safety. "Don't worry about it."

"No," Greg decided. "I should be with him. It's just that work is piling up, and I…never mind. I'll take him to the office with me."

"Okay," Blakely said, pensive, before telling him that she'd drop Chase off after a trip to the local substation. Greg had left the details of Chase's life up to Bethany. Still, it was surprising to see how disconnected he'd been with his own son. Had making a living blinded him to what was really important? His family? And how had Blakely missed it?

Easy. Bethany never talked about the cracks in her marriage. From the outside, she had a perfect life.

Blakely should have noticed how much effort it was taking to create the illusion. She might have been able to help.

"I'll swing by the hospital now," Greg said, sounding resigned.

"Why don't we meet there instead?" she offered. "That way, you can stay there as long as possible."

Greg's hesitation wasn't reassuring. Was she being too hard on him?

"See you there?" she asked.

"Okay," he agreed before ending the call.

She left the call with an unsettled feeling.

Chapter Ten

Dalton tapped his thumb on the steering wheel as he waited for Blakely to join them in his truck.

"I play soccer," Chase offered, filling the empty space.

"How's that going for you?" Dalton asked, unsure what the hell to say to a seven-year-old.

"I don't like it when I score and the other team cries," Chase said, like scoring a goal brought down the weight of the world on his shoulders.

"Do you like kicking the ball?" Dalton asked.

"It's okay."

"Have you thought about playing a different sport?" Dalton asked.

"Yeah," Chase admitted without enthusiasm.

"Or an instrument?"

Chase's face lit up. "Like guitar?"

"Sure," Dalton said, unsure if he'd just opened a can of worms. No one would accuse him of being a good parent. Or of being in a position to give advice to a kid. There was a reason he didn't spend much time with anyone under the age of twenty. He didn't have the first idea what to do with them or what to talk about with them. "Why not?"

"That would be awesome," Chase announced. "Do you think I can quit soccer?"

"What does your mother say?"

"That I can do whatever I want after I finish the season," Chase recited.

"Sounds like good advice right there." Dalton wouldn't argue with teaching a kid to follow through on his commitments.

"What about my friends?" Chase asked in earnest. "Won't I be letting them down if I quit?"

"A real friend would want you to be happy," Dalton said after a thoughtful pause. "Would you want your friend to stay on a team if they weren't happy?"

"No, course not," Chase responded. His eyes widened when it dawned on him. "And they wouldn't want me to play if I wasn't happy."

"Real friends will be there no matter what," Dalton said, wondering when the last time he could say that about another human being had been. Growing up, he'd been close with his family. Now, he had the occasional poker night with a few folks from work and not much else.

His life had never felt empty until thinking about it in those terms. Until now.

What was he going to do about it?

Out of the corner of his eye, he saw movement at the front door. Blakely stepped out, looking more beautiful than she had a right to.

After she joined them, he set out for the closest substation.

"What are all the policemen doing at your house, Aunt Blakely?" Chase asked. His innocence deserved protection.

"They're helping," Blakely said without hesitation. "Do you remember how we talked about how important it is to look for the helpers if something goes wrong?"

"Uh-huh," Chase said.

"Your mom had an accident, so a lot of helpers showed up to take care of her," Blakely explained. Dalton couldn't think of a better way to explain a stressful situation to a kid. She had a knack for parenting whether she realized it or not. An image of her holding their child stamped his thoughts.

Where the hell did that come from?

BLAKELY TOOK A deep breath. After giving statements while Chase played in a witness room and driving to the hospital, she fixed a second cup of coffee while waiting for her brother-in-law to show.

Dalton circled the waiting room a second time in a matter of minutes as they waited for word from the doctor. All they knew so far was that Bethany had lost a lot of blood and was in stable condition. The doctor wanted to speak to Blakely before allowing any visitors. Her mind kept snapping to wishing she could head to her chambers to check out her files. The identity of the bastard determined to kill her must be hiding in those documents.

She flexed and released her fingers a couple of times to work off some of the frustration. No one got to make her afraid anymore. The exception was this sick sonofabitch coming after her sister or nephew. Of that, she was scared beyond reason.

"Hey." Dalton's calm voice, his deep timbre, brought light to the darkest places inside her. "Bethany is going to be fine, and we'll find the bastard responsible if the law doesn't do it for us first."

She glanced over at Chase. "I'm more worried about him right now." Another dark thought struck. "And what if he comes back for Bethany? You heard the person we talked to at the substation. There aren't enough resources to monitor my sister's room twenty-four-seven."

"True," he agreed, and she appreciated him not trying to Pollyanna the situation. "I'll speak to the floor nurses and see if they'll keep an extra eye on your sister's room."

"Thank you," she said. She'd been planning to do that herself but didn't want to leave Chase in the waiting room until his father arrived. She checked her watch. Where was Greg?

Speaking of her brother-in-law, the man came zipping into the waiting room looking rough. His jeans and a button-down, collared shirt were the only casual things about him as he rushed into the room.

"Daddy," Chase exclaimed.

Blakely was careful to watch their interaction this time, making sure Chase felt comfortable with his father.

Greg shot an apologetic look in Blakely's direction before making a beeline to his son, who met him halfway across the room. Greg knelt down and embraced his son as a woman in her early twenties stood at the door, looking like she'd rather walk on hot coals than enter the room.

Did Greg bring his mistress to pick up his son from the hospital where his wife lay in a bed after being shot?

Blakely walked straight up to the hovering woman. "I'm Blakely Adamson. Bethany's sister."

The large-busted blonde stood a couple of inches shorter than Blakely's five feet seven inches. Her face flushed hot pink, matching her lip tint. "It's good to finally meet you. I work for Greg as his receptionist." Blakely picked up on the fact she'd said *his* instead of *his company's receptionist*.

Was she reading too much into it? Or did Greg bring his affair to the hospital? Because she couldn't imagine him doing that to Bethany, or Chase. It would mean she had no idea who this man was anymore.

"And your name is?" Blakely asked. She wanted a name.

After a pensive glance in Greg's direction, she responded, "Charlotte, but my friends call me Lotte."

I'll bet they do.

Blakely exchanged insincere pleasantries before turning to Greg. "Speak to you in the hall for a minute?"

His lips compressed, forming a thin line. A flicker of something that looked a whole lot like shame passed behind his eyes before he told Chase to stay put while the grownups talked.

Blakely didn't wait for him to finish before walking into the hall to wait for him. Toe tapping on the sterile white tile, she waited near the elevator bank so Charlotte would be out of earshot. The woman stuck to the waiting room door like glue.

"I know what the fight was about," she whispered to Greg as he joined her. "Is that…?"

"No," he defended, but she could see the real answer on his face in the way his eye twitched when he said the word. Clearly, he wasn't ready to admit it, and it wasn't her business.

"I told her to consider forgiving you, Greg." She shot him a glare that could refreeze Antarctica. "Are you going to make me regret it?"

"You did?"

"Why do you sound so surprised?" she asked, planting a fisted hand on her hip.

"I just thought…you and Bethany are so close… I didn't—"

"What? Think I don't count you as family too?" She didn't hide the disappointment and hurt in her voice. "That's where you're wrong. Because I consider you my brother."

"I'm sorry," he said with a wave of shame. "I let everyone down, and I can't make it right."

"Be the husband Bethany deserves, and the father Chase

can look up to," she said. "No matter what happens in your marriage. You can still be a good partner and dad."

Red-rimmed eyes stared back at her.

"I'll try," was all he said. She'd never seen him look so beaten down in all the years she'd known him. How had she missed this?

"Call me if you have questions about Chase's schedule, okay?" she asked, figuring he got the point.

"I will," he promised.

"Do you want to wait for the doctor?" she asked after explaining no visitors were allowed yet.

"I better take Chase home," Greg said, once again surprising her. Wouldn't a husband want to see with his own eyes that his wife was going to be okay? Maybe the marriage was dead. Or maybe he couldn't face Bethany.

Either way, Blakely's heart was breaking for her sister. Bethany might have gotten caught up in a big house and driving a fancy car, but she'd loved Greg very much at one time.

Was all love eventually lost?

Greg excused himself, retrieved Chase, and then left with his son and the receptionist as Blakely made her way back into the waiting room.

"I'd hate for my sister to wake up only to find herself alone," Blakely said as she walked over to Dalton.

In a surprise move, he hauled her against his chest and held on to her. As he whispered calm reassurances in her ear, tears trickled down her face. She couldn't remember the last time she had a good cry. Maybe she was overdue. Because the other option, the one where she felt at home in Dalton's arms, wasn't something she was ready to face.

"Do you want to stick around?" he asked.

"I want to," she admitted. "Except that staying here

means not making progress on figuring out who is responsible for all this."

"There's no wrong answer," Dalton said, bringing his hand up to cradle the back of her neck as she looked up at him.

The move might have been a mistake, but she couldn't regret it. Her gaze dropped to his lips—kissable, thick lips that broke over straight white teeth when he smiled.

"Would you kiss me?" she asked.

The question barely left her lips before his grazed hers. He feathered kisses on the corners of her mouth, the dimple in her chin, before covering her lips in a kiss that made her understand the term *weak in the knees*. She brought her hands up to his broad shoulders to steady herself against the wave of desire that slammed into her, sending heat swirling in her belly and on the tender skin of her inner thighs.

Bringing her arms up to loop around his neck caused her full breasts to press against a wall of muscle as sensations lit up her body like a pinball machine.

No matter how many days and weeks passed, she hadn't been able to erase Dalton from her thoughts. She'd dreamed of seeing him again. Although, to be fair, not under these circumstances. He was here now, causing her body to hum with anticipation as need welled up, a squall forming in her chest.

A man like Dalton could shred her.

The thought was the equivalent of a bucket of ice water being thrown on her. She pulled back enough to break their lips apart, instantly missing the way his had felt moving against hers.

"I'm sorry," she heard herself say, breathless. "I crossed a line. I shouldn't have done that."

"Am I complaining?" came the response, and she could

feel his smile as it spread sunshine over her. The fact he was breathless too shouldn't make her want him more. But she did. She'd never wanted anyone more than she wanted Dalton Remington right this minute.

Realizing she'd crossed a professional line—though was it, considering they'd already made love?—she took a step back to put some space between them. This close, she couldn't trust her fingertips not to smooth over his chest and back, mapping every muscle and scar, memorizing every curve and line on a perfect body as she had that weekend.

"We should go," she managed to say, clearing her throat to ease some of the dryness.

"Whatever you want," he said.

Tempting. Because she knew exactly what her real answer would be. *Him.* And that was out of the question.

Or was it?

Chapter Eleven

Dalton reached for Blakely's hand and then linked their fingers as they walked out of the hospital after stopping by the nurse's stand. They'd learned that Bethany was resting peacefully and would most likely be out of it for the rest of the night. The update calmed Blakely's nerves about leaving her sister alone at the hospital.

He was scratching his head as to how Greg could have walked out before seeing his wife and why the man would have brought the blonde with him. *Tacky* was the first word that came to mind. Others followed, but he didn't want to focus on those.

Halfway to his truck in the hospital parking lot, he got the prickly-hairs-on-the-back-of-his-neck feeling. The one you get when someone is watching you. A protective arm went around Blakely's shoulders after dropping her hand. He pulled her close so the shooter, if there was one, would have a difficult time figuring out where he stopped and she began.

"What is it?" she asked, going with the flow. She must have realized something was off based on his body language.

Dalton surveyed the area. The sun was high in the sky

on a late Sunday afternoon, blinding him when he looked in the direction he felt eyes on them. "A bad feeling."

Blakely froze. "Should we turn around?"

Dalton normally stared danger in the face instead of turning tail. Setting his pride aside, he couldn't risk a shooter watching them with the sun to his back. Rather than risk her safety, he said, "You go inside, and I'll grab the truck."

"Is that safe?" she asked.

"They don't want me," he said.

"What if they decide punishing me is better than killing me?" she asked with a vulnerability in her voice that caused his free hand to fist. She had a point. They had no idea who was doing this and for what reason. Though, he suspected this was someone she'd given the maximum sentence to while seated on the bench.

Until they had answers, she was right to be cautious. Even then, he wanted her to be cautious.

"I'll be careful," he promised before feathering a kiss on her forehead. Suddenly, he realized they were in public, and this wouldn't look professional for either one of them. He cleared his throat and dropped his arm from around her shoulder. "Go inside and wait by the ER doors. Stand behind a big planter. Okay?"

She nodded before turning and heading inside. For a second, he thought she might argue. The woman had an independent streak a mile long. It was one of many traits that made her sexy as all get out to his thinking. Strong women were sexy. Opinionated women were sexy. Intelligent women were sexy.

Blakely had it all.

Dalton stepped into what he guessed would be the line of fire as she doubled back to the hospital. Once she was in a secure location, he dodged in between vehicles on his way to his truck. Made it safely there.

Sliding into the driver's seat, he saw a glint of metal in the direction he'd gotten the heebie-jeebies from a few minutes ago. Keeping a low profile, he hunched down in the seat and then started the engine. Pulling out of the parking space, he half expected bullets to fly. Found himself tensing up in preparation for one of those bullets to break his passenger window and lodge itself into his flesh.

Thankfully, none of that happened as he made his way toward the ER bay and then positioned the truck in front of the glass doors, which opened with a swish. Ducking low, Blakely rushed out without a backward glance.

Again, no bullets flew. He'd take that as a win.

"I'm making a call to the nurse's station to let them know there could be someone out in the parking lot," she said as she lowered the seat until she was flat on her back.

"Good idea," he agreed as he mashed the gas pedal before someone came out and yelled at them for being in the ambulance bay. He didn't mind getting into trouble. Hell, he'd been in trouble most of his childhood. What bothered him was the fact someone could get caught in the crosshairs should this bastard decide to fire.

Shoving those thoughts aside, he navigated out of the parking lot as he double-checked his mirrors to make certain no one followed. Once clear of the hospital, he said, "It's safe to sit up now if you want."

She finished the call and then brought her seat back up. "I feel much better now that the nurses are aware."

"It might have been nothing, but it's better to be safe than sorry," he agreed.

"I hate that I dragged you into this mess," Blakely stated.

"Just doing my job," he said as he pulled up to a red light.

Glancing over at Blakely, he added, "And it's a job I happen to love and am damn good at."

The corners of her lips tightened in a frown.

"That, you are," she responded, turning her face away to stare out the passenger-side window. She glanced at the side mirror too. "You've kept me alive so far."

"We make a good team," he said, not loving the fact he'd been the one to make her frown. Something told him that she didn't smile nearly enough.

The rest of the ride to the courthouse was spent in silence. The face of this courthouse wasn't much to look at. It was mostly brick and mortar. Inside, by contrast, it was grander. The courtrooms themselves were smaller than he'd expected on his first visit, but he was used to them now. He'd been inside judges' chambers several times throughout his career, each with the same large mahogany desks. The Texas and American flags flanked leather executive chairs. Every judge had the same green law-library desk lamp. Did it remind them of their college days? When the law was an ideal instead of the reality they carried out every day? A time when most of the people they encountered were still good, instead of the horrors they came across in the courtroom in a defendant's chair?

Blakely's chambers had a wall of books on one side along with a pair of leather chairs that looked comfortable to sit in.

"I hope you understand that I can't let you sit next to me while I scan files for names," she said.

"Right," he said. "Of course. Do you want to talk through the kind of person you might be looking for?"

"I have a few cases in mind where I've forgotten details and names, but faces stick out," she said. "Figured I'd start there and with the ones who sneered at me while I handed down their sentences."

"Seems like a good place to begin," he concurred, taking one of the leather chairs that turned out to be as comfortable as it had looked. His cell buzzed in his pocket. He fished it out and then held it up. "I'll take this while you search."

Blakely's full attention was already on the screen that had come to life, casting a glow on her face in the otherwise dim room. She studied the screen, and he was almost certain she hadn't heard a word he'd said.

His first instinct was the call coming in must be an update about his grandparents. But, no, he didn't recognize the number.

"Hello?"

"Hello, Marshal Remington," the familiar voice said. He'd spoken to the investigator at the scene this morning. "Detective Harvey here."

"Right," Dalton said. Now he had a name to a voice. "How can I help you, Detective?"

"Got a call from Johnny Spear's parole officer a few minutes ago," Harvey said.

"Name doesn't ring a bell," Dalton responded as he watched Blakely scroll through case files. Was this what she had been like in law school? Quiet? Studious? Had she been the nose-always-in-a-book type?

"You might want to ask the judge if she knows it," Harvey continued. "Because there was a paperwork error that led to him being released by mistake."

Dalton lowered the receiver away from his mouth. "Do you know anyone by the name of Johnny Spear?"

Her lips compressed, and she brought her gaze up and to the right. "Sounds familiar. But recent." Her fingers danced across the keyboard. Then, she dropped her gaze to the screen. "Oh, wait. Yes. I do remember him. He is recent. I gave him the maximum sentence for murdering his family. He claimed self-defense against his seventy-year-old father." She looked at Dalton and seemed to realize he still had someone on the line. "Why?"

He held up a finger, telling her to wait.

Had they found their perp?

"HER HONOR KNOWS the individual in question," Dalton supplied as Blakely waited with bated breath. She distinctly remembered the threat he'd made as he was being hand-cuffed and then taken out of the courtroom by the bailiff. He'd dropped the f-bomb on her, made certain she could see that he was flipping her off despite the restraints and had warned her to watch her back from now on.

She'd taken this as another idle threat. Hardened individuals weren't all that happy with her when she handed down maximum sentences, which she only did when the situation warranted. Keeping honest people safe was the only legitimate reason to take away another person's rights. She didn't take the responsibility lightly. Still. If she had a nickel for every idle threat she received, she would someday be a very wealthy woman.

"I see," Dalton said into the phone. "Okay." He paused a couple of beats. "I'll let the judge know." More silence. "I appreciate the information, Detective."

Blakely had a bad feeling about this.

The second Dalton ended the call, she asked, "What has Johnny Spear done?"

The look on Dalton's face sent her blood pressure rising. "Turns out, he didn't show up for his parole appointment."

"I just sentenced him last month," she said with an arched brow. "He shouldn't be eligible for parole."

"I'm afraid there was a paperwork error," he explained. "Johnny Spear was released last Tuesday."

"He didn't waste a lot of time coming after me," she said, hearing the shock in her own voice. This wasn't good. Johnny had been clear with his intentions. "Do they have an address on him?"

"I'm afraid he's disappeared," Dalton said. "A BOLO is being issued right now as we speak."

Before she could respond, her cell buzzed. "Hold that thought." She grabbed her cell from her handbag and then checked the screen. "This is the nurse I spoke to earlier. I better take this.

"Is everything okay with Bethany?"

"Yes, sorry to scare you," Nurse Lena said. "There's a man here with flowers who says he's a friend of the family. Since your sister isn't allowed visitors that aren't blood relatives, I denied access to the room."

"Did he give a name?" Blakely asked, thinking this didn't sound so good.

"Dr. Canon," Lena supplied. *What the hell was he doing there?* "I can't let him into my patient's room."

"You did the right thing," Blakely stated, wondering if she should have ignored her former law professor's text this morning.

The nurse's voice dropped to a whisper. "He's standing here right now asking to speak to you. Should I hand him the phone?"

"Absolutely," Blakely stated.

Static came through the line.

"You've been difficult to reach lately, Miss Adamson," Dr. Ellery Canon's familiar voice sounded.

"What are you doing at the hospital?" she asked, ignoring his comment.

"I was worried about you since you haven't returned any of my calls or texts," he said like that should be plain as the nose on her face. "Then, your address came up, and I thought something might have happened to you."

"Oh, right, your scanners," she said, remembering how often he used to mention that scanners could be useful tools for a lawyer. The fact he recognized her address when it came up was just creepy. Blakely remembered overhearing a conversation once between a pair of female students about Dr. Canon. Midterm test results had come back. The front-row students had commented about their A's, saying the rumor was true. All a female student had to do in order to get an A in his criminal law class was to sit in the front row, wear a low-cut blouse and use cleavage to their advantage. They'd said he was harmless enough, and they didn't mind giving the old man a thrill. Even if Blakely wasn't a 34B, she would never have stooped so low to get a grade. For better or worse, she'd earned every single alphabet letter on her grade reports and was proud of the fact.

Still. He'd called her one of his prize students, had invited her along with a few male colleagues to his home for dinners a handful of times since graduation and had been a big cheerleader for her career since she'd left college.

"I brought flowers for you," he said. "But I guess these are for someone else now."

"The nurse can take them," she offered, not wanting to offend her former professor. He still had pull in certain circles, and she'd worked for and deserved a clean reputation. She was still too early in her career to make enemies, and the man had never been inappropriate with her.

"I'll make sure they get to the right place," Blakely offered. "It's not necessary for you to stick around."

"All right," he said. Right before ending the call, he delivered his favorite line. "See you in court."

Blakely ended the call with an awkward thank-you.

"Everything all right at the hospital?" Dalton asked, breaking through the thoughts rolling around in her head.

"Yes," she said, refocusing on him. Her stomach gave a little flip the moment their gazes touched. "My law professor showed up with flowers."

Dalton's face twisted. "You two must be close."

"Not really," she said. "He sometimes brings students to observe a trial for extra credit and has introduced me to some of his contacts, but I don't know him beyond a professional level."

"Bringing flowers sounds kind of personal if you ask me," he said.

"He listens to scanners like an ambulance chaser to illustrate how they can be used to find clients," she said.

"Does he find clients that way?"

"He's a professor, so it's an academic exercise to him," she explained.

A clank in the hallway caused them both to freeze.

Dalton moved, breaking through the temporary hold first.

"Hide underneath your desk," Dalton said, already to his feet as Blakely reached for the key that unlocked the drawer with her Sig Sauer.

It dawned on her just how poetic it might be for someone like Johnny Spear to kill her in her chambers. It was, after all, this courthouse where his life was changed forever.

Drawer unlocked, fingers curled around the butt of the gun, she'd be ready for whatever walked through that door.

Chapter Twelve

Dalton had his weapon drawn before he exited Blakely's chambers. He slipped out to the small reception area and flattened his back against the wall. Slowly, purposefully, he made his way toward the door leading to the hallway.

Stopping next to the door, he listened. A list of folks who might be at the courthouse late on a Sunday ran through his mind. Maintenance. Custodial. Another judge. Security guard.

Yes, it dawned on him that word could have spread about the judge's attack. Law enforcement circles ran small, sometimes shockingly small. It was another reason a relationship wouldn't be a good idea, especially now that he'd been assigned to protect her.

Approaching thirty had him questioning how much he loved his job despite what he'd said to her at the hospital. A growing piece of him missed working the paint horse ranch alongside his family members. He was realizing how lonely it could be moving to a new city where he worked much of the time. He volunteered for extra duty in order to fill his days.

Now, he was starting to wonder why. He'd had an independent streak a mile long growing up. Was he getting softer as he got older?

The clank of keys on a key ring sounded on the opposite side of the door. Could be custodial. Or security.

His truck was registered to him personally. It had been the vehicle he'd been driving when the protection assignment had come in. Security might red-flag his truck if they'd driven by.

The business end of his gun aimed at the door, he held steady as he waited to see if the door handle moved or a key slid into the lock. There would be a second or two for him to identify himself as a marshal before a decision to shoot might have to be made. Dalton had been forced into a position of discharging his weapon on multiple occasions. He never took it lightly that one of his bullets could end a life. Criminal or not, everyone's right to live was respected by Dalton.

Several seconds passed without another sound on the other side of the door. It felt almost like a standoff. But did the person out there even suspect that someone could be on the other side of this door?

His logical side kicked in, reminding him there were a whole lot of reasons someone might stop. The first of which was to read and respond to a text. There were other reasons. Like the person could be cleaning.

Being in law enforcement had tainted him in many ways. It made him suspicious of everyone and everything. It made him sit in restaurants facing the door so no one could sneak up on him. And it made him snap to worst-case scenarios.

Silence stretched on for what felt like an eternity. Patience won during times like these. Lucky for him, his stubborn streak engaged.

And then he heard someone whistling. He dropped down

to check the crack underneath the door. The small sliver offered enough of a view to lead him to believe someone from the custodial department was doing his job.

On a slow exhale, he pushed to standing and returned to Blakely once he was certain the man had moved down the hallway.

"False alarm?" she asked before setting a Sig Sauer on top of her desk. Even from here, seven feet away from her, he could see her hands trembling. Did she believe she could steady herself enough to hit a mark? A thump of adrenaline could cause her to shoot the wrong person. Or miss entirely.

"Looks like it," he said, keeping an ear toward the hallway. "Now that you have a name, do you think we should head out?"

"To go where?" she asked. "My home isn't safe any longer."

"We should have packed an overnight bag," he admitted.

"I have court in the morning," she said. Her stomach picked that moment to growl.

His place was a mess. Laundry was piled on the floor in his bedroom. His normal chores were put on hold once the call came in. Still, his apartment was safer than going home. "I have a spare bedroom. Can't promise much in the way of comfort, but—"

"No, thanks," she said, cutting him off.

"Do you have a better idea?" he asked, trying his level best to hide the fact his ego was bruised by the express rejection.

"I should probably stay at Bethany's house," she said. "I'd like to be there for Chase, especially in the morning before he's taken to school. It's been a hard weekend for him and…"

It seemed to dawn on her that a murderer was stalking her. She shook her head. "That's a bad idea, isn't it?"

"Not completely," he reassured her. "Chase probably does need you."

"But I could be bringing a murderer to his doorstep," she said. "He could end up in the hospital like Bethany. If she hadn't been at my house and we weren't on the couch this morning, she—" The helpless look she shot him was quickly followed by her squaring her shoulders and lifting her chin up. "I know what you're going to say. I can't think like that. But wouldn't you if the situation was reversed?"

Dalton started to speak but bit his tongue instead. After giving reality a few seconds to kick in, he said, "My initial response is no, but that's just the US marshal talking. As a human being who loves his family and would do anything to protect them if they needed protecting, I would blame myself just like you're doing right now." He paused for a beat. "It still wouldn't be true, but I'd do the same."

She took in a deep breath and smiled.

"Do you know how to use that weapon?" he asked, motioning toward the Sig.

"I've been to the shooting range," she admitted. "Can't say that I'm an expert marksman, but I've taken a couple of classes."

"Where was it?"

Blakely motioned toward a drawer. "I keep it locked inside my desk. It's just for emergencies."

"Do you want to lock it up before we head out?" he asked. "I can take you anywhere you want to go."

A surprising helpless look crossed her features for a split second before she recovered. "I have no idea where that is." She threw her hands up.

"Since you don't want to go to my place, I could see if I can call in a favor or request a safe house," he offered.

"No, no," she repeated. "Your place is fine if the offer still stands."

"I can make a mean steak," he said.

"I remember."

"Does that sound good?" he asked. "We can pick up a couple of ribeye on the way home."

"Okay," she said, tension lines forming around her mouth—a mouth that had burned against his a little while ago. "If you don't mind cooking. Because we could pick up something to take back, or I can order something for delivery."

"I don't mind," he reassured her.

It was probably more of his bruised ego talking, but he didn't like the fact her law professor had tracked her to the hospital. He must have believed that he would find her lying in the bed instead of her sister. He understood keeping up professional connections in a small world. But showing up at the hospital made Dalton believe the professor might be interested in more.

Blakely wasn't naïve, but he also didn't think she realized how desirable she was or how interesting she was to talk to. Dalton didn't do long talks after sex, and yet he had with her. They might have kept professional details out of the picture, but they'd discussed everything from favorite foods to favorite colors.

He didn't do that either. He didn't get too personal with the women he spent time with. Dinner and a movie, their pick on both counts. Walks in the park. One of the women he'd dated had been more into fitness than him. But his abs had never looked better than when they were together because her favorite activity was working out at the park.

He didn't argue. The workouts were intense. The sex was decent. But when he had to fight with the mirror for her attention, he'd drawn the line.

Then, there'd been the hairdresser who'd tried to convince him to shave the sides of his head and leave a thick patch on top. Not quite a mohawk or mullet. Definitely not him. He'd learned early on to walk away from anyone who saw him as someone they could change. She'd been into fashion and the latest trends while he'd been content to watch a game on his day off.

Lately, though, he was starting to feel like he was missing out on something. He blamed his family. All three of his cousins had found the loves of their lives. Until recently, he hadn't believed in such a thing. He and his brother, Camden, were the lone holdouts. Or, maybe the lone *missing outs*. He couldn't be certain which one.

Or had it been his time with Blakely that had changed his mind? Opened him to new possibilities?

"Ready?" Blakely said after clearing her throat while she closed and then locked the gun drawer.

"Mind if I step into the hallway to make sure no one is out there?" Dalton asked.

"Go for it," she said as she closed her laptop and then rounded the desk. She'd bought the Sig never in a million years expecting to have to use it one day. It was meant to be insurance. And like most policies, no one ever intended to need to cash them in before they were good and ready.

She wasn't ready to shoot someone. Being around guns at all ushered her back to that chilly Sunday morning when Eric, her fifteen-year-old ex-boyfriend, had shown up at her home wild-eyed and blank-faced. Distant. Like he'd gone somewhere far away mentally, and no one could reach him again.

She remembered his anger the moment he'd jumped her and put the sharp blade to her throat. He'd held her head back and threatened to call her sister outside so Bethany could watch as he sliced Blakely from ear to ear.

Somehow—she could never remember the exact details— she'd managed to drop down and avoid having her throat sliced. Her forehead was another matter. That had been cut while she'd fought Eric. He'd been strong. Stronger than she remembered.

"Hey," Dalton said to her, breaking through the memory and bringing her back to the present. "Are you all right?"

"To be honest, Dalton, I'm not real sure that I'll ever be all right again, but I'm going to do what I always do."

"What's that?" he asked.

"I'm going to keep on keeping on, no matter who tries to stop me or what bastard thinks they can take me out," she said, pulling on all her strength. After Eric, she'd promised herself that no one got to make her feel weak again. No one got to make her scared of her own shadow again. And no one got to take away her sense of safety and security again. "If Johnny Spear wants to come for me, he better be ready for a fight."

"Good," he said to her. "Because that's exactly the person I wanted to get to know more in Galveston that weekend. And since we'll be spending a lot of time together until this case is resolved, I hope to see more of that fight in you."

"Do you have any regrets?" she asked before adding, "Tell me honestly."

"About us?" he asked, cocking an eyebrow.

"Yes," she managed to say.

"I think it's unfortunate we met when we did," he said.

"And if I could turn back time, I'd rewind the clock and do things a whole lot differently."

"That's probably good," she said, his words the equivalent of a knife through the center of her chest. Despite the heat in the kiss they'd shared, which to be fair, might have been more on her side than his, he seemed to have a lot of regret when it came to her. It was good. It might keep them from making another mistake—though, she couldn't bring herself to categorize that weekend as a bad thing. Time waited for no one. It moved on. And she needed to move on with it. They'd shared a moment in the past. Key words being *in the past.* Today was a new day, and she needed to get with the program no matter how strong the pull was to this man or how damn good he smelled when they were close. She'd memorized his woodsy and spicy all-male scent. Her fingers had mapped the lines and curves in his back.

"Do you think so?" he hedged.

"I believe everything turned out the way it should have," she quipped, masking the hurt she felt in his words. In order to keep herself safe, she had to keep everyone else at arm's length. Since Eric, she couldn't afford to let her guard down with anyone. Even her relationship with Bethany changed after that day. Bethany became needier, and Blakely stepped even more into a parenting role.

Did she have regrets?

The short answer was yes. But since she didn't dwell on the past or mistakes, she pulled herself up by her bootstraps and moved on.

Except when it came to Dalton. For some reason, a reason she didn't want to acknowledge or examine, she couldn't seem to move on. The recent kisses they'd shared were right up there with the best of her life. No one had ever even come close to making her want to stick around or dig deeper into someone's mind until Dalton.

Leaving him again was going to open those still-fresh wounds. Was there an alternative?

Chapter Thirteen

Dalton's apartment was messier than he remembered. Or maybe he was just more embarrassed at bringing Blakely home to any mess when her home had been neat as a pin. He mumbled an apology as he moved to the patio to fire up the grill.

"Do you mind fixing those inside so you won't be exposed?" Blakely asked as her gaze swept the twin building out the window and the parking lot in between.

"Okay," he conceded. He had one of those fancy stoves with a grill top. It wasn't as good as outdoor grilling, but she had a point. No matter how much of a long shot, someone might have figured out the two of them were together and identified him. It would take both of those for someone to get his address since he was certain no one had followed them from the courthouse. *Better safe than sorry.* His grandmother Lacey's voice had a habit of popping up in situations like these. Thinking about her was too hard, so he stuffed the memory down deep.

"I'll do the baked potatoes," Blakely offered. "It'll give my hands something to do."

"Fair enough," he said. "Let me know when you're about twenty minutes out." In the meantime, he could let the steaks rest after peppering them with Lawry's Seasoned Salt.

"Will do," she said as she preheated the oven.

Normally, a cold beer would sound good about now. But his mind needed to be clear. Being around Blakely was distraction enough. Every time he walked past her or needed to stand beside her, he breathed in her clean floral and citrus scent. Every time their skin grazed, electricity pulsed through him. Every time his gaze dropped to her lips, an ache formed deep in his chest.

Rather than torture himself by focusing on someone he could never have, he excused himself from the kitchen to straighten up.

Blakely's cell buzzed in the next room. She grabbed it from her handbag and then checked the screen. The look that crossed her features before she dropped the phone into her purse again brought on questions. "Everything okay?"

"Yes," she said without turning to face him. Was she hiding her expression or was he reading too much into the situation?

Dalton finished straightening up by tossing clean and dirty clothes into a laundry basket that he set on top of the washer in the hallway between the two bedrooms.

"Did you just move in?" Blakely asked as he joined her in the kitchen.

"I just signed a lease for another year," he said.

"Oh," she said as her cheeks flushed with embarrassment.

"What gave you that impression?" he asked, doing his level best to keep a straight face. It was obvious to anyone who walked in, but he wanted to hear her version.

"I didn't mean to make an assumption," she said. Was she trying to spare his feelings? "But there's not one picture hanging on the walls, so I just assumed."

"Did anything else tip you off?" he asked, continuing with the blank-face routine to see how far he could push it.

"The packing box sitting next to the front door," she said, looking like she was choosing her words carefully.

Dalton broke into a wide smile. "This is my second year living here, but I haven't made the time to finish unpacking." He chuckled as she made a face at him. "What? I wanted to give you enough rope to hang yourself because you seemed so worried that I might get offended."

"Thanks for the save," she quipped, but then she laughed too. And then they both laughed in a manner that far outweighed the joke.

Blakely pinched her side but couldn't stop. "I really thought you might be doing your best here."

Dalton couldn't hold a serious face if he tried. "I might not have your decorating skills, but I do realize when a house hasn't been unpacked yet. I've got eyes."

"Really? Because for a minute, I thought you couldn't see that walls need pictures or art, or something on them so they don't look like dry-erase boards." More laughter broke out. It was good to see Blakely with a smile on her face for a change. The situation wasn't all that funny, but both needed a break in tension. Stress usually found an outlet in the form of tears or laughter. This time, Blakely was laughing so hard she cried, and he wasn't far behind.

When the laughter finally died down, Blakely said, "Why isn't there anything on the walls? Too busy?"

He shrugged. "The truth is that this place is a convenient location, but I can't say that it's ever felt like home."

"Why's that?" she asked. He resisted the urge to ask if she was sure about asking anything deemed too personal.

"I grew up on a ranch, so the land probably has something to do with it," he said. "I'm not sure what else the problem is, other than to say it doesn't feel like home."

"The building is tall and modern," she pointed out after careful thought. "What floor is this?"

"Seventeenth," he supplied.

"It strikes me as odd that you'd live so high in the air when you've always been a feet-on-the-ground person," she stated. The comment resonated. There was real insight in those words.

Dalton resisted the notion she might know him better than he knew himself. They'd spent a long weekend together before now, which wasn't nearly long enough to get to know a person. "Well, you have a point there, Your Honor."

It also dawned on him that she was most likely good at reading people and body language given her chosen profession. He could say the same about himself. It still had him scratching his head how he'd misjudged the situation that had happened with the two of them talking for hours about nothing the first night they'd met and then spending the night together making love. But that was probably coming from the bruised ego she'd left behind after walking, no, running, away from him.

Dating a coworker wasn't professional. Having sex with a coworker definitely wasn't considered professional. Technically, however, they weren't coworkers. They worked in the same district and in the same type of business. Their paths could cross. That was an obvious reality given the circumstances. It scorched him that she didn't believe he could be professional enough to handle the situation should they come face-to-face.

Now that he'd been assigned to protect her, having a fling was off the table. When they'd made love, she hadn't known him from Adam.

"We're twenty minutes out," she announced, cutting into his reverie.

Dalton moved into the kitchen, trading places while Blakely took his seat at the small table built for two. Moving around each other in the kitchen felt like a dance they'd rehearsed their entire lives. There was nothing more natural. "Hold on." He moved to the opened box in the living room, dug around and extracted a picture of all the cousins together at the paint horse ranch. They were young and fresh-faced, all sitting on top of a small stretch of wood fence, all smiling like they'd just been told they could eat nothing but ice cream for dinner. His cousin Crystal had found the picture years ago, had duplicates made and then framed for each one of them to put up in their homes since they all lived apart in different areas of Texas. This way, no matter where they were, they would always have each other. Or, at least, that was what she'd said while presenting the gifts.

He set the picture on the fireplace mantel, in the center. "There. Is that better?"

Blakely smiled. "Yes, it is."

He couldn't agree more.

BLAKELY WATCHED AS Dalton worked his magic on the stovetop grill. "Do you mind if I ask what drew you to law enforcement and becoming a marshal?"

"I'll tell if you will," he said. "And you go first."

These topics had been off-limits before, but there was nothing stopping them from sharing details about their private lives now.

"I had a run-in with someone when I was fifteen years old," she explained. "It resulted in the scar on my forehead." She paused a beat, realizing it was easier to talk about than she feared it might be. Was that the Dalton effect? "After that, it took a really long time to trust people again."

"I'm sure that must have left a huge imprint on you mentally," he said. "Being fifteen is hard enough without having a traumatic event to knock you off-balance."

He didn't know the half of it.

"I'm sorry that happened to you," he said with the kind of compassion that made her almost believe everything would be all right again. "It must have left a lasting impression."

"It did," she admitted. "But then I got strong physically and mentally, and I promised myself that I would do everything in my power to protect others from a similar fate."

"What happened to the person who did this to you?"

"He got off with a slap on the wrist because his family had enough money for an expensive lawyer. One who played golf with the judge who presided over the case," she said, realizing she hadn't spoken those words out loud in…ever.

"Sonofabitch," he mumbled, and she couldn't agree more. "So you studied law and decided to become a judge to protect those who can't protect themselves."

"Yes," she said, also realizing the irony in the fact one of those bastards was currently threatening her life after being released on a technicality. At least they knew who they were looking for now. There was a BOLO out. She had to trust law enforcement to do their jobs.

"It's noble," he said. "And I'm still sorry the bastard walked away without punishment."

"He self-destructed within a couple of years," she said before turning the tables. "How about you? Why did you become a US marshal?"

"Job security," he quipped. They both laughed at that. His job was one of the most dangerous paths in law enforcement.

"Seriously," she said.

"Okay," he said before flipping the steaks. They sizzled

on the grill, and the place already smelled like heaven. "Here goes. I had a no-good mother who abandoned the family not long after I was born."

"Oh," she said. "That's awful."

"Thankfully, I was too young to remember that," he said. "Except that my father then died young. He was a good person by all accounts."

The phrase *only the good die young* came to mind. Though, experience had taught her that wasn't always the case.

"So my siblings and I were brought up by extremely loving grandparents on their paint horse ranch," he continued as though that explained everything. When she arched an eyebrow, he continued, "My grandfather was a US marshal. He is the most stand-up person I've ever met." He shrugged. "That was how he saved the money to buy the paint horse ranch for my grandmother. They eventually built the business enough for him to work the ranch full-time. I guess I figured if I could be anybody, I'd want to model my life after his."

Blakely had heard everyone who worked in law enforcement had a story. "Thanks for telling me yours."

"I never talk about my family," he admitted as the steaks sizzled. "They're done."

"I'll grab plates," she offered.

Dalton motioned toward a cabinet as he pulled the steaks off the heat. Standing next to him felt like the most natural thing.

"Here you go," she said to him as she held out a plate. He tossed a gorgeous ribeye on top with a smile that could cut through ice. "I wasn't so sure I'd be able to eat with everything going on. My stomach usually rebels first when I'm under stress. But my mouth is already watering."

"It's good to eat so you can keep up your strength," he said.

"After we eat, I'll make a call to the hospital to check on Bethany," she said.

"While you do that, I should check on my grandparents. They're in the hospital," he said.

"I'm hoping that no news is good news for both of us."

"Couldn't agree more," he said as he plated the second steak. They fixed up baked potatoes standing side by side. His spicy male scent filled her when she took in a deep breath. It would be so easy to lean into Dalton's strength. But then what? What would she do if she learned to depend on someone else?

Not everyone will let you down. Those words coming out of nowhere shocked the hell out of her. Were they true?

"This food is amazing," she said, redirecting her focus after sitting down and taking the first bite.

"Steak is my specialty," he said.

"Do you mind if I ask you another question?"

"Shoot," he said, before adding, "Forgive the word choice."

"Have you ever thought about reaching out to your mother?"

"No," he said in a tone that said *case closed*.

The question was a mood killer. The rest of the meal was spent in silence. When Blakely had taken the last bite, she said, "I'll clear the table and do the dishes."

"I can help," he said. She knew better than to argue when anyone offered help in the kitchen.

They each took their dishes to the sink. Not a bite was left on either, so they didn't need the trash disposal. After rinsing plates, knives and forks, she placed them in the dishwasher while he put on a pot of coffee.

"Do you want a cup?" he asked.

"It's too late for me," she said. "All I want is to know that my sister is still in stable condition, a shower and a bed."

"Take the main bedroom," he said, again in the tone that said arguing would be a mistake.

"Do you have anything I can change into for sleeping?"

"I'll put something out while you make the call to the hospital." With that, he disappeared down the hallway.

Blakely made the call. It was quick and to the point. Bethany was stable. No one else had come to see her.

Dalton returned a few moments later. "Lay your clothes out, and I'll throw them in the wash. We can get up early tomorrow to swing by your house before court."

Cooking in the kitchen and making plans to go back to work tomorrow were reassuring. It was the little things, she'd learned, that gave a sense of normalcy in difficult times.

"Okay," she said.

"I put a robe out for you to use," he said. "And an oversize T-shirt."

She liked the sounds of those things. After thanking him, she headed into his bedroom. It looked similar to the other rooms, unfinished. The bed was big and had comfortable-looking blankets and pillows. She tested it as she walked past. This was going to be like sleeping on a cloud.

A pink robe that was her size hung on the door to the bathroom. A sting of jealousy caught her off guard. She'd been clear there was no future for the two of them. Dalton was honest and respectable. He was honorable, which seemed in rare supply with people these days. All she had to do was take one look at her brother-in-law.

That wasn't completely fair. She didn't know the real ins and outs of her sister's marriage. Greg, no matter how off he seemed or how desperate he looked, was a decent person.

He was clearly torn up about the affair he'd been having. He seemed…she didn't know the right word…maybe lost?

Seeing him at the hospital had been a wake-up call too. Bethany had been keeping secrets. She hadn't been confiding in Blakely. Guilt nearly consumed her at letting her younger sister down. If Blakely had known about the problems, she would have been able to help. It was possible the situation wouldn't have gone this far.

A shower helped wash the day away. Reluctantly, she wrapped herself in the pink robe after drying off. A toothbrush still in its wrapper waited on the counter. She brushed and then set her clothes outside the bedroom door for them to be washed.

When she opened the door, she heard the low hum of Dalton's voice. It reverberated through her, lighting all kinds of fires that didn't need to be lit. Was he talking to the owner of this pink robe? As much as she knew in her heart he wouldn't betray another woman by kissing her, they hadn't exactly talked about whether or not he was seeing someone.

Was it her business?

No.

Did a growing part of her *want* it to be her business?

Yes.

So, what did she plan to do about it?

Chapter Fourteen

Dalton wouldn't be able to sleep if he tried. The update from his sister, Jules, had his stomach burning and his mind churning. His grandfather woke up for five minutes. Unfortunately, Jules had been outside grabbing a little sunshine to rejuvenate after what had been a long night of sleeping in fits and starts.

Essentially, when their grandparents needed someone to be in the room, no one had been there. He didn't blame Jules. She was one person and doing a helluva fine job being "on" nearly twenty-four hours a day. She needed support. Maybe it was a mistake to have only one person on duty. The job might be too much for one individual to cope with. And yet, he couldn't leave Blakely right now either. Did that make him the worst human in the world?

For someone who claimed to always put family first, how many holidays had he been home for in recent years? Not many. In fact, he volunteered to work so others could be home with their kiddos. Murderers didn't take holidays off. In fact, they had a habit of striking when opportunity presented itself.

A cold chill raced down his back at the thought of Johnny Spear getting to Blakely.

Dalton shook off the thought as best as he could, took a shower in the hall bath and then routed for clean clothes in the laundry basket. He threw on a pair of boxers and cotton workout shorts, grabbed a blanket after washing her clothes, and then rested his eyes while lying down on the sofa.

He rarely needed more than a cat nap when he was on a protection assignment, so he got up before the sun and finished the small load of laundry. The least he could do was give her clean clothes to wake up to. Handling her pink silk panties had sent blood flowing south, but he was no longer a hormonal teenager. He was a grown man, who was capable of doing laundry without needing a cold shower afterward.

Remembering how silky Blakely's skin had felt under his touch was another story. It created a visceral memory that was more difficult to tamp down.

Dalton almost laughed out loud. Grown man, huh?

A fresh cup of coffee helped wake him up. He was still full from last night, so he grabbed his phone and checked to see if a message had come through on the group chat. When he'd talked to Jules last night, she'd sounded hopeful there was a chance their grandfather would wake up again.

Of course, they'd been going down this road long enough for him to be educated on the fact someone in a coma could wake up, seem totally fine and then go right back under, never to wake again.

Too many weeks had passed for Dalton to expect this situation to end well. Duke, his cousin, mentioned that they might want to think about what they wanted to do with the ranch if their grandparents didn't make a meaningful recovery.

Dalton just wasn't there yet. He couldn't see a world where his strong-as-an-ox grandfather wasn't at the helm of Remington Paint Ranch.

This wasn't the time to think about comfort food, but he couldn't stop himself from wanting a chicken-fried steak from Mama Bea's place in Mesa Point. Every time he thought about the ranch, Mama Bea came up. Her food was the definition of heaven. A little voice in the back of his mind picked that moment to point out that he'd found heaven in everything when he was with Blakely.

He reminded himself how fast she'd bolted before and how little use there was in thinking there was even a remote possibility she would let him in her life, no matter how much electricity charged the air in between them every time they were within arm's reach of one another. Or how much his mouth ached to claim hers, marking her as his, when their gazes met. Or how sexy she was in a jogging suit. Of course, she was even sexier with nothing on.

"Good morning," she said after clearing her throat. He hadn't heard her open the bedroom door. She caught him off guard, especially considering he'd just pictured her naked. She held out the pink robe, which was folded up. "This belongs to you. Or should I say your girlfriend?"

"No girlfriend," he said quickly and with a little heat as he met her across the room. "Is that how little you think of me?"

"I wasn't sure what to think when you left out a pink ladies' bathrobe for me, Dalton."

Was she jealous?

"The robe belongs to my sister," he said. "She slept over on her way to serve a warrant, got a tip her felon was about to move and hightailed it out of here so fast she forgot to take her favorite robe with her." He crossed his arms over his chest. "It looked to be about your size, so I thought you might want to use it once you got out of the shower. But I didn't realize—"

"Never mind," she quipped, handing over the bundle. "I just thought something else. That's all. No big deal."

Well, it sure as hell sounded like a big deal to him. Or was that wishful thinking on his part?

"For the record, if you were in a relationship with someone else, it would be a very big deal to me," he said before walking out of the living room to set the robe on top of the washing machine.

When he returned to the kitchen, the sun had begun to rise, and Blakely nursed a cup of coffee while standing in his kitchen looking better than she had a right to.

"Hungry?" he asked.

"Not really," she said. She seemed content to let his comment fly past without acknowledgment. "We should probably head to my house so I can grab clothes for work." She issued a sigh. "Though, nothing in me wants to go back there."

"We can always stop by a twenty-four-hour big-box store instead," he said.

"No," she said. "I need to face it even if I don't want to."

"There's nothing wrong with giving yourself a minute, Blakely. You don't always have to make the hard decision and push through if you need a little more time."

She blew out a breath. "I've been pushing through life ever since I can remember. It got me through the deaths of my parents. It got me through the responsibility of taking care of my sibling. And it got me through both undergrad and law school. I'm one of the youngest judges seated in Texas. What if I don't know how to take more time? What if this is just who I am?"

Dalton was beginning to realize how much the story you told yourself about your life shaped it. "I think you're amazing, and you can be anything you want to be."

"What if I can't do it?"

"It might be hard, but if you put your mind to it, I doubt there's anything you can't accomplish," he said and meant every word.

"Do you mean that, Dalton?"

"I've never been more certain of anything in my life," he reassured. "Plus, I've been told that I have a stubborn streak a mile long. Until I met you, I thought that was as far as a stubborn streak could go. You proved me wrong on that."

Blakely broke into a smile. "How is it that you can make me laugh so easily?"

"That's easy?" he shot back, matching her smile.

"Okay, tough guy," she said. "You better go get dressed while I come up with a plan to get in and out of my house without incident."

"I'll call to let my contact at Houston PD know we'll be heading that way so he can get eyes on the place," Dalton said before excusing himself and heading into the bedroom to grab clothes.

He dressed in a suit since he was taking Blakely to her courtroom. Once inside, it would be difficult if not impossible for Johnny Spear to get to her. On the way in was another story altogether, but he could alert the bailiff when they got close so extra eyes could be on her when Dalton dropped her off at the front door.

Leaving his apartment caused a bad feeling to settle in the pit of his stomach. Was he being overly cautious with Blakely due to their past?

Or their present?

WHOA! BLAKELY COULDN'T remember the last time she witnessed a man wearing a suit in the same way Dalton wore a suit. He filled out every thread of material that looked handspun by angels. What could she say? The man was perfection.

"You dress up nicely, Mr. Remington," she managed to say through a dry-as-desert throat. Was it suddenly getting hot in the apartment?

"Thank you, ma'am," he responded with a smile that could charm the pants off anyone with eyes. "After you." That same smile had been good at seducing her in Galveston. She'd been drawn to him like the magnet to steel cliché. The sister trip was supposed to be a chance for her and Bethany to catch up on each other's lives, spend some real time together. Except that Chase had gotten sick at the last minute, so Bethany had been needed at home. Since Blakely had funded the whole weekend and couldn't get her money back, she'd said *what the hell* and gone by herself on a whim.

Okay, she'd been feeling sorry for herself. She could admit that now. She'd realized how needed her sister was and how much the opposite was true for Blakely. No one would even notice if she disappeared off the face of the earth. That wasn't completely true. Bethany and Chase would miss her dearly. But they had each other, and they would be fine.

Sitting alone at the restaurant where she'd originally made a reservation for two had been beyond sad. Then, Dalton had walked in. He'd asked for a table for one and been told they couldn't seat him until after nine o'clock. He'd asked about placing a to-go order and had been told that could be arranged.

Without thinking, or in her case overthinking her next move, she'd waved him over and told him that she wouldn't mind the company if he wanted to eat with her. Eating at home alone every night was one thing. She was used to it. All she had to do was turn on the TV for background noise, and she was just fine. But eating out in public alone had just felt sad to her. The pity party she was having for herself had made her mad enough to ask a stranger to sit down. Dalton had thanked her and then told the hostess that he wasn't going to need to place a to-go order after all.

They'd made an agreement not to discuss work or anything too personal. But the night flew by. She couldn't even remember what either of them had said, but she remembered thinking, *This man is far too beautiful to be sitting here with me.*

The only information she'd divulged on a personal level was that she'd spent too many years in school but that she liked her job, so the long semesters spent with her nose in a book had turned out to be worth it after all.

He'd asked what her field of study had been. She'd laughed.

He'd asked if he could guess. She'd laughed.

He'd asked if he could walk her back to her hotel. She'd smiled and decided to take a chance.

After all, what was the harm in being escorted back to her hotel, considering she could see it from the restaurant? They'd sat in the lobby for another hour before she'd done something she never had before…invited him upstairs.

The next morning, he invited her to breakfast at the house he'd rented. "Were you on a stakeout when we met?" she asked him as the elevator dinged, indicating they were on the ground floor.

"No," he responded. "That would have been unprofessional."

She stepped out of the elevator and followed him through the first-floor lobby and to his truck. "Then what were you doing in Galveston?"

"It was work related," he said as he opened the door for her. She climbed in the passenger side and lowered the seat back to hide her face from view as much as possible. Dalton smiled approval at the move, and it gave her stomach a little flip.

He rounded the front of the truck and then reclaimed the driver's seat. "I was waiting for a felon to show up. We had good intel that he would be there any day, so we spread out and set up shop."

"How many of you were there?"

"From the Marshals office? Just me," he said. "But there was a task force on this one because he was on the most wanted list."

Blakely had been eating in a restaurant possibly with one of the worst criminals in America, and the man could have walked right past her and she wouldn't have known it. "Whoa. I'm guessing he never showed."

"You guessed correctly," he said. "In fact, he ended up on one of the cruise ships as staff two weeks later."

"So you wasted your time," she pointed out.

"Spending the weekend with you could never be considered a waste of time as far as I'm concerned," he said so low that she almost didn't hear him. Those words, though, sent more of that warmth circling through her, settling inside her thighs. Her body remembered his touch, craved it even now.

Where was logic when it came to matters of the heart?

Blakely cleared her throat. She couldn't think about how much she'd missed his touch in the weeks since. She couldn't think about how many times she'd had to force this man from her thoughts, especially at night when she tried to sleep but images of him kept popping into her mind. And she couldn't think about how right she'd felt in this man's arms and how safe, even if it only lasted a short time.

Blakely couldn't afford to give someone her safety. Besides, she'd gotten by fine on her own all these years. And she'd be fine moving forward.

So why did it feel like such a lie this time?

Chapter Fifteen

"Did you call the security company that patrols your neighborhood to let them know you'd be by this morning?" Dalton asked his now-quiet passenger. She'd been silent for longer than he was comfortable with. What was going on in that brilliant mind of hers?

"I should do that," she said, reaching for her cell. "I have a number that I can text so everyone will get the message. I'll let them know that we're on our way."

A few seconds later, she dropped her phone inside her purse again before leaning her head back.

"Did you sleep okay?" he asked.

"Sure," she said. "In fact, once I was out, I didn't open my eyes again until this morning. How about you?"

"I got in a couple hours of shut-eye," he said. "I don't need much." He hoped the small talk could keep her mind off returning to her house. Her body language had tensed once the subject came up. Talking had always calmed his sister and cousins when they had to face a scary task. He hoped the distraction would work for Blakely too.

"I'm normally an eight-hour girl," she said. "You don't want to talk to me before I've had my coffee either."

"Good to know," he said, remembering she'd had her

coffee in hand when he joined her in the kitchen. "What about breakfast? Should we run through a drive-through?"

"I can grab a couple of protein bars at my house," she offered.

He got it. She didn't want to risk being stuck in a line if Johnny Spear caught up to them. Innocent people could get hurt, not to mention both of them shot. "Sounds like a plan." His coffee had kicked in, clearing the cobwebs. Though, he had the ability to snap into action on fifteen minutes of sleep and no caffeine if needed. His sister teased him about it being his superpower.

The situation with his grandparents got him thinking about family a whole lot. And about whether he wanted to stay on the job or not.

"Did you ever want to be anything else besides a judge?" he asked Blakely.

"Not really," she said. "Not seriously or when I was old enough to know the variety of jobs out there. I went through the usual I-want-to-be-a-veterinarian stage that most animal lovers go through when they're young. What about you?"

"I've been thinking about that question since the accident," he admitted. Dalton hadn't spoken to anyone about a pull toward changing professions. Not even his family. "I loved the parts of my childhood that allowed me to run free on the land. The ranch is a special place."

"Have you spoken to the others about what it might look like if your grandparents have a long recovery?" she asked. He appreciated the fact she hadn't said "when they die." He couldn't bring himself to believe they wouldn't pull through this, even though time was running out and they weren't making meaningful progress.

"No," he said. "But I've been thinking that conversation is probably overdue. After this assignment, it's my turn and then my brother Camden's. I'm not sure how long we can keep rotating like this. Plus, decisions are going to have to be made about the horses. It keeps the person who is holding vigil at the hospital busy since much of the work can be done via laptop until it's time to arrange a pickup."

"Growing up on a horse ranch sounds like the coolest childhood ever," Blakely said with appreciation in her voice.

"It's not for everyone, but it was special to me," he admitted.

"Would you consider going back and taking over for your grandparents full-time?" she asked.

"It was never even a thought until recently," he said as he entered her neighborhood. "Now? I guess I'm considering all options."

"Would you regret leaving your job?"

"How will I know if I don't try it?" he asked before turning the tables. "Would you ever consider doing anything else for a living?"

"Never say never," Blakely said. "But, I've been so busy making my mark that I haven't taken the time to consider any other path. I'm proud of the work that I've done and how far I've come." She shrugged as they pulled up in front of her home where a squad car waited. "And I know that I don't want to be on the other side of the bench as a litigator. So what else would I do?"

"I don't know," he said. "Maybe work as a victim's advocate. I could see you doing something like that." His tactic to keep her talking worked. She'd relaxed enough to stop working her fingers into a knot. That was progress.

"Guess I never thought about it," she said. "Once I decided on law, I gave myself no other options because that was the only way to succeed in getting through law school."

A uniformed officer exited his vehicle to walk to the

truck, as Dalton did the same before rounding the front to open Blakely's door.

He surveyed the area and then tucked Blakely behind him.

After perfunctory greetings, the officer followed closely behind as they essentially formed a shield around Blakely.

She was in and out of the house in less than ten minutes. It had to be some kind of record for getting ready, and she shouldn't look this good without making much effort. Though, Dalton wouldn't complain.

Thick hair in a slicked-back ponytail, she looked every bit the serious judge. Except Dalton had never seen a judge as beautiful.

They made it to the truck without incident, thanked the officer and then doubled back toward the courthouse.

Once settled and out of her neighborhood, Blakely pulled a couple of power bars out of her handbag, as promised, and handed one over.

Dalton polished his off in a matter of four bites. Blakely ate hers slowly, staring out the window as she chewed on every bite.

"You might be right about becoming a victim's advocate," she said once she'd finished hers. Next, she pulled out a pair of bottled waters. "Thirsty?"

"What else do you have in there? A breakfast taco?" he teased.

Blakely's serious expression broke, and she smiled. "I threw everything in here but the kitchen sink."

"Oh, darn," he teased. "How will I wash my hands without a sink?"

Blakely exhaled. "Thank you, by the way."

He shot a confused look her way.

"First of all, you didn't ask to be reassigned the minute

you realized who you'd be protecting on this assignment," she began. "I might not have acted like it at first, but I'm glad it's you and not some stranger."

"You're welcome." He probably shouldn't be thanked for doing his job. Though, he appreciated the gesture.

"Secondly, you haven't run off after everything," she said. "I should have explained myself. I should have figured out your number and called or told you what I did for a living instead of taking off without an explanation."

"About that," he said, surprised she'd brought it up. "What happened there? Did you think I was such a jerk that I wouldn't understand?"

"No, not that at all," she quickly countered. "I panicked. Plain and simple. I have no excuse for my actions, and I'm sorry."

"Apology accepted," he reassured her.

"And then I kissed you yesterday, which I had no place doing," she continued.

"No, and it can't happen again." They'd been doomed from the beginning. She realized that before he did. And he'd nursed a bruised ego, but he'd moved past it all and had no intention of going down that road.

"I know."

Why the hell did those words inch their way through the wall he'd constructed when it came to Blakely?

BLAKELY HAD NO idea why she felt the need to explain her actions, except that Dalton deserved to know the truth. "It's just that I'm broken, and I'm no good for anyone for the long haul. You know what I mean?"

Before he could respond, she added, "That fifteen-year-old who put this scar here was my boyfriend. I thought I loved him. And, yes, I know that what I felt was puppy love, first crush, but you know, it sure felt like the real thing to me then."

"First love is powerful," he said, taking it all in without a hint of judgment in his expression. She loved that about him. He seemed to see the good in her.

"I haven't… I don't… I just don't think relationships are right for everyone," she said. "Take me, for instance. I'm completely happy alone. I have my sister and I have Chase." If this divorce happened like she feared it might, she would be seeing a whole lot more of Bethany and Chase. As it was, Blakely wanted to bring her sister home from the hospital to live with her until she sorted out her marriage. "They are going to need me more than ever."

Dalton nodded, but his grip tightened on the steering wheel.

"And I need to be there for them," she said. "Plus, my job is my life, and I spend the rest of my waking hours reviewing cases."

"You take care of everyone around you," he said in an unreadable tone.

"It's what I've always done," she said. Being the oldest, even by a few minutes, she'd stepped in to be there for Bethany after they lost their parents, and she intended to be there for her sister now.

"One question," Dalton said.

"Okay," she said.

"Who takes care of you?"

The question was simple. So why did it kick up a dust storm of emotions that caused hot tears to well in her eyes? "I do." Her voice cracked.

"As far as I can tell, you take care of everyone around you," he said, his voice wrapping around her like a warm embrace. It threatened to shatter all the carefully constructed walls she'd built around her heart.

Could she afford to let someone in?

Heart racing faster than if she'd just sprinted across the parking lot, she wished she could. It was too much, too soon, too unknown.

"I think I've been doing a decent job of managing my life," she said.

"I didn't mean to—"

"What? Imply that I wasn't? Because what other logic is there for making a comment like that one?" **Damn.** She could hear the defensiveness in her own tone. "You're saying that I'm not competent to take care of myself. And that I'm incapable of managing my life."

"Hold on a second," Dalton said, still calm as the surface of a lake on a clear day. "You got all that from what I said?"

"It's what you meant, isn't it?"

"No, seriously. You extrapolated a criticism of your professional life as well as your personal life based on what I said?" He white-knuckled the steering wheel.

When he put it in those words, she sounded off base. It had made sense in her head a few seconds ago. "Sorry, would you repeat your statement?"

"Why? You're just going to decide what I mean instead of hearing me out anyway," he said. The finality in his tone said they were done talking about this.

Had she jumped to conclusions?

Maybe. Okay, yes. Yes, she'd jumped to conclusions, but that didn't mean she was off base.

"It's all I know," she said quietly as she stared out the front windshield.

"My grandmother used to say, 'If it's not broke, don't fix it.' Sounds like the saying applies here."

Blakely doubted she could change if she wanted to. "I'm set in my ways, Dalton."

"Okay," he said. His quick agreement struck like a physical blow. "We're here." He pulled up to the front doors of the courthouse, as close as possible. Ralph, her favorite bailiff, waited at the door. "You should probably head on inside."

A moment of panic gripped her. "Where will you be?"

"I'll be around," he said.

Okay. She'd done it. She'd successfully pushed him away. She'd done this, without regret, to every person who came into her life for longer than she cared to remember.

Why did she suddenly feel hollow inside?

Blakely was midtrial on a robbery case. She expected closing arguments later today, and then the jury would go into the jury room and start their process.

As she passed by the men's bathroom on the way to her courtroom, her law professor stepped into the hallway. The move caught her off guard. She yelped and brought a defensive hand up to push him away.

"Your Honor," he began, tipping his hat and offering a slight bow.

Before he could continue, she asked, "Professor, what are you doing here?"

"I brought a couple of promising students to witness a trial," he explained. The professor had a full head of white hair. He was tall, roughly six feet, and in his midfifties.

"Extra credit?" she asked, unable to muster a smile.

"That's right," he said, standing a little too close. "I'd hoped to catch you." His gaze shifted from her to Ralph and back. "Might I have a word in private?"

"Is it urgent?" she asked as an icky feeling took hold. "Because I'm on my way to court."

"Of course." His smile was more like a sneer. "It can wait."

Blakely tried to shake off the grimy feeling on her way to the bench.

"Everything all right, Your Honor?" Ralph asked.

"Fine," she said, even though she felt anything but.

Chapter Sixteen

Dalton surveyed the area for a long moment after Blakely disappeared inside the building. There was no sign of trouble. None that he could see anyway, which didn't necessarily mean a threat wasn't there.

Once Blakely was safely inside, he parked and then walked the perimeter. The parking lot itself wasn't busy. Half the spaces were empty. Jurors were most likely already present. This new-construction building had a dozen courtrooms. Summoned jurors were being sorted through in a large room, given assignments. Others had cases underway and were already seated in court.

Badge visible on his belt clip, he walked corridors and poked his head in rooms to get a baseline. So far, so good.

He'd seen Johnny Spear's picture, so he knew what facial features to look for. There were countless ways to alter your appearance, but Dalton was skilled at sifting through hair color changes and the various other ways to conceal your real identity. Clothing was another big one. Throw on a dress, put on makeup and paint your nails, and someone like Johnny could walk around freely without being identified.

The probability that Johnny could breach the courthouse might be slim, considering all the ID checks and fail-safes implemented, but Dalton left nothing to chance.

When he'd dotted every *i* and crossed every *t*, he located Blakely's courtroom and found a seat in the back row. There was a small sprinkling of attendees. A gentleman with white hair sitting by three college-aged kids gave rapt attention not to the defendant or the litigators, but to Blakely.

Was this the law professor who'd shown up at the hospital? Didn't that make the tiny hairs on the back of Dalton's neck prickle? The man seemed to be stalking Blakely. This felt like more than just following her career. Dalton needed to have a conversation with her to get her take on the situation. This whole bit rubbed him the wrong way. Not once had any of his college professors tried to establish a personal connection outside of the classroom.

To be fair, she was remarkable and very successful at a young age. He was certain her university would want to keep a strong alumni connection.

Dalton's cell buzzed in his pocket. After checking the screen, he slipped out of the courtroom. "Hey, Jules. What's up?"

"It's Grandpa Lor," she began, emotion making the words come out strained.

"Everything okay?" His pulse spiked.

"He's awake," she managed to say clearly. "And he's asking for everyone."

"I'm on my way," Dalton replied before ending the call. His next was to his supervisor. "I need to go. Now. My grandfather's condition has improved."

"That's good news," Jamison Fox said. Most called him Foxy behind his back. The females on staff said he could pull off the name given his good looks. He wore a gold bracelet around his wrist with his wife and two young kids' names inscribed on it. His devotion to family, they'd said, made him *People*'s Sexiest Man Alive eligible in their books. "I'm happy for you, Dalton."

"I'm mid-assignment," Dalton began.

"Not a problem," Foxy said. "I'll pull someone and send them over. Where are you?"

"In court," Dalton said before explaining Blakely was well protected while in the courthouse.

"Go be with your family, Dalton."

He hesitated before thanking his supervisor. The thought of leaving Blakely sat hard on his chest. Harder than he expected. *A break would be good*, the little voice in the back of his mind reminded. They'd hit a wall on the personal front. Being with Blakely twenty-four-seven wasn't doing good things to his heart or his mind. A little time apart might help clear his head because their attraction was becoming a problem. For him, at least. She'd been clear about where she stood on having anything but a professional relationship.

"I'll have someone over before the end of the day," Foxy said. "Don't worry. I've got this. We'll protect the judge."

The reassurance helped, easing some of the guilt he felt for abandoning her.

"I appreciate it," Dalton said.

"Mesa Point is a couple hours' drive," Foxy said. "You should get on the road if you want to be there by lunch."

"Will do, boss," Dalton said, then thanked his supervisor once again before ending the call. He was torn right down the middle. Half of him wanted to give Blakely a heads-up before he took off. The other half reminded him that she'd been clear about taking care of herself. She'd been clear about not needing anyone in her life.

Walking away while his pride was still somewhat intact was his best bet. If it hurt now, imagine what it would feel like if he spent more time around her.

Closure. This was closure. So why did he feel like he had a big, gaping open wound where his heart should be?

OUT OF THE corner of her eye, Blakely saw Dalton slip out of the courtroom. Hours passed, and he didn't return. Had something happened? Had Dalton been called out? Was something happening in the building or parking lot?

Or had Johnny Spear been caught? Case closed?

At noon, she ordered a break for lunch. Ralph escorted her to her chambers, where she half expected Dalton to be waiting. Her heart sank to her toes when she found the space empty instead.

Still no sign of Dalton when it was time to head back into the courtroom. On the way, she leaned into Ralph and asked, "Have you seen my US marshal escort anywhere?"

"No, Your Honor," Ralph replied as he walked her back to the bench.

Was this bad news? Had something gone down?

"Have you heard any commotion?" she asked.

"No, I haven't," he responded before taking his post.

For the rest of the afternoon, there was no sign of Dalton. The trial concluded, and the jury convened to discuss a verdict. Once again, she waited alone in her chambers until the straightforward case was about to conclude. The jury was out for no longer than fifteen minutes before the announcement came that they were ready to deliver their verdict.

Still no sign of Dalton, and the day was almost over.

Would he be waiting in the truck?

At least the professor and his students were gone when court resumed. Blakely went through her usual bit before asking the jury foreman to read the verdict.

"Your Honor, we, the jury, find the defendant, Thomas

Dunn, guilty of armed robbery," the foreman said, reading from a piece of paper.

"Thank you," Blakely said as the door to the courtroom opened and a man in a suit slipped in. He had that law-enforcement swagger she'd learned was as much part of the job as a neat haircut. This man had military-short red hair.

Her stomach dropped because there was still no sign of Dalton.

She delivered the maximum sentence to the defendant and then dismissed everyone before returning to her chambers. Red immediately knocked at the door as she reached for her purse, ready to get out of there and back to Dalton's apartment.

"My name is Lenn Gunnard," Red said. "I'm here as a replacement for Dalton Remington."

"Oh," she said, trying not to sound panicked despite her pulse spiking. "Is everything okay with Marshal Remington?" Did he despise her enough after their last discussion to ask to be removed from the case?

"Yes, Your Honor," Lenn supplied. "Family emergency."

Was that an excuse or did something happen with his grandparents? "I understand. I hope everyone is okay." Suddenly, she couldn't find a better word to use than *okay*. Where did her extensive vocabulary go? The one she'd used at mock trial during law school that had impressed her professors so much?

"I'm not certain," the marshal said. "I have a truck in the parking lot. Ralph said he would wait out front until I texted it was safe to come outside."

"Okay," she said. There was that word again. "Thank you."

Lenn disappeared as Ralph stepped into view.

"Ready, Your Honor?" Ralph asked.

"Yes," she said even though her thoughts were with Dalton and his family. What if something bad happened? Could she reach out to him? Would he even take her call?

Probably not.

But he couldn't stop her from showing up.

"I have an idea, Ralph," she said. "Would you be willing to give me a ride home?"

"Yes, Your Honor," he said.

"Any chance we can slip out the back?" she asked.

Ralph stood there for a moment before answering. "We can do that."

"I'd owe you big-time," she said.

"No, you wouldn't," he said with a wink. She could guess what it meant, but she wasn't ready to go there and admit to having feelings for Dalton with anyone. If she thought their relationship had a snowball's chance in hell of surviving the long haul, Dalton would be the first to know. She just didn't want to explain that she needed to get to the hospital in Mesa Point, Texas, to a stranger. Whether he liked it or not, she wanted to be there for Dalton in case the worst had just happened. He deserved that much from her, especially because she couldn't give him anything else, even if she wanted to. And a growing part of her wanted to.

"Then, let's go," she said after grabbing her handbag. They made their way out the back and to his truck without incident.

"I have a back way out of the parking lot that should keep us from driving past your new bodyguard," Ralph said. The spark in his voice said he was up for the adventure.

"I appreciate what you're doing," she said to him. "And I'll text the marshal so he isn't waiting all night. But I'd like to get a head start first because I'm sure he'll head straight to my home, where I need to go to pick up my car."

"What about the docket?" Ralph asked.

"I might be back by morning," she said, realizing she hadn't gotten past ditching the marshal out front. "But I'll call out once I get on the road with my car. And I'll take all the heat for asking you for a ride."

"Wasn't worried," Ralph said.

When they had a ten-minute head start, she texted the new marshal and said she would meet him back at the courthouse in an hour. Then half expected him to blow up her phone with messages. He sent one.

Don't worry about it. You'll be reassigned.

Did that mean Dalton was being put back on the case? Her heart double-crossed her, flipping, at the thought.

Calm down. She couldn't be certain of anything right now, and there was no use getting worked up if the man refused to ever set eyes on her again.

Her home wasn't far from the courthouse. Ralph walked her to her car as she dug out the keys.

"Be safe," he said once she was in the driver's seat.

"I will," she promised before closing and locking the door. She started the engine and backed out of the driveway as Ralph waved.

He became smaller and smaller in the rearview until he disappeared altogether. She'd made it into her subdivision. Now, she needed to make it to the highway. This time of year, it was already dark outside. Her stomach growled, making her wish she'd thought to throw a couple power bars inside her purse. She could stop once she got down the highway. Houston traffic was relentless.

Almost out of her subdivision, an aggressive vehicle pulled up from behind. The cab of the SUV was dark, the windows tinted. Bright headlights made it impossible to see who was behind the wheel. Her heart jackhammered the inside of her ribcage.

Was she going to have a reaction every time something felt off? Hadn't she stopped panicking over every little thing years ago?

The engine behind her gunned as she approached a four-way stop. The next thing she knew, her back bumper was being rammed. The SUV didn't have a front license plate, which was illegal in Texas. However, many vehicle owners ignored the regulation, and police didn't have time or resources to pull vehicles over for every minor infraction.

The SUV pushed her out into the intersection as a vehicle came rolling up. She mashed the gas pedal and hooked a last-minute right, staying in her neighborhood. She knew these roads like the back of her hand.

Whipping down an alley and then making another right, the SUV kept close enough to watch her every move. Blakely released a string of curses that would have made her mother blush.

And then she wheeled left, cutting down a back road. She maneuvered through the alley that would dump her onto an outside street. The highway wasn't far. She would have a better chance of losing the SUV on the highway.

In the meantime, she tried to use her voice to have her phone call for help. Of course, the phone didn't respond. She'd never had much luck with that thing.

Glancing in the rearview, she realized she was alone. Hot damn. She'd lost the SOB who'd been on her bumper. The close call jacked her pulse through the roof and scared her. Losing the marshal didn't seem like the best plan in hindsight.

But she'd done it. She'd lost the SUV and could maneuver out of the neighborhood and onto the highway. Once she could exhale, she would call and report the incident to the Houston PD. If Johnny Spear was close, she wanted the law to know.

Halfway through the next intersection, a vehicle sped up and T-boned her. Her sedan went into a spin as the SUV hit Reverse, backed up to make another run for her, miscalculated and got momentarily hung up on a fire hydrant.

Gunning the engine, she made her move, speeding through the neighborhood toward the highway as she frantically checked her rearview mirror, expecting the SUV to show up any second.

The incident rattled her to the point where her hands shook.

And then she caught a glimpse of him speeding toward her.

She smacked the steering wheel with the flat of her palm as she neared the on-ramp. Freedom was within arm's reach. *Come on. Come on. Go faster.*

Could she get there in time?

Chapter Seventeen

"I can't believe you're here," Jules said to Dalton as they stepped into the hallway to head to the waiting room, where a fresh pot of coffee waited.

"It's good to be home," he said. *Home.* Oddly, he'd had the same feeling when he was around Blakely. But it was no use. Her mind was made up. He had no idea what he was offering her anyway. And even if he had a clue, she'd been honest about needing to be alone.

After hearing the reason behind the scar on her forehead, he couldn't blame her for going into protect-herself-at-all-costs mode. As much as he wanted a chance to see where a relationship might go between them, it took two to tango. She was both unwilling and unable to meet him halfway.

As much as he hated to admit defeat, it was time to cash in his chips when it came to the sexy judge.

"Grandpa Lor is looking alert," Dalton said, switching topics in an attempt to reroute his thoughts.

"The doctor says his cognitive tests are coming back looking very promising," she said. They'd wheeled him out of the room, promising to bring him back soon. Dalton wished the prognosis on their grandmother was better. She'd been having a difficult time. Much more so than Grandpa Lor. At least there was hope now, which was more than they'd had yesterday. "But it's getting late, and we should think about ordering in food."

"I can swing out and pick something up," he said. "No need to eat more hospital food."

"It wasn't too bad the first few days," Jules said. "But I can't stand the smell of it now." His sister stood there for a long moment. "He's awake, Dalton." Her voice held disbelief and shock rolled up into one.

"It's a miracle," he agreed, still trying to process the news. He'd bolted out of the courthouse quickly. Part of him felt guilty for not telling Blakely himself, but there'd been no time, and he'd needed to get on the road as quickly as possible.

"Don't take this the wrong way, but is everything okay?" Jules asked. "You seem distracted."

"I'm good," he said. "*Shock* is probably a better word for what I'm feeling right now." It was mostly true. There were other feelings mingled with regret.

Jules's gaze shifted to a spot behind Dalton's left shoulder. Her forehead wrinkled in confusion. "Someone is headed toward us, and her gaze is fixated on the back of your head. Should we be concerned?"

Dalton turned in time to see Blakely making a beeline straight toward him. Threads of hair had freed themselves from her slicked-back ponytail. Half of her white shirt was untucked from her navy pencil skirt. He blinked a couple of times to make sure he wasn't hallucinating. "What are you doing here?"

Jules cleared her throat and introduced herself to Blakely. "I'm Dalton's sister."

"I've heard about you," Blakely said, offering a handshake.

"Really?" Jules asked, wide-eyed. His sister needed to

get better about hiding her surprise when she was caught off guard by a comment. "Well, it's good to meet you." She turned to Dalton. "I'll run out for burgers. Do you still like the usual?"

"Yes," he said, pulling out a credit card and handing it to his sister. "But only if you let me pay."

"Can I get you anything?" Jules asked Blakely, ignoring him.

"No, thank you," she responded.

"Put that away," Jules said with a wrinkled nose before excusing herself and making an exit. That was Jules. She had a dramatic flair.

"You didn't answer my question," he said to Blakely.

"I heard there was a family emergency, and I was afraid something… How are your grandparents, by the way?" she asked.

"My grandfather woke up," he said. "Apparently, he just sat up and asked for my grandmother's potato soup. Said he was starving."

"And your grandmother?"

He shook his head. "There's been no change." It dawned on him that no one followed Blakely out of the elevator. "Where is your protection?"

"I'm sorry about your grandmother, but that's incredible news about your grandfather." She ignored the question.

"Thank you," he responded, then repeated the question, slower this time.

"Nice guy," she said. "I ditched him." She made a move to enter his grandmother's room. "Are visiting hours over?"

Did she think he was going to gloss over that response? "Not for family. And why the hell did you think taking off without protection was a good idea?"

"I didn't." She lowered her voice, fisted her right hand

and then planted it on her hip. "In fact, I didn't think at all. You were gone, and I didn't know if you were okay. So I slipped out the back, and Ralph drove me to my car. I had to check on you."

She'd been clear where he stood with her. Did she need a reminder?

"My supervisor is probably popping TUMS over this incident," he said through clenched teeth. "Coming here on your own is reckless, Blakely. Or have you forgotten that someone out there is trying to kill you?" He fished his cell out of his pocket.

"I needed to know that you were okay," she said. "Now that I have, I can go."

As she tried to stalk past, Dalton grabbed her wrist to stop her. Skin-to-skin contact wasn't his brightest idea. The sizzle of electricity nearly lit a fire. "Don't. Go."

She lifted her gaze to meet his.

"It's not safe for you to leave by yourself," he clarified. The last thing he wanted to do was give her hope. She'd crushed any fantasy he'd had about the possibility of the two of them being more than professional associates. "You get that, right?"

She compressed her lips and nodded.

"You have to take this threat seriously," he continued, firing off a text to his supervisor to let him know she was safe. The move might get him in more trouble, but it was the right thing to do.

"You don't think I am?"

"Ditching the person sworn to protect you isn't a good move, Blakely."

There was so much hurt and disappointment in her eyes that a knot tightened in his chest. Damn. He needed to get a grip.

"I SHOULDN'T HAVE come here." Blakely had made a huge mistake. It was clear to her now that Dalton had been doing his job and didn't want to see her again. As far as the couple of kisses went—kisses that had more promise than any she'd had before meeting him—he most likely got caught up in the moment. Besides, she'd been the initiator, and he'd been along for the ride.

When she put it like that, it didn't sound a bit like Dalton's personality. But it was easier to stick him in that bucket than face the fact she'd let a good person go because of fears she couldn't seem to conquer.

"You're here," he said, all business now. "You might as well stick around until someone can be sent for you."

His cell buzzed. He checked the screen and then excused himself to take the call.

While he was gone, Blakely sent the message to clear her docket for the rest of the week due to her personal safety being compromised. Johnny Spear, or whoever had been behind the wheel of the SUV that had rammed into her, would be able to set up on a nearby rooftop and make the shot as she walked up the courthouse stairs.

Disappearing for a minute to give authorities time to find him and catch him made the most sense to her now. But where could she go? She should have considered this before hopping into the car on a whim. Blakely didn't do "whim." She'd never done "whim."

What had gotten into her?

The short answer? Dalton Remington. He was a game changer. One she couldn't afford.

Speaking of the devil, he came walking up.

"How is your sister?" he asked after tucking the cell inside his pocket.

"Stable," she said. "Greg and Chase should already be

with her this evening. She's sitting up and able to talk on the phone. We had a good conversation on the drive over." Blakely issued a sharp sigh. "Looks like we're both getting positive news tonight." She wasn't sure how he would react to what she wanted to say next. "Would it be all right if I went inside the room and met your grandmother?"

"There a reason?" he asked.

"I'd like to be your friend," she said. "If that option is ever on the table. And if it isn't, then we both walk away once this is over."

"After you," he said with a small nod and a ghost of a smile on his lips—lips that she didn't need to focus on.

The room was softly lit. The steady beep of machines next to his grandmother's bed that were much like a heartbeat reassured her.

There were flowers and cards on every surface. The room smelled of lilacs and roses. "Wow." There was so much love surrounding this woman.

Who would care if Blakely was gone?

Her sister and Chase. At one time, she would have added Greg's name to the list, but she barely recognized her brother-in-law anymore. At her gravesite, there would be exactly two people.

How sad was that? And why did she suddenly care? She'd gotten by fine until now taking care of her sister and Chase. Wanting more out of life aside from her small family and work came out of the blue.

"I don't think it was the smartest idea to ditch your protection and drive here on your own," Dalton whispered. "But I'm glad you made it safely."

"My car took a hit, but I'm okay." She regretted the words the second they left her mouth. "Before you jump on me again, it happened in my neighborhood before I could get to the highway, and I called it in."

"Johnny Spear?" he asked, the corners of his mouth turning down in a frown.

"I couldn't get a good look at the SUV driver, but I assumed it was him," she said. "Who else would it be?"

Concern lines creased his forehead. "Did Houston PD report back?"

"As far as I know, he's still on the loose," she said.

"Consider me back on your case," he said under his breath.

"Is that a good idea?"

"Do you have a better one?" he quipped, raking fingers through his hair. He paced back and forth in front of the window.

"I haven't really thought about it," she admitted. "Ralph was able to keep me safe out the back of the courthouse, and he was the one who made sure I was behind the wheel with doors locked before he even thought about leaving."

"Johnny Spear could have followed you from the courthouse or been waiting for another opportunity to strike at your house."

"That's the reason I took Ralph with me," she tried to explain.

"Not good enough, Blakely. You could have been killed." The pacing quickened.

"But I wasn't," she said, trying to soothe him. As it was, she could almost see the wheels spinning as he retreated in thought. "I'm here. I'm in one piece. And I can't spend my whole life worrying about 'what if' because that would push me over the edge. A lot can happen. It didn't. I'm safe."

"Promise me that you won't disappear," he stated. "I'll request to be put back on your case, but you have to give me your word that you won't do anything to jeopardize your own safety."

Blakely raised her right hand. "Do you have a stack of Bibles?"

Because she was ready to take an oath that she would stay by Dalton's side and allow him to protect her.

Could she trust him with her heart?

Chapter Eighteen

The text came through approving Dalton's request to be re-instated on Blakely's case in a matter of minutes.

Are you sure this is what you want?

His response was direct: Never been more certain of anything in my life, boss.

Done.

Dalton glanced up at Blakely, who he was surprised to learn had been studying him like notes the night before a final. "I'm back on the case. You're my responsibility now, and I take my job seriously."

"So I've noticed," she shot back as she matched his glare. "You're the best. It's the reason I'm still alive, and I don't take that for granted."

"No more funny business. Period. Understand?"

Blakely looked more than a little put off by the comment.

"I have no intention of getting myself killed," she lobbed back with fire in her eyes. "And I feel a whole lot better with someone who I know is competent having my back than a stranger who is punching a time card." Daggers shot from her eyes now. "And no more funny business on your side either."

It wasn't the words she said so much as the way she'd said them that had him thinking she'd changed topics on him. Did she mean the couple of kisses they'd shared? Because he hadn't been the one to initiate them. Though, he'd been a willing participant. No way in hell could he regret those, or even stick them in the category of *bad ideas*. They were. But they'd also been the best kisses of his life and had held the most heat and promise. He knew exactly what happened next when he let those kisses run wild. Primal instinct took on a life of its own when his hands roamed her smooth, silky skin. She was the closest thing to heaven on earth he'd ever experienced, and he highly doubted he would ever have the pleasure of experiencing anything that came remotely close again.

"We're in agreement then," he said vaguely. Two could play games. Speak in veiled sentences. "No more."

Before Dalton could issue another response, he saw Grandpa Lor being wheeled toward him after the elevator doors closed.

Seeing his grandfather alert and alive filled him with emotion. Dalton's heart was so full it could burst open.

Blakely followed his gaze and turned around, and he could see a warm smile spread across what had been a serious face only a few seconds ago. "The family resemblance is strong."

"That's my grandfather, all right." Dalton had barely finished his sentence when his feet started moving of what felt like their own volition toward his grandfather, not stopping until he was bent over the wheelchair in a warm embrace. This was almost too good to be true after fearing too much time had passed with his grandfather in a coma for him to make a meaningful recovery.

There was something about seeing his grandfather that seemed to wash away all his anger and frustration from a few moments ago.

Blakely had taken a huge risk in coming to the hospital. The small but annoying voice in the back of his head reminded him that she'd taken that risk *to be with him* and *to make sure he was okay*. There was no way he could stay angry at her for risking her own life to see him.

He wasn't ready to assign a meaning to it either, like she was in love with him and unable to see it or cop to the fact.

"Welcome back, Grandpa Lor. Welcome back." Dalton whispered those words on repeat in his grandfather's ear.

"It's good to be back," Grandpa Lor admitted.

Sizing him up, Dalton could tell he'd lost a few pounds, but it wasn't anything Mama Bea's country-fried steak couldn't fatten up.

"Grandpa, I'd like you to meet my friend Blakely."

Blakely stepped forward and extended a hand. "It's my pleasure to have the honor of meeting you."

Grandpa Lor's gaze shifted from Blakely to Dalton and back. He said, "I'd be proud to shake your hand. However, we're huggers in the Remington family."

That was all he had to say for Blakely to close the distance between them and offer a warm hug.

A dozen campfires lit inside Dalton's chest at seeing two of the most important people in his life hugging.

"I've heard a lot about you," Blakely said.

"Don't believe any of it. I'm not nearly so wild as the rumors would have you believe." Grandpa Lor winked. His usual lightness and sense of humor was intact. His mind was sharp. For the first time since this whole ordeal began,

Dalton had real hope life might return to some semblance of normal. Grandma Lacey had to pull through. Life wouldn't be the same without her.

Blakely's wide smile as she practically beamed at his grandfather sent another jolt of electricity straight to Dalton's heart.

The nurse behind the wheelchair, gripping the handles, cleared her throat. "I hate to be the one to break up this family reunion, but we are in the hallway, and I'd like to get Mr. Remington back into his room so I can get him more comfortable in his bed."

Dalton and Blakely stepped aside at the exact same moment, parting like the Red Sea to allow the nurse to wheel Grandpa back inside the room.

As Grandpa passed Dalton, he reached for his hand and asked, "Has there been any change with my girl since I was gone?" If Dalton was ever going to commit his life to anyone, he would want to have the kind of love story his grandparents had. High school sweethearts turned life partners who'd built a small business from the ground up together. Ranching was hard work, and yet he never once heard his grandparents complain. Then again, complaining wasn't in their nature.

"No, sir," Dalton said, the nurse agreeing a moment later. She added, "But just like you, Mrs. Remington's condition could change at any minute now. You hang on to that. You hear?" Dalton heard the hopefulness in the nurse's voice and wished he felt the same way when it came to his grandmother. Having Grandpa Lor back was nothing short of a miracle. Did he dare hope for a second?

Dalton instinctively reached for Blakely's hand and linked their fingers as they followed the wheelchair inside his grandmother's room. He told himself the physical connection with Blakely made him breathe easier because he didn't want to let her out of his sight and not because her touch comforted him in ways he knew better than to allow. He wanted to know that she was always near so he could keep an eye on her. She needed to be within arm's reach at all times should anything serious go down.

They'd barely walked into the room when Dalton's cell buzzed. He fished it out of his pocket and checked the screen. "It's from Jules."

"Is everything okay?" Blakely asked.

"Yes, she's fine," he said. "She's asking for help to bring up all the food from the parking lot."

The thought of leaving his grandfather even for a few minutes docked a boulder on the center of his chest. What if he left and his grandpa Lor fell back into a coma? He'd just gotten him back.

Blakely, who was standing right next to him, nudged him with her elbow. Then she whispered, "I'll go down. You stay here with your grandfather."

Dalton bit back the urge to say no. Because this was Jules they were talking about. She was also a highly trained and damn good US marshal. And his sister wouldn't let anything happen to Blakely any more than he would.

"Okay," he agreed. "Thank you."

"I'll be right back," Blakely promised. He let go of her hand before he changed his mind. Besides, he never would have agreed if she hadn't outsmarted Johnny Spear to show up here in the first place. The fact she'd risked her life to come see Dalton wasn't lost on him. But he couldn't afford to let himself get wrapped up in the gesture.

Besides, he needed to help his grandfather out of the wheelchair and into the bed. Dalton moved beside the nurse. "I can lend a hand."

"That would be appreciated," she said.

This close, Dalton could assess just how much weight his grandfather had lost. Hoisting the man up was too easy. He stood on spindly legs, but that wasn't anything good Southern cooking couldn't fix.

"I'll leave you to it," the nurse said after reconnecting Grandpa Lor to the machines next to his bed. She paused at the door. "Lori-Anna has been calling every day to check on you and your wife. Am I allowed to call her back and give her a status update on your condition?"

Dalton hadn't heard his mother's name spoken out loud in longer than he could remember. He had no desire to see or hear from her again after what she'd pulled. Even hearing it now, after all these years, caused his hands to fist at his sides. What could possess a person to walk out on their infant son? Not to mention another son and daughter who were barely old enough to wipe their own backsides? She'd walked out on her husband and her children. Dalton had no use for the woman, despite the tug of curiosity deep in his chest.

"You have my permission to tell Lori-Anna about my status and tell her that I appreciate her calling and checking on me," Grandpa Lorenzo said, much to Dalton's complete shock and horror. Then added, "I'll give her a call as soon as I'm able."

He waited for the nurse to exit before he pulled a seat next to Grandpa Lor's bed and asked, "Do you really want that woman to receive an update, or are you just being kind?"

Grandpa Lor studied Dalton for a long moment. He motioned toward a big white pitcher with a straw poking out of the top next to his bed that was probably filled with ice water.

Dalton handed it over carefully.

After taking a sip, Grandpa Lor cleared his throat and said, "Your mother's situation was complicated. I understand why you wouldn't want to talk about her, so we didn't force the conversation on any of you."

"Does that mean you stayed in touch with her over the years?" Dalton asked, a hornet's nest of emotions buzzing around his heart. As angry as he still was, curiosity was getting the best of him. After almost losing his grandfather and with the possibility still looming that he could lose Grandma Lacey, his heart must have softened when it came to blood ties.

No. The subject was dead, and he should probably leave it alone.

"I won't pretend to condone what Lori-Anna did all those years ago," Grandpa Lor began. Speaking caused him to cough. He paused long enough to take another sip of water before holding the big jug in his once sturdy, now shaky hands. "Life is complicated. Families are complicated. Sometimes, finding a place of understanding is better than holding on to anger."

Dalton couldn't remember a time when either of his grandparents spoke ill about anyone in the family. His no-good uncle had ditched Dalton's cousins after his wife died. The good son, Dalton's father, had been killed in an accident on the ranch. His wife had walked out on their children a couple of years before his death.

So, yeah, he completely understood just how complicated families can be. Relationships fell into the same boat. He'd be a hypocrite if he said otherwise. Especially considering his relationship with Blakely. Or lack of relationship, he should say.

"I know it's probably hard for you to understand," Grandpa Lor continued before another small coughing jag.

"Maybe you should rest," he said, not wanting to wear his grandfather out.

"I'd rather talk, if that's all right with you," Grandpa Lor said. "I've been asleep too long, and it feels good to have company."

"All right then," Dalton said.

"Your mother had a lot of difficulty after you were born," Grandpa Lor said. "No one understood what was happening at the time, including her. Times were different almost thirty years ago. Difficulties were swept under the rug. She went inside herself. Got real quiet. Which wasn't anything like her normal personality."

"Does that excuse what she did in everyone's eyes?" Dalton couldn't help the question.

"I never said it did," Grandpa Lor said wistfully. "I think sometimes it helps to understand, even if it doesn't excuse someone's behavior, if that makes sense."

"It does," Dalton confirmed, not yet ready to let go of his feelings toward the woman who birthed him but couldn't stand to stick around long enough to raise him. She hadn't tried to reach out since then either. Not one birthday card over the years. Not one Christmas present. As a young boy, Dalton couldn't count the number of times he'd fantasized that he would wake up Christmas morning, run downstairs and find her sitting next to the Christmas tree with an armful of presents.

Too many.

Don't get him started on all the birthdays he'd spent waiting by the phone just in case she called. He'd wasted a lot of energy and a lot of time waiting for his mother to make an appearance. He'd cried himself to sleep as a little boy, wishing he had a mother like the other kids on the playground had.

And then one night, he made a promise to himself never to shed another tear.

That was the last time he'd cried.

"Time doesn't heal every wound," Grandpa Lor said.

It occurred to Dalton that he'd been talking to Grandpa for several minutes. Blakely should be back by now. He checked his cell. Nothing.

"Excuse me while I send a message to Jules, Grandpa," Dalton said.

Grandpa Lor gave the okay via a quick nod before he took another sip of water.

Dalton sent the text. Checked the time stamp on the one Jules had sent. It came in twelve minutes ago. *Fourteen minutes.*

The parking lot was a two-minute walk from the ER. There wasn't a lot of activity at the hospital today, so the elevators shouldn't take long. A bad feeling settled in his chest.

Panic slammed into him with the force of a two-by-four.

Where were they? Where was Blakely?

Chapter Nineteen

An arm came around Blakely as she approached the second row in the parking lot.

"Got you, bitch." It was the same voice from the other night. She was certain of it. She searched her memory bank for what Johnny Spear's voice had sounded like and came up without a match. Nothing made sense as a band tightened around her body, pinning her arms to her side.

Blakely tried to throw an elbow into her attacker's midsection. The band tightened.

The light closest to her was out. A glow in the distance was too far to make anything out by.

She wondered why Jules was still sitting in the driver's seat, facing forward. *Oh no.* Please don't let it be that something bad had happened to Jules. She wasn't moving. It was like a mannequin sat in the driver's seat instead of a real person. This situation was bad.

Blakely would never forgive herself if she got Dalton's sister killed because of her actions. But she couldn't focus on that right now. Not while this man's grip was around her like a vise, making movement impossible.

She *had* to break free. Blakely attempted to jerk her arms free.

No use.

He was strong. Too strong.

She attempted to drop down, forcing her legs to become rubber.

No use.

The trick didn't work. She needed to think. *Think. Think.*

Blakely couldn't get a good look at the attacker since he'd come from behind. She tried to memorize details about him. He had no particular smell that she could identify like a cologne or the stench of cigarettes. There was no alcohol smell either.

What else?

The man was tall. Roughly six feet. That much she could tell. Otherwise, he had on something thick, a hoodie. She could see the thick cotton material on his arm even in the darkness.

Struggling against her arm restraints, she tried to squirm out of the man's grip.

Once again, to no avail.

"Take this," he said in a growl.

The next thing she knew, a hard object slammed into the crown of her head.

The urge to vomit caused bile to rise up the back of her throat. She swallowed and tried to focus blurry eyes as she was being ushered toward Jules's vehicle.

Once again, she tried to fight.

"Hold still," the man growled.

Another blow to the back of her head made her dizzy. It hit with such force that her teeth rattled. A dark cloud was closing in over her brain, but she knew better than to give in to it. She knew 100 percent that she would be dead before she ever opened her eyes again if she allowed the darkness that was threatening to close around her like a heavy cloak.

No way in hell did this sonofabitch get to win. Not as long as she had air in her lungs.

She had to make a move. It was now or never.

Blakely fought like a wild banshee, pushing against the tight grip around her arms.

"I got you," came the voice. "You won't get away this time." There was so much anger and frustration in a voice that was so unfamiliar to her. "You'll pay for scratching me up before, honey."

Her next thought was this bastard had scared her nephew into hiding. Anger fired through her, giving her a boost of adrenaline. With it, she mounted another fight. This man had the strength of an ox. Fighting was no use.

So she screamed at the top of her lungs.

There was no one around in the parking lot, but she expected Jules to turn her head. When she didn't, all hope Dalton's sister might still be alive was dead. This animal had just murdered a US marshal. He would think nothing of doing the same thing to a judge.

Her thoughts immediately turned to Dalton and what losing his sister would do to him. It would destroy him, and she would be responsible for bringing this tragedy to his doorstep. It was her fault.

Blakely screamed again, more out of frustration than anything else.

Because no one came in or out of the doors on this side of the parking lot. It was getting late in a town that rolled up its streets by eight o'clock every night.

"Shut your mouth," Hoodie ordered.

The man was going to kill her.

Her first thought might have been about Dalton, but her second was for Bethany and Chase. How would her sister survive without Blakely's help? What would happen to

Chase? His family was already falling apart as it was. She couldn't let him lose his aunt.

Renewed determination to live filled her.

"Who are you? And what do you want from me?"

"Honey, you're my meal ticket. Nothing more," he said in a chilling tone. Those words, spoken with such detachment, sent chills racing up her spine.

Two words stuck out. *Meal. Ticket.* Was it possible someone had hired this man to "handle" her? Could she get this bastard to talk? Maybe trip him up? She had a law degree for heaven's sake. Maybe she could use it to her advantage.

"You want money?" she asked. "How much is my life worth to you?"

"I—uh," the man stuttered. "Just shut your trap, honey."

The word *honey* was the equivalent of fingernails on a chalkboard to her.

"No. It's only fair if you're going to kill me for money to give me a chance to buy my way out of it. I have a lot of money. Are you sure the person who's paying you does?"

"He does just fine."

"How do you know?" If she could just plant a few seeds of doubt in this man's mind, maybe she could talk her way out of this.

"Shut up!" His tone was final. She didn't like the panic in his voice or the anger. Her tactic could backfire on her and cause him to put a knife in her back right now, leaving her for dead like Dalton's sister.

Speaking of murder, why didn't this bastard just shoot her from a distance and leave her for dead?

Did he want to take her to a different location so he could dump her body or scrub it?

Had Jules gotten in the way?

None of this was encouraging, but she needed to dissect

the situation and search for an out. One thing was certain, this man meant business. He was very clear about that.

"You need to go to sleep," he whispered before another blow practically knocked her teeth loose. The next strike was harder than the first and hit the same spot at the crown of her head. What had he used?

The butt of a gun or possibly a knife handle?

His one arm, wrapped around her like a band, was stronger than both of hers put together. Now that he'd picked her up and was holding her to one side, could she throw her head back and cause the man some pain at the very least?

Get some of her DNA on him? Or his underneath her nails?

Screaming in the isolated parking lot wasn't doing any good. She had to try something.

DALTON KNEW SOMETHING was wrong. He fired off a text to his sister, asking what was going on and what was taking them so long. Then he waited. A minute passed with no response.

"What is it?" Grandpa Lor asked. "What's wrong?"

Dalton shook his head. "She should have been back by now. And Jules isn't returning my text. Something's off."

Dalton looked up and caught Grandpa Lor's stare. The second their eyes connected, Grandpa Lor's expression said he knew exactly what Dalton was talking about. Once a marshal, always a marshal. Those instincts never went away.

"Go get your girls."

Dalton nodded before standing up and rushing toward the hallway. He stopped at the door and looked back. It did the soul good to see his grandfather awake and alert.

He tapped the doorjamb a couple of times. "Watch out for anything suspicious while I'm gone, okay?"

Grandpa Lor reached toward the call button. "It isn't

much, but it should stir up a bee's nest of attention should the need arise." His mischievous smile was back, and it warmed Dalton's heart to see its return.

Dalton offered a small smile before making a beeline toward the elevator bank.

Blakely could be anywhere, but his money was on the parking lot since Jules hadn't returned his texts. The thought of anything happening to his sister was enough to cause his hands to fist. Add Blakely to the mix, and he was downright boiling over.

You should have gone down instead. The voice of shame shot daggers straight through his heart. Guilt consumed him. He should have been the one to run down to pick up the food. Now, he'd not only put Blakely in danger but his sister too.

If anything had happened to Jules...

Nope. He couldn't go there. Not until he assessed the situation.

But he had no time to deflect the shame as he tapped the elevator button for a third time in a row. Would constantly hitting the button make the metal machine move toward him faster? He didn't know and didn't care. It gave him something to do with his hands while he waited. Besides, his tombstone would never read: *Here lies a patient man.*

The elevator dinged and then the doors opened. His chest squeezed when it came up empty. He wanted Blakely and Jules to step out of that elevator and tell him what a worrier he was. He wanted to be wrong about the pair of them being in trouble. He wanted, no, *needed*, both of them to be safe.

Instincts honed by years of experience said he was about to find out just how badly he'd misjudged the situation. And he would never forgive himself for the mistake.

Chapter Twenty

Blakely brought her hands up to dig through the layer of thick cotton and find her attacker's skin. She managed to maneuver enough to slip a hand underneath the material of his hoodie, up the sleeve. It was then she realized he was wearing some type of rubber glove just like the other night. So he was still concerned about leaving any DNA traces behind.

This was no doubt the same person who'd attacked her before. He must have been following her up to now, biding his time. Was he the same person who'd driven the SUV?

The short answer was most likely *yes*.

If this man was going to kill her in this parking lot, she fully intended to have some of his DNA under her finger-nails.

Blakely made a claw shape with her hand before digging her nails deep into the flesh of his wrist and then scraping as far as she could go.

Hoodie bit out a few choice words but didn't loosen his grip.

She needed to break free. She needed to get loose. What could she do to stop this bastard from killing her?

Now that she was approaching the vehicle, she saw Jules's face muscle twitch. She was alive?

A burst of hope filled Blakely's chest. Dalton's sister was alive!

The realization gave her a boost. After bringing her chin to her chest, she threw her head back in one quick motion, connecting the back of her skull with his left jaw. A crack sounded as pain shot through her and a trickle ran down the back of her neck. Blood?

Better his than hers. However, she didn't connect with his nose. His jaw wouldn't bleed.

The blood had to belong to her.

Closing in on Jules's vehicle, Blakely wondered what this man had done to the marshal to make her sit so still. Until she got close enough to see the look of panic in Jules's eyes and the beads of sweat trickling down the side of her face.

"What the hell have you done to her?" she demanded.

Hoodie chuckled. The evil sound vibrated through her.

"You will behave from here on out, or she'll go *boom*." Those words cut through Blakely with the precision of a knife.

A bomb.

Jules was strapped to a bomb. It made sense now why she wasn't so much as turning her head despite the fact she had to know they were coming at her from the driver's side, and they were only a foot or two from the door. Jules's gaze was focused forward. Tension tightened the muscles of her neck and shoulders like an overstrung cello.

Now it made sense.

Icy fingers of panic gripped Blakely's chest.

"I'm the one you want. Let her go," she reasoned.

"Not a chance," he said with amusement. This was funny to him? The man was comfortable killing others, so he was most likely a lifetime criminal.

"How much are you being paid?" she asked for the second time.

"More than you can afford." His voice raked through her. "This is your own fault. You had to fight back, didn't you? Now you're a liability."

What the hell did that mean?

A liability?

Wasn't she the intended target?

"You have no idea how much money I have or what I'm capable of," she shot back. Keeping him talking was a stall tactic. He didn't seem to realize she was giving Dalton time to miss them and wonder what had happened.

Would he figure it out too late?

"You messed everything up, and now you have to pay," Hoodie said through clenched teeth. She'd hoped to crack a molar with the backward headbutt. Give him a fraction of the pain he was causing. "And you need to go to sleep so you can't cause any more trouble."

"The woman sitting in the car is a US marshal," she said out of desperation.

"And you're a judge," he snapped. "So what? Neither one of you are in control now, are you?"

Blakely made mental notes just in case by some miracle she survived. He was someone who resented the legal system. Someone who'd done time? Possibly with Johnny Spear?

She didn't recognize him as someone she'd sentenced, but that didn't mean much considering her caseload.

"Johnny's broke," she said in the equivalent of throwing spaghetti against the wall to see if it stuck. "I don't care what he promised you. He won't be able to deliver. I'm worth nothing, and you'll go to jail for him."

"You're right about one thing," he said before adding, "You're worthless. In the way."

In the way.

Of what? A payoff?

"And I don't know who this Johnny person is, but if he hates you, he's doing just fine in my book."

Now Blakely really was confused.

Why attack her if she wasn't the real intended target? Had someone made a mistake? Ended up in her driveway when they were meant to be somewhere else? And now what? She could identify someone in a lineup, so she couldn't be allowed to live?

No. That didn't make any sense either.

"Look, you're about to kill me anyway," she started, wondering how much information she could get from Hoodie. "Why don't you just tell me who is behind this? Why not let me know the name of the person who is having me killed? Don't I deserve to know that much before I die?"

Hoodie issued a disgusted grunt.

Wrong tactic.

"Or don't you believe you can get the job done, so you have to protect yourself?" Based on the fact he got really quiet, she realized she'd struck a nerve. Taunting him was risky, but the bigger risk was doing nothing and letting him carry out her murder. "Oh, you're not authorized to say, are you? You're just a pawn. The sacrifice should this whole thing go south. You're the one who goes to jail when the law comes after you for my murder, and believe me, they will. I already have plenty of your DNA underneath my fingernails. My murder will be connected to you. Law enforcement will hunt you down like a hunter stalks a feral hog. You're already in the database anyway. Your biometrics have been taken because you've already served time."

His grip tightened around her. She was scoring direct hits. Now to keep it going but not push so far that she shoved him over the edge, and he snapped her neck in half. She had no doubt he was strong enough to do exactly that with his bare hands.

He was angry enough to crack.

Blakely took in a slow, deep breath. If she couldn't overpower Hoodie physically, she had to win on a different level…the mental game.

"How do you plan to kill me anyway?" she continued.

"Boom!" he whispered as he walked her to the passenger door. "Get in."

This was so not good.

Blakely did as instructed, as Hoodie pulled a cell phone out of his pocket and smiled. His hood was on and cinched around his face, revealing precious little of the details of his features.

He held up the cell as he backed away into the darkness.

Blakely glanced over at Jules. "I'm so sorry."

CROUCHED LOW, LIKE A tiger about to strike, Dalton moved through the vehicles without making a sound. He overshot the bastard in the Hoodie who'd been carrying Blakely with one arm so he could come up from behind.

He also assessed the situation and determined there was a bomb either strapped to his sister or in her vehicle. Probably on Jules, if he had to guess.

One wrong move and two of the people he loved would go *boom!*

Dalton couldn't lose anyone else.

So he bided his time as Hoodie backed away. The phone must be linked to the detonator. Again, he was guessing, but it appeared that Hoodie had to tap the screen. He wouldn't do that until he was in the clear.

So Dalton waited.

A little closer.

Like a lion leaping toward a gazelle, Dalton dove at Hoodie, striking him from the side at the knees.

A crack sounded as the big man was knocked off-balance, and his cell flew out of his hand. Dalton flinched, half expecting the bomb to detonate. His moment of relief when it didn't was short-lived as Hoodie landed hard on the pavement and immediately threw a punch. His fist connected with Dalton's chin, causing his head to snap to the left.

The sound of car doors opening and closing broke through the ringing noise in his ears. Before Jules and Blakely could get to him, Hoodie pulled a gun and shoved the barrel on Dalton's right temple.

Dalton muttered a string of curses.

The man was fast.

"Back away or I'll shoot," Hoodie demanded as his gaze searched for his cell.

Hands up, both Jules and Blakely took a couple of steps back.

"Find my cell and give it back to me," he ordered. "Or I'll blow his head off."

"Are you sure you want to do that?" Jules asked, calm as anyone pleased. "Because that man is a US marshal. You'll do hard time."

"They won't catch me again," the man quipped. Had he altered his appearance with surgery? Removed his fingerprints?

There were ways for career criminals to erase the ability to match them in a database using biometrics.

"Stand up," Hoodie said to Dalton. "Now."

Dalton did as ordered, once again waiting for the right moment to strike. He'd taken a calculated risk by attacking Hoodie. Dalton had needed the element of surprise in order to stop him from tapping the screen and blowing up Jules and Blakely.

He hadn't anticipated the man recovering so quickly. Or being able to access his gun so quickly. But the risk had paid off. Jules and Blakely were safely out of the vehicle, and nothing had blown up.

"I think I see your phone," Jules said. "I'm going to walk over and pick it up."

"Walk slow," Hoodie demanded.

"Okay," she said. "You can watch me as I go." She took a few steps away from them then bent down. "It's underneath this vehicle. Okay? I'm going to crawl on all fours so I can retrieve it. Are we still good?"

"Yes," he said. "But do anything that makes me nervous, and I'll blow his head off."

"I got it," Jules said calmly before doing exactly what she'd said. "Bad news." She backed up and then sat on her heels. "Phone's shattered."

Hoodie cursed as she held up the screen so he could verify what she said was fact.

"Put your hands on the vehicle where I can see 'em," he demanded.

Jules stood up and did as he said.

Hoodie looked at Blakely next. "You do the same thing on the car next to her."

Blakely held her hands high in the air where he could see them.

The sound of sirens wailed in the distance.

The next thing Dalton knew, he felt a blow and then nothing.

BY THE TIME he came to again, he was in a hospital room, and his head felt like it had been split in two with an axe.

"He didn't act alone," Jules said as Blakely squeezed his hand. The women stood on opposite sides of the bed. Blakely pulled up a chair while Jules paced in front of the window.

"Do you mind doing that over there?" He pointed to the back wall.

"Oh," Jules said, realizing she was making herself an easy target. "Yes. Good point."

"What happened to him?" he asked Blakely.

She shook her head. "He's gone."

"How did it happen?" he continued, realizing he probably didn't want to know but couldn't help himself.

"The gun he pointed at you convinced us to stay put and count to ten slowly," she explained. "It gave him the head start he needed to disappear."

The gunman had used Blakely and Jules to disarm Dalton.

"What about the bomb?" he asked.

"There's a bomb squad outside right now," Blakely said. "We should be getting word at any moment that it has been defused. At least, that's the hope."

"How long have I been out?"

"Half hour tops," she answered.

Dammit. Dammit. Dammit.

The bastard slipped out of their grasp. At least they were all three alive and well. That counted for something. It was the most important thing. "He didn't kills us when he could have."

"I'm hoping some of what I said got through to him," Blakely said.

"Which is?"

She leaned forward and kissed the back of his hand. "He was being paid to kill me. I offered more money. When he didn't take the bait, I sowed seeds of doubt as to whether or not the person he's working for could pay up."

"Who would hire someone to kill you?" Dalton asked. "Johnny Spear?"

"I checked into his background and have no idea where he would come up with the money to hire someone to kill a judge," she said.

The price would go up based on the amount of time someone would serve. "Then, who?"

"That's the sixty-four-thousand-dollar question," Blakely said on a sharp sigh.

Chapter Twenty-One

For a few miserable moments down in the parking lot, Blakely feared Hoodie was going to shoot Dalton. A panic attack took hold. It was as though the air had been sucked out of the universe, and she couldn't breathe.

"We chased him, but he was prepared," she explained.

Jules piped in, "The jerk had a motorcycle stashed in between two cars. One of those crotch rockets." She shook her head. "We didn't stand a chance because there was no way I was getting back inside my vehicle." Jules smacked the flat of her hand against the wall. "We could have lost you, Dalton."

"I'm here," he reassured her, plucking at the cotton gown. "I'm good." He assessed his injuries. "Can't say my fashion sense is all that stellar." He cracked a smile, and it broke the thick tension in the room. "Who dressed me in this?"

Blakely raised her hand, feeling the red blush heating her cheeks. "That would be me."

"I helped," Jules broke in.

"Great." Dalton compressed his lips, looking like he had to bite back a snappy comment. "Then, you both must know where my pants are."

Jules looked to Blakely and shrugged her shoulders in dramatic fashion. "Beats me."

Blakely laughed. She couldn't help herself. Her relationship with Bethany had never been this light, this playful. This fun?

"Maybe you should hit that call button," Blakely said. "Ask one of the nurses."

"Okay, funny guys," Dalton said, putting his hands in the surrender position. "For the record, I've never felt better."

Jules nodded. "Sure. Is that why you squint when you look at me?"

"So I need glasses," he quipped. "Doesn't everyone at some point?"

"It's late, Dalton." His sister walked over to his bedside. "What do you think about staying put for the night and regrouping in the morning? This day feels like it will never end, and you know how I get when I'm running on E."

"Since I'd planned on spending the night at the hospital anyway, that's not such a bad idea," he conceded, much to Blakely's surprise. He shifted his gaze to her. "Will you stay here too?"

"I don't have anything with me," she said, unable to think up a better argument against the idea. "Not even a toothbrush."

Jules sized her up. "You look to be about my size. If you don't mind sharing my clothes, I always have an emergency overnight bag with me. I left one in Grandpa Lor and Grandma Lacey's room just in case I got permission to stay the night."

"Sounds good," Blakely said. "Besides, my adrenaline rush dissipated a while ago, and crawling into bed sounds amazing right now."

"Great. I'll be right back." Jules gave a little wave before disappearing into the hallway. The woman had a remark-

able resemblance to the actress Blake Lively when she was in her early twenties, great hair included.

Must be nice.

"Do you think the nurses would kick me out of the hospital if I took the bed over there?" She motioned toward the twin on the other side of the curtain that had been drawn back halfway.

"We can probably make some kind of arrangement," he said. "Or you could just crawl into my bed."

"We both know where that would end up." She couldn't deny the pull toward Dalton or the fact even thinking of being that close to him lit all kinds of wildfires inside her. But it would be a mistake.

"I'm not complaining," he said before shaking his head. "No. Never mind. We've done that dance. Haven't we?"

"We have," she said, not mentioning the part about it being the best dance of her life. Or that she wished more than anything she could figure out a way to trust men. Trust him.

"No use beating a dead horse, in a manner of speaking," he clarified.

"Nope." Even though her lips still burned with the imprint of his from the kisses they'd shared. She needed to change the subject before heat consumed her. "He won't come back tonight. Will he?"

"This guy is unpredictable," he said after a thoughtful pause. "I have no idea what the man is capable of." He paused another beat. "I would never believe someone would go after two marshals and a judge. You, of all people, know the kind of time he would do for that."

"The promised paycheck must be big," she reasoned. "For him to take that kind of risk."

"Who would have that kind of money?" he asked.

"That's a good question." Before Blakely could think too much about it, Jules came bounding into the room again.

"Everything you need should be in this bag." Jules held out the black gym bag.

Blakely took the offering and thanked her.

"I'm going home to grab a couple hours of shut-eye, but should be back at sunrise," Jules said before exchanging goodbyes and then leaving once again.

True to Jules's word, the bag had everything she might need for the evening. "Do you think we should ask permission for me to stay overnight?"

"Nah," Dalton said. "We should be fine."

"Do you need to shower?" she asked.

"Are you offering?"

Blakely's cheeks heated once again. It wasn't a terrible idea. But sex with Dalton would only leave her wanting more. And then what? The whole question of a relationship would enter her mind, causing even more confusion. She couldn't risk it. "I can hit the 'call' button for you if you'd like." She smirked. "Maybe one of the nurses with big, calloused hands will be on duty."

His laugh was a low rumble in his chest, and it was one of the sexiest sounds she'd ever heard. "One can only hope."

Blakely tightened her grip on the handle of the bag and then disappeared into the bathroom. A quick shower did the trick. Brushing her teeth with a clean, fresh toothbrush was beyond amazing.

She'd run out so fast from Houston that she hadn't thought of necessities like clean underwear or toiletries. After getting ready for bed, she brought the bag with her into Dalton's room. He was already asleep, softly snoring.

After climbing into bed, she did her best to shut down her thoughts as they spiraled. Who could hate her so much

they wanted her dead? Who would be willing or able to pay someone to erase her?

The same hamster wheel of questions spun through her mind. She turned on her side and then punched the pillow in an attempt to get comfortable.

Closing her eyes only served to bring up images of Hoodie. She'd seen his mouth, his thin-lipped sneer. The fact he had day-old stubble on his chin. She concluded he had dark hair based on his facial hair.

A determined killer stalked her. And she had no idea who or why.

At least she knew the man was someone's puppet.

But who?

THE SECOND DALTON opened his eyes, he checked to see if Blakely was still in the bed next to his. His heart raced until he received visual confirmation that she hadn't taken off while he was out. Then, he could exhale the breath he'd been holding. Still asleep.

As much as he'd wanted to have a relationship with the stunningly beautiful judge, could he ever be certain she wouldn't flip out and take off? Where would that leave him if he was always watching the door to see if she would bolt through it?

A soft knock at the door was followed by Jules entering.

"Good morning," she practically chirped. There'd been a lot of changes in her since Toby. The two had found love and each other while transporting a prisoner. Their chopper went down, and they'd had only each other to rely on. Toby had taken more of the brunt of the injuries and was healing nicely with Jules by his side.

"You've had your fair share of hospital stays of late, haven't you?" he asked as she set down the bag of bagels

from his favorite place along with one of those carrying trays that held multiple drinks. This time, there were three cups of coffee.

"Yes," she said on a sigh, taking the seat that had been pulled up next to his bed. "I have. I've been bouncing between floors, but Toby is home now, and Grandpa Lor is awake. It's a miracle. And I never believed in miracles."

"Good to hear Toby is recovering," Dalton said. He should really stop by more often to check on his family members. "When you say *home*. What do you mean?"

"The family ranch," she supplied, taking one of the coffees and handing it to him.

"You're an angel," he said, taking the offering. "I could stand to brush my teeth first."

"Do you need help going to the bathroom?" Jules asked.

"I got it," he said, grasping at the opening in back of his gown before a quick trip to the bathroom. Standing up made him woozy. He needed food in his stomach and caffeine.

"Thanks for the grub," he said as he climbed back under the blanket, tucking in the sides so he didn't accidentally give anyone a peep show.

"You're welcome," she said, taking out a bagel before slathering cream cheese on it.

"I've been thinking a lot lately," he started after she handed it over and he thanked her once again.

"About?"

"Coming back to the ranch," he said.

"I thought you loved your job," Jules said, surprised. She grabbed another bagel and opened it. Everything bagels were manna from heaven.

He acknowledged that he did. "I used to, but things have been changing for me lately. I think I'd like to put in notice and move back to the ranch full-time once this case is over."

"Seriously?" Jules stopped mid-slather.

"I'm dead serious." He regretted his word choice, but the sentiment remained the same. "I've been doing a lot of soul-searching since our grandparents' accident."

"And?"

"Don't you miss the ranch?" he asked.

"Yes, of course," she said. "But that doesn't mean I want to come back and work it full-time." She set down her bagel. "I have been thinking about becoming more involved again though. If I didn't have to give up my job."

"I wonder if everyone else is thinking along the same lines," he said. "Seems like we're usually in sync."

"Crystal would definitely do more," Jules said. "I've been talking to her about it. So would Abilene."

"Have you talked to Camden?"

"Not yet," she said. "He's been unreachable lately. I see that he's been reading the updates. But he doesn't comment."

"I can reach out to him," Dalton said. "Just to get a base-line of what everyone is thinking." He took a bite of bagel, chewed and then followed it with a swig of black coffee. "Grandpa Lor is feisty as usual, but I think he'd be thrilled with the help."

"Did you get a good look at him?" she asked.

Dalton nodded. "He definitely needs some home cooking to put some meat on those bones."

She smiled. "The bagels should help." Then, she added, "I'm proud of you, Dalton. I hope that doesn't sound too mushy or cliché."

He cracked a smile.

"The ranch will be lucky to have you back full-time," she said.

He nodded. "It just feels right. You know?"

"Then you have to do it."

"Any idea how long it'll take Grandpa Lor to be released from the hospital?" he asked.

"Do you seriously think he'll leave Grandma's side?"

"I guess not," he agreed.

"Can you imagine the two of them being separated from each other?"

"No," he admitted. He couldn't. He'd always believed the two of them would ride off into the sunset together. "I doubt death will part them no matter what vows they took on their wedding day."

Jules laughed.

"Agreed," she said before urging him to eat.

Dalton polished off a bagel and then his coffee. "You still haven't told me where they hid my clothes."

"Right. That."

"Do you intend to?" he asked.

"Have you spoken to the doctor about being released?" she asked.

"He stopped by last night after Blakely fell asleep," he said. "Turns out, I have a mild concussion, but I could have told him that."

"You and Camden should know what that feels like after our childhoods," she teased.

"Truer words have never been spoken," he said. "All of us played sports."

"And ran around the ranch like wild animals if memory serves," she added.

He couldn't help but laugh as memories filtered through of him falling out of a tree, Camden falling out of a tree, Duke falling out of a tree. "Our grandparents are saints for putting up with us."

"Yes, they were," she said with a spark in her eyes that he'd seen many times before.

"We had an amazing childhood that I completely took for granted," he said as shame filled him. "I should have been here for them."

"Don't blame yourself, Dalton. Any one of us could say the same thing, and you would be the first to tell us not to think along those lines."

She had a point there. One he couldn't argue.

And then she caught him off guard when she asked, "What about her?" Jules hooked her head in Blakely's direction. "What will happen with your relationship if you move back to Mesa Point?"

"Simple. We don't have a relationship to discuss."

"Really?" Jules asked. "Is that what you think? Because I had no idea my little brother was so oblivious."

Attraction didn't make a relationship, he wanted to point out. And Blakely had been clear about not seeing herself trust another person.

"It takes two to tango, Jules." And he was a one-man show.

Chapter Twenty-Two

"Are those bagels I smell?" Blakely stretched her arms and made a show of waking up. Was she being too obvious? She hadn't intended to eavesdrop on their conversation, but she woke up at "We don't have a relationship to discuss," and it had felt like the wrong time to make it known she could hear.

If not for her bladder forcing her to get out of bed, she would have pretended to be asleep for the rest of their conversation. However, she had to go.

Throwing off the covers, she stepped lightly on the tile flooring.

"Yes," Jules said with a look toward Dalton. "Help yourself."

"Bathroom first," Blakely said before disappearing into the adjacent room. She wished she could crawl through a crack in the wall and disappear after hearing Dalton tell his sister about their non-relationship. Clearly, the woman had picked up on a vibe between Blakely and Dalton.

Were they that obvious?

So much for playing it cool around other people. Blakely couldn't contain her attraction when she was one-on-one with Dalton, but she thought she was doing a decent job of covering in front of others.

Maybe not.

Their chemistry was undeniable. So much for being stealth about their past. Now, there were questions—questions she couldn't answer. Trying to be with Dalton didn't work. Trying to stay away from Dalton didn't work.

Right now, she was a big ball of contradiction. He must be confused as hell.

Blakely made a quick call to check on her sister before freshening up. Then, she joined the siblings in the next room.

"How'd you sleep?" Jules asked, and Blakely was grateful for the general question. She couldn't answer personal ones right now. Not when she was just as confused as everyone else about the nature of her and Dalton's relationship.

Blakely was handed a bagel and a cup of coffee almost the second she sat down. "Better than anyone should in a hospital."

The comment elicited a couple of laughs and a nod from Dalton, who probably didn't sleep much more than a few minutes here and there.

And then he turned his attention toward his sister.

"Jules, can I ask you a question?" Dalton started before adding, "It's off topic but important."

"Go ahead," she urged. "You know you can ask me anything."

"Did you know about our mother being in contact with our grandparents all these years?" he asked in a direct question.

Jules sat there for a long moment, quiet. She stared out the window and shifted in her seat.

"I did," Jules admitted. She shot a look of apology toward Dalton, who looked like he'd just been betrayed by his best friend.

"Am I the only one who didn't know?" he asked.

"I've never discussed it with Camden," Jules said. "So I can't speak for him."

Based on the look on Dalton's face, the response didn't exactly offer much in the way of reassurance.

"What about her?" he asked. "Are you in touch with her? Do you guys…what?…talk on a regular basis or something?" The rim of his cup suddenly became real interesting to him.

"Not really," Jules admitted.

"What does that mean exactly?" Dalton pressed. "You don't talk at all or don't talk on a regular basis?"

Beep. Beep. Beep. The heart monitor picked up.

Blakely glanced at the machine and then tried to catch Dalton's gaze. No use. His was fixated on his sister.

"Just that," Jules said on a shrug. "I asked our grandparents if they knew anything about our mother for medical history purposes a couple years back." Jules kept her gaze fixed on the window. "Once I opened the door, Grandma Lacey came to me and asked if I had any questions."

"You mean Pandora's box," he quipped. *Beep. Beep. Beep. Beep.*

Jules shot a warning look.

"I'm guessing you did have questions," he continued. *Beep. Beep. Beep.*

"That's right." Jules turned her attention to the sliver of bagel in her hand. She started to take a bite before thinking better of it and setting it down. "My curiosity started with medical questions, and then things spiraled from there. I wanted to know what she was like and if I got any of my traits from her. I look in the mirror, and I don't see a resemblance to Dad. I'm not like you and Cam. I've always felt like I looked like the black sheep of the family and—"

"No way," he countered. "You're *you*. You look like *you*."

Jules pinned him with her gaze. Blakely wouldn't want to go up against Dalton's sister in a bar fight, that was for sure.

"Haven't you ever looked at me and wondered where I got this hair color from?" Jules asked.

"No," he said, shaking his head. "I had no idea you felt that way, or I would have—"

"What? Reassured me?" She blew out a frustrated breath. "And force a discussion about our mother on you and Cam when you both seemed capable of letting a sleeping dog lie?"

"You could have given us the benefit of the doubt that we would have been able to handle talking about her," he pointed out. *Beep. Beep.*

"The subject never came up," Jules admitted. "It's not exactly something we ever discussed. I mean, you and Camden never mentioned anything about our mother, so I guess I figured that you just didn't want to know, and I should leave it alone."

"I'm sorry you didn't feel like you could come to me to talk about it," Dalton said. "I guess I haven't been the easiest person to discuss our parents with."

"Through no fault of your own," she said. "I just figured there would come a day when you would be ready to talk about her or ask questions, and part of me wanted to have the information and be ready should that day ever come. At least, that's another excuse I told myself before I was able to admit that I was just curious where I came from."

"Growing up, you always did put it on yourself to be the one to take care of Cam and I, even though Cam is the oldest," Dalton said.

"He has the most memories of our parents," she said. Blakely wondered if their older brother held on to the most pain too.

"Grandma Lacey did a really great job with all of us," Jules said, twisting her fingers together. This subject obviously made her uncomfortable. "Learning about our mother had nothing to do with the upbringing we had, which was the best."

"Our grandparents did the best they could with the hand they were dealt," Dalton said. "Can you even imagine being at that point in your life and taking on six children?"

Jules shook her head. "I guess I've been thinking about that a lot more lately now that Toby and I…"

Dalton's eyes widened to saucers. "What? Are you telling me that you're—"

"No," Jules said with an expression that made it look like she'd just bitten into a sour grape. The look on her face immediately shut down any notion that she might be pregnant. "We're engaged, not yet married." She paused for a few beats. "I know babies don't necessarily wait, but I've always been on the fence about having children because of our situation."

"I'm not on the fence at all," Dalton stated with finality. "I never intend to have a family."

What was it about that statement—a statement Blakely would have wholeheartedly agreed with a week ago—that caused her stomach to sink and a sense of hopelessness to settle in her chest?

She didn't want a family. Did she?

"Have you met her?" Dalton asked his sister.

"Haven't decided if I want to or can handle it," Jules admitted.

"Grandpa Lor said there's a lot we don't know about our mother's 'situation,' as he called it," Dalton said. "Do you know what he's talking about?"

"I haven't heard anything from her perspective," Jules said. "But I know she was suffering when she left."

"What do you think about setting up a meeting with her to ask questions?" he asked.

"It's crossed my mind," she said. "If only to hear her side of the story. And, I don't know, get closure."

DALTON NOTICED BLAKELY hadn't said a word in several minutes. Then again, he and Jules had been discussing family. He needed to shift gears because he still wasn't sure what to think about his mother being in contact with his grandparents or any member of his family after the stunt she'd pulled. *Anger*. Now, there was a word. *Confused*. It fit.

Was closure possible or a pipe dream?

Either way, Dalton set his empty coffee cup down and turned his attention toward Blakely. "You probably don't want to hear all this about our family."

"I don't mind," she said. He realized she'd lost her parents too. "Families are complicated. I get it. Mine is beyond messy right now."

"Speaking of your family, is there any word on Bethany?"

"My sister lost a lot of blood, so they're keeping her at the hospital after the surgery to remove a bullet fragment from her neck," she explained. "If the bullet hit a few centimeters to the left, there would have been no surviving it."

"It's strange to think of being lucky when you're talking about taking a bullet," Jules conceded. "However, in this case, it sounds like your sister was very lucky."

"She has a lot of thinking to do about her marriage, so being away from home probably isn't the worst thing right now," Blakely continued.

Dalton nodded. "The hospital is secure, and the nurses are watching her room like a hawk."

"There's some peace of mind in that knowledge," Blakely said. Based on the tension lines scoring her forehead, there wasn't much. He understood. If Jules were in a hospital and he couldn't be near... Dalton couldn't even think about it. Everyone in his family had a dangerous job. Everyone was good at what they did, which didn't rule out the possibility something catastrophic would happen. In order to work the job and sleep at night, he couldn't let himself go there mentally about everything that could go wrong.

"It's not much," he conceded. "Which is why we need to figure out who is behind these attacks so we can put an end to this once and for all."

"As long as Bethany is in the hospital, she's safe," Blakely stated. "Which also buys us some time to figure all this out."

"Speaking of which, I can get a whole lot more done out there than trying to stay in here," he pointed out.

"Hold on there," Jules said. "Where do you think you're going?"

"Out of here," Dalton said firmly.

"What do you think the doctor will say?" Jules asked.

"I think he'll tell me to stop taking up bed space when I'm fine and don't need to be here," Dalton said, a little heated.

"Whoa!" Jules teased. "I'm just trying to be the voice of reason."

"Didn't mean to get riled up," Dalton said.

"Where will we go?" Blakely asked. He liked the fact she wasn't trying to bolt. He'd promised to protect her, and that was exactly what he intended to do.

"My place should be safe," he said.

"That means you have to leave the hospital," Blakely said. He could tell she felt guilty by her expression.

"My grandfather is awake, and we have every reason to believe he'll stay that way," Dalton said.

"You could take Blakely back to the ranch," Jules offered, but both Dalton and Blakely were already shaking their heads before his sister could finish her sentence.

"Too dangerous for everyone else," Blakely said before he could.

"Toby's there, recovering," Jules said. "I'm staying there when I'm not here at the hospital. We'd be ready."

"Someone could light the barn on fire, damage the property or set a blaze just to flush me out of the house," Blakely said. "You already experienced a bomb last night."

"I wasn't ready for it," Jules said a little defensively. Dalton understood how frustrating and embarrassing it was for someone in law enforcement to be tricked. She had nothing to be embarrassed about, but Jules wouldn't see it that way and neither would he if the situation was reversed. Hell, he couldn't forgive himself for letting Blakely go downstairs or not warning Jules of the possibility in the first place.

"It's my fault, not yours," he said to his sister.

"Agree to disagree," Jules said. "But arguing or assigning blame doesn't fix anything."

"Now we agree on something," he said.

"I really hate getting your family involved in any of this mess," Blakely stated.

"We don't," Dalton and Jules said simultaneously.

Dalton added, "It's what we've chosen to do for a living. You're not putting us in any danger that we didn't already sign up for."

Blakely conceded with a slight nod. "This feels more personal."

He knew exactly what she was talking about. Their fling. It made this situation more personal for him too.

There wasn't anything they could do about it now.

"Suffice it to say, I'm not going anywhere until this is resolved," he said, wishing for more but knowing Blakely couldn't give it.

Chapter Twenty-Three

Blakely needed to have a serious conversation with Dalton once this ordeal was over. Right now, all she could think about was keeping everyone safe until law enforcement caught up with the bastard who was determined to kill her.

Her cell buzzed. She checked the screen, and her stomach fell. "It's my brother-in-law."

Locking gazes with Dalton, even for a few seconds, gave her a boost of confidence before she answered the call.

"Hey, Greg. Everything okay?" she asked.

"Aunt Blakely," came Chase's small voice. She listened for any signs of sadness or panic, decided she was searching for something that wasn't there. "Can you come pick me up?"

"Where are you?" she asked.

"Home," Chase said. "I don't like it here without Mommy."

"Are you alone?" she asked.

"Gotta go," Chase whispered. "Daddy's coming."

"Chase?" she asked, but he was already gone. She locked gazes with Dalton. "I need to get back to Houston."

"Is that a good idea?" Dalton asked.

"What choice do I have?"

Dalton seemed at a loss for words.

"Someone bring me up-to-date on what's going on, please," Jules said.

"Blakely just got a call from her nephew," Dalton started.

"Asking me to pick him up," Blakely finished.

"Where?" Jules asked.

"In Houston," Blakely responded.

Jules pushed to standing and started pacing again. "We can get there with some planning."

"I'm sorry to be the one to say this considering I know how much you love your nephew, but you have to consider the possibility you'd be placing him in harm's way," said Dalton.

Right. Like Bethany.

Blakely bit out a curse. "What else am I supposed to do?"

"Catch this bastard so you can get your life back," Dalton said. If only it was that easy.

What if this guy escalated? Then again, he'd tried to blow up her and a US marshal. How much further would this go?

"Chase is safe with his father," Dalton said.

As much as she didn't want to admit it, Dalton was making sense, whereas she was being irrational. Her emotions were at the wheel. Despite the couple hours of sleep last night, she was still bone-tired. Caffeine helped. Some. But she needed an IV of dark roast if she wanted to be alert and awake for the rest of the day.

"You make a good point," she finally said to Dalton.

"My apartment might be the safest place for us right now," he said.

That was true for them and everyone around them.

"I'm coming with you," Jules said.

"Your plate is full already, taking care of Toby while being here for our grandparents," Dalton said. "Grandpa Lor is awake now. He'll need your support even more."

Jules opened her mouth to speak but then clamped down on her bottom lip instead.

"I'll have your truck swept before the two of you leave," Jules said. "Are you sure it's safe to go to your apartment? Because I can arrange a safe house to get you by until this blows over."

Going to an unfamiliar place where there would be strangers didn't exactly feel warm and fuzzy to Blakely. Not being able to go pick up Chase when she desperately wanted to be there for him was the hardest thing. Not being there for Bethany made her want to scream. What choice did she have? "It's hard to kill someone you can't find."

Jules looked to Dalton, who gave a slight nod.

Okay, then. They were going to a safe house.

"I can get you near Houston," Jules said as she retrieved her phone from her handbag. "How do you feel about Galveston?"

"Good," Dalton answered.

"Okay, then I think I have a place for you to hang out that should keep you off the radar," Jules said.

"While you're getting a sweep done on my truck, maybe I can take one of the ranch vehicles instead," Dalton said.

"No one should be expecting it," Jules said. "Give me half an hour, and I'll set everything up. In the meantime, dear brother, make sure you get clearance from the doctor to leave. Okay?"

He saluted. "Yes, ma'am."

The next hour was a blur of activity as Dalton cleaned up and got dressed, nurses scrambled around getting him ready for release, and a doctor was summoned to give the final okay for him to be discharged. He'd been clear about his intention to walk out with or without the doctor's per-

mission. Waiting would get him in the least amount of trouble with his boss.

An apartment at The Waterfront on Bayou Shore Drive was arranged, and a ranch vehicle was parked at the side of the hospital. Jules would oversee the bomb sweep of Dalton's truck, drawing attention there while he and Blakely slipped out the side door and to the waiting vehicle.

Dalton stared at his cell. "Johnny Spear has been arrested at Lake Texoma, where he was hiding in a fishing cabin with no contact to the outside world."

"I'd started to move on from him as a suspect anyway," Blakely admitted. "It's good to know that I'm on the right track."

"Have you considered the professor?" Dalton asked before they were interrupted by a thumbs-up from Jules. "Go time."

Within a matter of minutes, they were racing down a staircase before hitting the side exit. An older gentleman scooted over to the passenger seat before exiting the truck with the engine left running.

"Shiloh Nash has worked the ranch since long before I was a twinkle in my parents' eyes. Grandpa Lor hired him at fifteen, and he's been there ever since," Dalton explained as Blakely crouched low in the seat. "Folks say all he needs to do is put his hands on a horse to hear its thoughts."

Despite his age, the man looked strong. He still had a full head of white hair.

"Sounds like he has a gift," she said, checking the side mirror to see if anyone was paying attention to them or if a vehicle was following them. So far, so good. Did she dare hope they would make it to Galveston?

"He's quite the character too," Dalton supplied. It was nice to talk about something so normal for a change.

"I wish we could stay here so you could have more time with your grandparents," she said.

Dalton tightened his grip on the steering wheel and kept his eyes on the patch of road in front of them. "They have Jules. Grandpa Lor is awake. Now we just need miracle number two."

Blakely could use one of those miracles about now.

THE DRIVE TO Galveston was quiet. They only made a lunch stop, eating fast food in the truck while parked across the street from the taco place. Apartment 4D of The Waterfront luxury apartments afforded a view of the Gulf of Mexico that Dalton might have appreciated more if he was on vacation. As it was, he checked the one-bedroom along with the perimeter with a wary eye. Once he deemed it safe, he joined Blakely inside, where she was rummaging around in the fridge.

"I meant to ask more about your relationship with the professor," he said to her.

"What relationship?" she asked.

"He shows up in your courtroom. Keeps track of your schedule. Surely you don't think it's for professional reasons only."

"He has a reputation for liking busty blondes, which I am not," she said, a little too quickly to dismiss his concerns. The guy did exhibit a stalker quality. "I admit he's made me uncomfortable on a couple of occasions, but I choose not to read too much into our interactions." She pulled out ingredients to make sandwiches. "I can also admit that seeing him in my courtroom yesterday was uncomfortable. Though, it wasn't the first time he's brought students." She closed the fridge door. "Do you see him as a threat?"

"I don't like his fixation on you," he admitted. "Has he ever made an advance?"

"I've been very clear where I stand with the professor," she said as she assembled dinner. Didn't mean the professor was on board or that he didn't resent her for refusing him. Would he resent her enough to come for her?

Dalton sent a message to Jules to see if she could pull up any dirt on the professor, like sexual harassment claims by current or former students. Any indications of escalation of stalking behavior.

He received an immediate response that Jules was on it.

After a quiet dinner, Blakely excused herself to take a shower. Dalton sat at the table and stared out the window. Now that Johnny Spear had been eliminated as a possibility, they were back to square one. The professor bugged Dalton. The man's actions raised red flags. Did it mean he was a murderer? Was he trying to scare Blakely? Get her to run to him in some twisted scenario in the man's mind?

Would he hire someone to hurt her? Abduct her?

It didn't add up.

Blakely's cell buzzed. Dalton resisted the temptation to check the screen. She would be out of the shower in a few minutes and could see for herself.

The darn thing barely stopped buzzing before kicking off a new round. An emergency?

He got to his feet and moved to the counter to check the screen. If he was going to read the messages, he needed her facial ID.

Since this seemed important, he picked up the phone and took it to the bathroom with him. Standing in the hallway, he knocked on the door as the cell went off again. "Sorry to interrupt, but your cell isn't letting up. Someone must want to get a hold of you desperately."

The water turned off.

A few seconds later, the door cracked enough for him to slip her phone through.

"Everything okay?"

"It's my sister," Blakely said. "She wants me to pick her up. Says she is being discharged first thing in the morning but doesn't want to go home and doesn't want anyone to realize she left the hospital in the middle of the night."

A minute later, she emerged from the bathroom dressed and still dripping wet.

"What should I do, Dalton?"

HIDING WAS GOING to drive Blakely out of her mind. Doing nothing was the absolute worst. "Tell me what to do because I can't leave my family hanging like this. There has never been a time when I wasn't there for them."

Dalton raked his fingers through his hair. "How tired are you?"

"I'm wide awake now," she admitted.

"Let's go get Bethany."

"How?" Did she dare hope he had a plan? Could they grab Bethany and bring her back to Galveston with them to hide out for a few days? What would that do to Chase? *Chase.*

"We'll figure it out on the drive over," he said.

"I'll grab clothes for her," Blakely said before throwing another jogging suit in her handbag along with the only other shoes she could find, ballet flats she'd packed.

Within a matter of minutes, they were back on the road.

The drive didn't take long at night with no traffic.

"You're authorized to go in the room, so maybe we arrange a swap while the nurses aren't looking?" Dalton asked after parking in the lot.

It could work. "I can change clothes with Bethany, and then she can walk out with you."

"We'll pretend to be a couple so I can hide her face," he added. It was cover, so the idea shouldn't bother her as much as it did.

"And then, I'll come out and say goodbye," she said. "Make a show of them seeing my face so they won't suspect anything."

"As busy as the nursing staff is, we have a good chance a different one will be at the station if we hold off for a few minutes," he reasoned. Someone was always at the station, but the nurses moved in and out of rooms.

"Let's do this."

Chapter Twenty-Four

The first part of the mission was a success. Dalton and Bethany waited in the parking lot. Now all Blakely had to do was give it a few minutes, and she could make her exit.

The sound of feet shuffling outside of her door sent her pulse flying. She climbed into bed, turned away from the door and pretended to be asleep. She forgot how often nurses came in and checked on patients. Bethany had complained about getting no sleep while in the hospital after having Chase.

This was so not good. Could she reach for her cell without drawing attention?

Footsteps sounded after the door was closed. The nurse was inside the room.

Hold on.

Something was off.

Would a nurse close the door behind her after entering the room?

No.

Someone was here.

Dalton would have made his presence known.

Squinting, she searched for something to use as a weapon on the nightstand next to the bed.

"You just won't die," came a growl from the familiar voice. A jolt of shock rocketed through her. A *whoosh* sound filled her ears as panic gripped her. Now she knew who was behind the attempts to kill her. And she couldn't believe who it was.

Blakely stayed quiet. She couldn't reach for the vase on the table without being caught. The voice was too close. Her heart pounded the inside of her ribcage. She could only hope the bastard couldn't hear it.

White-hot anger filled her as she clenched her fists. How could he?

As he came close enough for her to hear his breath, she hit the call button and burst from the covers. "Greg! You sonofabitch! I'm not Bethany."

He dove for her, ramming her in her midsection as voices sounded in the hallway. She crashed into the nightstand, cracking her head against the hard wood. The vase tipped over, slamming into her head first and then the tile floor, where it burst.

"What the hell?" Dalton's voice cut through the room as the light flipped on.

A nurse rushed into the room beside him.

But it was too late. Greg had pinned her to the floor and had a piece of glass to her throat.

"Back up or I'll cut her carotid artery," Greg demanded. The wild look in his eyes said he was desperate and would kill her if need be, despite the look of apology he shot her. "This isn't supposed to happen this way." He rocked back and forth, his elbow jabbing her in the chest as he held her down.

"What then? What was your plan? Kill your sister-in-law? For what reason?" Then it dawned on her.

"You were a decoy," he said. "Bethany is the one who is supposed to die."

"For what reason?" Blakely asked, distracting Greg while she prayed everyone else was coming up with a plan. "My sister has nothing to give."

"Life insurance," Bethany said from behind them. Her tone said he'd drained her of any love she might have had for him over the years. "You asked me to sign the policy that you took out a few months ago. If everyone thinks my sister is the real target, and I'm accidentally killed, you'll get to play the grieving husband role. Is the money for your mistress?"

"I didn't… I don't…" Greg stuttered.

"Was I that awful of a wife that you wanted me gone? Dead?" Bethany asked. Now Blakely could hear the hurt.

If only she could somehow wiggle free or get hold of a piece of the vase to turn the tables on Greg. Could she make a move without triggering him?

The desperate look in his eyes, his actions—this wasn't the Greg she'd once known. How could she have missed the signs of his mental decline?

Busy. Being busy was a lousy excuse, even if it was true.

"I owe people," Greg finally said. "And they're coming for me if I don't pay up. These aren't the kind of people who let missed payments go unnoticed."

"How is that possible?" Bethany asked.

"You have no idea what it's like to try to keep up your lifestyle," he practically spat out. "I tried to be a good husband. I worked but you were never satisfied." There was nothing but anger and accusation in his tone now. Like a teapot boiling over.

Blakely made eye contact with Dalton, who gave an al-

most imperceptible headshake. He didn't want her to make a move.

Could she buck Greg off without causing him to slice her throat?

"You. You wanted the world handed to you on a silver platter." Greg's voice was almost hysterical now. "And you didn't care enough about me to see that I was drowning."

"Is this about your mother?" Bethany asked, panicked. "Because I tried to help with her when she was sick."

"She was all I had," Greg said.

"That's not true," Bethany argued. "You had me and you have a son. Remember Chase?"

Greg's wild eyes searched the room. "You'll never find him."

Oh. No.

"Did something happen to Chase?" Blakely managed to ask as Bethany's knees buckled and her legs came out from underneath her. Before she could hit the floor, Dalton scooped her up.

"I'm going to set her on the bed, okay, Greg?" he asked, taking a slow, measured step inside the room.

Greg's body stiffened. The sharp point pressed a little harder into Blakely's neck.

"Please, Greg," Blakely managed to say. "Don't do this. We'll get help for you. You still have a family." The thought this man could have hurt Chase had to be pushed out of her thoughts. She had to find a way to win him over. "We'll be there for you."

"Where have you been?" Greg asked. "You're just saying that now because you don't want to die."

"No, I don't," Blakely admitted as Dalton set Bethany on top of the covers.

"Back off," Greg said, his full attention on Dalton.

Could she make a move?

Distracted by Dalton, Greg released the pressure on her neck. It was now or never.

Blakely bucked. Greg lost his balance. He brought his hand down to stabilize himself but ended up grabbing a handful of glass.

He bit out a string of curses as she rolled away, out of reach.

Dalton stepped in between them and drew his weapon. He identified himself to Greg and read the man his rights.

Bethany came to. "Where's Chase?"

"You'll never find him," Greg spit out as hospital security flooded the room. "He's gone."

Blakely felt sick. She grabbed her stomach as Bethany leaned over and threw up.

"No," her sister said. "You couldn't hurt our baby. Could you?"

Greg sneered as he was being placed into zip cuffs.

Please. Please. Please be bluffing.

"Where is he?" Bethany chanted as she managed to push off the bed and throw herself toward Greg. "I wasn't perfect, and neither were you. But Chase is innocent. He's just a boy."

Seeing her sister plead ripped Blakely's heart out.

"Let's go," she said to her sister. "We need to find Chase."

Dalton helped, asking security to have the police meet them at Bethany's home.

Fear and anger balled up together as Blakely managed to help her sister to the truck. A decoy. It made sense. The shot had come through the window after Blakely's attack.

Dalton drove like the street was on fire behind him. Blakely called out directions. Was the stranger who Greg

had promised a payout to at Bethany's house right now? Did he have Chase? Or was Chase…

Blakely couldn't let herself think her nephew was gone.

All three of them flew out of the vehicle as Blakely fumbled for the key to unlock the door. All the lights were out. From the outside, it looked like a normal home. What were they going to find inside?

Dalton took the lead, flipping on lights as they ran through the downstairs, checking rooms.

"Chase," Bethany called out.

A sleepy little boy appeared at the top of the stairwell.

"Mommy?" he asked, rubbing his eyes.

Despite everything she'd gone through physically, Bethany found a reserve of strength as she practically flew up the stairs. Adrenaline could do that to a person. Give them a burst of superhuman strength.

Dalton continued checking the home while Blakely joined her sister and nephew, wrapping them in a hug.

"Where's Daddy?" Chase asked.

"He's not coming home for a long time, baby," Bethany said. "But I'm here. I'm not going anywhere. Neither is your aunt Blakely."

"That's right, buddy," Blakely calmly reassured him.

Dalton joined them, cell to his ear. He said a few uh-huhs into the phone before thanking the caller and giving Bethany's address. "There's been an arrest. Kyle Newt is an ex-con who a certain person promised half the insurance money to for his help in removing a certain person from this life." He was intentionally speaking in vague terms that a seven-year-old wouldn't be able to follow. Greg might be a bastard for what he'd done, but he was still Chase's father. The boy would have to be protected as best as the family could.

Greg had been desperate. Desperate people did desperate things.

He was now a criminal.

"Are you coming home, Mommy?" Chase asked.

"What do you think about moving in with your aunt for a little while?" Bethany asked before turning toward Blakely and whispering, "I don't think I can stay here."

"You'll live with me until you figure it all out," Blakely said.

Bethany wrapped her in a hug.

THE LAW HAD taken statements, and it was time to go home. Except Dalton had no idea where home was now. Because it felt a whole lot like Blakely.

"Are you leaving?" Blakely asked Dalton as Bethany pulled together a few items to take to her sister's house.

"I can drop you off at home if you'd like," he said.

"Here's the thing," Blakely said before capturing his gaze and holding on to it. "My definition of *home* has changed now that you came back into my life. In fact, it changed the weekend we spent in Galveston, but I was too scared to admit it."

"What are you saying?"

"That my home is here." She reached out and placed the flat of her palm on his heart. "If you'll let me back in, I promise to love you for the rest of my life."

Dalton covered her hand with his. "There's only one thing I've ever been certain of in my life and that's you. You are the only thing that makes sense. I'm in love with you, Blakely. But you need to know that I'm leaving my job to work the ranch full-time."

"Sounds like the perfect place to retreat to on the weekends if you ask me," she said without hesitation.

"Are you saying that you could see yourself splitting your time between the ranch and your home in Houston?" he asked for clarification.

"Only if you mean *our* home in Houston," she stated. "I'm in love with you, Dalton. And I don't want to waste another day without you."

Dalton dropped down on one knee. "Then, I have a question to ask."

She brought her hand up to cover a gasp. When she removed it, all he saw was her beautiful smile.

"From the moment I met you, something inside me changed. Something clicked. And I know it sounds cliché, but I knew right then and there I was supposed to be with you for the rest of my life." He kissed her hand. "Would you do me the incredible honor of marrying me?"

"Yes," she said. "I'm so in love with you, Dalton, that it scared me. But I'm not afraid anymore. And I don't want to wait another day to make us official. I'll marry you any time, any place and any day."

Dalton stood up and hauled his fiancée against his chest, wrapping her in a warm embrace. "What are you doing tomorrow?"

"Marrying you," she said. Those words sent warmth spiraling through him. He dipped his head and claimed his fiancée's lips.

"One more thing," Dalton said. "What do you think about asking for a meeting with my mother?"

"If that's what you want, I'll be right by your side the whole time," she said. With her by his side, he felt like he could pull off anything.

"Do you think it's a good idea?"

"I think you won't know until you do it," she said before pressing a small kiss to his lips.

"Will you come with me?" he asked.

"Yes," she said. "From now on, you couldn't get rid of me if you tried."

"Good." Because he'd finally found home.

Dalton kissed Blakely tenderly at first and then hard, marking her as his as she did the same to him. One word came to mind...

Home.

* * * * *

COLTON ON GUARD

KAREN WHIDDON

To all my faithful readers who enjoy the books
I write—thank you from the bottom of my heart.
Your emails make my day.

Chapter One

"Yes, ma'am, I apologize that we left your son off the booking for this tour," Parker Colton told the red-faced, mean-eyed woman. "I'll get them added immediately, so all three of you can join the group leaving in ten minutes. I'll just need to collect the payment. Will it be cash or credit card?"

His perfectly reasonable question only appeared to infuriate her even more. "You know, you might be used to skating by on your good looks and charm," she ranted, "but that's not going to fly with me. You made a mistake and you need to fix it!"

As her voice rose and the other guests stared, Parker interrupted to tell her fine, they'd let her teenager go along without an extra charge. Since this appeared to be what she'd wanted and expected, she jerked her head in a nod and closed her mouth.

Then, as tour guide Hetty Amos got everyone rounded up and herded them outside, Parker sagged against the counter in relief. Hetty made sure to circle back around and clap Parker on the back. "It's okay, Pretty Boy," she said, grinning. "Even with those good looks and charm, you got everything handled."

Before Parker could come up with a response, Hetty

waved and sauntered outside to join her group. They were all going on a wildlife tour.

Watching them leave, Parker smiled ruefully and shook his head. As part owner of the family business Rough Terrain Adventures, or RTA for short, he usually handled taking tourists on tours. Hiking, climbing, four-wheeling and fishing. He wasn't usually the one working the front counter and handling bookings, which might explain how that awful woman's son had been inadvertently left off the reservation sheet.

Parker loved RTA and, most of the time, his life. At this very moment however, he'd have gladly traded places with anybody else. Running tours had always been the ideal occupation for someone who'd always preferred to spend every possible waking hour outdoors, no matter the weather. The beautiful mountain town of Shelby, Alaska, offered ample opportunities to enjoy nature. RTA specialized in allowing tourists to enjoy outstanding hiking trails, world-class fishing, unbeatable backcountry skiing, recreational cycling, kayaking, northern lights viewing, snowmobiling, and glacier cruises in stunning Prince William Sound.

No wonder Parker's job in the family business working as RTA guide and manager often felt like an extended vacation with pay. He got to take people on adventures, doing things he himself loved and enjoyed. Talk about fun. Never a dull moment. He couldn't have asked for a better, more enjoyable career.

Until now. His sister Lakin, who'd been basically the brains of RTA and kept everything running smoothly, had left them high and dry to renovate an old hotel with her longtime boyfriend. Parker had zero patience for juggling the various office tasks she'd previously taken care off. Reservations, phone calls, logging both accounts receivable and accounts payable

were time-consuming and, frankly, he found them tedious and unpleasant. He'd rather be outside where he belonged.

Add in the fact that his father and his uncle had taken to constantly dropping by to check on things, and Parker thought he might lose his mind. Which is why he felt desperate enough to consider calling Genna MacDougal and asking if she wanted a job. She'd worked at RTA for the entire four years she'd been in high school. Part time during the school year and full time in the summers. She'd been Lakin's assistant the entire stretch and knew how to do everything Lakin did. Everything Parker and Spence and Hetty now took turns doing.

Genna with her light blond hair and luminous green eyes. Beautiful didn't even begin to describe her. She was, Parker thought, everything he'd ever wanted in a woman. And the fact that he knew he couldn't have her only served to make him want her more.

Despite the truth that facing her again made him wince, hearing she'd moved permanently back to Shelby had felt like an answer to a prayer. He needed help and he'd heard she needed work. It would be a win-win situation.

As long as they could both get past what had happened between them a little over a year ago. And as long as Parker could figure out a way to regard her as just another employee and not the woman of his dreams.

About to pick up the phone, he looked over when the bell above the door jingled. His cousin Spence, who also co-owned RTA and worked as a guide, strode in.

"I'm here to help," he said, his broad grin and sideways glance inviting Parker to share in the joke.

Except Parker wasn't in the mood for games. "Good," he said. "You can take over checking the online reservation system. I'm way behind on that."

Though Spence's smile never wavered, he did a double take. "Do you really think that's the best idea?"

"We don't have a choice," Parker snapped. "Now that Lakin left, someone has to do it."

Spence didn't move. "I thought we were going to hire someone."

"If I do, will you be able to train them?"

"Me?" Spence scoffed. "Call Lakin and make her do it. Or you could call Genna MacDougal? She worked here for four years. It's been a while, but she probably knows how to run this place better than you or I do."

Since none of his family was aware of Parker and Genna's one-night stand, Parker shrugged. "I'm still thinking about it."

"We need the help. Call her."

"I don't have her number," Parker lied. Once upon a time, he would have given anything to have located a way to reach Genna, but he'd managed to lose her number because he hadn't bothered to enter it into his phone. Now that Lakin had actually provided Parker her contact information, he hesitated to use it.

"I do," Spence said, pulling out his phone. "Let me send it to you."

Once he'd done so, he crossed his arms and waited. Parker made a show of opening the text and saving the contact.

"Well?" Spence finally said. "Are you going to reach out to her or not?"

Parker thought for a moment. Maybe he was making too big of a deal out of nothing. After all, an entire year had passed. They'd both been consenting adults and a good time had been had by all. No doubt Genna had moved on.

He met his cousin's gaze and slowly nodded. Then, taking a deep breath, he made the call.

WHEN HER CELL phone rang, Genna MacDougal glanced at the screen and took a second look. Parker Colton. Almost a year too late. Funny, she'd saved his number and must have forgotten to erase it. She'd figured he'd long ago tossed hers.

Naturally, she debated not answering. But curiosity won out in the end. "Hello?"

"Hey, Genna." He sounded nervous. *Good.*

"What do you want, Parker?" she asked, not even bothering to try to sound nice. She had no idea of the etiquette when speaking with a man who'd ghosted her after a one-night stand, but she really didn't care. Parker had figuratively kicked her when she'd been down. That wasn't something she'd easily forget or forgive.

"I'd like to offer you a job," he said. "Temporary, but still… We need a new general manager at RTA and since you worked for us before—"

"Go to hell," she said, cutting him off. Then she ended the call. The sudden flare of anger she'd felt surprised her.

Hanging up on Parker should have felt good. Better than that, it should have felt great.

Except it didn't. Instead, a wave of remorse swept through her. One year ago, she'd been at her absolute lowest. When Parker had come up to her at the bar, he'd not only been the sexiest man she'd ever seen, but was physically the polar opposite of her ex-husband. Still stinging from Chad's betrayal, she'd acted solely on impulse when she'd gone home with Parker. And she couldn't even blame the passionate night they'd spent together on too much alcohol since she'd barely had two drinks.

Nope. She'd been raw and needy. Having the guy she'd crushed on back when she'd been in high school and home from college take an interest in her had been exactly the boost she'd needed. He'd been witty, charming, and oh so

easy on the eyes. They'd shared one magical evening, laughing, dancing, and she'd given him her phone number. But then, just as she'd been about to leave, he'd pulled her into an embrace. His kiss had made her head spin.

Hand in hand, when he'd led her out to his truck, she'd gone home with him without hesitation. Even though she'd never, not even once, had a one-night stand. Until then.

It had been a magical night. Exactly what she'd needed to make her feel like a desirable woman again. Parker had given her just the right amount of passion combined with respect. Nearly reverence. They'd made love over and over again until they were both spent and she'd fallen asleep in his arms.

And when she'd woke in the morning, he'd been gone. He'd scrawled a note and left it on the nightstand. *I'll call.*

Except he never had. Part of her hadn't really expected him to. She'd left town without ever hearing from him again.

Until now. She couldn't believe the mofo had had the nerve to call and offer her a job. Even though she really needed one.

These days she was putting all her effort into getting her life together. With her messy divorce and dissolution of property behind her, she'd taken her parents up on their offer to house-sit here in Shelby, Alaska, while they tried living in a long-term rental in Hawaii. Though she had the funds to survive indefinitely, she wanted to keep as much money in her savings as possible. Therefore, she needed to get some sort of job.

She hated that Parker's offer actually tempted her.

Sure, working at Rough Terrain Adventures had been fun back in high school, but no way would she be able to spend her days side by side with Parker after what had happened.

That kind of humiliation wasn't easy to forget, especially when she'd just been shattered by her cheating husband.

Nope. Some other kind of work would come along. It had to. She didn't want to blow through her savings, so she needed a source of income. Shelby might be on the small side, but she knew the right opportunity would open up in time.

Less than an hour after hanging up on Parker Colton, her doorbell rang. Frowning, since she wasn't expecting anyone, she opened the door to find her old friend, Lakin Colton, on her doorstep. Still a stunning beauty, Lakin wore her brown-black hair long and straight. Her brown eyes sparkled with friendliness.

"Genna!" Lakin exclaimed, pulling her in for a hug. "It's so good to see you again."

Smiling, Genna invited her in. Tall and athletic, Lakin dressed to hide her curves. She wore her long, dark hair straight.

"You haven't changed a bit," Genna said.

"Neither have you!"

They chatted for a while, Lakin full of enthusiasm for a hotel renovation project she was doing with her boyfriend Troy. It took a few minutes, but Lakin finally got to the reason for her surprise visit.

"I understand my brother called you to talk about coming to work at RTA," she said. "They've kind of been floundering since I left."

Genna stiffened. "He did," she replied. "I turned him down."

"But why?" Leaning forward, Lakin regarded her earnestly. "You know that business better than anyone outside of my family. We need you, you're looking for work. The pay is decent. So why on earth would you say no to what seems like the perfect fit?"

Not wanting to go into the sordid details, Genna shrugged. "I just don't want to," she said.

Naturally, Lakin shook her head. "That's not a good reason. Now, what are you not telling me?"

Before Genna could think up a nonresponse, her doorbell rang again. This time, Lakin and Parker's cousin Spence stood outside. "We need your help," he said, not bothering with pleasantries. "We can even bump up the salary, if that would help."

"Why do I feel like you Coltons are ganging up on me?" Genna asked, only half joking. "Surely you can find someone else?"

"You're already trained!" Lakin and Spence replied in unison. "And our family knows and trusts you."

The doorbell chimed yet again. "This is getting ridiculous," Genna muttered, going to answer. Sure enough, two more members of the Colton family had arrived. "Abby and Sasha," she said, stepping aside and gesturing them to enter. "Did you all plan this or is it a spontaneous gathering?"

Seeing Lakin and Spence there, the two new arrivals burst out laughing. "Definitely not planned," they said. "We all just really would appreciate you coming to run the office at RTA. You're perfect. We heard you'd turned the job down, so we stopped by to see if we could change your mind."

Now resigned, Genna crossed her arms. "The only person not here is Parker," she said, not bothering to hide her irritation. "Is there a reason for that?"

Spence shrugged. "I think he's a little upset that you hung up on him. What's up with that anyway?"

Though she felt her face heat, she refused to air her dirty laundry to Parker's family. Clearly, he hadn't told them anything about what had happened a year ago. Therefore, neither would she.

"Everyone, I'm very sorry, but I'm just not interested," Genna said. "I hate that you wasted your time coming over here, but me working at RTA just isn't going to happen."

Spence looked at Lakin, who nodded. "Do you happen to have a pen and paper I could use?" he asked.

Perplexed, she went into the kitchen, grabbed a pen and the pad she jotted her grocery list on and brought it out for Spence. "Here you go."

He jotted something down before handing the paper back. "We can pay you that," he said.

The number he'd written was far higher than she'd expected. "You must really want me to work for you," she said. "I'm not sure what to say."

"Just say yes!" Lakin exclaimed. "You know you want to."

Though Genna knew no such thing, she was also well aware she couldn't make that amount of money working anywhere else in Shelby.

"I'll think about it," she said, hoping this attempt at compromise would be enough.

Apparently, it wasn't. No one made a move to leave. Abby and Sasha exchanged a quick glance. "We're sorry," Abby said. "But we really need you to agree to take the job before we go."

"No pressure," Lakin added, clearly tongue in cheek.

Spence shook his head. "This is serious. At least, to our family. Rough Terrain Adventures is important to us. And to the town."

She almost took pity on them. Almost. She understood where they were coming from and, if not for the fact that she'd have to work alongside Parker, she would have accepted their offer the moment she'd seen the salary.

"I don't like being bullied," she finally said. "And the

more you all try to pressure me, the less likely it is that I'll accept your offer. I need some time to think."

"How long?" Spence asked, appearing worried.

"I can let you know by morning."

Spence nodded, the others murmured their agreement, and they all trooped toward her front door. Only Lakin lingered. She waited until the others were gone before turning to face Genna. "There's something you're not saying. What is it?"

In years past, Genna might have blurted out the truth. Now, she simply shook her head. "I'm sorry, Lakin. I promise to decide quickly. I'll call Spence the second I know."

Expression crestfallen, Lakin nodded. "It's just that I feel so guilty. They're all acting as if me leaving is a death knell for our business. I'm finally doing what I've long dreamt of and, while I know they don't begrudge me that, apparently RTA is having difficulty functioning without me."

"I'm sorry." Genna gazed at her old friend. Lakin would be shocked if she knew the reason for her hesitation. Lakin clearly adored her brother and Genna refused to say or do anything to change that. "I'll let you know as soon as I decide."

Lakin nodded. "I'm sorry for the intrusion." Tugging on her long braid bashfully, she smiled. "I promise I'll still love you, no matter what you do."

"Right back atcha," Genna said. "Isn't it nearly the end of the season anyway? Snow will be starting soon."

"That's true and, yes, it does mean some of our adventures will be coming to an end until spring. But there are a lot of snow enthusiasts. We've added snowmobiling, ice fishing, ice-skating and snowshoeing to our ski trips."

Which ensured RTA didn't have to close down for winter. In other words, Genna would still have a job.

Once Lakin had also left her house, Genna locked the door behind her and then sank down onto her couch. This shouldn't be so difficult. She'd loved working at RTA back in the day and imagined she would still. She'd worked with Lakin and knew how things ran, so there wouldn't be a long learning curve. Not to mention the salary. Considering that she'd been out of the work force for a number of years and had a huge gap in her résumé as a result, she felt positive she couldn't make that amount elsewhere. And she definitely needed to find a job.

Those were the pros. And there was only one con. Parker. *It has been a year*, she told herself. The man probably didn't even remember much about that night and, if he did, he obviously wasn't embarrassed about the way he'd ghosted her. Maybe she was making too big a deal out of nothing, getting worked up too much inside her own head.

Still, while she understood they were probably used to getting their own way, the fact that the Colton family had descended upon her en masse spoke to their own desperation. While she'd found them all showing up on her doorstep unbelievably pushy, she got where they were coming from. When you truly cared about something, you went all out.

The fact that she couldn't make a simple decision really bothered her. She needed to go ahead and accept the job offer. After all, since she'd be living in Shelby, she couldn't avoid Parker forever.

Instead of waiting until morning, she decided to drive over to RTA and let Parker know in person. His reaction to her would go a long way in helping her decide if they could manage to work together.

She grabbed her car keys and headed off before she could talk herself out of it.

As she approached the RTA building, a sprawling log

cabin just outside the center of town, her heart rate accelerated.

Pulling into the drive, she parked. She took a moment while sitting in her car to eye the place. The large cabin with the metal roof looked welcoming, especially the numerous porch areas with railings. Someone had placed potted flowers around the spaces and this gave off a cheery, summery vibe.

As the number-one tour company in town, RTA was extremely popular. Their customers came from all walks of life. Tours included rafting and camping along mountain rivers, hiking the glaciers, helicopter skiing, seaplane trips to out-of-the way fishing spots, and other sorts of outdoor adventures. Right now, in peak tourist season, they were open seven days a week.

Like all the other tour companies, RTA tended to close down during the heaviest snow, December through February, though they had added a few snowmobile adventures to their already large catalog.

Each of RTA's ten or so employees was extensively trained in their own area and knowledgeable about whatever activity they were assigned. Prices were high, but reasonable, and they were usually booked out six to nine months in advance.

If she took the job, Genna would be in charge of coordinating all this. It sounded incredibly complicated and fast-paced, but since the guides—including Parker—spent most of their time out of the office on adventures with clients, she'd have a lot of alone time.

This knowledge reinforced her decision to accept the job. She remembered the reservation software, the way they used GPS to keep tabs on their guides and their guests. She had the organizational skills to manage all of it.

Now to face Parker and let him know she'd be coming to work on Monday.

Pushing the door open, a little bell on top announcing her arrival, she looked around at the apparently empty office. A man popped up from behind the counter. "Sorry, I was trying to fix the…" His words trailed off as he took in her presence.

To her dismay, Parker Colton looked even better than she remembered. If anything, his dark brown hair seemed shaggier, his blue eyes sexier, and his unshaven face gave him a rugged, bad-boy appearance. At six-two, he towered over her and his muscular body made the room seem smaller somehow. If she'd never seen him before, she suspected her knees would have gone weak. Even being prepared, the first sight of him felt like a punch in the stomach and she struggled to catch her breath.

"Genna," he said, his gaze searching her face. "It's good to see you."

"Is it?" Remembering she'd be working with him, she had to rein in her snark. "Uh, anyway. I just stopped by to tell you that I've decided to accept your job offer."

"You do?" Confusion flitted across his handsome features. "What changed your mind?"

"Spence, Lakin, Abby and Sasha. They all came to visit."

"And convinced you to work here?" He crossed his arms. "How?"

"The salary. It's too good to pass up. Even if I have to—"

"Work with me?" he finished for her. "It's okay, I get it."

Deciding it would be safer and more professional not to go down that road, she nodded. "I can start this coming Monday."

To her surprise, he groaned. "Monday? That's an entire week away. Is there any chance you could start right now?"

"Today?" Not sure how to react, she shifted her weight from one foot to the other. She hadn't dressed for work, though from what she remembered, RTA issued all employees several green work shirts emblazoned with the company logo.

"Yes. Today. You're already here, so why not?" He swallowed hard. "Please."

Was that a trace of panic she detected in his tone? She glanced at her watch, as if she actually had some place else she was supposed to be. "Fine," she finally said. "You might as well tell me up front. How bad is it?"

He smiled, his amazing blue eyes crinkling in the corners. Everything inside her went still for a few heartbeats before she remembered to breathe. Did this man have any idea of his effect on her? Somehow, she doubted it, because if he did, no doubt he'd use that to his advantage.

"Come take a look," he replied. "Lakin had everything pretty organized, but since she left and all the rest of us have been trying to alternate between being guides and keeping the place running, it's gotten way out of hand. How much do you remember from when you worked here before?"

"I'm sure it will all come back to me." The moment she walked behind the counter, Parker handed her a three-ring binder. "Lakin made notes about everything. We've all been referring to them constantly, but once you get into a routine, you'll probably have them all down pat in no time."

He reached under the counter and pulled out a cardboard box. "New work shirts are in here. Find your size and take as many as you need."

Standing this close to him, his scent brought back instant memories of that night she'd spent in his arms. The masculine combination of outdoorsy evergreens and something less tangible made her briefly close her eyes as she battled a sudden longing.

No, she told herself, straightening and making a show of rummaging through the box of green shirts. *No attraction, no love affairs, none of that.* She'd decided to focus on herself and figure out what she wanted from life. Parker Colton with his bedroom eyes and magnetic smile would be nothing more than a coworker from now on.

A couple of cars and a small tour bus pulled up out front. As people began exiting, milling about in the porch area, Parker smiled again, his relief evident. "There's my next tour group. I'll leave this in your very capable hands." After grabbing a clipboard with a checklist from the counter, he took off, the bell over the door tinkling merrily behind him.

Taking a deep breath, she grabbed a green RTA shirt out of the box and hurried off to the bathroom to change.

Chapter Two

Greeting the tour group, Parker began checking everyone in, using the list he'd printed out and attached to his clipboard. He'd never been happier to have a distraction than right this moment. When Genna MacDougal had walked through the door, he'd taken one look at her and his entire body had gone on full alert. Everything had come rushing back; the steamy sex they'd shared, her perfect body, and how sensual and uninhibited she'd been.

Since she'd made it clear she wanted to forget about that night, he'd have to figure out a way to do so. They needed someone to keep RTA running way more than he needed to rehash what had been a pretty spectacular night one year ago.

At least it had been to him. Obviously, Genna didn't feel the same. When her deep green eyes had met his, he'd seen no hint of the desire that had been coursing through him. Though not unfriendly, she'd been detached and professional. Exactly as any new employee might be.

He finished checking in the guests. In the future, Genna would be doing this task. Once he knew he had everyone, he gave his standard safety speech and then they all followed him toward one of the storage barns to collect their four-wheelers. This adventure consisted of a lot of off-road driv-

ing, which had always been one of his specialties. Just what he needed to take his mind off their new office manager.

Two hours later, as he led the group back to the RTA storage barn, he went through the motions of signing everyone out as they returned their four-wheelers. Once everything was done, he sent them all back inside to speak with Genna and check out. He had to clean the vehicles and make sure the gas tanks were full so they'd be ready for the next group. Which would be tomorrow. Since the end of season neared, everyone seemed determined to pack in as many adventures as possible. Which was great for business. Lakin had claimed she'd hated to leave while RTA was so busy, but since there rarely was a time when they were completely slow, this would be as good a time as any.

Even though winter had always been their quietest season. Most people tended to hunker down with family, choosing to take their vacations in better weather.

Except for the snowbirds and the native Alaskans. As soon as the first flakes of snow started to fly, they geared up for fun. Skiing, snowboarding, ice fishing, all of that. It might be cold, but these clients were too busy having fun to care.

RTA had been under a lot of pressure to add guided hunting to their expeditions, but so far, they'd resisted. There were a lot of hunting guides already operating in the area and in such an overcrowded field, the competition was fierce. Safety shortcuts were routinely taken and the Colton family wanted no part of a client getting hurt or, worse, killed.

Instead, they stuck to the tried-and-true winter activities. This decision had worked well for them so far. For RTA employees, winter had become a time of rejuvenation and peace.

Parker always got restless this time of the year, though

he wasn't sure why. Certain activities had begun to wind down though others had picked up. Aurora season was at a prime and RTA took advantage of that, leading numerous and popular late-night expeditions. October also brought in several guests to take fall sightseeing and wildlife tours, and since trout were abundant, Parker led a lot of successful fishing trips.

The change of seasons hovered on the horizon and the temperatures had begun to drop. The gray skies became more frequent, though there were often a few brilliantly gorgeous days full of sunshine. The scent of snow often swept in on the crisp north wind, though when moisture fell, it was rain. Nature seemed to be waiting, holding her breath.

Since Parker loved winter almost as much as summer, he waited impatiently for the first snow. He'd always loved the comforting ritual of building a fire in his woodstove and kicking back to watch the white flakes fall. If he felt lonely, which he did sometimes, he brushed it off. His job kept him busy and, for now, that had to be enough.

He moved on to the next four-wheeler. This one needed air in one of the tires, so he took care of that before topping off the gas tank.

Since this was mindless work, his thoughts returned to Genna. Once he'd learned she'd returned to Shelby, he'd never taken the time to seek her out and explain what had happened and why he'd never called her.

After the wild night they'd had, he'd had to get up at the crack of dawn to meet a 6:00 a.m. tour group and then realized when he'd gotten back that he'd lost her number. RTA had been super busy that weekend, so by the time he'd found a minute to go look for her, Genna had already left town. And then he'd learned from Lakin that Genna was married. No wonder she'd said she wasn't looking for a relationship.

She'd already had one. She'd been in town visiting her parents before returning home to her husband.

While he had no idea what kind of man her husband might be, she must have needed that single hot and passionate night as badly as he had, maybe even more. Though he'd found it difficult to think of her as the kind of woman who'd cheat on her husband, the passion that had blazed between them had revealed the truth.

Since he hadn't wanted any part of being the other man, he'd put Genna from his mind. Until she'd returned to Shelby. And even then, he'd managed to avoid her.

But then Lakin had revealed that she'd learned Genna had been going through a nasty divorce the last time she'd been in town. Which meant she *hadn't* been having an affair with Parker. She'd been dealing with a lot at the time of their hookup. His ghosting her had likely made her feel even worse.

The thought made him wince. No doubt about it, he owed her an apology. That way, they both could move on with their lives.

Once he'd finished up with the four-wheelers, he locked the shed and headed back toward the office. By the time he got there, most of the tour group had gone. Only one vehicle, a large, jacked-up truck, remained in the parking area.

Pulling open the front door, which sent the little bell tinkling, he saw the remaining guest leaning on the front counter, talking to Genna.

"Jeff Prentiss, right?" Parker said, letting himself in behind the counter. The tall, broad-shouldered man had been a bit of a show-off on the trails, but at least he'd listened when Parker had given instructions.

"Right," Jeff replied. With all his attention fixed on

Genna, he barely looked at Parker. "So, what do you say, Genna? Drinks tonight or tomorrow?"

Expression tight, Genna nonetheless managed a smile. "Thanks, but like I said, I'm not interested. Here at RTA, we appreciate your business. Now, if there's not anything else, you're all finished up and you can go."

Jeff didn't move. As if he thought by standing his ground, Genna would somehow change her mind.

Parker took a step forward, his hands balled into fists. "Is there something else you need?" he asked, allowing a hint of warning to enter his voice. "If not, I'll be happy to escort you to your vehicle."

Finally, Jeff turned his head to look at Parker. The open hostility in his ruddy face made Parker straighten. "I'd appreciate you giving us a little space," he said. "I'm still talking to Genna."

"No, we're all done," Genna countered. "As a matter of fact, I'm about to go back to my office and start getting caught up on things."

"But you haven't agreed to go out with me yet," Jeff said. "I can't leave until I know when we're meeting."

About to open his mouth to tell the guy off, Parker closed it when Genna shot Jeff a withering look. "First off, I'm not going out with you. Not tonight or tomorrow night. Not ever. I don't know how to make that any clearer."

She took a deep breath and then pointed to the exit. "Since you don't seem to understand how to take no for an answer, let me make things clear. You need to go. You're finished with your trip. If you want to book another, you can do that online. Have a nice day." With that, she spun around and disappeared into the back office.

For the space of a few heartbeats, Parker thought Jeff

might be foolish enough to go after her. He got ready, just in case he needed to physically stop him.

"She needs to listen to me," Jeff muttered. "I know I can convince her."

"No, you can't, and no, she doesn't."

Jeff narrowed his gaze, focusing on Parker. "I just need five minutes." He made a move, like he intended to slip in behind the counter and head for the back office.

"I wouldn't if I were you," Parker said. "You need to leave. Right now."

"How about you and me settle this outside?"

"I'd be glad to." Though Jeff wasn't a small man, Parker had several inches and at least twenty pounds on him. Maybe a fight would be just the thing to help him get over his jumbled feelings.

Clearly, Jeff hadn't been expecting Parker to take him up on his offer.

"Let's go," Parker said, moving out from behind the counter to the door and holding it open. "I'm suddenly in the mood for a fight. My only rule is no weapons—no knife or gun or anything other than fists."

Jeff mumbled a curse and stalked past him. Parker followed him out. But instead of turning to make good on his threat, Jeff strode over to his lifted truck and left.

Since the next group wasn't due to arrive for an hour and Spence would be taking them river rafting, Parker locked the dead bolt. When he turned around, he saw Genna had come back out front.

Remaining behind the counter, she watched at Jeff drove off in his SUV. "I don't think he should be allowed to book again," she said once the vehicle had gone. "If you hadn't been here, I don't think I would have been safe." The slight quiver in her voice made his gut clench.

"I agree." Dragging his hand though his hair, Parker swallowed. "I'm sorry that you had to deal with that, especially on your first day."

Eyeing him, some of the tension left her face. "He sure was pushy," she said. "Thanks for getting him to leave."

Though he wondered if she had to deal with stuff like that often, he also knew it wasn't any of his business. "After the Fiancée Killer started murdering women, Lakin had a panic button installed near the computer," he told her. "Thankfully, guys like that are rare. But if you press that button, it sends out an alert to the police station and also to mine and Spence's phones."

"Good to know." Green eyes pensive, she shrugged. "I sure as heck didn't expect something like that to happen on my first day. And, yes, with four women dead, that serial killer has just about every single female in Shelby nervous."

"Justifiably so. Hetty is our only female tour guide, though she's also a pilot, and she's nervous, too. We've instituted a policy where no female, whether employee or guest, is ever left alone at night on the premises."

"Good." She glanced around. "I'm guessing that's not possible in the daytime."

"We try, but mostly it's not," he answered. "The good thing is, since we're super busy, there will nearly always be a guide either coming in or out, not to mention constant groups of guests."

"Good. I confess, I wasn't too worried until you brought up the Fiancée Killer."

"I'm sorry," he said. Deciding now would be as good a time as any, he swallowed. "There's something else I need to apologize for."

"I doubt it." After this clear dismissal, she turned to head into her small office.

"Wait," he said then softened his voice. "Please."

She turned slowly. "What's up?"

Slightly nervous, he cleared his throat. "Back when we, uh, got together. A year ago. I said I'd call you, but didn't. I wanted to explain why."

"Oh, there's no need—" she began.

"But there is," he interrupted. "I lost your number. Then, when I went to ask my sister for it, she told me you were married. Since I didn't want any part of being the other person in an affair, I didn't even try to call you. It was only when you came back to town that Lakin realized she'd been wrong."

"I was going through a pretty nasty divorce," she said. "But it's been a year and you shouldn't even give that a second thought. I wasn't upset that I didn't hear from you. Not at all. You were exactly what I needed at the moment—a good time. Nothing more." She laughed. "Don't worry about it. I haven't."

Then she turned and disappeared inside her little office in back, leaving Parker staring after her, his ego bruised. No, more than bruised. Battered.

If she hadn't hung up on him when he'd first called to offer her the job, he might have believed her. He'd explained why he hadn't contacted her. That's all that should have mattered. What had he expected anyway?

Despite the fact that he hadn't ever stopped thinking about her, he knew he should figure out how to put her out of his mind.

Maybe working side by side with her, day after day, would help. Though, when Spence had first come up with idea, Parker had felt it would be almost a kind of torture.

He'd have to get over that. And pronto. Because, like it or not, she worked for RTA now. And he wouldn't do anything to jeopardize that. The family business had to come first.

ALONE IN THE small manager's office, Genna tried to focus on getting used to everything. Lakin had always been organized; so, mostly, Genna needed to familiarize herself with the system. The detailed notes in the binder would definitely help with that.

The reservations were all online, as were the schedule of the tours. As she scrolled through the upcoming groups, she saw that Parker's assessment had been right. RTA appeared to be booked solid. Most days had back-to-back tours.

Good for them. Might as well get as much done before the snow started falling.

Scrolling ahead to the month of December, she saw Lakin hadn't been kidding. While the types of outings had changed, each weekend was marked "Full." During the week, things slowed quite a bit, but Genna imagined the employees were glad to have a bit of a break from the non-stop bookings.

She remembered from working here before that the summer was the busiest season. Tourists flooded the area in good weather; families on vacation and work groups needing a bonding activity. Since school wasn't in session, RTA made sure to have child-friendly activities such as whale watching and wildlife tours.

She heard the bell tinkle over the door and realized Parker must have unlocked it. The sound of voices told her the next bunch of clients must have arrived.

Putting down the binder, she hurried out to greet them.

By the end of the day, exhaustion had Genna dead on her feet. She'd met four of the ten RTA guides, not including Parker and Spence, whom she already knew. When Spence had arrived for his group and had walked into the building to see her working, he'd grabbed her up into a laughing bear

hug. After twirling her around, he set her back on her sneakers. "You're here!" he exclaimed. "Thank you so much."

His enthusiastic greeting made her grin. "It's been busy. Luckily for me, Lakin made detailed notes. I remembered quite a bit from when I worked here, but she made it easy for me to look things up and double check to make sure I was doing everything correctly."

The front door opened then. A large group that appeared to be several families, including six teens, came inside. They were all talking at once, the teens roughhousing, and Genna simply waited at the front counter for them to choose one person to speak to her.

"You've got your hands full," she muttered to Spence.

He smiled. "Just the way I like things."

Once she'd checked the group in, she watched as Spence herded them off to a bus to ride out to where RTA docked their boats. Since the days were still long this time of year, RTA took full advantage of the sunlight. This group would be doing some fishing, which ought to be interesting with so many rowdy teens.

Taking a final glance at the schedule to make sure that was the last group, Genna dropped into a chair and sighed.

The bell above the front door tinkled again, making her look up. Parker strode in, glancing back over his shoulder and shaking his head. Once again, she caught herself melting at the sight of him.

"Spence should have a time with that group," he said, smiling.

Her stomach clenched.

Pretending that his smile didn't affect her, she nodded. "That's what I told him. He didn't seem to mind."

"He doesn't." Moving closer, he studied her. "Personally, I think he thrives on chaos. How was your first day?"

"Part day," she corrected, trying not to let her eyes roam over him. How any man could look so sexy while just standing there bemused her. "This job is definitely fast-paced. It's not for the faint of heart."

Her choice of words had his smile widening. "But do you think you'll enjoy it? Or at least find it tolerable?"

Not sure how to respond to that, she made busywork organizing a stack of brochures and settled on a noncommittal answer. "It's fine. I like it so far."

"I'm glad." He came a little closer, though he stayed on his side of the counter. "Listen, would you like to go have a drink with me after we shut this place down? My treat?"

As tempting as she found the idea, she knew she had to decline. Opening her mouth to tell him no, she lost the capacity for thought when his gaze met and held hers.

"Strictly as coworkers," he continued, possibly noticing her hesitation. "I thought I'd invite the rest of the gang, too, so you can get to know everyone a little better. I know you already know most of them, but you've been gone awhile and might want to get reacquainted."

Despite being tired, she appreciated the thought. "How about we do that, but maybe on Friday night instead? With this being my first day, I'm really tired."

Immediately, he nodded. "Friday sounds great. I'll let everyone know. Maybe we can do dinner and drinks."

"I'd like that," she replied. Hopefully, she'd have grown accustomed to being around him by then and she wouldn't feel that low-key electric buzz under her skin every time he got close.

Gathering her things, she waved goodbye and left.

Her parents called shortly after she arrived home. Though they'd both lived in Alaska their entire lives, they'd decided to make a major change. Shortly after Genna had

asked to move back home once her divorce was finalized, they'd decided to move to Hawaii. "We're not getting any younger," her father had announced, grinning from ear to ear. Her mother had been giddy with excitement. Now that they were retired, they said it was time to live somewhere warm. They'd leased a modern condo near the beach and were loving the tropical weather.

They were thrilled when Genna told them about her new job.

"That's wonderful, honey!" her mother exclaimed. "You loved working there before."

"I did," Genna agreed. "And I'm sure it'll be the same this time. Right now, I'm just relearning how the operation is run."

"The Colton family do a great job with RTA," her father said. "They treat their employees right and they have a great reputation around Shelby. Heck, around all of Alaska, the Lower 48, and even into Canada. People come from all around to go on one of their adventure tours."

"I see that." Genna dropped onto the sofa, wishing she'd thought to pick up a bottle of wine.

"Any news on that serial killer?" her mom asked, not hiding her worry. "I hate that they haven't caught him yet."

"Me, too," Genna answered. "But the police and FBI are actively searching for him."

"But what about you? Are you being careful?"

"Yes. Me and every other woman in Shelby."

They chatted a few more minutes. Her parents told her how much they loved their rental house, the tropical weather and the Hawaiian culture. "I do miss the beautiful wildness of Alaska," her father admitted. "But not the cold."

After the call ended, Genna wandered around the house where she'd grown up. Since the move had been more of an

experiment, her parents had taken very little with them. The furniture and artwork made Genna feel as if she'd stepped back into the past.

This had been comfortable at first. Now, she found it stifling. Since her parents had needed a house-sitter and she'd been looking for a place to stay, the situation worked. For now. Though, lately, Genna had found herself aching to paint a wall here or there, add some color, brighten the dark rooms up. With wood-paneled walls, wood floors and dark furniture, the house often felt somber and stifling. The exact opposite of the colorful life her parents were now living in Hawaii.

Though they'd told her she could use the master bedroom, that had felt weird. Instead, she slept in her old bedroom, which her parents had blessedly changed into a generic guest room. Here, she'd decorated to her own taste, bringing in items she'd salvaged from the home she'd once shared with her ex-husband.

The one thing she really wanted to do was to have an alarm system installed. Once, Shelby had been relatively crime free. But with this serial killer on the loose, and being a single woman, she felt the need to protect herself. She knew she'd certainly sleep better at night once she had some kind of protection. She just hadn't gotten around to calling someone to come out and do it.

Genna had even considered getting a dog. Something big with a loud bark. But she wanted to adopt and didn't want a puppy. So far, she hadn't made time to make the trip into Valdez to check out the animal shelter.

Despite telling herself she wouldn't be in any danger from the Fiancée Killer, the truth was that no one had figured out what exactly his type might be. So far, four bodies had been found. Each of them had been clothed in a little black

dress, a fake diamond on their ring finger. They'd been strangled before being partially buried with the head and left hand always visible. Thinking about this scenario kept Genna, and likely most of the women of Shelby, up at night.

As all women everywhere did, living in a larger city, she'd always stayed super aware of her surroundings, kept her keys in her hand when walking to her car, and if she thought even remotely that someone might be following her, she never went directly home.

That had all been in a larger city. Honestly, coming home to Shelby, she'd thought life would be different. The way she remembered it being. But the Fiancée Killer had changed all that.

Like everyone else in town, Genna hoped he or she would be caught soon. Sooner or later, a mistake would be made and it would be over. Until then, all she and everyone else could do was be careful.

The rest of her first week at RTA went by quickly. As she got used to the various aspects of her position, she started to relax. She expanded the customer satisfaction survey that Lakin had instituted and made sure to ask each guest about their experience. On the rare occasion that a problem arose, she made sure to take care of it with courtesy and kindness.

Though the tour guides were in and out, she got to know several of them. As Friday approached, she found herself looking forward to hanging out with them for a meal and a drink.

Except for Parker. Though on the surface he acted friendly, she could sense him going out of his way to avoid being alone with her for any longer than absolutely necessary. She understood, sort of. She guessed she must have bruised his ego when she'd told him she'd never given him

a second thought after their torrid night together. A bold-faced lie to be sure, but she knew a man as hot as Parker would have had no shortage of females vying for his attention. To be honest, she'd been surprised that he'd even remembered their one-night stand.

As for Genna, she wondered if she'd ever be able to forget it.

Luckily, her job kept her too busy to dwell much on Parker. Tuesday and Wednesday had been a flurry of guests, meeting other guides, and making sure everything ran smoothly. Reservations were coming in for winter as well as for next spring. She had to update the software, make sure each tour group wasn't overbooked, and handle the schedule months in advance.

She loved every freaking second of it.

As she became accustomed to the routine, her confidence grew. She'd always loved customer service work, especially here. The guests were universally in a great mood, excited about their adventure to come. And since RTA did exactly as they advertised, Genna had yet to have an unsatisfied customer.

Lakin's notes in the computer helped Genna identify repeat customers and some of the personal details enabled her to ask about their children or pets. Genna loved the way some of the guest's faces lit up when she mentioned their family.

All of the guides seemed friendly, too. With RTA so busy, often with back-to-back groups leaving for different adventures, she'd met most of them. Even if their interactions were necessarily brief, most mentioned how much they were looking forward to their planned dinner out on Friday.

Despite her full days, her entire body knew every single time Parker was near. She didn't understand it, but her nerve

endings would prickle, her skin would flush, and despite trying not to, she was uber aware of his movements. If he happened to glance at her, she felt the heat of his gaze all the way to the soles of her feet.

Hopefully, that would be only temporary. She was bound to get used to being around him eventually.

At the end of every workday, even though the sun wouldn't fully set until almost seven, she appreciated how one of the male guides always hung around the place to make sure she wasn't alone. The last tours usually came in around six and once she'd finished processing everyone, it would be time to close for the day.

They'd had to figure out her schedule, because she couldn't work twelve-hour days every day of the week. Since she lived fairly close to the building, she volunteered to do split shifts, but in the end, she'd decided to base her daily schedule on what tours they had booked. Their slowest days seemed to be Mondays and Thursdays, so she said those would be her days off.

Everyone seemed relieved and Parker and Spence promised to make sure her desk was covered when she wasn't there.

Teamwork, she thought. Always a good thing. Now she just needed to figure out how to think of Parker as just another coworker and she'd be all set.

Chapter Three

The next morning, which was Friday, Parker arrived at RTA shortly after sunrise. He'd slept well and grabbed breakfast and coffee on the way in to work. His first tour group would be a morning hike finishing up with some trout fishing, but they weren't due to arrive for another hour.

Even though they'd agreed that Genna would have Thursdays off, her new schedule wasn't set to start until the following week. Selfishly, Parker was glad. Though he didn't spend a lot of time inside the office, when he did, he found himself constantly wanting to be near her.

He didn't understand how she could have such a strong effect on him, especially after all this time. Since she'd clearly moved on and regarded him as just another coworker, he wanted to do the same.

But he couldn't. And for good reason. Not only was she beautiful, but there was something about her. When she smiled, the woman freaking *glowed*.

The guests adored her. The other RTA guides did, too. No wonder Parker still struggled with a fierce rush of attraction every time they shared the same space.

He wondered how long it would take for him to get past that. If he would *ever* be able to change the way he felt about her. He had to.

Tonight, they'd all be going out for an informal meal and a drink or two. He'd already told himself several times that he needed to keep his distance from her and to let the others all get to know her.

Even if he wanted to do exactly that more than he would have ever believed possible. In the few days that she'd worked for RTA, she'd been politely professional. Nothing more. Nothing less.

Once at the office, Parker made a pot of coffee and poured himself a second cup.

Genna walked in about thirty minutes later. "Good morning," she said, smiling. "You sure are here early. If I remember right, your group isn't scheduled to leave for another half an hour."

Though his heart leapt into his throat the instant her bright green gaze found his, he managed to smile back. "The weather is looking iffy," he said, pulling out his phone and opening the weather app. "See. Look at the radar."

Accepting his phone, she studied the screen before handing it back. "It's a few hours out," she said. "Hopefully, it will break up before it reaches us."

After pouring herself a cup of coffee, she flashed an impersonal smile and disappeared into her office.

Which left him alone in the front counter area, with nothing to do but wait for his group to arrive.

The tour went off as planned, and even though he made sure to be attentive and give his guests the best possible time, his thoughts kept returning to Genna. He didn't know what it was about her, but he'd thought about her more than he should have.

He had three more tours after this one. He'd better keep his attention focused where it needed to be.

When he returned with the morning group to headquar-

ters, Genna had already left for lunch. Spence was filling in for her. He laughed when he noticed Parker looking around for her. "She'll be back, cuz."

"Who?" Parker asked, fooling no one. "I need to eat something before I go back out. I was hoping I could get Genna to bring me something."

"So call her." The phone rang just then and Spence went to answer it.

Pulling out his own phone, Parker scrolled through his contacts until he found Genna's number. Then, shaking his head, he decided he'd just go grab something to eat himself. He had another batch of clients due to arrive in an hour. Who knew? Maybe he'd even run into Genna when he was out.

After asking Spence if he wanted anything, Parker jumped into his truck and headed off. The closest fast-food place also happened to be his favorite. Pulling into the parking lot, he did a quick scan to see if he could spot Genna's car. Once he realized she must have gone somewhere else for lunch, he decided to go through the drive-through and take his burger back to eat at RTA.

He'd barely finished eating when he spotted Genna's little red car pulling up. His heart rate accelerated as he wadded up his wrapper and tossed it in the trash. He couldn't help but watch as she crossed the parking lot. With the sun in her gold hair and her jaunty walk, she embodied everything he found attractive in a woman.

As she breezed through the front door, Spence looked up from the computer and greeted her. "I'm glad you're back. It looks like my next group and Parker's are back-to-back."

"Great," she said, smiling at him. She barely even glanced at Parker. "I like being busy."

As if on cue, several SUVs pulled up.

"That's probably my group," Parker said, keeping his voice casual. "Let me know once you get them checked in, please."

"Will do," she chirped, still avoiding eye contact.

"Thanks." Stung, Parker went back into the storeroom, pretending he needed to get supplies.

Spence followed him. "What the hell was that?"

Not even bothering to pretend he didn't know what his cousin meant, Parker shrugged. "I'm not sure. She seemed fine when I left this morning."

"You didn't do something, did you?"

"No," Parker replied. "I did not."

"Is it like this every day between the two of you?" Spence crossed his arms.

"No. Maybe she just had a bad lunch. No idea." He glanced at his smartwatch. "I've got to go. I'm due to take my group out in ten minutes."

"Wait. Are we still all meeting up as a group tonight for dinner and drinks?" Spence asked.

"Yes." Parker didn't tell his cousin that he'd been looking forward to tonight all week. Maybe once Genna was out of the office, the two of them would be able to interact in a friendlier manner.

The instant Parker stepped into the main area, several of the guests greeted him. As regulars, they always made sure to book tours with him. All of the tour guides had their favorites and, honestly, seeing the familiar faces from years past just made the outing more enjoyable.

"Is everyone checked in?" Parker asked, directing his question to Genna.

Without looking up from her computer, she nodded. "Yes. You all are ready to go."

"Excellent." Looking around at all the guests' excited faces, he grinned. "Let's head out."

They all followed, talking at once.

The rest of the day went in similar fashion. He brought back one group, had a small break, during which he did his best to avoid Genna, and then his next batch arrived.

The overcast skies had threatened rain all day. Parker kept an eye on the clouds while taking his latest group four-wheeling up the mountain. When they reached their destination, a meadow with a small lake, the wind swirled the colorful leaves. Several of the guests dismounted, walking around and taking pictures.

When Parker pointed out the black bear on the other side of the water, cautioning guests to remain close, more people got out their phones to snap photos. This group had traveled from the Lower 48, where the sight of any kind of bear was uncommon. They all seemed thrilled.

The rain held off for the trip back down, too. Parker counted his blessings as they parked the four-wheelers in the storage barn and made their way back to headquarters. This time, instead of getting everything ready for the next trip, Parker followed the group into the building. He hung out in the waiting area while Genna checked the guests out one by one. All of the other employees, including Spence, had left for the day. With her broad smile and efficient process, she somehow managed to make each individual feel special. He marveled at the way each person reacted to her charm.

As the last guest said his goodbyes, thunder shook the building, followed by a bright flash of lightning. Startled, Genna squeaked then flashed him a sheepish smile. "I hope he makes it to his car," she said as they both watched the guest break into a run.

As the man drove away, the sky opened up. Rain came

down in sheets, the wind sending it sideways. More thunder, several rounds this time in succession, several lightning flashes and a loud boom.

"That sounded like an explosion," Genna said. Just then the power went out.

When she made another tiny squeak, Parker fought the urge to go to her and pull her into his arms. "It's going to be all right," he said instead. "Lightning struck somewhere close." He went to the front window and tried to see out. "As long as it didn't start a fire, we'll be okay. We can just hang out here until the storm passes."

She made a sound that might have passed for agreement.

Another crack of thunder and immediately a lightning flash illuminated the room, showing him she remained on the backside of the counter.

"That was close," he commented. The need to hold her, touch her, tell her he'd keep her safe, consumed him. Instead, he reminded himself that they were only coworkers, nothing more.

"I don't like this," she said, sounding disgruntled. "I checked the weather this morning before I came to work and it wasn't supposed to rain until later tonight."

Since RTA had a fireplace, he knew he could light a fire. They often did, especially in the winter when they needed to chase away the chill. If the day hadn't ended, he might have. He could imagine himself and Genna, sharing a glass of wine on the couch with a fire blazing in the background.

Clearly, he'd gone over the edge. Digging out his phone, he pulled up his weather app. "Judging by what I see on the radar, it's going to rain for a good while."

"Great, just great. I guess we'll need to cancel the get-together tonight."

The disappointment in her voice matched the way he felt.

"I think we should. Let me send out a group text and let everyone know. We'll reschedule it for next Friday."

She nodded, waiting in silence while he sent out the text. Her phone pinged, too, since he'd included her in the group. She glanced at the message and sighed. "I've been looking forward to this all week."

"Me, too," he admitted, earning a startled glance from her. "Since it's still pouring out there, how about I drive you home?"

"I can drive myself," she said, though she didn't sound certain. "As long as the roads don't wash out."

Which she knew as well as he did, they would in this kind of storm. "My truck sits up higher than your car," he pointed out. "Also, if you were to run into any trouble on the way home, I'd hate for the wrong person to find you."

"Like the Fiancée Killer." Her loud sigh told him what she thought of that. "I doubt even he'd be out hunting for victims in this."

"You never know," he replied. "Please, let me take you home."

"What about my car?" she asked. "I don't like the idea of being stuck at the house without transportation."

"I can pick you up in the morning and bring you to work. You can get your car then."

Outside, the sound of the rain increased, becoming a roar. Parker had always loved the sound of rain drumming on the metal roof of the RTA building. But right now, it sounded more threatening than soothing.

"At least we don't get tornadoes here," Genna commented. "I spent some time in Texas in the springtime and those tornado warnings are scary as heck."

He loved that she didn't swear. "You lived in Texas?" he asked. "I didn't know that."

"My ex-husband's family lives there," she said. "We were visiting them."

The mention of her ex only reminded him of the night they'd spent together. He swallowed hard, forcing away the stab of longing. To distract himself, he tried opening the front door.

The wind nearly blew it out of his hands. Struggling, he managed to pull it closed. Turning, he wiped the rain off his face with his sleeve. "I don't think we're going anywhere for a bit," he said, pulling out his phone and turning on the flashlight app. "We keep some camping lanterns in the storeroom just for this purpose," he said. "I'm going to go get them."

"Okay," she replied. "I know I saw a couple of three-wick candles on the bookshelf in my office. If I can find a lighter, I'll get those lit, too."

When he returned with the two battery-operated lanterns, he saw she'd gotten the candles burning. Between their flickering lights and what the lanterns provided, they could actually see each other. Definitely a step up, he thought. And kind of cozy, too.

Outside, the storm continued to rage, rain pounding the metal roof. "That's really loud," Genna commented.

"Yes, it is," he agreed. "Since we're going to be here awhile, I know we have a bottle of cabernet somewhere, from our last open house. Want to have a glass while we wait this out?"

When Genna didn't immediately respond, he glanced at her. Shadows danced across her face in the flickering candlelight, making her eyes seem huge in her delicate face. "I'd rather just go home," she finally said. Then, before he could comment, she strode over to the front door and opened it.

The rush of wind and rain nearly knocked her off her feet. Parker helped her push the door shut.

"I guess not," she muttered, using the bottom of her shirt to dry her face. "I thought maybe it might have died down a little since you tried to go out."

Instead of commenting, he went to the small kitchen area. She trailed along after him. He located a bottle of wine and two plastic cups. He had a corkscrew on his pocketknife, so he used that to open it. After pouring himself some, he took a sip. "It's not beer, but it'll do," he said. "Do you want some?"

She came closer. "Maybe just a little."

He poured her some and handed her the cup. To his surprise, she drank all of it in one swallow. "Okay," she said, a hint of a smile playing on her mouth, "we had wine. How about we try to get home?"

What could he do but smile back? "Let me close this wine up first."

"If you can do that, do you mind if I take it with me?" she asked.

That made him chuckle. "Sure. No problem." He located one of the wine stoppers that Lakin always kept lying around. "Here you go." He handed her the bottle.

"Thank you."

"It sounds like the rain is letting up," he said. This time, when he opened the door to check, the wind and rain didn't beat him back. Though still pouring, the gusts had died down. "I think we can make it home now."

Plastic cup still in hand, she crossed over to peer out. "Good. As long as no trees are down, it looks drivable."

"In my truck, yes." He kept his voice firm. "Please, let me take you home."

"I just can't be without a vehicle, even if it's just over-

night," she said. "How about you follow me instead? That way, you know I get home safely."

Though he'd rather they just went together in his truck, he nodded. While she blew out the candles, he returned the camping lanterns to the storeroom, using his phone flashlight to make his way back to the front.

Genna waited near the door. She'd donned a yellow rain slicker that she must have grabbed from storage. Since the thing was at least two sizes too big, she'd rolled the sleeves up. With the hood up, she looked achingly vulnerable, a fact that he knew she'd hate.

"Ready?" she asked. At his nod, she stepped out onto the front porch that, now that the wind had died down, provide ample shelter from the rain.

Once he'd locked the office up, they both eyed the rain. The damp cold seeped into his bones, making him long for snow.

"Follow me," she said before dashing out into the deluge.

He waited until she'd gotten into her car before running for his truck. Though he would have preferred to take her home, he had to respect her wishes. He only hoped she remembered how to drive in the mud.

Paved roads or not, this kind or rain brought flooding, which in turn coated some of the roads in mud. Parker had only seen this happen a few times in his lifetime, but he'd never forgotten the indignity of once as a teen having to call his cousin to tow him out when he'd gotten stuck.

As he followed Genna from the parking lot, he kept a tight grip on the steering wheel. He was able to turn his windshield wipers down a bit from high. More proof the rain was slowing.

Driving, he kept his attention on the road, despite the distraction of emotions whirling inside him.

When they turned onto Genna's street, he shook his hands out one by one. They'd actually started cramping. And when she pulled into her driveway, the last of the tension left his body. He exhaled, more relieved than he should have been.

Pulling up behind her, he kept his truck running. He'd wait unto she got inside before backing out and heading home.

Except, when she exited her car, instead of going in, she stopped halfway. And then she turned and moved toward his truck instead of the house.

She went around to the passenger side, opened the door and climbed in. Her stricken expression made him instinctively reach for her. "What is it? What's wrong?"

"My front door is wide open," she said, her voice shaken. "I know I locked it when I left for work this morning. What if whoever broke in is still inside the house?"

HEART POUNDING, Genna sucked in her breath. Inexplicably, her eyes filled with tears.

"I'm calling the police." He immediately dialed 9-1-1.

"But—" She gripped his arm.

Still giving information to Dispatch, he shook his head. "A unit is on the way," he said. "You stay right here with me until they arrive."

Though she struggled to keep herself from shaking, she did as he asked. Her legs would likely be too weak to carry her anyway.

In less than five minutes, two squad cars pulled up, lights flashing. Parker grabbed his umbrella and got out in the steady rain, crossing over to her side. Before he could open her door, Genna joined him. She kept her rain hood up, even though he made sure to keep his umbrella over her, which she appreciated.

The policemen got out slowly, taking care to open their own umbrellas. Genna waited patiently, glad of the time to collect herself before explaining to the officer what she'd seen.

"I'm glad you didn't go inside," the one officer said once she'd finished. "Let us take a look and make sure it's safe."

Genna nodded. She stepped closer to Parker, aware he'd think it was to make better use of his umbrella. She would have given much to have the right to let him put his arm around her and pull her close. They both watched silently as the officers disappeared inside.

"Why my parents' place?" she asked, proud that she managed to keep her voice steady. "I mean they've owned this house for thirty years and never once had a break-in. Not just that, but there's very little of value inside. They aren't big on updating. The only thing new is the TV and those aren't even that expensive anymore."

"I don't know," he replied. "I'm sorry this happened to you."

He still didn't touch her. While she understood, she really wished this time he would make an exception. Just this once.

A few minutes later, both police officers emerged. "We did a thorough search. No one is inside and, quite honestly, nothing appears to be damaged or missing. Are you absolutely positive you didn't leave the door ajar and maybe the wind blew it open?"

"I'm sure," Genna responded. "And the front door looks damaged to me. Like someone kicked it in. Even from here, I can see that part of the frame is broken."

"High winds can also do that." The officer scratched his head. "It seems kind of odd that anyone would bother to kick your door in and then not touch anything."

She bristled, but decided it would be best not to respond.

"I take it you don't have any kind of burglar alarm?" the other officer asked, his expression kind.

"No," she replied. "I've been thinking about getting one ever since that serial killer started going after local women. Now I really wish I'd gotten one installed. I'll start making calls first thing in the morning."

The older of the two policemen nodded. "Now might definitely be a good time to do that." He handed Genna his card. "Call us if you need anything."

Accepting it, she thanked him.

She and Parker stood silently and watched them drive off.

"Do you want me to walk you inside?" Parker asked.

"Yes, please." Feeling extremely vulnerable, she clutched at his arm. When he covered her hand with his, her heart squeezed.

"Stay near to me," he said, tugging her a tiny bit closer. Then they stepped into the house.

"Wow," he commented. "It's very neat. I get why the police officers thought no one could have broken in."

"Yeah, I get it. It's also very dated. Since I'm housesitting for my parents, I've been afraid to change anything."

"Late nineties?" he asked. "Just to hazard a guess."

"Let me put it this way. This room looks exactly the way it did when they brought me home from the hospital for the first time. They've never bought anything new."

She pointed to the couch, covered with one of her mother's old comforters. "When things wear out, they simply cover them up. I guess they like the comfort of having everything stay the same and familiar. That's why their decision to move to Hawaii was such a big shock."

Reluctantly, she let go of him and began to inspect the place.

He followed her from the living room to the kitchen, then

down the hallway to check on each of the three bedrooms. Everything appeared undisturbed, including the guest bedroom. "This is mine," Genna told him. "Notice the splashes of color?"

"I do."

"As far as I can tell, nothing was stolen." Perplexed and worried, Genna shook her head. "This is making me question why someone would go through all the trouble of breaking in."

"Since the policeman already asked you if you're sure you locked the door, I'm not going to repeat the question."

"I appreciate that," she said, meaning it. Despite feeling traumatized, when she looked at him, she still found herself battling an aching sort of longing.

If he realized this, he didn't show it.

"Well…" he said, swallowing hard and turning to go. "I'll see you in the morning," he finished. "Make sure and lock up after me."

"Wait." Not wanting him to leave, she hurried over and touched his arm again. Still in her yellow rain slicker, she looked up at him, hoping he could somehow sense her fear. "I can't lock up. The door won't even close properly. Look." She showed him.

"Judging by the way the wood had splintered around where the lock had been, it does look like someone busted in the door," he said. "Wind wouldn't do that."

"I know." Exhaling, she fought to keep her voice steady. "There's not a chance I'm staying here alone with no way to keep an intruder out. What if they were to come back?"

His gaze found hers. "You have a point."

"I feel…violated," she said, breathing hard.

As if unable to help himself, he pulled her close and held her.

Offering comfort, nothing more, she told herself.

"I'm not going to let you be alone," he said, smoothing her hair away from her face. "Would you be willing to go back to my place with me? You can stay there tonight. We can work on getting your door repaired in the morning."

"Separate rooms?" she asked, her face still pressed against his chest.

"Of course," he promised. "I'd never try to take advantage of you, especially when you're down. If we ever get together again, you'll be the one to initiate it. Sound good?"

"Well, that will never happen," she said, her tone dry.

That made him chuckle.

Again that wild rush of attraction. Even now. Grappling with her mixed emotions, she attempted to summon up a smile, and thanked him. "I appreciate you offering to help me, more than you could ever know."

His glance met and held hers. "Does that mean you're coming with me?"

"Yes," she replied. "I just need to pack a few things. Give me a few minutes and I'll be right back."

"Okay," Parker replied. She could feel his gaze on her as she turned to go.

In her room, she tossed a change of clothes and some toiletries into a backpack. Despite everything, she found she actually liked the idea of spending nonworking time with him. On a friendly basis, of course. Maybe this would help her get over her constant awareness of him. She certainly hoped so.

When she returned to the living room with her backpack in hand, he turned and eyed her. "Listen, I should probably ask if you'd rather have me stay here with you rather than go to my place."

Her gut clenched. "That's even more kind of you, but no.

It wouldn't be safe," she said, hoping he couldn't see her terror. The howl of the wind and the rain made it even worse.

"It sounds pretty nasty out there," he pointed out. "But if you're sure, let's go."

Chapter Four

Outside, the wind had picked up again, rattling the partly closed front door. Rain drummed in a steady fury. Just to make sure, Parker crossed to the window. The storm had definitely intensified once more. Rain came down in sheets. He couldn't even see his truck parked in the driveway.

Which meant the drive home might be tricky, to say the least. Again, he debated the possibility of simply staying put. If not for the thread of fear he'd heard just now in Genna's voice, he might have tried to convince her.

While he tried to figure out the best course of action, she joined him. "Wow," she said.

"See what I mean?"

"Yes." She turned to face him. "But, honestly, I'd much rather brave the weather than risk being here when the intruder comes back."

He noticed she said *when* rather than *if.*

"I can keep you safe." He meant every word.

"Maybe so, but even if you stayed here with me, I'd be jumping at every single sound. Best to just go somewhere else, at least until I can get the front door repaired and an alarm system installed."

Slowly, he nodded. "What about securing your belong-

ings? We can try to put something to block anyone from coming in the front door."

"And leave through the garage." She looked around the room. "How about we just pile up a bunch of furniture against it. I know that wouldn't really stop someone determined to enter, but it might provide a bit of a deterrent."

"Good plan."

Once they'd moved everything in front of the front door, he stepped back. "That'll have to do."

"It's better than nothing."

They went out through the garage. Genna grabbed a spare opener from a hook on the wall. As soon as he used his remote to unlock his truck, they exchanged glances and ran for the vehicle.

Despite the short distance, they both got drenched. Or he did. Genna still wore her rain slicker with the hood up.

Inside his truck, they turned to look at each other. With one hand, he pushed his soaked hair away from his face. "I wish I had a raincoat like yours," he said.

Her smile made everything worth it. "You'd look good in yellow," she teased.

"Not as good as you," he replied, perfectly serious. He noticed she lowered the hood finally, fluffing her wavy blond hair with her fingers.

The mad urge to kiss her went through him. He froze, took a deep breath and waited until it passed. Then he started the truck and drove out of the parking area.

Headed back to his place, Parker focused on getting them there safely. He could not afford to be distracted by the beautiful woman sitting next to him. The wind-driven rain made it difficult to see, even with his windshield wipers on high.

They inched slowly forward, caution over speed. He could feel Genna's tension, hear it in the quick shallow breaths she

took. He didn't dare take his hands off the steering wheel or his attention from the road, so the only comfort he could offer was words. "It's going to be all right," he said.

They rounded a curve and slowed. Ahead, the road was washed out, water coursing over the pavement, making it impossible to tell the depth. *Turn around, don't drown* had been drummed into everyone's heads since childhood. Yet, every time they had a flash flood, there were always numerous individuals who ignored that warning and found themselves stuck in several feet of water. First responders were kept busy saving these people.

Parker didn't want to become one of them. Yet with an already tense Genna next to him, he didn't really have a choice.

He stopped the truck and shifted into Park, considering his options.

"Is there another way we can go?" Genna asked nervously. "Driving through all that water doesn't look safe."

"There is," he answered, finally able to look at her. "But not only is it about thirty minutes out of our way, there are several areas of that particular road that are likely to be washed out even worse. This is our best bet."

Slowly, she nodded. "I trust you," she said, catching and holding his gaze.

His heart squeezed. "Thanks," he managed to respond. "With this lift kit on my truck, it sits a bit higher than normal. I feel reasonably confident we can make it through."

Reasonably confident. He hoped she didn't ask the odds.

"Okay. Like I said, I know you'll keep us safe."

"I'm definitely about to try," he told her, shifting back into Drive.

One final quick glance at Genna, who'd gone back to gripping the door, and he gently pressed the accelerator, sending them moving toward the water.

Between the swift-moving current, the rain and wind, it took all of his strength to keep the truck on the road. *Slow and steady*, he reminded himself, using continuous pressure on the gas pedal.

Despite their slow speed, water plumed up, splashing the windows and making it even more difficult to see.

Still, they continued to plow forward. Foot by foot, with the water rising the farther they went.

They must have reached the middle, because just when he thought it might make it to his running boards, it began to recede. And then finally they came out onto the other side, eventually reaching dry road.

Once they had, he coasted to a stop for the moment and looked back. "That was easier than I expected," he quipped. "Though I don't want to have to do it again."

"Me neither." She gave a sigh of relief. "Hopefully, this storm will pass and the roads will clear up by morning."

"My house is just a few hundred yards past here," he said. "We'll be there in no time."

When they pulled up into his driveway, he used his automatic garage door opener and got ready to pull in. Since he had to park his truck at an angle due to the length, he only tended to use the garage in the cold months. But this downpour warranted the extra effort.

Genna sat up and watch with interest as he maneuvered his truck inside. He got it parked on the first try.

"Nice," she commented, smiling. "I'd hoped you'd figured out a way to get this huge truck inside your garage."

"I'm just lucky there's extra height in here. Otherwise, being able to fit the length of it wouldn't matter."

He got out, intending to make his way to her side to open her door. But by the time he got there, she'd already grabbed her backpack and jumped out.

"I really appreciate you letting me stay here," she said, her expression earnest. "I promise you won't even know I'm here."

Though he doubted that, he simply nodded. Pushing the button on the wall that closed the garage, he opened the door to the house. "Come on in," he said, gesturing at her to precede him.

Once inside, he flipped the wall switch so they could see. They were in his laundry room, just off the kitchen. "This way."

He led her past the kitchen, which opened up to the living room, and down the hallway. The second door on the left had been designated his guest bedroom. Though it rarely got used, he'd recently put fresh sheets on the bed because one of his old friends who'd moved away had been supposed to come back to Shelby for a week. The visit had been canceled at the last moment, but everything had been made ready for a guest.

"Serendipity," he said, telling her the story as he turned on the light. "This will be where you'll be sleeping."

She brushed past him on the way in, her body making brief contact with his. That small touch was enough to send desire blazing through him.

His swift intake of breath had her turning to look at him. When she met his gaze, she took an almost involuntary step closer. Then, as if she'd realized what she'd done, she moved away, placing her backpack on the bed with great care.

Of necessity, he moved to the doorway, not wanting her to see the physical proof of his sudden arousal. With effort, he found his voice. "Since we didn't have dinner, I'm going to look around the kitchen and see what I can rustle up for us to eat," he said.

Pretending not to notice his voice sounded like rusty nails, she nodded. "If you'll give me a few minutes to freshen up, I can come help you."

"Sounds good." Stiffly, he moved away. He also needed a few minutes of alone time, so he could get his body's reaction to her under control.

Mentally berating himself, he opened the refrigerator and began inspecting the contents. Since he cooked for himself most nights, he kept it pretty well stocked. A few minutes of perusing the dinner choices and he'd managed to return to normal.

"So, what are you thinking?" Genna asked from behind him. Then, without waiting for an answer, she continued. "I'm thinking you should let me make dinner. It'll be my way of thanking you for helping me out."

Since the idea of the two of them cooking side by side now felt too intimate, he nodded. "Okay. The fridge and freezer are stocked up, so is the pantry. The only thing I'm sick of eating is salmon."

This comment made her laugh. "Isn't everyone? Honestly, I've tried so many different recipes, trying to make it taste different."

"That's what happens when something is so plentiful," he said. "I heard people in Maine are like that about lobster."

"Not me. I can always go for a fresh lobster tail and butter." As she smiled up at him, this time his heart did a little flip-flop. "I'm thinking a steak, baked potatoes and maybe asparagus."

Impulsively, he hugged her, a move he instantly regretted. Releasing her as fast as he could, he stepped back. "That's my kind of meal. I even thawed a nice Porterhouse, intending to grill it tomorrow. It's big enough that it should feed both of us."

"Sounds perfect," she said, keeping her gaze averted. He found himself wondering if he should apologize for the quick hug, just in case. Good thing she didn't know how close he'd come to kissing her.

"Genna," he began. "I'm sorry if—"

"It's all good," she said, cutting him off. "Now, I'd better get busy doing my thing. I'll holler if I need you."

Dismissed, Parker did the only sensible thing. He retreated.

If it hadn't still been raining outside, he'd have gone for a walk. Getting outside always eased his tension. Instead, since he was confined to the house, he took an early shower and changed into comfy clothes.

When he emerged, the smell of steak broiling made his mouth water.

In the kitchen, Genna had set the table and had just removed two foil-wrapped baked potatoes from the oven. "You're just in time," she said, smiling.

Somehow, this made him feel worse. "Genna, I never want to make you feel uncomfortable."

His words wiped the smile from her face. "You're over-thinking things. Please, sit down and let's have a nice meal. It's been a spectacularly bad day. I'm really not in the mood to make it any worse."

Damn, he liked her attitude. Quietly nodding, he asked her if there was anything he could do to help.

"Nope. Just sit and eat," she replied.

"Yes, ma'am." He sat.

She picked up their plates and carried them to the stove. When she returned and placed them on the table, they each had a perfectly cooked portion of steak, baked potato and asparagus.

"This looks way better than anything I could have made," he admitted.

"Thank you." She took a seat and gave him a mock stern look. "Dig in."

GENNA WASN'T SURE if it was because of the handsome man sitting across from her, but the dinner they shared tasted better than anything she'd ever made.

Parker definitely appeared to like it. Making appreciative sounds as he ate, he cleaned his plate in record time. "That was amazing," he said, sitting back in his chair and watching her eat.

Once she'd finished, he grabbed both plates and carried them to the sink. "I'll wash up."

"Thanks." Suddenly exhausted, she didn't move. Instead, she covertly admired his backside while he washed off their plates and everything she'd used to cook.

When he finally finished and turned around, he studied her. "Did you want to watch some TV?"

Though she really wanted to crawl into bed, it was still early. "Sure," she said, rising and stretching. "I don't care what we watch. You choose."

They settled in the living room. She took the couch and he sank onto his recliner. Using the remote, he chose a crime drama. "I've watched a few episodes of this," she said. "It's pretty good."

Appearing lost in thought, he nodded.

Relaxing slightly, she grabbed a throw blanket from the end of the couch and used it to cover up.

She must have dozed off because the next thing she knew, Parker gently shook her. Confused, she sat up, blinking sleepily. The room had gone quiet, the television turned off.

"Did you want to sleep here?" he asked quietly, bending

over her. "I wasn't sure if you'd rather I left you alone, or woke you so you could move to the bed."

Heaven help her. Maybe her defenses were in tatters due to her being only half awake. Without really thinking, she reached up, pulled his face down to hers, and kissed him.

Oh, what a kiss. It was everything she'd thought it would be, just as passionate and perfect as she remembered. Tongues tangled as they deepened it. Desire, which always seemed to be simmering inside her when he was around, blazed to life.

It would have been a simple thing to tug Parker to her, his full body on top of hers. Though fully clothed, shedding those would have been a simple thing.

Except she knew doing so would be a terrible mistake.

To his credit, Parker kept himself back. Only their mouths met, though he tangled one hand in her hair. If he wanted more, he made no move to take it. Instead, he continued to thoroughly kiss her, letting her make the next move. Which, despite how badly she wanted to, she couldn't take.

Finally, they broke apart, both breathing hard.

Talk about awkward. She didn't know where to look, what to do with her hands. Meanwhile, he waited, clearly giving her time and space to choose what she wanted to do next.

What she wanted had nothing to do with anything.

"I guess I ought to go to bed," she managed to say. "Thank you for waking me."

Instead of responding, he straightened and nodded. Moving stiffly away, he glanced back over his shoulder at her. "Please turn the lights out when you go."

A moment later, she heard the sound of his bedroom door closing. The slight click made her wince.

Well, she'd certainly made a mess of things.

Feeling an uncomfortable combination of both arousal

and embarrassment, she briefly considered spending the rest of the night on the sofa. But aware she'd likely regret that decision in the morning, she pushed herself up and made her way toward the guest room. She shut off the lights as she left.

After a quick detour to the guest bathroom to brush her teeth, she returned to her little room and closed her own door. Quickly changing into her pajamas, she slid between the cool sheets and gave a sigh of relief.

When she opened her eyes again, it was morning. The instant she woke, sitting up in Parker's guest bed, she immediately realized she'd made a huge mistake.

She'd kissed him.

Moving on autopilot, she tried not to think. Today was another workday, and they'd be working side by side for large chunks of it. There couldn't be any lingering awkwardness between them. She had to clear this up. Somehow.

While she showered in the guest bathroom, she tried to think of what to say. Should she apologize? Explain that she'd been barely awake and…what? Acted on the constant, simmering desire he aroused in her? No, that wouldn't work. It sounded too much like an invitation to try again, or to take things even further.

She definitely didn't want to lead him on. Because, plain and simple, they were coworkers. Nothing more. Nor could they ever be. She wasn't willing to risk this blowing up in her face yet again. Especially since her livelihood would be affected.

After finishing, she shut off the water, toweled dry, and tried to clear her mind. She hadn't been able to come up with much and decided she'd simply apologize and leave it at that. Decision made, she ignored the butterflies in her stomach, dried her hair and got dressed. As a general rule,

she didn't wear a lot of makeup, just mascara and lip gloss, which meant it didn't take her long to get ready.

Sadly, Genna didn't feel refreshed. She hadn't had much success sleeping. The kiss and the break-in had weighed heavily on her mind, making her toss and turn all night long. Every time she'd managed to drift off to sleep, booms of thunder had yanked her back into awareness. The storm had continued into early morning, finally moving on right before dawn.

Because thinking about the break-in terrified her and dwelling on the kiss made her want to cry, she wished she could get through the morning without thinking. At least until she got to work. Once at RTA, she could keep herself busy enough so she wouldn't have to dwell on anything. Except, she did need to have the front door repaired and call an alarm company and make an appointment to have a system installed.

But first, she had to face Parker. He'd been kind enough to offer her a place to stay, and then she'd kissed him. What if he'd taken that to mean she wanted more than just a kiss?

And what if she did? Too much to consider, especially since she'd always been a fan of weighing all her options.

She'd kissed him. Damned if she hadn't wanted to do a whole lot more.

Admitting that brought to mind visions of their night together. She relived every moment, wondering how it could be seared inside her brain. Their tangled bodies, the passionate kisses and the way he'd made her feel sexy, beautiful and whole again. Special. At least until he'd disappeared without a call or text.

In retrospect, that had turned out to be a good thing. She hadn't wanted to go straight from her disastrous marriage into another relationship. She'd needed to learn how to live

on her own and rebuild her self-respect, especially after being betrayed not only by her husband but by a woman she'd considered her best friend.

Genna never wanted to feel that level of pain again. Yet when she'd gone slinking back home to her parents to lick her wounds, and she'd been ghosted after she'd indulged in one amazingly carnal night with the sexiest man she'd ever met, it had hurt nearly as much. Maybe because she'd been vulnerable.

Even though Parker had belatedly, one year later, offered up an excuse, the rejection still stung. Likely more than it should have. Maybe she needed to finally let it go.

Giving her hair one final swipe of the brush, she stared at herself in the mirror. Then she took a deep breath and opened her bedroom door. The scent of coffee brewing drifted down the hallway, making her mouth water. When she made it to the kitchen, Parker was standing at the stove, his back to her, stirring something.

Dang, he looked good. Flushing, she remembered she owed him an apology. Not yet though. She needed to be fully awake for that. Needing fortification, she made a beeline for the coffeepot.

"Morning," Parker said, turning to smile at her. "Mugs are in the cabinet to the left of the coffee maker. I have half-and-half in the fridge and sugar in the smallest of those canisters on the counter."

"Thanks," she replied, pretending that his smile hadn't knocked the breath from her. "Any reports on storm damage?"

"Not yet." He filled two bowls and carried them to the table. "Since we're opening RTA, we can fill everyone else in once we get there."

Slowly, she nodded. "What are you cooking?" she asked, feeling ridiculously tongue-tied.

If he noticed, he gave no sign. "I made some oatmeal with raisins."

Though she usually nursed a cup of coffee until fully awake, since she felt like she'd been up for hours, she appreciated the hot meal. "That's very kind of you," she said, grabbing a mug from the cupboard and filling it. Once she'd added her cream and sugar, she took a seat at the table and took a sip. He'd already placed a couple of spoons there, along with paper napkins.

The aroma of oatmeal, cinnamon, and raisins made her realize she was starving. No one had made her breakfast since her mother when she'd lived at home. The small kindness made her insides go all gooey. She decided maybe she'd wait on the apology, at least until after they'd eaten.

"Dig in," he said, dropping into the chair opposite hers.

Though she tried not to watch him through her lashes, she couldn't help herself. He ate quickly and efficiently, the way he did most everything—except make love. Again, the thought made her entire body flush. She concentrated on finishing her breakfast, glad he couldn't hear her thoughts.

"Do you think the roads have cleared?" she asked, wondering if she should offer to help with the dishes. Since doing so felt too intimate, she stayed put while he carried their bowls and utensils to the sink and rinsed them before placing them in the dishwasher.

"Yes," he replied, turning back to face her. "Despite the early morning clouds, it looks like the sun is trying to come out."

His phone rang before she could comment. She sipped her coffee, watching as his expression changed. The grim sound of his one-word responses sent a shiver up her spine.

"Thanks for letting me know, Eli," he said. "Please keep me posted if you learn anything else."

"What's going on?" she asked. She knew his brother Eli was a state trooper.

"Another body was found. This time on a remote hiking trail outside of town. Young woman, same scenario as the other four. Black dress, and cause of death appears to be strangulation."

Genna swallowed. "That's awful. They haven't even identified the fourth victim and now there's another. Even more reason to worry me and all the other women in Shelby."

"They need to catch the bastard." A muscle worked in Parker's jaw. "I know Eli is frustrated. I'm sure everyone working the case is."

Just then, a ray of sunlight broke through the clouds and beamed through the sliding-glass door. Parker turned, walked to the door and opened it. He stepped out onto his back porch, leaving the door open.

Unsure whether or not to follow, Genna pushed to her feet. After getting a second cup of coffee, she ventured outside, walking on the balls of her feet. She wanted to be ready to turn and go back in at the first sign that he might want to be alone.

Leaning on the railing, he drank his coffee and eyed the forest. "This used to feel like the safest town on earth," he said. "At least, growing up here. We used to ride our bikes and explore the woods from sunup to sundown. No one worried we might be abducted."

She walked up to stand next to him. "All the bonfires we had near the river in high school. My parents always knew I'd make it home safe."

"Yeah." He glanced at her. The dark shadows in his eyes made her heart ache. "Now everyone has to worry. Lakin

has promised to never go anywhere alone. Would you mind doing the same?"

Though touched, she had to shake her head. "That's not possible," she replied. "I live by myself. I have to buy groceries and go shopping. There's no way I can live my life if I have to constantly look for someone to accompany me everywhere."

He acknowledged the truth of her statement with a dip of his chin. "Okay, but don't take any solitary hikes until this killer is caught."

"Now that, I can do," she murmured, cupping her mug with both hands. In the distance, an eagle circled, hunting. "I've never been much of a hiker." She didn't tell him that she'd gone once as a teenager with a boy she'd thought she'd liked from school and had nearly been raped. She'd been able to talk her way out of danger and had made it home unscathed, but the experience had made her understand how dangerous the wilderness could be. Not solely from wild animals, either.

"Really? It's one of my favorite activities when I'm not working."

"Isn't that one of the things you do when you *are* working?" she asked, her tone dry. "I know you take out a lot of hiking expeditions."

"True." He shrugged. "I enjoy being outdoors. There are too many fun activities, no matter the season."

She eyed him briefly. For a second, she considered asking him if he'd ever enjoyed sitting in front of a blazing fire in a warm and cozy living room, watching the snow fall outside. But then she realized it wasn't anything she needed to know. Better to think of Parker as someone completely incompatible.

Chapter Five

Parker took a deep breath. With beautiful Genna standing beside him, raw longing nearly took him out at the knees. How easy to imagine what they could be, if she'd just allow him in.

She'd kissed him. And the kiss had rocked him to the core. For one moment, one shining moment, he'd believed she'd wanted him as much as he did her.

At least she hadn't apologized.

Putting his attention back where it belonged—on the discovery of yet another likely victim of the Fiancée Killer, he took a deep, shaky breath. That woman, whoever she was, had been someone's daughter, sister, friend. To have her life snuffed out in such a horrible way was gut-wrenching.

"I hate that another woman lost her life at that serial killer's hands," Genna said, her voice somber. "I sure hope they figure out who he is and soon."

"Me, too. I think everyone does," he replied.

Taking another sip of her coffee, she looked up at him. "We'd better head for the office," she said. "I need to get the place opened up and ready for the first group. It's going to be a busy Saturday."

He glanced at his watch, saw she was right, and turned

to walk back inside. "I can go whenever. How long do you need?"

"I'm ready now."

Surprised, he nodded. "Let me grab my keys and we'll go."

She followed him into the kitchen, setting her mug down next to his in the sink. The simple act made his heart squeeze. *Ridiculous*, he chided himself, snatching his truck keys off the counter.

"Let's go."

As they drove toward headquarters with the sun shining, it was hard to believe the road had ever been under water. Everything—the trees, the grass, even the pavement—glistened.

Next to him in the passenger seat, Genna fidgeted.

"Are you okay?" he finally asked her.

"Yes," she replied. "No. Not really. Listen, we need to talk about what happened last night."

"No, we don't. Don't worry. Everything is all right."

She sighed loudly. "But it's not. You were kind enough to let me stay in your home. You fed me, too. And while I deeply, deeply appreciate that, I'm afraid I might have given you the wrong impression when I—"

"Nope," he interrupted. "No wrong impressions were made. You were asleep. You acted without thinking. If anything, I took advantage of you by kissing you back."

"Oh, please." He could almost hear her rolling her eyes. "Would you at least let me finish? I owe you an apol—"

"No." He stopped the truck, glad no one else was out and about on this road so early. "Don't you dare apologize to me. At least let me hang on to what shreds of dignity I have left."

Eyes huge, she stared at him. "I don't get it. I'm confused. What do you mean?"

As their gazes locked, again that pull of attraction passed between them. At least for him. He found it difficult to believe this could be one-sided.

"I wanted that kiss as much as you did," he elaborated. "Probably even more. If you'd have invited me into your bed, I would have gone without hesitation. To put it mildly."

Heaven help him, his blunt words not only made her swallow hard, but he swore he saw a flare of desire in her green eyes. She swayed toward him, making him realize she wasn't as immune to their connection as she pretended to be.

Now was not the time. For both their sakes, he knew he had to be strong. Turning to face the road, he shifted into Drive and continued on. Genna sat silent beside him.

They reached headquarters without incident. Everything appeared to have returned to normal and, aside from standing water in some of the ditches, he couldn't tell that there had been any flooding.

As soon as he parked, Genna had the passenger door open and was out. He followed at a more leisurely pace while she used her key to unlock the front door. Once inside, she turned on all the lights and booted up both front-counter computers before going into the back.

"Would you mind getting the coffee started?" she called out, her voice professional as she continued on her way to her office. "I need to check the schedule, but I'm pretty sure we have a tour group arriving in under an hour."

"We do," he answered. "It's my group."

"Hiking?" She turned and grinned at him.

"Not this time. Four-wheeling. Demand is high this time of the year to head up the mountain and see the fall foliage."

"Got it." And she disappeared into her office, leaving him staring after her. This wanting, this craving, made him restless. Uncomfortable in his skin. He didn't have any idea

how to cure it or to make it go away. To be honest, he wasn't even sure if he wanted to.

After turning on the coffee maker, he wandered back outside to make sure no trees had been felled by the storm.

Spence arrived just as Parker returned from making sure the path up the mountain hadn't been blocked. As far as he could tell, it had looked clear.

"I'm worried about the river," Spence said after they exchanged greetings. "I'm supposed to take a small tour group out fishing. But after that storm, I'm concerned."

"I hear you. You might end up river-rafting instead," Parker quipped, only half joking.

"Exactly." Spence checked his wrist. "I'm going to drive down there. Want to go with me and check it out?"

"I wish I could, but my group will be here in fifteen minutes," Parker answered.

Spence responded with a wave and strode off to his truck.

The rest of the day passed in a blur. As always, Parker enjoyed the hell out of the four-wheeling expedition. He'd always liked mud and, after all the rain, there was plenty of that to go around.

Lots of laughs, cheers, especially when they had to tow one of the four-wheelers out of the mud. Sunburned, mud-splattered and happy, the group finally returned to RTA headquarters where Parker turned them over to Genna. She raised a brow at their appearance, but didn't comment.

Instead of taking himself off for a shower, Parker stood near the door and watched Genna interact with the customers. Her friendly smile clearly charmed them. Several of the guys flirted with her, which caused a muscle to twitch in Parker's jaw.

As they finished checking out, one by one they left. Sev-

eral high-fived Parker on the way out. One guy gave him a fist bump and a few just waved.

Finally, they were all gone, leaving Parker alone with Genna.

"You should see yourself," she said, still smiling. "Every single one of your group looks like they took a mud bath."

"We kind of did," he admitted, grinning back at her. "It was a blast."

He could have stood there for eternity and allowed himself to get lost in Genna's gaze.

Instead, the door opened behind him and Spence walked in. The instant he caught sight of Parker, he burst out laughing. "Damn, I wish I'd had that trip instead of mine. Though with the river as high as it is, I might get a little bit wet."

"Do you think it's safe?" Parker asked.

"As far as I can tell, yes. We'll turn back if we encounter anything concerning."

Spence's group started straggling in and Genna busied herself with checking them in. Hetty Amos, their pilot and guide, arrived, laughed at Parker, and signed on to the other computer. Parker asked her quietly if she would be around awhile since Spence would be taking his group out and Parker wanted to run home, shower and change.

"Sure," she replied. "I know the rule. No females are to be alone. I got you. Go get yourself cleaned up. I'll be here for the next couple of hours."

Relieved, he thanked her, waved at Genna, and headed out.

Once home, he shed his muddy clothes and jumped into the shower. An image flashed into his mind of Genna, naked in the shower with him, water sluicing off her perfect, glistening body. Forcefully, he shoved the thought, and the instant bolt of heat it brought, away.

After drying off, he dressed in clean clothes and wandered into the kitchen in search of something to eat. He made a sandwich and ate it alone at the kitchen table. While he did, he realized his house felt…empty. In the brief time Genna had been there, her vibrant presence had filled the space with something he hadn't even realized had been missing.

He really had it bad. Grimacing at his own foolishness, he finished his meal, washing it down with a big glass of water. When had he become so lame, sitting around mooning over a woman who alternated between wanting no part of him and pulling him down for a kiss?

That kiss. Heat had instantly consumed him, taking him right back to the night they'd spent together. They'd feasted on each other, laughed and made love and slept before making love again. Parker had never lacked feminine attention, but what he and Genna had shared had been on an entirely new level.

Then last night, alone in his bed after she'd kissed him, achingly aware of her asleep in the room down the hall, he'd burned with wanting her.

Now he couldn't stop thinking of things he wanted to do to her, with her. Most of them carnal.

But some of them, surprisingly, were not. He dreamt of sharing things with her. A sunrise at the top of the mountain, a quiet moment in a double kayak out in the middle of a serene lake. Dinner and drinks, holding her close as they swayed to the music of the band.

In short, he wanted more. In fact, he realized all of it sounded an awful lot like a relationship. Something he'd avoided like the plague the last several years.

He had his reasons, most of them centered around how badly he'd been hurt when he fell for Genna the last time.

Also, he told himself that he liked his freedom far too much to give any of it up for another person. Now, he had begun to understand that maybe he simply hadn't met the right one.

Shaking his head, he pushed such foolish thoughts away. Genna had made it crystal-clear that she had no desire to pursue any kind of romantic anything with him. Except, then why had she kissed him?

Unsure what to take away from all of that, he decided it would be better not to dwell on it at all. Otherwise, her simple kiss might give him false hope. Which could be painful. He'd never been the type to moon over a woman and he didn't plan to start now.

Yet he couldn't seem to stop yearning for her.

The way he saw it, he had two choices. He could work hard to force himself to see her only as a friend—unlikely. Or he could try his best to get her to open herself up to the possibility of a fresh start between them.

Because right now, he had to believe they were meant to be together.

ONCE GENNA FINISHED checking in the latest group of excited tourists, Spence loaded them up and drove them away. Needing to avoid how the quiet office made her worried thoughts resurface, she made small talk with Hetty. Both Shelby natives, they were close in age. Genna didn't know her well, being a couple of years older than Hetty and they hadn't hung out together in high school. She did know Lakin was dating Hetty's youngest brother Troy.

The fact that Hetty had become a pilot fascinated Genna and she told the other woman so.

"You'll have to come up with me some time," Hetty said, smiling. "It's beautiful, so peaceful and serene. I do my best thinking when I'm high above the ground."

"I'd love that." Genna checked the time. "But right now I've got to make a few personal calls. I need to call a door repair place and an alarm installation company."

"What happened?"

Genna told her about the break-in, though she omitted the fact that she'd spent the night at Parker's.

"I've got a guy," Hetty said, "both for the door and the alarm. Let me give you their names and numbers."

Grateful, Genna thanked her. Hetty scribbled down the information on a slip of paper and handed it to her.

"Does Parker know about this?" Hetty asked, her expression serious.

Genna slowly nodded. "He does. He said something about repairing my door himself, but I'd rather just hire someone."

"If they can get out today, I get it. But if they can't, let Spence and Parker see what they can do. As I'm sure you're aware, it's not safe."

"I know. And thanks for the idea. I'll definitely talk to one of them if I don't have any luck," Genna replied, meaning it. Especially since it was unlikely she'd find anyone who could come out and do the repair today. Maybe if she'd had time to call earlier in the morning. She'd have to try and see.

To her surprise, both the door company and the alarm place sounded eager to have her business, especially when she told them Hetty had referred her. They each promised to be out between five and eight that same evening.

After agreeing, she hung up and marveled at her luck. Then she told Hetty she'd need to leave a little early to meet the workers.

"I'm just glad it worked out," Hetty said. "And don't worry, I can cover the front desk for the rest of the night."

"I appreciate that. But we've got to make sure you're not here all alone."

Drumming her fingers on the counter, Genna thought for a moment. "Hopefully, Parker or Spence or one of the other guides can stay here with you once I leave."

"I'm sure we'll find someone." Hetty didn't seem concerned. But then she looked up at Genna and frowned. "What about you? Is anyone else going to be there at your place when you meet up with the door and alarm companies?"

Surprised, Genna shook her head. "I live alone," she explained. "I'm sure it'll be fine. I don't know if both companies will be there at the same time, but I'm just relieved I can get someone out tonight. Once I get all of that done, I should be able to sleep safely in my own house."

Hetty shook her head. "Girl, you are missing the point. What if one of those workmen aren't on the up-and-up?"

Dumbfounded, Genna stared. "But you referred both companies to me. Are you saying they aren't reputable?"

"That's not what I'm saying at all. Don't you watch any true crime TV? What if the Fiancée Killer took out one of the legitimate workers and traded places, just so he could get to you?"

"Seriously?"

"Yes." Hetty nodded. "Heck, even serial killers have jobs. You never know what that guy does when he's not going around murdering women. You have to be prepared for any possibility, even if it seems unlikely."

The front desk phone rang just then, saving Genna from replying. After she dealt with the caller, she turned to see that Hetty had gotten on her phone, too.

Though she thought Hetty's scenario disturbing, once uttered, it took root inside Genna's mind. Suddenly she found herself nervous, unsure if she should go through with her plans for that evening.

Except, she really needed to have her front door repaired. And an alarm system wasn't something she was willing to put off any longer.

Parker's truck pulled in. She watched through the front window as he got out and strode up to the front porch. She needed to check the schedule, but she thought he had one more trip that afternoon. He'd be taking a group of hikers up to look for wildlife and fall foliage.

Which meant he'd likely finish before she had to leave.

Maybe she'd ask him to go meet the workmen with her.

Entering the room, Parker greeted her and Hetty with a broad smile. "It's a beautiful day," he said. "Hard to believe it was storming so badly yesterday."

Genna nodded. Hetty ended her phone call and frowned. "Genna's leaving a little early. She's having two different workmen at her place tonight. With everything that's been going on, I don't think she should be alone with them. Don't you agree?"

He swung his blue-eyed gaze to Genna. "Definitely," he replied. "Genna, would it be all right with you if I come over and help? Just in case?"

She liked that he'd asked her instead of just insisting. "That'd be great, but we also need to make sure Hetty isn't alone here after I leave."

"Spence will be back by then," Hetty noted, dismissing her concern with an elegant wave of her hand. "He'll stay."

Two vehicles pulled up and parked. "I think your next group is starting to arrive," Genna said.

"I'm ready." Parker rubbed his hands together. "It's a small group this time. There are only six. Once you get them checked in, we'll take off. It's a two-hour hike with a break at the top of the mountain. When I get back, after they're all processed, we'll head out. I'll follow you to your place."

The front door opened before she could respond. Six people filed through the door, all talking at once. She checked them in one by one, enjoying their obvious excitement.

Finally, they were ready to go. Parker gave them a brief talk, made sure everyone had what they needed in their backpacks, and led them out the door.

Genna watched him leave, unable to look away until he and his group disappeared from sight.

"So that's how it is?" Hetty teased, grinning. "The sparks flying between the two of you just about set this place on fire."

Though Genna felt her face heat, she managed to play it off. "You definitely have a huge imagination," she replied, trying to keep her voice level.

"Whatever." Hetty shrugged. "Not any of my business."

The rest of the afternoon passed swiftly. Spence and his bunch returned with plenty of fish. They were a group of happy customers. As Genna checked them out in the system, several volunteered that they planned to write glowing reviews.

"We appreciate that," Genna said, smiling. Even Hetty looked up from scrolling her phone and grinned with approval.

Nonchalant, Spence strolled around to the back counter. "I aim to please," he announced with a cheerful wink.

After they'd all left, Genna filled Spence in on her situation.

He nodded with approval when she told him Parker would be following her to her house. "Good," he said. "And I'll stay here and help Hetty close the office. Right now, no female in Shelby needs to be around strange men when she's alone."

"That's what I said," Hetty chimed in.

"Then I'm glad Genna listened." Spence's cell phone rang and he stepped outside onto the front porch to take the call.

Since she'd be leaving early, Genna got busy filing all her electronic paperwork and setting everything up for whoever would be opening tomorrow. She had the day off; something she was actually looking forward to.

The last part of the afternoon seemed unusually quiet. She answered a few phone calls inquiring about tours, directed them all to the website, and checked a few times to see if there'd been any new reservations.

Hetty had gone outside to talk to Spence. Genna could see the two of them sitting in the oversized wooden chairs enjoying the sunshine. They made a cute couple. The love they shared was palpable.

This job, this place, and these people, felt like family, she realized. This sense of belonging, of camaraderie, was exactly what she needed at this stage of her life. Even if she had some definitely different kinds of thoughts about Parker.

Eventually, Parker and his group wandered back in. Some of them were red-faced and perspiring, other seemed out of breath, but they all appeared happy. She began the checkout process, asking each one about their experience. Without exception, the guests raved about the wildlife and the colorful autumn foliage, glad they'd taken the hike and gotten the exercise.

After they'd all cleared out, she looked up to see Parker and Spence deep in conversation. Hetty had answered the phone and, from the sounds of it, had signed the caller up for one of the winter snowmobile tours.

Heart full, Genna began gathering up her belongings, getting ready to leave. When she straightened, backpack over her shoulder, she noticed Parker watching her. The heat in his gaze made her knees weak.

"Are you about ready to go?" he asked.

"I am." She nodded, looking away. "How about you?"

"Ready when you are."

After waving goodbye to Spence and Hetty, Genna headed outside with Parker right behind her. She got into her car and started it. Driving away, the sight of Parker's large pickup truck in her rearview mirror comforted her.

As she pulled up into her own driveway, hitting the button to open her garage door, she wondered if their strategy to block the front door had worked. If not, she realized the possibility existed that an intruder might still be inside.

After turning off her engine, she waited for Parker to get out of his truck. Catching sight of her expression, he lightly squeezed her shoulder. "Do you want me to go first?" he asked.

"Yes, please."

Staying close to him as he stepped inside, she fought the urge to reach for his hand. Instead, she focused on switching on the lights.

In the living room, the furniture they'd carefully piled against the front door appeared to be undisturbed. Relieved, she exhaled.

"It doesn't look like anyone tried to force their way in," Parker said. "Let's get all this moved so your door guy can work on this."

Once they'd done that, she offered him a soft drink or an iced tea. He asked for water instead.

Right after she'd brought him a glass, her doorbell rang. Since the front door wouldn't close all the way, she was glad they hadn't knocked.

"I'm with Shelby Alarm Service," the young, bearded man announced. "I understand I'm here to do an installation."

"Come in," she said, suddenly glad Parker had insisted on keeping her company. "I'm sure they told you already, but I signed up for the full package. Window and door sensors and motion sensors. With monitoring."

He consulted his clipboard. "Yes, ma'am. That's what I show on my work order."

"Perfect." She stepped back. "Then I'll let you get to it. I'm expecting someone else to repair my front door."

That contractor arrived a few minutes later. He took one look at the splintered frame and damaged door and shook his head. "You're going to need to replace all of this," he said. "It's not repairable."

Hearing him, she glanced at Parker for confirmation.

"I don't know about that," Parker said. "Can you show me why you can't just replace the frame?"

Genna went to check on the alarm guy while the other two men discussed the front door.

She found him installing sensors on all her windows. "When your system is armed, if anyone tried to open a window, or a door for that matter, it will alert."

"Just here?" she asked. "Or at the monitoring center, too?"

"Both. Once it alerts, if you don't deactivate it, we will call you and ask for your password. If you don't answer or give an incorrect response, we contact the police."

Which was exactly what she wanted.

"I heard another body was found," the man said, not looking up from his work. "I bet we get a ton of installation calls now. It's not possible to be too safe."

"I agree." That said, she left him alone to work and went back to check on the front door.

Parker smiled when he saw her. "Looks like you're getting a new everything," he said. "He's putting in a reinforced steel door instead of a wooden one."

"Perfect," she told him. Then, because she imagined installers would much prefer to do their work without the homeowner standing over their shoulders, she took herself off to the kitchen.

To her surprise, Parker followed her. "When all this is done, how about we go out and grab dinner together?" he asked.

Surprised, she looked up at him. When she saw the heat in his eyes, she sucked in her breath. "As friends?" Her answer came out a bit shakier than she would have liked.

"Sure. Why not?" But the hint of mischief in his smile said otherwise.

She almost turned him down. Almost. But the part of her that had made her kiss him had her deciding to go. After all, she could either spend the rest of her life attempting to ignore the attraction between them and keep things on a friendly level, or she could go along with the flow. Judging by the way her luck with men and relationships went, it wouldn't take much to make Parker realize they'd be better off as simply coworkers. Possibly even friends. But nothing more.

"Sure," she answered, looking down so he couldn't see the conflicted emotions in her expression. "As long as it's not too late."

She opened the refrigerator and grabbed the leftover bottle of wine they'd shared during the storm. "Do you want a glass?" she asked. "I'm about to pour myself one and go sit out on the back porch. You're welcome to join me."

Since her yard was enclosed by a six-foot-tall cedar fence, she figured she'd be safe enough alone for a few minutes. Even if she wasn't, this was her home. She refused to spend every waking moment inside her house quaking in fear.

"I'll be out there in a few," he said, evidently reaching

the same conclusion. "After I check on both contractors to see how much longer they've got."

"Let me know," she replied, pouring a generous glass. "And help yourself if you want wine."

Taking a small sip, she made her way outside. Already, she'd begun to reconsider agreeing to go out to eat with him. But then again, doing so seemed like the least she could do after all he'd done to help her.

She shook her head. She'd never been in the habit of lying to herself and didn't intend to start now. If she ever intended to regard Parker as nothing more than a friend, she had to get whatever this was out of her system. Starting tonight.

Chapter Six

When Genna agreed to have dinner with him, Parker felt like he'd won the lottery. He couldn't help but be glad she'd looked away, because he didn't want her to realize how stoked he was.

Actually, he hadn't really thought she'd say yes.

But since she had, he didn't want to take a chance he'd inadvertently give her any reason to change her mind.

The front door guy was nearly finished. He'd removed the splintered door frame and installed a new one. "It'll need to be painted," he told Parker. "She can also paint the new door. It's white. Most people like some color."

Since Parker had no idea what Genna would like, he simply nodded.

"It's a shame another body was found," the guy said, continuing to work. "I hate the way this serial killer has everyone in town on edge."

"Me, too." Parker replied. "And they haven't been able to identify that fourth body yet. Now there's been a fifth."

"Yeah, it's awful." Finishing with the bottom hinge, the worker started on the middle one. "I should be done in just a few minutes. Then I just have to write up the invoice."

Parker wondered how Genna would react if he simply

paid for the door. Not well, he suspected. "I'll go get her when you're done," he said.

Then he went to see how the alarm installation was going.

"I'm just about done with the window sensors," the installer said as soon as he saw Parker. "Obviously, I can't do the front door until it's in place. But I can work on getting the control box set up."

"How long will that take?" Though Parker didn't want to seem impatient, he couldn't wait to take Genna out to dinner. Even though neither had called it a date, just spending time with her in a nonwork setting sounded amazing. They could get to know each other, without pressure.

"Maybe thirty minutes."

Satisfied with the answer, Parker left to check on Genna outside. He found her kicked back in a wicker chair, feet up on an ottoman, sipping on a glass of wine.

The sky had barely started to darken, the setting sun coloring the western horizon in vivid shades of pink and orange. He walked to the porch railing and looked out over Genna's large, fenced backyard. A raised bed for vegetable took up one corner and strategically planted evergreens gave the space a balanced ambience.

"I've been thinking about getting a dog," Genna said. "Partly for companionship, but also as an added layer of protection. A dog would alert me if someone was skulking around outside."

Surprised, he turned to look at her. "Have you ever owned a dog before?"

"Growing up, we had Binx. My dad got him from the city animal shelter in Fairbanks. No one knew for sure what combination of breeds he was, but he was big and lovable. He lived to be nearly fifteen." She sighed. "We all missed

him so much. My mom said she never wanted to feel that kind of pain again, so they didn't get another dog."

"What about you?" he asked, genuinely curious. "Once you moved out on your own, you never thought about it?"

"I did. But you know how it is. I never had the time, didn't want the responsibility. I wasn't ready."

"And now you think you are?"

She nodded. "Yes. Now, I think I am." Taking another sip of wine, she eyed him. "What about you? Do you have any pets?"

"Not currently. I lost my boy Trooper to cancer this past winter. He was my buddy. He and I went everywhere together. Hiking, fishing, four-wheeling—he loved it all. He was the unofficial RTA dog." He didn't even try to keep the sorrow from his voice. "That's his photo in the lobby. I miss him more than I can say."

"I'm sorry," she said, her gentle tone matching the compassion in her gaze. "I have an idea. I'm off tomorrow and have been thinking about driving over to Valdez to check out the dogs in the shelter. Would you like to go with me?"

Though he knew he had two tours booked the next day, he nodded. He would move the tours. "I would," he said, taking care to sound as casual as possible. "When were you thinking of going?"

Her smile lit up not only her face but sent a bolt of raw desire through him. "We can work around your schedule. It's only about a half-hour drive there, so just let me know when you're available."

Mouth dry, he managed to nod. Right then the front door installer came looking for Genna.

"All done," he said, handing her an invoice. "We take credit cards, Venmo or Zelle, however you want to pay."

She sat up, looking over the paper before nodding. "Let

me get my wallet." Pushing to her feet, she headed inside, the installer right behind her.

Parker went, too. While Genna paid with one of her credit cards, he went to check on the alarm guy's progress.

"Almost done," the man said cheerfully as soon as Parker appeared. "I just need to run a quick test." He looked around. "But I'll need the homeowner here. We've got to set up her password."

Genna and the door installer appeared, just in time for her to hear the last comment. "I'll be right there," she said. "I need to check out my new front door."

Parker decided to go with her.

"You can paint this any color you like," he told her, noting the way she eyed the white door. Her former door had been emerald green.

"Good. I'm thinking red." She made a show of inspecting it. "Looks good. Thank you so much for coming out quickly."

"No problem." The man turned to go, but at the last moment appeared to remember something. "Extra keys," he said, pulling them from his pocket. "Here you go."

Accepting them, she watched as he got into his truck and drove away. Then, closing the door behind her, she returned to the hallway where the alarm control panel had been mounted on the wall.

When she chose her password, she made sure no one, including Parker, stood too close. Instead of feeling hurt, he wanted to clap. He liked that she took precautions to protect herself, even as he hoped she knew she had nothing to fear from him.

After a demonstration that involved having the alarm go off and the monitoring company calling, the installer de-

clared he had finished. Genna paid him, too, and showed him to the door.

Finally, they were alone.

"Expensive day," Genna drawled, placing the invoice on the counter with the other. "But at least I'll have peace of mind."

Parker waited in the living room while she went to get ready to go out to eat. When she returned, she had changed out of her RTA shirt into a bright green T-shirt. The color matched her eyes.

She looked stunning.

"Where do you want to eat?" Parker asked, hoping she hadn't noticed his reaction. More than anything, he wanted to keep things casual. He sensed anything else would only frighten her away.

"I don't care," Genna responded. "Surprise me."

Briefly, he considered asking her what she liked and disliked, but decided not to. He didn't want to get in to one of those long discussions where one person suggests something, the other one vetoes it, and nothing is ever decided.

"You're sure you want me to choose," he asked, just to clarify.

"Yes. I'm too tired to even think about it. I just want to eat and relax. I'm sure you know where the best places to eat are. I'm down for whatever."

"Then let's go." He pulled out his keys. "I'll drive."

"Perfect."

He decided on sushi. A new place had opened up downtown and he hadn't tried it yet, though he'd heard good things. If for some reason, Genna didn't like sushi, there were several other items on the menu for her to eat.

As he drove, with the radio on KVAC, playing country music, he enjoyed the way Genna didn't feel the need to

fill the silence with chatter. But as they pulled into the restaurant's parking lot, he glanced at her and realized she'd fallen soundly asleep.

When she'd said she felt tired, she hadn't been exaggerating.

Hating to wake her, he wasn't sure what to do. Should he drive around awhile, hoping she woke on her own? Or park and see if the simple lack of motion might do the trick?

His stomach rumbled, reminding him that he needed to eat. He decided to go ahead and park. Hopefully, she'd wake up.

Once he'd pulled into a slot and turned off the engine, Genna stirred. Not awake. Not yet anyway. She sighed, still sleeping, and then slowly opened her eyes. When her drowsy gaze found him, he sucked in his breath. A different kind of hunger filled him. He knew better than to act on it, so instead he allowed himself sit and watch her while she slowly came awake. "What happened?" she asked, stretching. Then, clearly realizing they were in his truck, she smiled sheepishly. "I'm guessing I fell asleep."

Before he could answer, she yawned, covering her mouth. "Sorry."

He found her so endearing that he ached. "No need to apologize. Do you want to go in and eat or would you rather I take you home so you can sleep?"

For the first time, she appeared to realize where they were.

"Sushi?" she asked, her voice incredulous. "You like sushi?"

"Yes. Do you?"

The brilliant smile spreading across her face made him think that she did. "I love it, actually. And I've been dying to try this place. I've seen good things about it online."

Just then, his stomach growled, loudly enough to make her laugh. "I can see you're hungry. I think I'm finally alert enough to go inside and eat."

Successfully fighting the urge to lean over and kiss her, he hopped out of the truck instead. Going around to her side, he managed to get the passenger door open before she did. When he offered his hand, she took it, sliding her fingers into his and allowing him to help her down.

When she didn't immediately pull away, he decided to go with it. They walked into the restaurant, hand in hand.

Inside, the place seemed fairly crowded. Busy, but not packed. They were immediately showed to a booth near one of the floor-to-ceiling windows and given menus.

Though he hated to let go of her, Parker helped her take a seat. He then slid across from her in the booth. Opening his menu, he began reading. When he glanced at her and she smiled, he felt the power of that smile all the into his bones.

"How about we try several different rolls and share them?" he asked. "That way we can sample a variety of things."

She nodded, appearing to like the idea. "That's fine with me as long as we split the bill half and half," she answered. "Sushi is expensive, after all."

He suspected she didn't want him to think this evening was an actual date. Which, as far as he was concerned, it definitely was.

"Sure," he said without hesitation. "I was thinking it was your turn to treat, but we can split it if that's what you want."

It took a moment for her to realize he was joking, though he'd made sure to keep his tone light. He saw the moment she got it. Her mouth tightened and she frowned.

"You know what?" she said, her voice firm. "I think I'll

let you treat this time. I haven't gotten my first paycheck yet, so your kindness would be greatly appreciated."

He couldn't help but laugh. "That's what I wanted to do all along."

"You played me," she told him, wagging her finger at him but apparently unable to keep from smiling. "But that's okay. I'll get it next time."

"I'll hold you to that." Still smiling, he leaned back. "I'm just glad you agree there will be a next time."

Genna didn't respond. Instead, she glanced up at him through her lashes and smiled.

He decided to take that as a yes.

SITTING ACROSS FROM Parker Colton at one of the newest and trendiest restaurants in town, Genna felt rejuvenated. Whether from her brief nap or simply due to his presence, she wasn't sure. Either way, she felt more alive in this moment than she had since the kiss. And there it was again. *The Kiss.* An action she should have regretted but instead wanted to repeat. And more.

Parker wanted more, too. She could tell from the heat in his gaze when he looked at her, the way she caught him studying her when he thought she wouldn't notice. She had no idea what to make of the chemistry between them, but she could no longer deny it existed.

Part of her wanted to see where it led. But she loved her job. She really hadn't thought she'd find something she enjoyed that paid so well. And if she and Parker developed a relationship and it went south, then she'd lose her job.

The question she needed to answer was if she wanted him enough to risk that.

Which is why she hadn't responded when he'd hinted that he wanted a "next time."

The waitress arrived to take their order. Shaking her head, Genna gestured toward Parker, letting him order what rolls they'd share. She'd never have been able to decide anyway. All of them sounded amazing.

Taking another small sip of her wine, she studied the handsome man across from her. With his tousled mane of sun-streaked hair and bright blue eyes, he drew more than his fair share of glances from women walking by.

He looked both comfortable in his skin and at one with the outdoors. The kind of man who knew how to be gentle yet would place himself between her and a pack of hungry wolves and fight them off with his bare hands.

And in bed... A flash of heat shot through her entire body. Despite how much time had passed since they'd shared a bed and their bodies, she didn't think she'd ever forget how his lovemaking had made her feel.

Blinking, she realized Parker had tilted his head and was regarding her with a quizzical expression. "Are you all right?" he asked. "You look like you went very far away just now."

Since she definitely couldn't tell him what she'd been thinking, she simply shrugged.

The first of the sushi rolls arrived. One entrée had been arranged into an elaborate tower of sushi. "That looks too beautiful to eat," she said.

He grinned. "Not for me." To prove his point, he plucked one off the tower and plopped it into his mouth. Rolling his eyes, he made sounds of appreciation as he chewed.

What could she do but laugh and then try it herself?

They ate and talked and ate some more. She finished her wine and switched to hot tea. When all the platters of sushi had arrived, she'd figured there wouldn't be any possible way they'd eat it all. Turns out, she was wrong.

Replete, they passed up the waitress's offering of saki. When the check came, Parker paid. "Are you ready to go?" he asked.

So full, she could barely move, Genna nodded. She figured she'd waddle out to his truck and hope she didn't fall asleep on the way home.

"I feel like we kind of gorged ourselves on sushi," she mused.

Her comment made him grin. "I love watching you eat."

Unsure how to take his comment, she cocked her head. "What do you mean?"

Leaning in, he lowered his voice. "It's sexy as hell."

A jolt of pure lust lanced through her. To hide it, she looked down, fiddled with her napkin and her empty wineglass.

He held out his arm and she took it.

The simple act of being close to him kept her heart racing, though she hoped he couldn't tell. As they walked to his truck, her thoughts were a jumbled mess. Should she invite him in? Suggest a nightcap? Or maybe instead of taking her home, should she see if he might want to go someplace for a drink?

In the end, she decided to let him take her home. Then, depending on whether or not he acted reluctant to leave, she'd play it by ear.

When they pulled up into her driveway, he shifted into Park and killed the engine. "I'll walk you up to your front door," he said, his tone leaving no room for disagreement. "I want to make sure your new alarm system is working before I head home."

Hiding her disappointment, she slowly nodded. "Thanks. I appreciate that."

Using her key, she unlocked the front door. Immediately,

her alarm began beeping. She hurried over to the keypad and keyed in her code to stop it. Turning, she eyed Parker standing near the threshold, as if reluctant to enter.

What the heck. She decided she might as well go for it. "Do you want to have a drink before you go?"

His easy smile once again kindled that spark low in her belly. "Normally, I'd love to. But I know you're exhausted. How about I take a rain check on that drink? I'll see you tomorrow when we drive out to Valdez."

"Sounds good." Despite it being anything but, she kept her tone light. Walking him out, she stood in the doorway and watched as he got into his truck.

His taillights had just vanished from view when her phone rang. Her mother. She stepped back inside, closed and locked the door before answering. "Hi, Mom."

"Why didn't you call and tell me about the break-in?" her mother demanded. "I had to hear it from Gladys. I called her a few minutes ago to catch up and she told me."

Proving once again how efficiently gossip spread in a small town.

"Honestly, I haven't had time," Genna said. "I had to work, and then schedule an appointment to get the front door repaired. The good news—that's done. I also had an alarm system installed."

For once, her mother was speechless. "You what?" she finally asked. Then, before Genna could answer, she turned and told Genna's father. "I'm putting the phone on speaker, dear," she said.

"Ok, Mom. Hi, Dad."

"I think you should close up the house and come stay with us in Hawaii," her father said, his gruff voice tinged with concern.

Surprised, Genna wasn't sure how to respond.

"I do, too," her mother said. "It's not safe for you there. I understand a fifth body was discovered."

Though Genna had always wanted to see Hawaii, leaving Shelby now would feel too much like fleeing. Which is exactly what she'd done when she'd left Anchorage as soon as her divorce had been finalized. Plus, she loved her job. Finally, she had to admit the thought of never seeing Parker again made her stomach hurt.

"I feel relatively safe," Genna said. And then she explained all the measures RTA had taken to ensure their female employees were never at risk.

"That's great, honey," her mom replied. "But someone broke into the house. You live there alone. How do you know that this Fiancée Killer isn't targeting you?"

The notion sent a shiver up Genna's spine. "I don't," she admitted. "But if it makes you feel better, I'm driving out to Valdez to visit the animal shelter. I've been wanting a dog for a while."

"A dog?" Both her parents spoke at once, sounding dismayed. They'd never been the kind of people to have pets.

"Yes. I'd like to adopt a large dog in need of a good home. Not only will he and I keep each other company, but he'll also be an added deterrent if anyone tries to break in here again."

"That does make sense," her mom said slowly. "Just don't let it on the furniture."

"Of course not," Genna lied. "Anyway, it was great to hear from you both. I promise to keep you posted."

"And check in more," her father said, his voice stern. "Your mother and I worry."

"I know you do. And I love you for it," Genna replied. "But please, try to understand. I'm just now finding my

feet after the divorce. I don't want to go somewhere else and start all over yet again."

"Well, if you change your mind, you're always welcome here." Her mom sounded a bit teary.

"I will." Ending the call, Genna swallowed past the lump in her throat.

The rest of the night, Genna found herself jumping at every little sound. She set the alarm as soon as darkness fell, well before bedtime. Turning the TV on despite the fact that she felt too restless to sit down and watch anything, she found herself constantly picking up her phone. Hoping Parker would text or, even better, call.

Even though they were riding into Valdez together tomorrow, tonight she really needed to hear his voice. Quickly scrolling to his contact info, she pressed the button to call him.

When he answered on the second ring, her heart lurched. "Hey," she managed, feeling like a fool.

"Hey, yourself," he replied. How he managed to make two simple words sound so sexy, she had no idea.

"I just wanted to firm up our plans for tomorrow," she managed to say.

"I figured." His easy response went a long way toward settling her nerves. "What time does the shelter open?"

"Eleven," she replied. "They're open until four thirty."

"I'll see you at ten thirty," he said. "Sleep well."

She told him the same and then ended the call.

As she got ready for bed, to her relief, she realized she felt drowsy. Crawling in between the sheets, she switched off her lamp and hoped to fall asleep quickly.

A sound woke her, dragging her out of a deep slumber in the darkest part of the night. Sitting upright, she listened. Nothing. Then, reminding herself that she had an alarm

system now, she put her head back on the pillow and tried to go back to sleep.

Just as she'd started to drift off, the loud shriek of her alarm had her jumping up. She started to turn on the light, but realized that if someone had actually broken into her house, that might make it easier for them to locate her.

Sixty seconds seemed to take forever. She thumbed down the volume on her phone, so when the monitoring company called, the intruder wouldn't hear. She wasn't sure if she should answer or not since she wanted them to call the police.

Halfway through her waiting, her mind still slightly groggy from sleep, she realized she should call 9-1-1. She did that and told the dispatcher in a quiet voice that she thought someone was inside her house.

A loud clatter from the living room made her freeze. "There's definitely someone here," she murmured. "They haven't turned on any lights so far. I'm hiding in my bedroom in the dark."

"Can you get out?" the dispatcher asked. "As in, leave now?"

Since to do that she'd have to go through the living room, she answered no. "Just send someone right away. I'm worried it might be the Fiancée Killer."

"We have officers on the way," the dispatcher said. "Please stay on the line until they arrive."

Another sound, louder and closer, nearly made Genna drop the phone. Juggling it to keep it from hitting the floor, she accidentally hit the button to end the call. Aware they'd call back, she struggled not to hyperventilate. Now, she actually found herself regretting not taking her parents up on their offer to go to Hawaii.

Parker. She sent him a quick text, figuring he was probably asleep.

Someone is in the house. Alarm went off and I can hear them. Called 911. Police are on the way.

Not expecting a reply, she set the phone down on the carpet. As expected, the police dispatcher called back, but Genna didn't answer. Instead, she let the call go to voicemail.

Sirens sounded, still distant, but clearly getting closer. Though she wondered why they didn't try to be stealthier, she was grateful for the prompt response. Every breath, every heartbeat, the way she tensed at every sound, and how impossible it was to keep herself from trembling, spoke to her absolute terror.

Flashing lights reflecting on the wall announced the police car's arrival. Another loud crash from downstairs and then she heard the police rapping hard on her front door.

Should she risk leaving her hiding place to let them in? Since, otherwise, she knew they'd likely damage her brand-new front door, she decided to take the chance.

As she sprinted from her bedroom down the hallway to the front of the house, she prayed no one would reach out from the shadows and grab her.

Flicking on the light, she opened the front door. Two uniformed officers stood on her front porch, and as she stepped aside so they could enter, another squad car pulled up, lights flashing.

As she quickly explained the situation, the second officers joined the first two. Asking her to stay put, they told her they'd conduct a thorough search of her house.

"Genna?" Parker sprinted up the front steps and swept her into his arms. "Are you all right?"

Clinging to him, she nodded. "Now I am. They're search-

ing my house. The alarm went off right after I heard a loud sound. It must have been someone breaking in."

"And they had no idea you'd installed an alarm."

Despite him holding her, she couldn't stop trembling. "Why?" she asked, not really expecting an answer. "Why is someone doing this to me?"

"I don't know." Pressing a kiss against her temple, he smoothed the hair away from her face.

A sound made her back out of Parker's arms.

Two of the police officers had returned. "Looks like the intruder busted in your back door. And, likely, that's how they left. It's sitting wide open."

Not another broken door.

"Can you tell us if anything is missing?" the second officer asked. "Would you mind just taking a quick look around?"

At first, she couldn't seem to make herself move. But then Parker took her hand and squeezed her fingers. "Come on," he said. "You can do this."

Slowly, she nodded. "You're right," she replied. "I can."

With him by her side, she walked through her parents' house. Once again, everything appeared undisturbed. "I don't think anything is missing," she said. "Which means the intruder…"

She couldn't finish the sentence.

"We'll need you to sign this, ma'am," the first officer said. "We'll file a report once you do. My suggestion to you is to install a stronger lock on that back door. A dead bolt, like the one you have up front. But for now, it should be secure enough."

"Thank you." She took his tablet and signed, deciding not to mention that "secure enough" had done nothing to

keep the intruder out. "I'll get that done first thing in the morning."

Parker squeezed her fingers again. "I'll do it for you."

Grateful, she thanked him.

Together, they watched the police officers leave.

No way did she want Parker to go and leave her there alone. In fact, she didn't know that she could ever spend another night alone in this house again.

Chapter Seven

Glancing at Genna, standing ramrod-straight and clearly struggling to hold it together, Parker clamped his jaw shut. He hated nothing worse than seeing a strong, capable woman like her reduced to fighting back tears.

When she raised her gaze to meet his, he saw the shattered emotions and terror in her eyes. Immediately, he pulled her close, noting how fragile her slender body felt. Trembling, she clung to him.

"I can't," she muttered, against his chest. "I just can't."

Unsure what she meant, he made a sympathetic sound and continued to rub her back. He'd offer her comfort until she let him know she didn't need it any longer.

And, despite the heat simmering in his blood as he held her close, he refused to take advantage of her distress. Not in any way, shape, or form.

When she pulled out of his arms, he quickly released her. Stepping back, he jammed his hands into his pockets so he wouldn't touch her. "Are you going to be okay?" he asked gently.

"No." She swallowed hard. "I'm not. In fact, I have a huge favor to ask. Would you mind if I stay at your house again?"

"Of course, I don't mind," he replied. "You're welcome to stay as long as you need."

"Thank you." Glancing around as if she expected some-one to step out from the shadows, she met his eyes. "Until the police figure out who is trying to break into my house and why, I'm going to take you up on it."

Though his first reaction—joy—made him want to grin, he knew that was the last thing she needed right now. Instead, he gave her a grave nod. "Why don't you go get packed? Take as much as you need, but remember, we can always come back and get more clothes if you need them."

"Thank you." She didn't bother to hide her relief. "Give me a few minutes. Go ahead and help yourself to a drink or snack or whatever you want."

That said, she hurried out of the room.

When she returned a few minutes later, she not only had her usual backpack, but pulled a medium-sized duffel bag with wheels. "I think I got everything," she said. Her tremulous smile tugged at his heart.

"Let me help you." He grabbed her duffel, which she released without protest. Outside, he waited while she used her remote to set the alarm before locking the front door.

He waited while she got into her vehicle and started it, then jumped into his. She followed him to his place. He drove in silence, matching the quiet darkness of the middle of the night. The streets were mostly deserted, the stoplights flashing red.

When they arrived at his place, she got out of her car slowly, almost as if she were sore and hurting. Parking, he grabbed her duffel while she shouldered her backpack, and he led the way into his house.

Inside, he walked down the hall to the guest bedroom. "I washed the sheets and remade the bed," he told her, turning on the light.

"Thanks." She took a step past him into the room. Look-

ing around, she exhaled. "You know, someday, if you want, I can help you with a little interior decorating," she said, looking around the impersonal setup.

He chuckled. "You don't like hotel room chic?"

"It's okay," she said, her voice cautious. "I'm sorry, I'm being rude. You've been kind enough to let me stay here and then I critique your décor."

His chest squeezed. He couldn't help but notice the way her hands still trembled as she set her backpack on the bed.

"It's fine," he replied. "I admit, I hired a designer to do some of the house, but only focused on the areas where I spent a lot of time. Until you, no one has used this guest room, so there hasn't been much of a need to spruce it up."

Nodding, she covered her mouth to mask a yawn. He took that as his cue to go. "Get some rest," he said. "We'll sleep in since we're off. We can head up to Valdez once we're up."

She didn't even try to disguise her exhaustion or her relief. "Thank you," she murmured. "I'll see you in the morning."

When he stepped into the hall, she closed the door behind him. He stood out there in the hall for a minute, realizing how lucky she'd been. If not for her new alarm, the outcome could have been a lot worse.

The only reason her earlier text had pulled him from sleep had been that his smartwatch had vibrated. Late-night texts were rare and usually only brought bad news. Which meant, of course, that he'd sat up, turned on his lamp, and read it.

Pure adrenaline had jolted through him the instant he'd seen her words. Without conscious thought, he'd pulled on some clothes, grabbed his truck keys and sped to her house. He'd known better than to call to ask her to clarify. She'd said someone was in her house. He hadn't wanted to take a chance of giving away her hiding place.

He got undressed, slid into his bed and turned off the lights. She was safe and that's all that mattered. Except, he couldn't stop thinking of her, alone and frightened, trying to sleep in the room down the hall.

Finally, he somehow managed to drift off to sleep.

A tortured scream woke him. *Genna!* Leaping out of bed, jumped into the jeans he'd tossed on the floor and sprinted down the hall to the guest room.

He found her sitting up in bed with the light on, wide-eyed, her arms wrapped around herself. Even from the doorway, he could see how violently she was shaking.

"I'm sorry," she stammered. "With everything that's been happening, I think this triggered some past trauma."

Aching to comfort her, he moved closer and sat carefully on the edge of the bed. When she reached for him, he froze.

"I'm giving your words back to you," she whispered. "If anything happens between us, I'll have to initiate it. Well, I am. Now." She pulled his face down for a kiss. "Make love to me," she murmured. "Make love to me now. I need to feel alive."

Though it crossed his mind that he might be dreaming, the press of her sweet and perfect body against his set him aflame. When she pressed her lips against his, he kissed her back with reckless abandon.

The savage intensity of her response brought instant, nearly violent arousal.

Still kissing her, he struggled to maintain control. First, he managed to grab his wallet, fumbling to retrieve the condom. Once he'd put that on, he looked up to find her watching, passion clouding her gaze.

Climbing back into her bed, he slid his hands under her T-shirt, across her silken belly, down the curve of her hip, to find her ready for him.

One touch and she clenched against his finger, her entire body shuddering. Aware he needed to slow things down, he helped her to pull her T-shirt over her head and then stepped back to remove his boxers.

Pupils huge and dark, she looked on as he undressed. He liked that she'd left the light on so he could watch her. Crawling back into her bed, he covered her body with his. Flesh against flesh, he pressed his rigid arousal into her thigh and slanted his mouth over hers.

Wild, untamed, when their mouths met, they devoured each other. "Inside me," she rasped, guiding him to her. "I need you inside me."

She was ready for him. As her body sheathed his, he lost the last shredded remnants of his remaining self-control. Passion pounded with each thrust. Her eager response matched his in savage intensity.

They were one in that moment. Joined in more than just their bodies, he felt that zing of connection between their souls.

Certain that she felt it, too, he managed to hold back his release until she shuddered, her body clenching around his.

Only then did he let himself go. When he did, pure and explosive pleasure rocked his world, the intensity unlike anything he'd ever felt.

Except once before, with her. Only with her. As he gave himself to her, surrendering, an amazing feeling of completeness washed over him.

Sated, they clung to each other while their rapid heartbeats slowed and the sheen of perspiration cooled and dried from their skin. She curled into him, a perfect fit, making him realize there would be no coming back from this. His life would never be the same again. He could only hope she felt the same way.

How could she not? Both physically and mentally, they'd stumbled across something rare and special, a once-in-a-lifetime chance at love.

He fell asleep with a smile on his face, Genna beside him in the bed.

The next morning when he woke, he slipped from the bed, leaving her asleep and still tangled up in the sheets. He turned once and looked back at her, his heart full.

They made a good couple. She might not realize it yet, but he had a sneaky suspicion that if they could manage to work things out, a long and happy road lay ahead for them.

Whether or not they discussed this now or later, he decided he wouldn't press her. Instead, he'd follow her lead.

After a quick shower, Parker headed to the kitchen to make coffee. Then he started breakfast, figuring he'd make something basic and hopefully she'd like it. Bacon, eggs and toast. Plus orange juice, if she wanted it.

Whistling while he worked, he realized he could get used to this. Though he knew she intended her stay to be temporary, just until whoever had been breaking into her house was caught, he couldn't help but hope she'd be there a while. Even though he fully intended to put the pressure on the Shelby police force to make sure they caught the guy. No one, especially not a woman he cared for, should be made to feel unsafe in their own home.

PLEASANTLY SORE, Genna opened her eyes and reached for Parker, only to find his side of the bed empty. As she sat up, she realized she smelled bacon and coffee, two of her absolute favorite morning things in the entire world.

Locating her discarded T-shirt, she pulled it over her head. She grabbed a change of clothes from her duffel and went down the hallway to the bathroom to shower.

Standing under the hot spray, she wondered how she should act around Parker now that they'd made love. Could they go back to the casual friendship they'd begun to enjoy? Did she even want to?

And what about her job? If the two of them started some kind of relationship, would her employment status suffer if it didn't work out? While she hated to be pessimistic about their chances, she also had to be realistic. Her husband, the man who'd pledged "'til death do us part," had cheated on her with a woman she'd considered her best friend.

Not only that, but things had been rocky between her and Chad for a while before they'd ended. Which was an understatement. No way did she want to go through anything like that ever again.

She decided to be upfront and let Parker know she wasn't in the market for any kind of relationship. Though she wasn't fond of the term, if they could make a friends-with-benefits situation work, she'd be open to that. But nothing more.

Decision made, her nerves settled. She dressed, combed through her wet hair and headed to the kitchen to see what he'd rustled up for breakfast.

The moment she entered, he turned and smiled. She felt the power of that smile all the way to the soles of her feet. For a split second, her resolve wavered.

"Good morning," he said. "Did you sleep well?"

Heaven help her, but she blushed. "I did," she replied, her voice surprisingly steady. "How about you?"

"Fine." His intent gaze seemed to peer into her soul. Her stomach turned over and her knees turned to mush.

"I still can't have a relationship," she blurted. "I'm just not ready."

"I understand," he said. Since she'd expected him to argue, she wasn't sure how to react.

"My marriage was pretty awful," she finally admitted, turning her back to him while she grabbed a cup of coffee. Bracing herself for a bunch of questions, she carried her drink to the table and took a seat, all without looking at him.

Finally, when he didn't probe, she raised her head. "I'm sorry."

"Don't be."

She had no idea how to respond, so she didn't.

"Do you want to talk about it?" he asked, his gaze steady.

To her surprise, she realized she did. "I met Chad in college," she said, sitting back and taking a sip of her coffee. "At first, he was everything I wanted in a partner. He was attentive, considerate, and he seemed to anticipate my every need."

She sighed and took another drink. "Later, I learned that's something narcissists do. It's called love bombing. I didn't know that then, though."

"How long were you married?" he asked, his voice as gentle as his expression.

"Seven years." She didn't even have to think about it. "Once I had that ring on my finger, he changed. Or maybe he just allowed his true self to show."

Thinking of all his rules, his little punishments if she failed to follow them, and his escalating temper, along with all the insults and snide comments designed to put her down, she felt ashamed.

Something of her thoughts must have showed on her face.

"It's okay." Reaching out, he covered her hand with his. "You don't have to talk about it if you don't want to."

Eyeing the quietly handsome man across from her, she realized that she did. "He had anger issues," she said, waving her hand as if those simple words didn't convey a wealth of trauma.

Parker's jaw tightened. "Verbal or physical?"

"Both. I survived. But what matters is that I became a shadow of myself. Where once I'd been happy and outgoing, I withdrew inside." Her self-conscious laugh hid so many emotions; none of which she felt ready to reveal. "You wouldn't have recognized me. I was a docile, quiet person. Head down, withering away into a shell without any heart or soul."

Hand still on top of hers, he squeezed. "I'm glad you got out."

Those words had her lifting her chin. "I am, too. I suspect if I hadn't, I wouldn't be here on this earth any longer."

He swallowed hard. "I'm sorry you went through that."

"I am, too, but I'm not proud that I stayed so long. Looking back, it's unbelievable that it took him having an affair with my best friend to make me leave. All the abuse, the way he treated me, and it took his cheating to finally gave me the courage to leave."

Hearing herself say it out loud, she had to shake her head. "Actually, I didn't have the energy to leave. I learned in therapy that depression can do that."

Getting up the courage to meet his gaze, when he only nodded instead of commenting, she felt grateful.

"Anyway, long story short..." She gave a wry smile. "That's why I'm not in the market for a relationship right now. Maybe not ever. I think I might be too damaged."

Bracing herself, she waited for Parker to explain that he wasn't that guy and would never treat her like that. If he did, that'd mean he completely missed the point.

Instead, he simply nodded again. "That's understandable. Thank you for trusting me enough to share that with me."

Dumbfounded, Genna got up to make another cup of coffee, certain words would fail her.

"Do you still want to drive up to Valdez and check out the animal shelter?" he asked.

She waited until she'd finished fixing her coffee before she turned. "I don't know. Maybe getting a dog right now isn't the best idea, since I'm your temporary houseguest."

"I think you should still consider it," he said. "But, of course, that's completely up to you."

Sipping her second cup of coffee, she thought about it for a moment. "We can go look," she finally conceded. "But I doubt I'll bring one home. The timing is wrong."

Though he shrugged, something in his gaze told her he believed she'd go, take one look at some poor dog in need, and fall instantly in love with it. The old Genna definitely would have done such a thing. The woman she used to be, who'd believed in happy endings and rainbows, trusted her heart and acted on impulse, believing everything would work out in the end.

Not anymore. Now she knew better.

"What about you?" she challenged. "You said you'd been wanting to get a dog. Maybe this is your chance."

He grinned. "Could be, you never know. Let me get these dishes cleaned up and we'll head out."

"I'll get them," she offered. "You cooked, I can clean."

Though he appeared uncertain, he finally gave in.

It only took her a few minutes to rinse everything and put the dishes in the dishwasher. When she finished, she dried her hands off on a towel and turned to find him eyeing her. The intensity in his gaze sent a bolt of desire through her.

"Ready to go?" he asked, a slight smile curving his mouth as if he knew her thoughts.

"Sure. I'm driving." She already had her keys in her hand. "Since I invited you to go with me."

He nodded. "Sounds good. Lead the way."

Once they were settled in her car, she glanced at him in the passenger seat, unaccountably nervous. The drive would be a straightforward one, with a lot of beautiful scenery in between the two towns. There were two ways to get there. The quickest route was inland, but she preferred the meandering road that went by the water. She waited until they'd turned off Parker's street before asking him which route he'd like to take.

"That's up to you," he answered immediately. "You're driving. I'm good with whatever way you choose."

Since she was in a bit of a hurry, she chose the more direct route.

The City of Valdez Animal Shelter sat on a picturesque road with jagged mountain peaks behind it. The smallish wooden building had been painted blue, she guessed in an effort to make it look more cheerful. A white-lettered sign hung over the double glass doors, advertising pet food and supplies. Only one other car sat in the parking lot.

"Did you check online to see what kind of dogs they have available?" Parker asked once they'd pulled up to the building and parked.

"I meant to, but with everything that happened, I forgot," she admitted. "Since I'm not ready to adopt today, I guess that doesn't matter. We'll just go inside and take a look around."

"Okay, but before we do, what kind of dog are you looking for?"

She shrugged. "I don't know. Something big and intimidating, but secretly gentle and kind. In my situation, I need the kind of dog that would make an intruder think twice before breaking in to my house."

"That makes sense." He got out of the car. "Let's go see what they have."

The busy shelter worker hurried up front when they entered. "Are you looking for a lost pet?" she asked, tucking a wayward strand of gray hair behind her ear. "If so, I'm going to need you to fill out some paperwork."

Genna found her voice. "No. Actually, we came to take a look at the dogs available for adoption."

This made the woman beam. "Perfect. Just go through that door. All the dogs in those kennels are available. Just holler if you need any help." That said, she hurried off.

"Let's do this." Parker held out his hand. Without thinking, Genna took it. Together they went through the door.

They stepped onto a concrete walkway dividing two long rows of metal kennels. Immediately, all the dogs started barking. There was a smell that no amount of cleaning could erase, which made Genna sigh. Most of the cages were occupied, and dogs of all sizes, breeds and colors had rushed to the front, begging for attention.

Still clutching Parker's hand, she stood frozen, unable to make herself move forward.

"Are you all right?" he asked, looking down at her.

"I think so." Wide-eyed, she took a deep breath. "I don't know what's wrong with me."

"It's okay to feel bad for the dogs," he said, his voice gentle. "And just because you don't plan on adopting one today, doesn't mean you can't visit with them while you're here. I'm sure they enjoy the attention."

Though she nodded, she still couldn't make her feet move. Only Parker's gentle tug on her hand had her taking steps forward.

There were a few large dogs, though most of them seemed to be medium-sized. Some barked furiously as she approached, others leapt onto the metal mesh, desperate to be noticed. As she moved down the row of cages, she saw

black dogs and brown ones, white-and-tan and multicolored. Most had short hair and short snouts, though she noticed one or two with long fur.

Releasing her hand, Parker stopped in front of more than one cage, visiting with its occupant. While he was having a conversation with a huge black dog, she spotted something in the corner of the kennel at the very end of the row.

She hurried down to get a better look. Inside, she saw a small dog cowering in the corner. She couldn't tell if it was a male or a female. Its long white fur looked dirty, tangled and matted. When she approached, it didn't get up to greet her or even acknowledge her presence in any way. Head down, the poor animal appeared defeated, without hope. Something about that reminded Genna of the way she'd felt after her divorce.

Telling herself that this small creature was the opposite of what she needed and that she'd decided she wouldn't be adopting a dog today, she turned away. Further down the aisle, Parker had stopped to converse with a shaggy brown dog of unknown age.

Just then, the shelter worker appeared. "Find anything you like?" she asked, smiling. "We have something for everyone."

Once again, Genna glanced back at the forlorn little dog. Almost as if the words were being pulled out of her, she heard herself asking "What about that one? What's his or her story?"

"That's June Bug," the woman answered, her smile widening. "She's a staff favorite. We all love her. She's a poodle/sheltie mix, spayed, and around five years old. Her owner died and the family didn't want her, so they brought her here."

Hearing her name, the little dog lifted her head. Her sad eyes momentarily brightened.

"Most people come in here wanting a large dog," the worker continued. "It being Alaska and all that. Sadly, she's become used to being overlooked."

"That's a shame." Still, Genna hesitated. She, too, had thought she preferred a big dog. Mainly for protection. Yet somehow she felt an overwhelming need to help this girl.

"Would you like to meet her?"

Genna nodded, at first still a little unsure, and then absolutely certain. "I would," she replied. "Please."

Down at the end of the aisle, Parker continued his dialogue with one of the other dogs. If he had any idea what Genna was considering, he gave no sign. Either that, or she figured he was giving her space.

The worker unlocked the kennel. Though June Bug raised her head, she didn't move from her spot in the corner.

"You can go on in," the woman said, waving her hand. "Spend some time with her, get to know each other. Just go ahead and call me if you need me."

With that, the worker moved off.

Slowly, Genna opened the door to the kennel. Though June Bug stayed in her spot, she kept her stare fixed on Genna.

About a foot away, Genna stopped and dropped down to her haunches. "Hey there, pretty girl. How'd you like to get busted out of here today?"

Gaze locked on Genna, June Bug wagged her tail.

"But you're going to have to get up first," Genna continued, keeping her voice soft. "Will you please come over here and let me pet you."

To her disbelief, the little dog got to her feet and hesitantly came over. She sniffed Genna, her tail still wagging.

Deciding to take a chance, Genna gently picked June Bug up, holding her close while crooning to her. "It's going to be all right, I promise."

June Bug tilted her head and then, as if she understood Genna's words, she licked her on the cheek.

That sealed the deal. "You're my dog now," Genna said. Still holding the little dog, Genna got to her feet and stepped out of the kennel.

"What do you have there?" Parker asked, still hanging out with the dog at the end of the row. "Is that a puppy?"

He sounded so horrified she had to laugh. "No, she's around five years old. Her owner died and the family didn't want her. Isn't she precious?"

"She is," he admitted, moving closer so he could get a better look. "But I thought you were wanting a dog for protection."

"I was." Trying not to be defensive, she gazed down at June Bug. "But this one needs me. And I need her."

Studying her face, Parker nodded. "You fell in love."

Surprised, she held his gaze. Instead of condemnation or mockery, she saw only understanding. "I fell in love," she repeated.

"Then she's coming home with us," he said. "Let's go fill out the paperwork. What's her name?"

He chuckled when she told him. "That suits her."

At the front desk, the shelter worker beamed when she realized Genna intended to adopt little June Bug. Once Genna signed the forms and paid the fee, she received some papers showing June Bug's vaccination history.

"Do you have dog food and treats? A collar and leash?" the worker asked. "We sell all of that here to make things easier."

Since Genna had never owned a dog before, she asked for

recommendations. Once all the necessities had been purchased, she put June Bug's new collar on her before carrying her out to her car. Parker trailed behind, carrying the shopping bags.

"Are you going to let her walk?" he asked once they reached the parking lot. "Maybe she needs to go before she gets in the car."

"Good point." Walking to a grassy area at the edge of the pavement, she clipped the brand-new leash to June Bug's collar and gently set her down. "Go potty," she said.

Tail wagging, the little dog pranced over and took care of her business. When she was done, Genna praised her and picked her up again. "Would you mind driving?" she asked Parker. "That way I can hold her."

"Sure." He smiled and held out his hand for the keys. "Let's take her home."

Chapter Eight

Glad he had to keep his gaze mostly on the road, Parker couldn't resist occasionally glancing over at Genna, crooning sweet nothings to her new pet. The little dog appeared to be eating it up, tail constantly wagging, eyes bright and alert. If he didn't know better, Parker would have sworn June Bug was smiling.

At first glance, the dog wasn't much to look at. Scruffy and in need of a bath, she looked more like a gremlin-type creature than a pet. But despite her lack of conventional cuteness, the tiny animal had a sweet vulnerability to her. Parker felt certain she'd blossom with a little love and TLC. And he knew Genna would be just the person to give that to her.

As he drove, with the beautiful woman radiating happiness sitting in the seat next to him, he realized he'd never been happier. Sure, he loved his job and the house he'd renovated until it completely suited him. But he'd never realized that something had been missing, the difference between simply living a good life and living one that actually felt complete.

Damn. Hell of a revelation to have about a woman who'd made it clear she wasn't looking for anything serious.

When they finally turned onto his street, he realized he'd been so lost in his thoughts that he had very little memory of most of the drive home. Once or twice, Genna had caught him looking over at her and her tremulous smile had made it difficult to breathe.

"What was your life like living in Anchorage," he asked, partly to pass the time but also because he genuinely wanted to know.

She grimaced. "Do you mean while Chad and I were married? Or after?"

"After," he replied. Since he couldn't bear the thought of her married to another man, especially one who had abused her, he wanted to hear how she'd rebuilt her life.

"I rented an apartment," she said. "It was new and modern and close to the center of town. It didn't take long to realize Chad and my former best friend Ann intended to make my life hell."

"Why?" This made no sense to him. "You gave him his divorce. Your so-called friend got what she wanted, your former husband. I don't understand why they'd feel the need to bother you."

When she spoke, her voice sounded level and matter-of-fact. "I can talk about this now," she said. "Because the time I spent in therapy helped me deal with it and dispel any lingering darkness. Chad lied to Ann. He told her I wanted to win him back, that I still considered him mine."

She sighed, glancing down at her sleeping dog before looking back at him. "Ann believed him to the point that she started harassing me. This gave Chad a kick, so he encouraged it. He even called me several times to gloat. Getting away from them was my only recourse, especially when Ann broke into my apartment and destroyed most of my belongings."

"Then you came back home," he said.

"Yes. I came home. Evidently, this made Ann realize I truly wasn't after my ex, because neither of them has attempted to contact me again."

"Did you change your phone number?" he asked.

"No. But I did block both of them. If they'd gone on to get disposable phones or something, then I would have changed my number. But as it turned out, I didn't have to."

If he hadn't been driving, Parker would have kissed her. She'd been through so much. And yet she'd managed to continue making a new life for herself and grow stronger.

"To be honest," Genna continued. "When I saw the broken door to my house, my first thought was Ann. But then I realized she would have had to drive all this way, or fly, and find a place to stay overnight, just to harass me—when I've made it as clear as I can that I have no interest in getting Chad back. It doesn't make sense."

He agreed and said so. "But then we have to figure out who actually did try to break into your place. Twice."

Stroking her little dog's fur, she nodded. "It's like choosing the best of two evils. I have to say I'd rather deal with Ann than the Fiancée Killer."

This made him chuckle. He decided not to tell her what he'd like to do to the man to whom she'd once been married. Like it hadn't been enough to cheat on Genna with a woman she'd considered her best friend, but then to taunt and badger her after she'd given him the divorce he'd wanted?

He managed to bring his anger under control after focusing on driving and taking several deep breaths. Genna didn't need to know how her words had gutted him.

As he pulled up into his driveway, he realized little June Bug had fallen asleep. Genna gazed down at the dog, her eyes shining with love.

"Isn't she just perfect?" she asked, clearly not really expecting an answer.

Nodding, he went around and opened her door, ready to help her out. Instead, she waved him off, moving carefully so as not to disturb June Bug.

He grabbed the bags with the food, bowls, toys and the fluffy round dog bed she'd purchased and hurried ahead of her to unlock the front door.

"Thank you," Genna murmured. As she moved past him, the little dog raised her head and looked around with interest. "I want to give her a spa day first thing."

A little mystified, he locked up behind them before asking her what she meant.

"You know, a bath, brushing her down, making her look beautiful. I bought some scented dog shampoo. Would you mind bringing it to me?" Without waiting for an answer, she headed into the bathroom. A moment later, he heard the sound of her filling the tub, all the while keeping up a steady conversation with June Bug.

He unpacked the supplies, located the bottle of coconut and passion fruit dog shampoo, and took it to the bathroom. She thanked him and he retreated, thinking of all the other dogs he'd seen in the shelter. They'd been all kinds, big and small, young and old. The one thing they'd all had in common was their desperate need for attention. Many still had remnants of hope shining in their eyes, though others appeared to have long ago given up.

In one way or another, people had failed them. They all needed homes.

Parker had been drawn to an elderly Lab mix in the very last run. Silver decorated the dog's black muzzle and when Parker had opened the run to go inside, the dog had been slightly unsteady on his feet, no doubt from lack of exer-

cise. He'd still wagged his tail though, the entire time he sniffed Parker from head to toe.

Reading the kennel card been posted on the outside of the cage, Parker saw that his name was Revis and he was eleven years old. His owners had surrendered him because they'd no longer had time to devote to a dog they'd had since he'd been a puppy. While Parker felt sure that each of the other dogs had their own sad stories, for the life of him, he'd never understand how people could treat a canine family member that way. Never.

By the time Genna emerged with her clean and completely transformed pup, Parker had reached his decision.

"I'm going back to the animal shelter," he told her, glancing at his watch. "Since they're open until four, I have time."

"Why?" she asked, clearly not understanding. "What did we forget?"

"My dog," he replied, smiling. "He's an older black Lab whose owners no longer had time for him."

Genna's eyes widened. Both she and her new pet looked at him. Then she slowly nodded. "Go get him. June Bug and I can't wait to meet him."

Truck keys in hand, he dipped his chin. "I'll be back."

The drive seemed to take longer when he made it alone. Either that, or time stretched out because he was in a rush to get back to the shelter.

Halfway there, his phone rang. "Hey, Lakin. How are you?"

His sister chuckled. "I've never been better. What about you? How is Genna working out?"

He took a few minutes to tell her all about the multiple break-ins at Genna's place. "We still don't know who it is or why they're targeting her. She even had an alarm system installed, which helped alert the police."

"Wow." Lakin exhaled. "I wouldn't feel safe being in the house."

"She doesn't. That's why she's staying at my place."

"Say what?" Lakin sounded incredulous. "Whose idea was that?"

He felt slightly defensive, but had no idea why. "Mine. It's all aboveboard. She's using the guest room."

"The one that looks like a cheap hotel room?" Lakin asked, laughing.

He decided to ignore the dig. "Look, I'm just about to Valdez. I'm going to have to let you go."

"Valdez? Why are you doing there?"

Since he and his sister had very few secrets, he told her. "I'm adopting a dog."

And then, while she sputtered and demanded more details, he told her he'd pulled into the shelter parking lot and ended the call.

The same shelter worker sat at the front desk when he entered. Her brows rose. "I'm surprised to see you so soon," she said. "Is everything all right with little June Bug?"

"Yes, she's living the life. I'm not here about her. I came for Revis."

The woman's entire face lit up. "Seriously? He's the best dog."

Parker nodded. He thought of Genna's little pup. "I do need to know if Revis gets along with other dogs."

"He *loves* other dogs," the woman said. "Revis loves everything and everyone. He's one of the friendliest dogs I've ever seen. He couldn't be more perfect. People keep overlooking him because he's black and because he's older."

"Because he's black?"

"Yes. It's well known in rescue, though we're not exactly sure why. Some people associate the color with evil, like

black cats and bad luck. Often it's because they're difficult to photograph. Either way, people pass black animals up."

"Not this time," Parker replied. "I want to adopt him."

"You've just made my day. First little June Bug, who also is good with other dogs, and now Revis." Glowing, she went to her computer and printed off the paperwork. "I just need your signature. His adoption fee is reduced since he's a senior."

After signing and paying the fee, he purchased a collar and leash, as well as a large bag of senior kibble and a raised feeder with two bigger bowls. "Let me take these out to my truck and then I'll go back and get him," he said.

When he returned, the worker had fetched Revis herself. The big, black dog sat at her side, alert and watching the door, his long tail sweeping the floor.

"There he is," Parker said, feeling a rush of happiness. The instant he spoke, Revis climbed to his feet, his regal calmness at odds with the furious tail wagging.

"Let's put your new collar on you," he said, scratching Revis under the chin. Once he'd done that and attached the matching leash, the shelter worker removed the slip lead.

"Looks like you're all set to go," she said, still beaming. Then she crouched down and kissed the top of Revis's graying head. "Have a great rest of your life, sweet boy."

AFTER PARKER DROVE OFF, Genna sat down on the couch, still holding June Bug. Gazing down at her scruffy little dog, she had a brief moment of panic. What had she been thinking? She'd wanted to get a big, loud dog for protection. Instead, she'd let her heart overrule her common sense.

Just then June Bug raised her head and licked Genna's chin, her large brown eyes luminous. And Genna knew

she'd done the right thing. She and this scruffy little dog belonged together, no matter what.

Next to her on the sofa, with her head on Genna's leg, June Bug fell asleep. All of her previous tension appeared to have vanished from her small body. She felt, Genna realized, secure.

Then, curled up with her dog sleeping beside her, Genna allowed herself to doze off, too.

The sound of Parker opening the front door had her sitting up, rubbing her eyes. June Bug lifted her head and yawned, but apart from that, she barely stirred.

"Here we are," Parker said, grinning. "Revis, meet Genna and June Bug."

A stately black Lab with ancient eyes and silver sprinkled on his muzzle, walked at Parker's side. "I checked to make sure he likes other dogs," Parker said. "The lady at the shelter said he does. She also mentioned June Bug does, too."

The sound of the larger dog's toenails clicking on the wood floor finally got June Bug's attention. She sat up, her gaze locked on Revis, who was easily ten times her size. She whimpered, though judging by her alert posture, the sound was not from fear.

Immediately, spotting June Bug, the giant dog let out a low woof. Tail wagging, he took a few steps closer until he and the tiny dog were nose to nose. Parker kept him leashed, just in case, though Genna didn't fool herself by thinking he could do much if Revis decided to eat the smaller pup.

But both dog's tails were wagging and they genuinely seemed excited to meet one another. After a moment or two of sniffing, June Bug climbed back on top of Genna and fell back asleep. Revis sighed and laid down on the floor, his gaze fixed on the other dog.

"I think he's in love," Parker commented, smiling.

"Maybe so," Genna replied. "But who could blame him?" She grinned, petting June Bug's head. "If this first meet is anything to go by, I think they'll be getting along just fine."

"I agree." Parker sounded relieved. It dawned on her that he'd been really concerned that the two dogs wouldn't like each other. Since she and June Bug were simply guests in his home, if that turned out to be the case, she'd simply have no choice but to try to return to her own house. Even though the idea terrified her. Luckily, she didn't think that would be happening.

"My sister is probably going to be calling you," Parker said, his gaze alternating between the two dogs and her. "She seemed a little surprised to learn that you're staying here."

Genna couldn't help but laugh, imagining Lakin's reaction, especially after practically having to beg Genna to even consider working with Parker. "I bet she was," she said. "But I also have a feeling she understands. There's not a single woman in town who wouldn't get why I don't want to stay alone in my house when someone keeps trying to break in. And there also happens to be a serial killer lurking around town."

He nodded. "I agree. But that doesn't mean she doesn't want to tease you. She would have with me, but I told her I had to go and hung up."

"If I don't hear from her, I'll give her a call tomorrow," Genna said.

They had sandwiches for dinner. Genna ate on the couch with a very interested June Bug watching her every move. Revis stayed close to Parker, who'd announced his plans to keep the bigger dog in his room at night. She wondered if he'd be allowing Revis to sleep with him in his bed, like she planned to allow June Bug.

Either way, having two dogs would help make sure one

wound up in the other's room at night. Though Genna supposed this was a good thing, she couldn't help but feel a twinge of regret. But when she went to bed, having her little dog curled up by her helped.

The next day, though Parker had to go in to RTA since he'd been scheduled for a couple of tours, Genna had the day off. Two days in a row, which made her feel both decadent and guilty. She couldn't help but worry about how things would run while she wasn't there. Even though it had only been a short time since she'd started working there, she'd implemented a system. Everything ran like clockwork. Both the guests and all the other employees seemed happy.

As for Genna, she couldn't imagine a better job. Or better coworkers. If not for the break-ins at her house, she'd have to say her life felt pretty damn perfect.

Since she had the day to herself, she decided to stop by her house to make sure it was still secure. Since she'd activated the alarm system, she knew she'd get a notification if anyone set it off, but she'd feel better seeing everything with her own eyes.

Then she figured she'd go into town, maybe have lunch at one of the places with outdoor seating. Usually that meant dogs were allowed. And since she intended to take her new pet with her, finding that kind of place to eat would be necessary.

Getting up from the kitchen table, she carried her coffee mug and cereal bowl to the sink. June Bug immediately trotted after her. Everywhere Genna went, the little dog went, too. Genna had taken to calling her JB for short.

Which was why she totally understood Parker's decision to take Revis into work with him today. While the aging Lab might not be able to take part in some of the more strenuous hikes, she'd bet he'd be fine lounging around the office.

Once she'd cleaned up her dishes, Genna went to her bedroom and emptied out her largest tote bag. One of the benefits of June Bug being so small meant she'd be able to carry her around with her.

"This tote should do nicely," she said out loud. June Bug immediately began wagging her tail. With the bag on the bed, Genna picked up her little dog and set her in it. JB sniffed around and then sat. When she did that, she wasn't visible at all.

"Perfect," Genna said. "Are you ready to go downtown with me?"

Grabbing the backpack she used instead of a purse, she slung it over one shoulder and picked up the tote and her dog. When she looked inside, she saw JB had fallen asleep. Obviously, she just might have the most perfect dog in the universe. With a sappy grin, she headed toward the door.

Driving to her parents' house, she couldn't shake a feeling of dread. At first, she assumed it had to do with returning to the place where an intruder had so recently been. But as she drove, she caught herself constantly checking the rear-view mirror and she realized she couldn't shake the feeling that someone might be following her.

The closer she got to Shelby, the more unsettled she became. The two-lane road changed to a four-lane and some of the vehicles behind her passed her.

Nothing looked really out of place. But still… She decided to take a random right turn and circle back around just to see if anyone followed her.

No one did. Breathing a sigh of relief, she turned onto her parents' street. Pulling into the driveway, she sat in her locked car with the motor running. In the bright sunlight, the house looked welcoming and undisturbed. She got out, keeping her keys in hand, and picked up the tote with her

sleeping dog. Then she took a deep breath and headed for the house. As she stepped up onto the porch, she turned and did a second check of the street. She didn't see anything suspicious; no unusual vehicles parked by the curb, nothing.

It all must have been her imagination. Though she felt slightly foolish, she couldn't deny she also felt immensely relieved.

Inside the house, she turned off the alarm and sighed. Since it was still set, that meant no one had been inside since she'd left.

Still, she walked around to check. Everything looked the same as it had when she'd left it. The busted back door that they'd jammed closed appeared undisturbed, though she figured another swift kick from outside would send it crashing open. Pulling out her phone, she put in a call to the door repair company she'd used earlier, but had to leave a voicemail. Whenever she was able to get the door replaced, she planned to have them reinforce it with multiple dead bolts if necessary. Between that, and the redone front door, along with her new alarm system, she knew she should be able to feel secure in the house where she'd been raised.

And she could leave Parker's place so he could go on about his life.

The thought made her feel sad. Shaking her head at her own conflicted emotions, she checked on JB, who somehow was still sleeping, and then let herself out through the garage.

Again she checked the street and, again, saw nothing out of the ordinary. She got into her car and after securing JB and her tote in the front passenger seat, she backed from her driveway and headed into town. Only then did she notice a black SUV pull away from the curb as if following her.

Chapter Nine

To Parker's surprise and relief, Revis fit right in with the crew at RTA. Everyone loved the older dog and with all the people petting and loving on him, it seemed his tail never stopped wagging.

"We have a mascot," Parker proclaimed. He couldn't seem to stop smiling. Between having Genna staying at his place in such close proximity and his new family member, he felt happier than he had in a long time.

Spence went home and came back with a large, well-worn dog bed, which he placed it in a corner behind the front counter. As soon as Revis saw it, he claimed it as his own. Curled up with his head on his large paws, he kept an eye on everything. At least, when he wasn't dozing.

"The office dog," Spence said, grinning. "Great idea."

"Thanks."

"But I thought Genna was getting a dog," Spence continued, checking the computer to see who would be in his next group. "How'd you end up with one instead?"

"Long story," Parker replied, really not wanting to go into it at the moment. "Since your tour is about to start arriving, I'll save it for another time."

Reluctantly, Spence nodded. "I'll hold you to that. What about you? When's your next outing?"

"Not for a couple hours. I had one scheduled earlier, but they all canceled. It was a family outing. Turns out they've all come down with strep throat."

"Ouch." Spence grabbed his own throat. "Which means I'm guessing you're planning to hold the fort down here then?"

"Yeah, for now. Hetty is due in soon. She's taking out a small group this afternoon. I should be back before she has to leave. And you can fill in also. Between the three of us, we should be able to keep this place covered."

"Four of us," Spence corrected. "You can't forget Revis."

"As if I could." Parker's phone rang. Seeing Genna's name on the caller ID made his heart skip a beat. Answering, he barely got out a quick hello before she started talking.

"Someone is following me," she said, an edge of panic in her voice. "I stopped by my house to check things out, and when I left, this black SUV pulled away from the curb. I've been driving around downtown taking random turns and it's sticking with me. I don't know what to do."

"Are you close to the police station?" he asked. Though his heart rate accelerated, he tried to sound calm.

"No, I'm on the other side of town. But I can get there. It will take me about twenty minutes though. I'm just worried whoever this is might ram my car or try to force me off the road. I have June Bug with me."

Was she crying? Jaw tight, he battled the intense need to defend her, to help her, and hold her close.

"Keep driving." He took a deep breath, not wanting to let her know how alarming he found this situation. "How far are you from here?"

"From RTA? Maybe ten minutes."

"Then come here." Decision made, he asked her to stay

on the phone while he went back to the gun safe and retrieved his pistol.

"What's going on?" Spence asked. With Genna still
on the phone, Parker filled him in. Once he had, Spence
cursed under his breath before he also went to the gun safe
and armed himself. "We've got you, Genna," he said, loud
enough for her to hear,

"How far out are you now?" Parker asked.

"Five minutes. And the car is still with me. They're not
even trying to hide it now."

The slight tremor in her voice had him clenching his jaw.
"Spence and I will be outside waiting for you. Pull up right
in front of the building. And stay on the phone."

"I will," she promised.

Tense and trying like hell not to be, Parker jogged down
the steps from the covered porch and waited for her at the
edge of the parking lot. He wanted to be able to see her car
the moment she turned into the driveway.

Right by his cousin's side, Spence's grim expression told
Parker that he'd do whatever he had to, to help. If Genna's
stalker was foolish enough to follow her there, they'd make
sure he never followed Genna again.

"There," Parker said, pointing at Genna's red car, just
about at the driveway. And like she said, a black SUV followed right on her bumper.

When she turned, the SUV slowed but then kept driving on past.

As Genna pulled up and parked, Parker rushed over to
open her door. When he did, she made no move to get out.
Instead, she sat frozen, gazing up at him, her expression a
mixture of relief and terror.

"Come here," he said, his voice rough. He held out his

hand. When she made no move to take it, he reached in and hauled her out of the car and into his arms.

"You're trembling," he said, smoothing her hair away from her face. "Are you okay?"

"No," she admitted, clutching on to him as if she might fall. "Do you think that was the same person who broke into my house? What if it was the Fiancée Killer?"

"That's highly unlikely," Spence interjected, startling Parker, who'd managed to forget all about his cousin. "It's not his normal method of operation. If you have a stalker, it's someone else."

The instant Spence spoke, Genna stiffened. She made as if to pull out of Parker's arms, but he tightened his hold. "You're still too shaky on your feet," he murmured.

She reared back, glaring at him, but made no other attempt to move away.

"Well, well, well," Spence drawled, grinning. "Is there something you two want to share with me?"

This comment did it. Genna stepped out of Parker's embrace and shook her head. "Your cousin is just being kind to a friend," she said, her tone daring either man to contradict her. "And I appreciate it greatly."

Just then, the tote back on her front seat moved. A furry little head poked itself out and then barked. "JB!" Genna cried. "I hope you're all right." She reached into the tote and scooped the tiny dog out.

Spence's brows rose. "What the heck is that?" he asked.

"Meet June Bug," Parker replied. "Genna's new dog."

"JB for short," she said, kissing her pet on the top of her head. "Isn't she adorable?"

When Spence didn't immediately respond, Parker elbowed him.

"She's something else," Spence finally said. "Um, Parker,

don't forget you brought that beast of a dog into work with you today. He looks like he could eat this one for lunch if he wanted to."

Genna shook her head. "They're already friends. Revis really seems to like JB and vice versa."

"They've met?" Spence glanced from one to the other. "I thought you just got the dog yesterday," he said, eyeing Parker.

Parker figured he might as well tell him. If he didn't, he knew Lakin would. "Genna's staying with me for a few days," he said. "She and I went into Valdez, which is where the dogs came from. The shelter had them both listed as dog friendly, and so far that seems to be the case."

Though Spence's eyes widened, he simply nodded and refrained from commenting. Parker figured for sure he'd be peppered with questions later, when Genna wasn't there.

"Let's get you inside so you can sit down," Parker suggested, taking Genna's arm. "Spence's group should be arriving soon, so unless you want to be put to work, maybe you should hide out in the break room."

Genna perked up at the mention of work. "I suppose I could do some—"

"No." Parker cut her short. "You're off today. No working. I'll check Spence's group in. Hetty will be here soon and she'll cover the office when I take my people out."

Smiling slightly, Genna nodded. "Parker, when is your expedition? I'm hoping maybe you can go with me into town at some point. As strange as it sounds, I'm a bit weirded out of going anywhere alone."

Just as Parker opened his mouth to reply, three vehicles pulled into the parking lot in rapid succession.

"Looks like my bunch has started to arrive," Spence said,

rubbing his hands together in anticipation. "Time to get this show on the road."

As soon as they got inside, Genna went behind the counter and directly toward the break room. Revis lifted his head when he saw her, tail swishing. As she passed, he got up and followed her.

Positioning himself behind the computer, Parker began the process of logging their guests in. Spence watched from the lobby, eyeing his cousin and clearly bursting at the seams with questions, but unable to ask them. Which Parker considered a good thing.

Once he had everyone checked in, Parker turned the small group over to Spence. As his cousin walked everyone outside, Parker breathed a sigh of relief. Then he headed back to the break room to check on Genna.

When he entered, she looked up from her phone and smiled. The smile didn't reach her green eyes. Her little dog sat in a chair right next to her, and Revis had curled up at her feet.

Relieved, Parker jammed his hands into his pockets so he wouldn't hug her. "You look like you feel better now," he commented, pulling out a chair and taking a seat.

"I do." She put her phone down and regarded him gravely. "I've almost convinced myself that I was imagining everything."

He wanted to tell her that he didn't think so, but also didn't want to get her worked up again. So, in the end, he simply nodded.

"As a matter of fact, I'm going to go ahead with my plan to head into town." Getting to her feet, she picked up JB, who appeared to really enjoy being carried. Revis got up, too, tail wagging, clearly ready for an adventure.

Conflicted, Parker wavered. He couldn't expect her to sit

around and wait for him to take out his tour and return, especially on her day off. "The black SUV did go on past," he said, thinking out loud. "So, hopefully, you should be safe."

Something in his tone must have revealed his concern because her eyes widened.

"It'll be fine," she said. He wasn't sure whether she was trying to convince herself or him. "I can't let this person, whoever they are, make me stop living my life. As long as I stick to town and more populated areas, I should be fine."

He knew then that she was thinking of the Two Bears River Trail, where the most recent victim had been found.

"I just won't go hiking," she said, confirming his suspicion. "It's not like I hike anyway, so I should be safe."

Though he wished he could cancel his next tour and go with her, he couldn't. Nor could he realistically ask her to wait.

The front door opened. He jumped to his feet and looked out. "Hetty's here," he told Genna.

"You bet I am." Hetty sauntered into the break room. "Hey, Genna. What are you doing here? I thought you were off today."

"I am," Genna replied. "I just stopped in to say hi."

Hetty narrowed her eyes and glanced at Parker. He simply smiled, not wanting to say anything if Genna didn't want to elaborate. He'd fill Hetty in later. Since they all looked after each other, he felt strongly everyone needed to be aware of anything weird going on.

"Are we still planning to have that get-together?" Hetty asked. "I know when it got canceled due to weather, you talked about rescheduling."

"Maybe soon," Genna replied. "Honestly, I've got so much going on right now. But even though I've met every-

body by now, I definitely want to do it. I just don't know when."

Hetty frowned at first then shrugged. "I get it," she said. "Have a nice rest of your day off."

"I plan to," Genna chirped.

If Hetty noticed her overly upbeat tone, she didn't show it.

"Let me walk you out," Parker said.

"No, that's okay." Waving him away, Genna headed for the door. "I'll talk to you later."

Slowly, he nodded. "Stay safe."

Watching her walk away, he ached. He didn't know what he would do if anything happened to her.

Once the door closed behind Genna, Hetty touched his arm. "How long have you been in love with her?" she asked. "And more importantly, does she return your feelings or are you on your own?"

GENNA KEPT UP a brave front, strolling outside as if she didn't have a care in the word. She maintained her brave front until she reached her car and climbed inside. Promptly locking the doors, she made sure JB's tote was secured with the seat belt before starting the ignition.

Then, because she had a feeling Parker and Hetty might be watching her out the front window, she forced herself to put the shifter in Reverse and backed up enough to turn the car around.

Though leaving was the absolute last thing she wanted to do, she squared her shoulders, lifted her chin and drove away.

She'd barely reached the first streetlight on the outskirts of Shelby when little JB poked her head out of the tote and whined. Chagrined, Genna realized she'd forgotten to let her pet outside to relieve herself.

Though tempted to pull over and take care of that right now, her location felt too isolated. For all she knew, she'd get out of the car and that black SUV would come racing around the corner. Might be foolish, but she didn't want to take any chances. JB would have to wait until they were actually in town. The restaurant Genna had in mind for lunch had an actual dog park out back. There'd be people and other dogs around, and she didn't think her stalker would dare make a move under those circumstances.

At least, she hoped not.

By the time she got to the restaurant, the usual lunch crowd had begun to thin. She parked, grabbed the tote and went directly to the dog area out back. Once JB had taken care of her business, Genna decided to walk her over to the patio area. The little dog made an immediate beeline for one of the strategically placed water bowls, which also had Genna realizing she'd forgotten to make sure her dog had water.

"I'm sorry," Genna said, scratching JB's neck. "I promise I'll get better at this dog mom stuff."

"I bet you're excellent," a masculine voice said. Startled, Genna looked up to find one of the wait staff smiling at her. "Can I show you to a table?" he asked.

"Thanks, Ty," she replied, reading his nametag. "I appreciate that. June Bug and I would like to sit out here on the patio. It's such a beautiful day."

"It is," he said, leading her to a small table in one corner near the railing. "Will this work for you?"

"It will." Sitting in the chair he pulled out, she accepted the menu he offered. When he also handed her a smaller pet menu, she laughed out loud. On it were things like bone stew and mac and kibble.

Since she didn't want to mess up JB's digestion any more

than she had to, she didn't order anything for her dog. For herself, she chose a strawberry, fresh greens and chicken salad, with light dressing on the side.

While she waited for her food, she people watched. The pace in Shelby felt different than it had in Anchorage. Maybe because the town was popular with tourists, it had a more relaxed, accepting vibe. Growing up, she'd never realized this, and it had taken living in the hustle and bustle of a larger city to make her appreciate her hometown.

Her food came. She took a moment to admire the beauty of the salad, which looked so fresh and colorful, before she dug in. It tasted as good as it looked.

While she ate, JB lifted her head once or twice, but didn't try to beg for anything. The little dog just seemed happy to be there, out in the fresh air with her new owner, the sun on her fur.

"You're such a good dog," Genna said, resisting the urge to slip her a tiny piece of chicken. JB gazed up at her and wagged her tail.

After finishing her salad, Genna pushed away her plate and exhaled. It had been a nice lunch. With the sun on her skin and a light breeze keeping her cool, she'd been finally able to relax and enjoy the beautiful weather.

The muted conversations going on at other tables merged with birdsong and light traffic in the street nearby. From her seat, she could not only see the snowcapped mountains in the distance, but the beautiful cloudless sky. People strolled the sidewalk out front, and customers entered and exited the restaurant. She watched food being served and tables being cleaned. Her server checked on her, asking if she'd like anything else, before removing her plate.

Just because she felt like she deserved it, Genna asked to

see a dessert menu. Ty immediately brought it, telling her he'd be back after giving her time to decide.

JB had stretched out on the cool pavement under the table and watched people with interest, though she never barked.

"Such a good dog," Genna murmured. She thought Revis, despite his much larger size, might also be great to take out in public.

Maybe because they'd come from the same shelter and had been adopted on the same day, Revis and June Bug would always be linked in Genna's mind. Remembering the unabashed joy Parker took in his new dog made her insides go all soft and squishy. A special dog for a special man.

She couldn't help but miss Parker. He would have enjoyed this place, she thought. She'd even spent far too much time guessing what he might have gotten to eat.

Clearly, she, who wanted to steer clear of any romantic entanglements, had it bad. She'd be seeing the man that evening, for Pete's sake. She was staying at his house. Seeing him every day at work. And now she couldn't even enjoy a solitary lunch without missing him?

To be fair, he'd been the first person she called any time she'd been scared. And he'd showed up every single time she'd needed him. Like today, when she'd thought that black SUV had been following her.

Now that some time had passed, she'd halfway convinced herself that she'd imagined it. After all, the SUV had driven on once she'd turned into the RTA drive. If it had been some random stalker, they would have continued on with her, maybe boxing her in with their vehicle so she couldn't escape.

Even thinking this made her shudder.

"Have you decided?" Ty asked.

Since she'd barely even glanced at the menu, she asked him what he recommended.

"The chocolate lava cake," he immediately answered. "It's to die for."

"Then I'll have that," she decided, passing him back the menu.

"And would you like a dog biscuit for your June Bug?" he asked. "On the house."

Beaming at him, she nodded. "Thank you, I would." She had to give him points for even remembering JB's name.

When her dessert arrived, along with a baked bone for JB, she almost clapped. "That's stunning," she said, admiring the cake. She even went so far as to pull out her phone and take a picture of it before picking up her fork to dig in.

She'd just taken her first bite, briefly closing her eyes to savor the blast of chocolate sweetness, when the sound of tires screeching had her turning toward the road. She was dimly conscious of other diners around her doing the same.

Two cars had nearly collided, only narrowly missing hitting each other because one had slammed on their brakes.

It wasn't this that made Genna freeze though. When she realized one of the vehicles involved was the same, black SUV, she nearly dropped her fork.

"Is something wrong?" Ty materialized at her elbow, his concerned gaze taking in her no-doubt pale expression and barely eaten dessert. "Is the cake not to your liking?"

Though her appetite had now completely deserted her, she managed to reassure him that the cake was, in fact, wonderful. "I'm just full," she lied.

"I'll get you a to-go box," he said. A moment later, he returned with one. "Here you go."

She thanked him and nodded, glad he hadn't brought the check. She wasn't about to tell him there was no way

she'd be leaving while that black vehicle was anywhere in the vicinity.

Instead, she continued to watch, waiting for the driver of the SUV to emerge. She had her phone out, camera at the ready, intending to take as many photos of him or her as possible. While she waited, she got several pics of the SUV itself, though she didn't have a good view of the license plate.

But while the driver of the other car immediately got out to look for any damage, no one got out of the black vehicle. Instead, it reversed, swerved around the intersection, and sped off.

Hands shaking, Genna's first impulse was to call Parker. But she figured he'd be heading out with his tour group about now and she didn't want to bother him.

The other driver had noticed her watching and waved. "Did you see that?" he asked, walking over to the wrought iron that bordered the restaurant's patio area. "I didn't even think to get his license number."

She nodded, explaining she hadn't been able to get it, either.

"Luckily, there's no damage to my car," the man said. With a friendly nod, he walked away.

Though she no longer had any appetite for her dessert, Genna forced herself to take a few more bites, eating slowly, trying to get her heart rate to slow. She didn't understand why this person had decided to single her out, but this all needed to stop.

Now, the thought of leaving the restaurant terrified her.

Petting JB, she stared at the mostly uneaten cake, making no move to put it into the to-go box. Ty materialized and offered to take care of that for her.

Once he had, he smiled and left the check, telling her, "No hurry." Good thing, because she had no intention of

moving just then. She honestly wasn't sure she'd be able to walk.

But eventually, she had to get up and vacate the table. It wouldn't be fair to the restaurant or to her server for her to sit there so long after she'd finished her meal.

First, she clipped the leash to JB's collar and walked her over to the grassy, shaded, fenced area that had been designated for dogs. Once JB had gone potty, Genna picked her up and carried her out to her car, continually scanning the parking area for any sign of the black SUV.

As soon as she got inside, she locked the doors and started the ignition. Slowly backing from her space, she drove slowly around the lot before exiting to the street.

A few blocks down she saw a large pet store. Since she could bring JB inside, this seemed like a safe place to pass a little more time. She needed to stock up on a few more dog supplies anyway.

June Bug appeared to enjoy riding in the shopping cart. Genna grabbed several more toys, another fluffy dog bed, this one for the office, and the perfect, pink harness. She wheeled up and down every aisle, including the fish and reptile area, hating that she had to constantly check over her shoulder. It didn't help that she had no idea what her stalker looked like, so she simply avoided everyone, male or female.

When it came time to check out, she tried to make small talk with the cashier, acting as though her heart wasn't racing. Once she'd paid for her items, she left the cart in the front of the store and loaded JB up in the tote bag. Taking a deep breath, she paused just outside the entrance and once again searched for any sign of the black SUV. She hated being so jumpy and on edge. And angry, she realized as she loaded the bags and her dog into her car. It was not only

frightening, but infuriating to be made to feel like a target. There had to be a safe way to put an end to this.

Right now though, she just needed to avoid the stalker. No way did she intend to confront him alone.

She took another quick scan of the parking lot before getting into the driver's seat. Once inside, after immediately locking the doors and starting the ignition, she tried to figure out where to go next.

Her first thought—RTA headquarters—she immediately discarded. It looked bad enough that she'd already put in an appearance there on her day off. Yet she couldn't go to her house and she didn't want to take a chance on driving to Parker's while he wasn't there in case someone followed.

As she drove slowly down Main Street, her anger subsided and she realized she wanted to cry. Since she didn't consider herself a weepy kind of person, this only increased her irritation. Swiping at her eyes, she tried to blink the tears away while she decided where to go and what to do.

Chapter Ten

As usual, Parker thoroughly enjoyed taking his eager group on the hike. Not only did he love the physical exertion, but it was fun watching the tourists' reactions to the beautiful foliage and the occasional wildlife sightings.

But he couldn't stop worrying about Genna. With two house break-ins and now a vehicle following her, the threat seemed urgent. Even if she had no idea who might be doing this or why, with a serial killer terrorizing young women, she couldn't afford to take risks with her safety.

The thought of something happening to her made his blood run cold. And Hetty, ever perceptive, had asked him how long he'd been in love with Genna.

He'd managed to blow the question off, acting incredulous that she'd even suggest such a thing. In reality, he knew he'd been fooling no one. If Hetty thought she knew, it wouldn't be long until everyone at RTA would be talking.

For himself, he knew he could live with gossip. With a business like theirs, run by family and employees who'd been there so long they were like family, it seemed there was always some rumor going around.

Parker and Spence tried to ignore them. Lakin had always delighted in them, claiming she found the talk hilarious.

But Parker didn't know how Genna would handle the rumors. She'd just started working for RTA and while she'd made everyone's acquaintance, she'd likely still feel like an outsider. With everything else she had going on, he wanted work to be a safe haven.

Returning after the hike to headquarters, he let Spence handle the checkout. He went back to the break room to grab a bottled water.

He wondered how Genna's afternoon in town had gone. Hopefully, there'd been no more incidents with someone following her. Pulling out his phone, he saw no missed calls or texts, so he had to assume everything had been okay.

Once the last guest had trundled off, Parker made his way out front. "I'm going to head home," he said. "You all set here?"

"Sure." Spence grinned. "Is Genna waiting for you to get home?"

Parker should have been surprised that Hetty had already spread the news, but he wasn't. Spence and Hetty were super close. "It's not like that, and you know it," he said, shaking his head at his cousin. "She's staying in the guest bedroom after someone has tried to break into her house twice."

At his words, Spence's teasing expression vanished. "And now she's had someone following her." He clapped Parker on the back. "Sorry, man. I just wanted to give you a hard time. You know I'm all in to do whatever you need to help catch this guy."

"I appreciate that." Barely able to contain his need to rush home, Parker said his goodbye. He called Revis and, after his dog jumped up into the back seat, got in his truck and headed home.

As he pulled up in front of his driveway, disappointment mixed with worry as he realized Genna wasn't there. With

the truck still running, he got out his phone and called her. She answered on the second ring.

"Are you home yet?" she asked, her voice shaky. "I've been driving around with JB, and didn't want to go to your place unless you were there."

"I'm sitting in my driveway," he said. "Did something else happen?"

"Yes and no." She sighed. "Would you mind watching for me? I'm about five minutes away. I'll only stop once I'm absolutely sure that I'm not being followed."

"Revis and I will wait right here," he promised. "Please stay on the line until I can see you."

"I will. Right now, no one is following me. I've been on the lookout for a black SUV. I haven't seen it since lunchtime."

The fact that she had seen it again wasn't lost on him. Though he wanted to press her for details, he knew it could wait until she was safe and sound with him and ready to talk.

"How was your tour?" she asked, her voice still shaky. Understanding her need to discuss something ordinary, he told her about the group. They'd been repeat visitors, two families who lived next door to each other somewhere in California.

"I'm almost at your place," she said once he'd finished. "Thank you for talking." She paused for a moment. "I really just needed to hear the sound of your voice."

Stunned, he told himself what she really meant was the sound a friendly voice. Anyone would do.

While he waited, he opened the door so Revis could hop out, which he did, tail wagging and panting happily. For an older dog, Revis moved well. Parker ruffled his fur, telling him they were watching for Genna and June Bug. Revis's ears perked up, almost as if he understood every word.

Finally, Parker spotted Genna's car making its way down the road. Both he and Revis watched, waiting while she pulled into the driveway and parked.

She got out slowly, waving. Crossing around to the other side, she let June Bug out before reaching into the back seat and retrieving several shopping bags.

"Do you want some help?" he asked, ready to take some of the bags from her.

"No, thanks. I'm good."

He noticed she'd left something in the back seat and asked her if she wanted him to grab that. She told him no, it was JB's bed for the office and she'd leave it there until she went back to work.

Genna and her tiny pet led the way into the house, Revis a few steps behind and Parker bringing up the rear. He couldn't help but reflect on how domestic all of this felt. Or would have, if not for Genna having a stalker.

Once inside, Genna carried her purchases to her room, both dogs following right behind her. She closed her door, JB and Revis still with her.

A sharp, staccato set of knocks on the front door, followed by multiple presses of the doorbell, told Parker that his brother Eli had come to visit.

Which could be a good thing or bad.

Opening the door, Parker motioned Eli in. At least his brother wasn't in his law enforcement uniform, which meant this call likely wasn't on official business.

"Evening," Eli said, his eyes scanning the room. "Where's your new dog? I've heard all about him and can't wait to meet him."

"He's around here somewhere," Parker replied, keeping his tone casual. He figured Eli had also come to check out

the current living situation, since the gossip about him and Genna had no doubt made the rounds of the family.

"Oh. I want to meet him," Eli said.

Since Revis had gone with Genna, Parker wasn't about to go get him. "Do you want a beer?" Parker offered.

"Sure." Eli dropped onto the couch. "They finally were able to figure out the identity of the second victim. It was a woman named Allison Harris."

Parker got their beers, opened them and handed one to his brother. "I can't believe that guy still hasn't been caught."

"He will be." Accepting the bottle, Eli spoke with confidence. "Sooner or later, he's going to make a mistake. And we'll get him."

Genna appeared, evidently hearing voices, Revis and JB hot on her heels. Parker introduced Genna, and then each of the two dogs. They stayed close to Genna, both of them regarding Eli with thoughtful expressions.

"You're with law enforcement, if I remember right," Genna said, her expression hopeful. "Are you here to tell us that the Fiancée Killer has been arrested and will be brought to justice?"

"I wish." Eli shifted in his seat. "But I hear you've been having some trouble yourself. Your house was broken into?"

She nodded. "And now someone seems to be following me. It was a black SUV. Mercedes, I think. I wasn't able to get the license plate."

"Following you?" Eli asked, frowning. "For how long?"

Genna sighed. "Just today. They almost caused an accident at an intersection in front of the restaurant where I was eating lunch out on the patio."

"And you don't have any idea who it might be?"

"No," Genna replied. "I don't have any clue who or why."

Though Parker had hesitated to mention it before, he

thought now might be a good time. "Didn't you say your ex-husband's new girlfriend was harassing you before you left Anchorage?"

"Ann?" Slowly, she nodded. "But that was back in Anchorage. There's no way she'd drive six to seven hours just to stalk me."

Sipping his beer, Eli appeared thoughtful but he didn't comment.

"Maybe not," Parker allowed. "But still, it wouldn't hurt to have Eli look into them."

Genna looked from one man to the other. "I'm sure Eli has enough to deal with, working on the serial killer case. I don't want to be a bother."

"You're not," Eli assured her. "If you'll just write down your ex-husband's name and address, as well as his girlfriend's, I can check them out."

"We'd appreciate that," Parker interjected when it appeared Genna might protest. "Just a few minutes of your time would go a long way to helping Genna feel safe."

Genna met his gaze, her expression troubled.

"Please," Parker said. "It can't hurt."

"Okay, I'll write their info down," Genna finally said. "But I'm telling you, it's not them. First up, they were cyber bullying me before as well as calling and texting. They're not now. Even though I've blocked both their numbers, they'd buy disposable phones just so they could reach me. All of that has stopped."

"Interesting." Eli shrugged. "Maybe they decided to torment you in person this time."

"They did that before, too. It accomplished nothing. And I'm here in Shelby now. They have jobs and lives in Anchorage. While it's a beautiful drive from there to here, it's also long. I honestly think Ann celebrated when she succeeded

in running me out of the area. Now Chad is all hers. She has no reason to follow me here and torment me."

"Maybe not," Eli answered. "But you never know with some of these kinds of people. They can become so wrapped up in vengeance or whatever it is that they're trying to accomplish, all logic flies out the window. Let me check into them."

"As long as they aren't made aware, I'm fine with it," Genna said. "I don't want to do anything to bring me to their attention and potentially start things up again."

"They'll have no idea," Eli promised.

With a curt nod, Genna turned and disappeared into her bedroom. To Parker's surprise, both dogs remained where they were, their attention fixed firmly on Eli, though they turned their heads as Genna walked by. When she reappeared, she handed Eli a folded piece of notebook paper. "Here you go. I've included their home addresses and cell phone numbers, as well as places of employment."

If her thoroughness surprised Eli, he didn't show it. He tucked the paper in his pocket and thanked her before turning back to Parker and asking a question about RTA.

Taking a seat on one end of the couch, Genna listened. She made no move to join in the conversation, which would have concerned Parker if not for her relaxed demeanor. She'd had one hell of a day. More than anything, he wished he could sit down next to her, put his arm around her and pull her close. But then he could only imagine his brother's reaction of he did. More fuel for the family gossip.

This made him think of their sister. "Have you talked to Lakin lately?" he asked. "How's that hotel renovation project going?"

Eli smiled. "She says she's having a blast. Living the dream, in her own words."

"Good for her." Parker glanced again at Genna before turning his attention back to Eli. "I've been meaning to go by and take a look at the place. See what they've done so far."

Eli chuckled. "Good luck with that. She told me she doesn't need me looking over her shoulder."

"Maybe Genna should go," Parker said, smiling. "What do you think, Genna? You and Lakin were old friends back in the day."

Though she smiled back, she chose not to answer the second question. Instead, she made a noncommittal comment, saying she just might have to pay Lakin's hotel a visit. Parker couldn't tell if she meant it or not. He hoped she did, because as far as he could tell, Genna kept to her own company. It might be good for her to have a friend. Of course, that would be totally up to her.

Eli changed the subject again, telling them a little about the ongoing investigation. What information he could give them was limited, he said, but he promised he and his colleagues were all hard at work on it.

Genna excused herself, heading into the kitchen to get something. Eli took the opportunity to give Parker a look, one brow raised. "Is there something we—meaning the family—need to know?" he asked.

There were several responses Parker could have given. Luckily, he didn't have to give any of them because Genna returned, carrying a glass of wine.

"WHY THE SERIOUS EXPRESSIONS?" Genna asked, looking from one man to the other. She figured they'd been discussing her and her situation, and she couldn't blame them.

For whatever reason, giving Eli information on her ex-husband and ex-best friend had made Genna feel conflicted.

Almost as if by doing so, she was dragging her old life into her new. Which she most definitely didn't want to do.

Had she somehow managed to make them think less of her? Surely not, since Parker already knew her story and she and Eli had only just met.

No doubt her moment of self-doubt was all in her head. They'd definitely gone right back to their conversation, a few seconds after a pause that might or might not have been awkward.

Watching as Parker and Eli talked, the way they spoke so affectionately about their sister, made her relax. Instead of feeling like an outsider, she felt...accepted. She also appreciated that Eli didn't make a fuss over her staying with Parker. Instead, he treated her presence as if it wasn't a big deal, which she appreciated, since it really wasn't.

Eli finished his beer and got to his feet. "I'd better go," he said. "I'll keep you both posted if there are any new developments on the Fiancée Killer."

"I hope you get a good lead soon," Parker said, walking him to the door.

"You and everyone else in Shelby," Eli replied.

Once the door had closed behind Eli, Parker returned. "How are you feeling?" he asked, settling next to her on the couch.

She shrugged. "Okay, I guess."

Parker took a deep breath. "I guess I should warn you. My family likes to gossip. I'm sure they'll be talking about you staying here with me."

"Why?" she asked. "Surely, once they find out the reason I'm here, they'll understand."

He shifted in the seat, clearly uncomfortable. "Yeah, they'll definitely get it. But that's not going to stop them

from giving me hell. They all want to make this more than it is."

While she could have pretended not to understand, she did. Slowly, she got to her feet, scooping up JB. "I'm sorry that my being here is such an inconvenience. Give me a few minutes to get packed and I'll go stay in my own home."

"That's not what I meant," he protested.

Ignoring him, she carried her dog into her room. Revis lifted his head as they passed, but made no move to follow. As she set JB down on top of the bed and reached into her closet for her duffel bag, she realized she was crying. Tears streamed down her face. Furiously wiping them away with the back of her hand, she wondered what the hell was wrong with her. Usually, she considered herself even-keeled.

"Genna, please. I don't want you to leave. I really don't." Parker stood in her doorway, clearly keeping his distance.

She couldn't blame him. She was a hot mess right now. Keeping her face averted so he wouldn't see, she tried to pretend she was fine. "It's all good…" she began. To her absolute horror, her voice broke. "There's just been a lot lately."

"It's me," he said, gently pulling her into his arms. "Not you. That was my awkward attempt to let you know that my family will be giving both of us a hard time, even though it's completely unwarranted."

Though she held herself stiffly, she didn't pull out of his embrace. He smelled good, a combination of mint and outdoors. And the Parker she'd come to know would never be so callous. Clearly, she might possibly have misunderstood.

"Why?" she asked, finally lifting her face to his. "Why would it bother you so much if your family teases us?"

"You're crying!" Gently, he smoothed her hair back, using his finger to awkwardly wipe away her tears. "Genna, I

never meant to hurt you. I just wasn't sure how to handle it. Obviously, I handled it wrong."

She didn't get a chance to respond, because he covered her mouth with his and kissed her. The kind of kiss that made her entire being melt. Deep and slow and sure, he showed her more than words ever could how much he wanted her.

When she finally broke away, they were both breathing heavily. "I was mistaken, wasn't I?" she asked.

"Yes." He nodded, a slight smile playing about his mouth. "I meant well, but completely botched things. What I need you to understand is that I don't want you to leave."

Since she didn't really want to, for a multitude of reasons, some of which she had no reason thinking, she bobbed her head. "I'm not going anywhere."

"Good." His smile made his blue eyes sparkle. "It's not safe."

It felt like he'd tacked that last statement on for good effect. Since it happened to be exactly what she'd needed to hear, she smiled back.

"Come here," she told him.

She didn't have to ask him twice.

Kissing, caressing, they helped each other shed their clothing as they made their way to her bed. Just like before, when they came together, the explosive passion made her forget everything but Parker.

Afterward, he continued to hold her close. She liked that he didn't immediately jump up, but treated her as if he thought her precious.

The realization stunned her. So much so, she pushed herself away from him and went to clean up. After that, she told him good-night, waiting while he headed into his own room to sleep. The moment he left, JB jumped up onto her

bed to sleep. The little dog raised her head when Genna got in, her tail wagging.

The next morning, Genna got up and began a routine that had started to feel comfortable and familiar. She met Parker in the kitchen and nearly laughed out loud when he handed her a mug of coffee, already fixed the way she liked it.

"Thanks," she said, her heart light. Honestly, the roller coaster of emotions that had been buffeting her almost gave her whiplash.

"You're welcome," he replied, drinking from his own mug. Revis lay curled up at his feet. "Are you glad to return to work?"

"I am." She glanced at her bedroom door, wondering when JB would stir her little self. As if thinking about her had summoned her, the small dog came trotting out to the kitchen, tail wagging. She and Revis touched noses before Genna took JB outside for her morning constitutional.

When she returned, Parker had placed two toasted bagels and a tub of strawberry cream cheese on the table. "Breakfast," he said. He looked so pleased with himself that she wanted to kiss him.

Better if she didn't. Instead, she fed JB and, once her dog had eaten, sat down at the table to break her own fast. Funny how making love the night before could improve one's outlook on life.

They decided to ride into work together. Once both dogs were in his truck, Revis in the back and JB in Genna's lap, they headed to the office.

When they arrived, they walked in together, both dogs trotting along side-by-side.

"I have the first excursion of the morning," Parker said, his boyish smile tugging at her heart. "I'm taking a large

group out fishing. That's perfect for an overcast sky like it is now."

He stretched, drawing her gaze. Then, realizing where her thoughts had inevitably gone, she shook her head at herself and blushed. "Well then, we'd better get busy," she said, making her voice brisk. "Let me get signed into my computer so I can get everyone checked in and you all can be on your way."

Not five minutes after that, a private bus pulled in and parked. At least fifteen people got out, all rushing for the front door. Though the sign clearly asked people to form a single line, several of new arrivals rushed the counter, all talking at once.

Though this sort of thing tried her patience, Genna got everyone sorted out, politely insisting they all wait their turn.

It turned out most of folks were guests of one man named Miles Franklin, who owned a large vacation property in town. He'd booked the fishing trip as a treat, one last thing to do before his guests left. He insisted on being first, and since he'd paid, Genna figured that made sense. He had an exaggerated sense of self-importance, but aside from that, he seemed decent.

Either way, she treated each person the same way, with her usual mix of friendly efficiency. They all seemed excited about the possibility of catching fish and a few confessed they'd never been fishing before.

Once she'd checked everyone in, Parker took over, shepherding everyone outside and down the path that led to the boat docks.

Watching them go, Genna breathed a sigh of relief. This particular group seemed as if they might be a bit challenging and, honestly, if she'd been Parker, she would have en-

listed Spence's help. But Parker hadn't appeared concerned and he'd been doing this long enough to know what he could and couldn't handle.

Spence arrived about an hour after Parker had left. "Good morning," he said, heading directly to the break room to grab a cup of coffee. When he returned, he settled in one of the office chairs and rolled up next to Genna.

"I checked the bookings today. Parker has a large group right now, doesn't he?" He grinned. "We switched. I get tired of taking people fishing. So he's doing that and I'm taking the next group on a nature hike."

Though she hadn't known that, she nodded. "Well, your group isn't too shabby, either. You leave in twenty minutes, right?"

"Yep." He glanced at the parking lot, which so far only contained the private bus from earlier. "If they show up, that is."

Almost as if his words had summoned them, several cars turned into the drive. As they parked, Genna opened the check-in software. "I'm ready," she told Spence. "I'll get them logged in and turned over to you in a hurry."

As people filed in through the front door and arranged themselves in a single line, she processed each one. Marveling at the difference between the two groups, she processed them quickly.

Once the last person had been logged, she gestured to Spence. With very little fanfare, he herded them outside and they started on the path that went up the mountain.

A short time later, Parker and his group returned. Just like before, they pushed through the front door, jockeying to be the first at the counter. Their mood seemed markedly different, and she caught herself glancing at Parker several times, just in case he wanted to give her a hint.

Instead, he crossed his arms and watched from the back of the room, his smile decidedly forced. Several of the customers grumbled loudly while waiting in line.

This time, Miles Franklin hung back, letting all his guests check out before him and sending them all out one by one to wait on the bus.

Finally, he was the only one of the group left inside. "I'd like a full refund," he demanded, glaring at Genna. "Not a single person in my party caught a fish."

Since this request had come up before, as unbelievable as it seemed, Genna had her answer prepared. "I'm so sorry, sir, but the agreement you signed clearly states that catching a fish is not guaranteed. We are not responsible for nature."

As she finished speaking, his expression darkened. "I don't care. I paid you people a lot of money to make sure my friends had a good time. We've already informed my cook that we are having a fish fry tonight. How can we do that if we don't have any fish?"

The anger simmering underneath his measured tone sent a chill through her. She glanced at Parker, very glad he was there. He watched silently, arms still crossed, but, judging by his intent expression, she could tell he'd jump into action if the situation got out of control and turned into something she couldn't handle.

She could only hope it didn't go that far.

Chapter Eleven

Watching while Genna tried to calm Miles Franklin down, it took every ounce of self-restraint Parker possessed to keep from intervening. This was definitely a case where the customer was not always right. Plus, the guy was needlessly being a total jerk.

But Genna's role as the office manager meant handling the customer interactions, both good and bad. Though this type of situation luckily had been rare, he needed to make sure she felt comfortable dealing with it. Unless she indicated the wanted him to step in, he'd let her handle things.

"Well?" Miles demanded, rapping his knuckles sharply on the counter. "Did you lose your voice?"

Revis, who'd been sleeping in his bed behind her, growled. Expression startled, Genna swung around to look. Not only had the big dog gotten to his feet, but her little JB had joined him. The two canines stared Miles down. The hackles on Revis's back were raised and they both looked decidedly unfriendly. Anyone who had any knowledge of dogs would take this as a clear warning.

Parker couldn't help but approve. It appeared he wasn't the only one watching over Genna.

After a brief irritated glance, Miles paid no attention to

the animals or to Parker. Instead, he continued to focus all his attention on Genna. "Well?" he demanded again.

Straightening, she took a deep breath. Parker guessed she was determined to keep her response cool and composed. "Since you are asking me how you're going to have a fish fry, I can suggest a couple of markets that stock an ample supply of fresh fish. Beyond that, there's really nothing else I can do for you."

At that, Parker had to stifle a laugh.

Miles bristled, likely about to hurl another set of insults or demands at Genna. Just then, the driver of the bus waiting out front honked the horn.

"You'd better get going," Parker drawled, unable to help himself. "It sounds like they might be getting ready to leave without you."

Face red, Miles looked from Genna to Parker. "You haven't heard the last of me," he declared. "I'll be posting a review online." He took two steps toward the door before whirling around. "And I will be contacting my bank to dispute the credit card charges."

With that, he bulldozed out the door and stomped off to the waiting bus.

Watching him go, Genna sagged against the counter in relief.

Parker sighed. "Please make a note in his file not to allow him to book with us again."

"Already done," Genna responded, shaking her head. "I can't imagine being so entitled that you think you shouldn't have to pay if you don't catch a fish."

"It happens. But luckily, not very often." He thought for a moment. "But it did remind me why I'd rather Spence take the fishing groups. At least when I stick to hiking or four-wheeling, people don't have unreasonable expectations."

As the bus drove off, Parker finally relaxed. Genna appeared to be trying, but she couldn't hide the way her hands trembled.

Just knowing how badly that customer had upset Genna made his entire body clench. "Are you all right?" he asked, his voice gruff.

Gaze locked on his, she slowly nodded. "It was all just so unexpected," she said. "I still don't understand why he got so angry."

"Some people are just like that. Like I said, it's rare."

"Is it? You're telling me that no one gets upset if they go out on a wildlife trip and don't see any? Or a whale-watching thing with no whales?" Genna asked, some of the color finally returning to her face.

"Oh, we have had some who might make a few snide comments here and there, but it's rare that someone demands their money back. And not just their own payment, but that of everyone in the group."

She glanced at her computer. "That would have been a significant amount of money. And he signed the disclaimer."

"Exactly." He moved around behind the counter and squeezed her shoulder, aching to do more. "Don't worry about it. He's gone. Hopefully, he'll move on with his life. And if he writes a bad review, once he explains his logic, no one will take him seriously."

"True." Finally, her tense expression relaxed and she smiled up at him. "I'm just glad you were here. You and the dogs."

They both turned to look. Revis and JB had returned to their beds and had curled up comfortably.

"Best decision I ever made," Genna said, her smile widening.

"Best decision *we* ever made," he corrected, barely able

to keep from touching her again. "You did well handling all of that."

"Did I?" Apparently completely unaware of how she affected him, she got busy typing something into her computer. "I wondered if you would have preferred I offer him something. Like maybe a free pass to come fish again."

He snorted, about to comment, until he realized she wasn't serious. "Only if you guarantee he could catch a bunch of fish next time."

Brows raised, she met his gaze. "Thank you. Just being able to joke around about this has made me feel a lot better."

"I'm glad." He thought for a moment. "After Spence's group comes back, are there any more going out today?"

"Nope," she replied without even having to check the schedule on the computer. "It's a slow day."

"Which means maybe you can I could go to dinner after?"

She froze. "Maybe," she finally said. "Though, to be honest, I'd rather get takeout and go home and eat."

The way she referred to his place as home brought a lump to his throat. "That sounds good, too. Let me know what you want and we'll order ahead."

In the end, they decided on fried chicken. "I need comfort food," she told him, her expression serious. "Mashed potatoes and gravy, and those rolls with honey."

After Spence and his group returned, Genna put them through checkout, which went smoothly. Spence appeared distracted and left as soon as his tour did, which meant Parker never had a chance to tell him about their irate customer.

"We can fill him in tomorrow," Genna said, correctly reading his mind.

"We'll definitely have to," he replied. He could only imagine Spence's response.

After Genna set her computer up for the morning, they turned out the lights and locked the door. They picked up the meal on the way home. Both dogs immediately perked up at the smell of fried chicken. Their intent fixation on the large paper sack made Genna laugh.

"None of this for you," she said. "But I promise I'll feed both of you your kibble as soon as we're home."

There it was again. *Home.* While he figured calling his place "home" wasn't a big deal to her, he couldn't help but like it. A lot.

He'd just pulled into the driveway and parked when she made an odd sound low in her throat.

"What's wrong?" he asked, killing the ignition and pocketing the key fob before turning to face her.

"Look at my car," she said, fumbling with the door handle so she could get out. "What the heck happened to it?" The urgency in her voice had him jumping out his side.

"Someone slashed my tires." Expression incredulous, she made a slow circle around her car. "All four of them."

Following her, Parker cursed. More than just jabbed, someone had repeatedly used a knife to create large gashes in each tire. Not only were they flat, they were in shreds. "Who would do such a thing?" he asked, unbelieving.

"I'm guessing my stalker figured out where I'm staying." A combination of fear and sadness colored her voice. "Until he's caught, no place is safe for me."

Pulling her into his arms, Parker kissed her forehead. "We don't know that this is the work of your stalker," he pointed out.

She lifted her head to look at him. "Oh, really? Who else could it be?"

"I'm thinking that irate customer from earlier today. It's

a simple thing to find out where I'm living. Maybe he decided this would be a good way to act out his frustration."

Her eyes widened. "I didn't even think of that. I'd pretty much forgotten about him. But honestly, I'd rather it have been him than my stalker. I hate not feeling safe."

"I get that." What Parker didn't tell her was that he planned to pay Miles Franklin a call. No way could he let anyone get away with ruining the property of one of RTA's employees. She might work there, but she wasn't responsible for company policies.

"A new set of tires isn't cheap," Genna mused. "And as badly as these are slashed up, I'm thinking they're not repairable."

Right then and there, Parker determined if Miles Franklin had done this, he'd either be replacing all four of Genna's tires or they'd be pressing charges.

"Let's go inside, feed the dogs and have our meal," he said, arm still around her shoulders. "After that, let me see what I can find out."

She didn't comment.

They fed the dogs and then spread out all their fast food on the table. He'd gotten several sides, all comfort food. In addition to the mashed potatoes, he'd ordered macaroni and cheese, baked beans and small salads. Plus, he'd ordered extra rolls, butter and honey.

Despite expressing her eagerness for the food earlier, Genna barely picked at it now. "Having my tires slashed messed with my appetite," she said. "But, hey, at least we have lots of leftovers. Maybe I'll feel like eating later."

He understood. While she packed everything up to put in the refrigerator, he left the room and stepped outside to the back patio. If he intended to pay Miles Franklin a visit, he would need company.

He'd just taken out his phone to dial Spence when Eli called. "I did some digging into Genna's ex and his new wife, Ann," Eli began.

"Wife?" Startled, Parker scratched his head. "I thought she was his girlfriend."

"Well, they got married," Eli replied. "I'm not sure when. Anyways, Ann is a piece of work. She's had a few assault complaints against her, but they were all dropped. I suspect her wealthy family had something to do with that."

"Assault charges?" Parker asked. "For other people? Not just Genna?"

"Yes. And some of the notes indicate Ann is a bit unstable, to put it mildly."

Parker scratched his head, digesting this. "Do you have any reports that she might have left Anchorage and traveled to Shelby?"

"None whatsoever. But that's not unusual. Unless she did social media posts or made a point out of telling a lot of people, there isn't any reason anyone would know or think anything of it. She's not breaking any laws by traveling."

Parker told Eli what had happened with Genna's tires, though he also made sure to mention the irate customer.

"Miles Frankin?" Eli asked, his voice thoughtful. "He has that huge summer house in town."

"That's him. I'm thinking about going over there and confronting him. If he slashed Genna's tires, he needs to pay for her new ones."

"Are you sure that's a good idea?" Eli sounded concerned. "Someone that gets that irate about not catching fish might not appreciate you coming on to his property."

He had a point.

"Maybe I should go pay him an official visit," Eli suggested. "Just to hear what he has to say."

Though Parker itched to confront Miles himself, sending someone who worked in law enforcement packed a much more powerful punch.

"Would you mind doing that?" Parker asked.

"Not at all. I'll be sure to keep you posted as to what I find out."

HAVING HER TIRES ruined felt like that last straw. In the time since her marriage to Chad had ended, Genna had endured countless harassment. She'd finally been able to get some peace after fleeing Anchorage and coming home to Shelby.

And that's actually what made all this worse. Enjoying a normal life for a few weeks before the tormenting had started up again.

The respite had given her a false sense of security. She'd finally believed she had been able to move on, to rebuild her life, with hopes she could make it a good one.

When Parker came back inside, she walked right over, wrapped her arms around him and held on tightly.

"It's going to be all right," he said, his deep voice rumbling through his chest as he hugged her back. "Eli is going to pay Miles Franklin a visit. If it appears for even an instant that Miles is the one who did this, I've told Eli that you're pressing charges."

"Thanks." Stepping away, she thought for a moment. "It has to have been him. I'd rather that than have it be my stalker. I don't like to think of the possibility that he might have found me."

"I don't like that, either." Parker admitted. "But I really think it was Miles. It's too much of a coincidence that it happened right after his blowup at you at RTA."

"Either way, it looks like I'm on the hook for new tires. I don't want to file a claim with my insurance company be-

cause, when Ann and Chad were harassing me, I had to file a couple. I don't want to get canceled."

"I see your point."

She considered a moment. "There's a possibility this is work-related. And maybe not Miles, though I can't for the life of me think of anyone else that go super angry at me."

"What do you mean?" he asked, glancing back at her over his shoulder.

"There have been quite a few hang-up phone calls lately," she replied, trying not to sound as nervous as she felt.

Her attempt mustn't have worked because Parker swung around to eye her. "When you say a few, how many do you mean?"

She shrugged, still attempting to be casual. "More than ten a day. At first, I thought it was someone dialing the wrong number. But now it seems deliberate. I've even started making a note of the time they come in. There's definitely a schedule."

"Like every hour?" He moved closer.

Grabbing her notebook, she slid it over toward him. "Take a look. As far as I can tell, they happen every forty-five minutes."

Frowning, he studied her notations. "That's really weird."

"I know." She shrugged. "It might be nothing. I don't know. I've been meaning to check with some of the others to see if it's also happening to them."

"Good idea."

She checked the time. "By the way, I have a hair appointment after work. I don't know how I'll get there, but if I figure it out, would you mind taking JB home with you so I can go directly there?"

"I don't mind at all." He smiled. "In fact, you can bor-

row my truck. Indulge in a little bit of pampering. You deserve it."

"Oh, it's just a haircut. No pampering. But I'm going to enjoy it nonetheless."

When it came time for her to leave, she felt surprisingly torn about leaving her little dog. "I'll see you when I get home," she said, crouching down and kissing JB's adorable little nose. "I promise."

She looked up to find Parker watching her, smiling. "She's a lucky girl."

Touched, she thanked him before getting up. "You take good of her for me. I'll see you later."

"Sounds good." Handing her his keys, he hesitated a moment. "Keep your eyes open, okay?"

"Always." With a wave, she hurried outside to his truck.

As she drove away, even though she had to constantly check her rearview mirror to make sure she wasn't being followed, she turned up the radio and began singing along. Her mood light, she decided that after her haircut, she'd do a little retail therapy in one of the boutiques that lined the street next to her salon. A new outfit would do wonders for her self-confidence.

She found a parking spot right near the salon entrance. Smiling at her good luck, she got out, locked the truck, and headed for the door.

Inside, the cool air smelled slightly of lavender. Classic rock played softly in the background. The receptionist, a young woman with purple hair and a nose ring, smiled as Genna approached. Her nametag read Willow. "May I help you?"

"I have a four-thirty appointment with Shannon," Genna said and gave her name.

Willow's smile faltered. "I'm sorry, but I show that appointment was canceled."

It took a moment for the words to register. "Canceled? By who?"

"I don't know. Whoever took the call likely assumed it was you."

"When was it canceled?" Genna pressed. "I made this appointment several weeks ago."

"That, I couldn't tell you." Chewing the end of a pen, Willow met Genna's gaze. "Since you seem surprised, I'm guessing you didn't cancel. Is it possible a family member might have?"

"No. I don't suppose there's any chance that I can still have that spot?"

Slowly, Willow shook her head. "I'm so sorry. Shannon already took another client. What we can do is make a new appointment."

"Today?" Genna asked hopefully, even though she knew that possibility was highly unlikely.

"No, I'm sorry. Shannon has an opening in two weeks. Same time. Would that work for you?"

"Since I don't seem to have a choice, yes. I'll take it. And please make a note not to cancel it under any circumstances."

"Will do." Willow's smile had returned, full-force. "I'm so sorry about the misunderstanding."

"It wasn't your fault." Still perturbed, Genna turned to go. Out in front of the salon, she realized shopping no longer held its earlier appeal. Instead, all she wanted to do was go home, cuddle her dog, and fill Parker in on what had happened.

Whoever had been stalking her clearly had moved on to

other ways to make her life miserable. At least she could take the truck back to RTA and pick up Parker and the dogs.

Though she wanted to head straight to RTA, her recent concern over being followed had her driving past her parents' place instead. She slowed, but didn't stop since her heart started pounding the closer she got.

This was her parents' home. The place where she'd grown up. This house had always felt like a safe haven. She'd retreated here immediately after her nasty divorce and again when she'd decided to relocate to Shelby.

And now she couldn't even bring herself to sleep in the place. This made her heart hurt.

Continuing past, she took a roundabout route to work. While driving, she constantly checked her rearview mirror to make sure she wasn't being followed. As far as she could tell, she wasn't.

What should have been a fifteen-minute drive turned into thirty. Finally turning into the parking area, she pulled up, hoping he was still there. Even though, technically, she could consider herself safe, she still sat in her car for a moment longer, the doors locked and the engine running.

She didn't like who she'd become. Paranoid, stressed, too worried about the possibility of something else happening to enjoy the moment.

Parker must have noticed her arrive because the front door opened and he hurried out. Only then did she finally turn off her motor and get out of the truck.

"Everything okay?" he asked, the concern in his eyes warming her heart. "Why are you back so soon?"

Instead of replying, she swiftly crossed the distance that separated them into his arms. Holding her, he made soothing noises while she told him what had happened. "This is

exactly the kind of thing that was happening to me back in Anchorage."

Steering her toward the building, he waited until they were inside with the door locked behind them before speaking. "I think it's time you have to consider that your ex and his wife might have something to do with this."

"Wife?" she blinked. Then, without waiting for his response, she grimaced. "That makes sense. Ann and Chad are exactly the same. Of course they got married as soon as our divorce was final."

He studied her. "Does that bother you?"

"No." She didn't even have to think about it. "I just hate having to consider the idea that they might be the ones tormenting me here. They're the main reason I moved. I'm far enough away from Anchorage that they'd really have to make an effort. And neither of them are the type to want to exert themselves. That's why I don't think this is them."

Considering her words, he nodded. "Maybe they have friends or family here in Shelby who are doing things for them."

The idea didn't make sense. "Who would want to get involved with something like that?"

He started to say something but she reached out and touched his arm to stop him. "I don't want to talk about this anymore," she said. "Would you mind taking me home? Also, giving me a ride to work tomorrow?"

His gaze locked on hers, making her knees go weak. "Yes, I will," he replied. "Let's lock up and we can go. And I'll call my buddy Mike at the tire shop to see if he can get someone to come here and change out all four of your tires."

Relieved, she gave in to impulse and hugged him. When he tipped her face up to kiss her, she met him halfway.

When they broke apart, they were both breathing heavily.

"We'd better get going," he said, his voice husky.

She nodded, waiting while he gathered his things. They called the dogs and once they were safely in the backseat of the truck, drove home.

When they go there, he kissed her again. This time, they didn't even make it to the bedroom.

The next morning, she woke up in her own bed, pleasantly sore. Smiling, she began the now-familiar routine of shower, coffee and breakfast. Parker grinned and winked at her when she strolled into the kitchen. Happy, she found herself grinning back.

As they rode into the office together, she caught herself wondering if life could get any better. Instantly, she chided herself for letting her clearly foolish heart get ahead of her common sense. This—whatever it was—would be fun while it lasted, but it was only temporary. Not the kind of thing she needed to be building hopes and dreams on. She'd already learned her lesson about things like that.

They arrived at RTA early. True to his word, Parker had called his friend in tire repair, ordered the set of tires and arranged for them to be installed on her car as soon as they came in. She'd handed over her credit card, trying not to wince at the amount.

They'd barely finished that transaction when vehicles started pulling into the parking lot. She'd powered up her computer and checked the schedule first thing. Today promised to be a busy day with back-to-back tours this morning and again after lunch.

A steady stream of guests kept her too busy to think.

After logging in each of Parker's, Spence's and Hetty's groups, Genna went around and tidied up the office. Since they had a weekly cleaning service, most of the difficult work had been done, but she liked to keep busy.

As there were no new groups scheduled to go out for at least a few hours, Genna immediately tensed up when she saw a car pull up and park out front. Though her first impulse had her wanting to run to the front door and lock it, she remained behind the counter. Grabbing her phone, she was ready to dial 9-1-1 if she had to.

When she saw Lakin step out of the car, she nearly sagged against the counter with relief. Instead, she waited, wondering what had brought Parker's sister here. Lakin hadn't visited since Genna had started working at RTA.

When Lakin sauntered inside, the two women hugged. She followed Genna back to the breakroom. She grabbed a bottle of water from the fridge and took a seat at the table.

For a few minutes, they chatted about inconsequential things. Finally, Lakin pinned Genna with her gaze and got to the point.

"I understand you're staying with Parker." Though Lakin asked her question in a casual voice, Genna stressed inside.

"I am, for now. It's only temporary. I just haven't felt like it's safe to go home."

"I hear you. But I heard you put in an alarm system and new front and back doors. How much safer could your house be?"

Ah, now Genna understood. Though she and Lakin had always gotten along, Lakin asked the hard questions because she was looking out for her brother. Instead of upsetting her, this made Genna like the other woman even better.

Genna decided there wasn't any point in beating around the bush. "I'm not taking advantage of Parker, if that's what you're thinking," she said.

Though Lakin's surprised expression felt gratifying, Lakin didn't back down. "I think he has feelings for you."

"If he does, that's his business," Genna shot back. "And mine. Both Parker and I are adults."

Lakin could have bristled, or come back with some kind of sharp retort. Instead, she did none of those things. She stared at Genna for a moment before her mouth curled up and she laughed. "Dang, you're every bit as prickly as he is."

"Maybe," Genna allowed. "But Parker warned me that his family would be talking about this. I suggest, if you want any more detailed information, that you should speak to him."

Admiration shone in Lakin's eyes. "I always liked you," she said. "So, relax. As long as you don't hurt my brother, I think you and I will get along just fine."

"You know how Parker is. He does what he wants. Once he makes up his mind to do something, I don't think anyone can change his mind."

Lakin nodded. Expression delighted, she clapped. "Oh, wow! You have feelings for him, too."

Again, Genna didn't want to start any more gossip. "We're friends, okay? Don't make this something it's not."

After a brief pause, Lakin sighed. "Fine. It's just that Parker has been alone for so long, I've just been hoping he'd find love."

"Then take that up with him," Genna quipped. Then, after a deep breath, she got serious. "Lakin, I've always liked you, too. But I need you to understand what's happening here. I have a stalker. Someone who has broken into my house twice. And slashed all the tires on my car."

She took a deep breath and then continued. "Someone is calling the office and hanging up numerous times during the day. I went to get my hair cut and someone had canceled my appointment. Eli looked into it, but so far we don't have any idea who might be doing this. Honestly, I don't feel safe.

That's the only reason Parker offered to let me stay with him, in his guest bedroom, I might add. That's all there is. Nothing more."

Though Lakin grimaced in disappointment, she finally nodded. "Fine. I get it. That said, is there anything I can do to help?"

"I appreciate that." Genna squeezed Lakin's arm. "But I think I'm good right now."

"Were you able to get another hair appointment?" Lakin asked. "If not, I can call my hairdresser and see if she can fit you in."

"That's kind, but I was able to rebook. I did tell the salon not to cancel it under any circumstances."

Finally, Lakin got up to leave. She hugged Genna again, holding on a bit tighter this time. "You take care of yourself, okay?"

Genna promised she would.

"And while you're at it, take care of my brother, too." With a broad smile and a wave, Lakin went out the door, leaving Genna staring after her.

Chapter Twelve

Parker couldn't shake the feeling that he'd overlooked something. The entire time he led his group up the steep trails, he tried to figure out what.

Hell, he wasn't even sure what his feeling related to. What had happened at Genna's house? Or to her car? Or the multiple hangs-ups as she answered the phone at RTA.

All around him, the sights and sounds of nature. This trail had long been one of his favorites. This group, which consisted of avid birdwatchers hoping to check a few more species off their list, made appreciative noises at all the usual places. They paused at the halfway point, overlooking a small waterfall.

As the guests milled around, talking quietly among themselves, Parker gazed out over the familiar landscape and all he could see was Genna's beautiful face. He didn't notice one of the women moving closer until she bumped elbows with him.

"Penny for your thoughts," she said, smiling.

Blinking, he stared. It took a moment for her words to register. "Can I help you with something?" he asked in his best professional voice.

"Not really." Tone breezy, she casually touched his arm. "You just seemed really deep inside your head."

Somehow, he managed not to jerk his arm away. Realizing she was flirting, which had happened more than once over the years, he managed to murmur some banal nonsense about just taking in the scenery. Then he moved away, cleared his throat, and informed the group they were moving on.

This trip, the wildlife sightings were abundant, which meant no one should have a reason to complain. Not that anyone ever did. With one notable, recent exception. Miles Franklin. He wondered if Eli had talked with him yet.

They saw a black bear, from a respectable distance, across the water. Several bald eagles put in an appearance, as well as two river otters. A number of guests voiced their hope of seeing a wolf, but none was visible this day. Even so, between the gorgeous scenery and the wildlife, everyone seemed happy.

The woman who'd come up to him earlier stayed close, made sure she was first to comment when he addressed the group, and slipped him her phone number. He almost made her take it back, but didn't want to humiliate her in front of the others, so he pocketed it. He'd toss it later.

When headquarters came into sight through the trees, the overwhelming sense of relief made him shake his head at himself.

It wasn't that he didn't appreciate the flirting, though he—and RTA—had an ironclad rule of not dating guests. Even if the company didn't, he just couldn't imagine himself with anyone else besides Genna.

His feelings for her no longer surprised him. The more time they spent together, the more he realized how well they meshed. Not only the sex, though that alone was amazing, but everything else. He'd come to love her. Even though he

didn't believe she felt the same way about him, he'd do just about anything to make sure she was happy and secure.

Once everyone had filed inside, he left them with Genna for checkout and took himself off to the break room. Once there, he grabbed a cold can of cola from the fridge and sat down to drink it.

From the other room, he could hear Genna talking sweetly to all the guests. He took the folded piece of paper from his pocket, tore it in pieces and dropped it into the trash.

Just that simple act made him feel better.

Before he had time to think better of it, he called Eli. When Eli answered, he sounded tense. "What's up, Parker?"

"Is this a bad time?" Parker asked, already regretting making the call.

"No. Well, maybe a little."

Parker could envision the other man checking his watch. "If you're calling about the cookout, I already told Lakin I'd attend."

"Cookout?" Since Eli sounded busy, Parker decided to let it go. "No, I wanted to see if you'd ever had a chance to talk to Miles Franklin about Genna's slashed tires."

"I did. He vehemently denies having anything to do with that." Eli sighed. "Oddly enough, I believe him. He said he got his revenge by posting bad reviews online."

Parker made a mental note to check. "Okay. Then I guess we'll have to keep trying to figure out who did it then."

"You know, it might have just been vandals. I'm sorry I can't be of more help. This Fiancée Killer case is taking all of my energy and time."

"How's that going?" Parker asked, genuinely curious.

"Not good. The killer is becoming more dangerous. There have been five bodies discovered so far and I keep expect-

ing every day for there to be another." He exhaled. "I've just learned one of the victims is the sister of a friend."

"Who?"

"Noelle Harris."

Parker winced. Eli had been in love with Noelle back in college. "Damn, I'm sorry."

"Me, too. I'll always regret losing her."

Though Eli had never said this before, most of the family had long suspected. "That's why you've always said we should always go after someone if we truly want them."

"Exactly." The sadness in Eli's voice made Parker think. "And that's why I'm going to say it again. Go after what you want, Parker. Don't hesitate or wait too long. If you do, it might slip from your grasp."

"I have no idea what you're talking about," Parker lied.

"Yes, you do. We're not blind. Everyone knows how you feel about Genna. But I suspect she has no idea. If you truly want a chance with her, you've got to make a move."

"Sometimes, Genna reminds me of a wild doe," Parker said, surprising himself for speaking his thoughts out loud. "She's beautiful but easily spooked. I don't want to do anything that might make her run."

"Then take things slow. But at least let her know you care about her."

Since his brother had his well-being at heart, Parker mumbled something noncommittal and attempted to end the call.

"Wait," Eli ordered. "I thought you were calling about the cookout. Did you know that Lakin is organizing a cookout. Sunday afternoon, at RTA headquarters? She made sure there aren't any tours on the books. If you haven't heard, I'm sure you'll be hearing from her soon. She expects everyone to be there."

Parker wasn't sure how to react to that. "Even you?" he asked, aware of Eli's busy schedule and how seriously he took this investigation.

"Yes, even me. She thinks it's time everyone in the family got reacquainted with Genna. I've got to run. Talk to you later." And Eli ended the call.

No one ignored a direct order from Lakin, but since she hadn't spoken to him yet, Parker briefly considered trying to avoid her. But that would be pointless. When Genna had first come to work at RTA, Parker had tried to organize a get-together at a restaurant. The weather had thwarted that effort and then he'd never attempted to reschedule anything.

A cookout would be fine, he thought. Casual, in a familiar setting, which would set Genna at ease. Truthfully, he wanted his entire family to meet her. Even if she didn't know it yet, he hoped someday she'd be part of them.

Right now though, he needed to figure out who was stalking her and why. Eli had to focus on the Fiancée Killer, which in the grand scheme of things had a much greater urgency. But Parker wanted to find out who was tormenting Genna. As soon as possible, he planned to put a stop to it once and for all.

WHEN ANOTHER VEHICLE pulled into RTA's lot and parked, again Genna found herself stiffening. She had to get past this fear, she knew. She didn't intend to live the rest of her life terrified.

When the tall, graceful woman wearing an Alaska State Trooper uniform emerged and headed toward the front door, Genna allowed herself to relax.

It must have been Colton female visit time. First Lakin and now Kansas Colton. Maybe, just maybe, Kansas had come here on official business.

"Welcome," Genna said, smiling as Kansas strode up to the front counter. Like all of the Coltons except Lakin, who'd been adopted, Kansas had vibrant blue eyes. With her long dark hair pulled back, she looked both competent and professional.

Though Kansas and Lakin had both been several years behind Genna in school, when Genna had worked at RTA during high school, she'd gotten to know them since all of the Colton siblings had either worked there in some capacity or made a habit of stopping by.

Like Eli, Kansas had gone into law enforcement. From what Genna heard, she was damn good at her job.

"Any news?" Genna asked, not even trying to contain her hopeful eagerness.

"On the Fiancée Killer case?" Kansas shook her head. "Eli is taking the lead on that one." She came back around the counter. "I just came by to see if you have a minute to talk."

"I do," Genna replied. "Let's go back to the break room. I just made a fresh pot of coffee, but we have soft drinks and bottled water in the fridge." She glanced around. "Parker's group just left. He's around here somewhere, if that's who you came to see."

"Nope. I wanted to talk to you," Kansas answered. "Though I can say hi to Parker, too, if he puts in an appearance."

"I'm sure he will."

Kansas grabbed a water and took a seat at the table. Genna, who'd just finished her coffee, poured herself another cup and joined her.

"I heard about what's going on with you," Kansas said, covering Genna's hand with hers. "About your stalker and everything. Lakin told me and then Eli. I'm really sorry you're having to go through all that."

"Thanks." Figuring the next comment would be about her living situation, Genna decided she might as well mention it first. "I'm sure you've heard that Parker was generous enough to let me stay in his guest bedroom."

Kansas nodded. "I did. That's really kind of him." A quick smile flashed across her pretty face. "And I'm sure he has no ulterior motive whatsoever."

Startled, Genna reluctantly laughed. "He's a good guy. I really appreciate the way he's helping me."

"You know my entire family is talking about it." Kansas thought for a moment. "As they should. Do you have any idea how long it's been since Parker brought anyone to a family function?"

Before Genna could respond, Kansas answered the question herself. "High school. Since he's a year older than me, and the last girl he brought home was at senior prom, that's almost ten years."

Not sure why Kansas had brought this up now, Genna shrugged. "That's a long time. But Parker isn't bringing me home to meet the family. I'd think I would know if he was."

Kansas stared. "He didn't tell you about the cookout we're having here on Sunday? RTA is closed for the afternoon and the entire family is coming, along with their significant others."

"No." Perplexed, Genna swallowed. "Is Parker the one organizing it?"

For some reason, Kansas found her question amusing. "Parker? No. Have you ever seen a man organize a family get-together?"

Genna couldn't help but smile. "I guess not."

"Lakin decided to do this, kind of on the spur of the moment. She's pretty much ordered everyone to attend. In fact,

she started a group chat and is assigning each of us dishes to bring."

"Weird that she hasn't mentioned it to me," Genna said. Then she pushed to her feet and went to look for her phone. She'd left it on the shelf under her computer. The screen showed there was one missed call, a voicemail and several text messages. She'd heard none of the notifications. Checking, she realized that somehow she'd managed to accidently put her phone in silent mode.

"Lakin has been trying to reach me," she said, feeling sheepish. "No doubt to invite me to the cookout."

"I told you." Kansas kicked back in her chair and took a long drink of water. "I have to say, I've never seen Lakin happier. It's funny how all of this kind of flipped a switch with her."

Curious, Genna eyed her. "What do you mean?"

"Turned out, she's always wanted to renovate a hotel. Or so she claims. Either way, she's in her element. And I think the place will be fabulous when it's all finished."

"I've been meaning to stop by and take a look at it," Genna said. "I told Lakin I would."

"I kind of envy her, just a little," Kansas admitted. "Relationships are hard."

Genna nodded. "That, they are. Does that mean you're seeing someone?"

"Not really. I'm getting pressure from a guy named Scott at work, though he's in the Wasilla office. But he doesn't really do anything for me. Not like—" She seemed to catch herself, abruptly going quiet.

Since Genna didn't want to pry, she simply waited to see if Kansas would continue. When she didn't, Genna smiled. "I take it you are interested in someone else."

Kansas's casual shrug fooled no one. "Not really. I just

want to be prepared for when the right person does come along." She took a deep breath. "How about you?"

"What about me?" Genna asked, making a face. "My divorce was brutal. And he and my ex best friend harassed me so badly that I had to leave Anchorage and come back home to Shelby." She shuddered. "I'm in no hurry to go through anything like that again."

"I don't blame you," Kansas said. "And that's why I won't bug you to try and find out if you have any feelings for Parker. But I can't speak for the rest of my family. Once we're all together at that cookout..."

Genna sighed. "Point taken. All I can do is tell them the truth."

"And what would the truth be?" Kansas leaned forward, her gaze intent. Despite claiming she wouldn't ask, Genna could tell the other woman really wanted to know. She didn't mind. In fact, she found the Colton family's dedication to Parker admirable.

When Genna didn't immediately answer, Kansas shook her head. "Sorry. I'm not trying to pry, honestly. I'm just curious to hear what you plan to say to the rest of my family."

"What am I going to tell them?" Genna lifted her chin. "That's it's none of their business."

Both women laughed.

"I like you, Genna MacDougal," Kansas said. "RTA is lucky to have you."

"Thanks." It had been so long since Genna had an actual friend that she wasn't quite sure how to react. Early in their relationship, Chad had gradually isolated her from all of her friends except one. Ann. Now she knew why. By the time they'd dissolved the marriage, Genna hadn't been able to lean on a single friend, because she'd had none left.

To be honest, since she'd returned to Shelby, she hadn't

made any effort to befriend anyone. At first, she'd been too busy wallowing in self-pity. Then she'd gotten this job, realized she had a stalker, and somehow she and Parker had become friends. *With benefits*, she thought, glad Kansas couldn't read her mind.

When she looked up, she realized Kansas was studying her.

"Are you okay?" Kansas asked quietly.

The sound of the front door opening saved Genna from answering. She pushed to her feet. "It sounds like Parker is back."

Kansas stood also. "I'll say hi to him, but then I've got to run. It was great chatting with you. I'll see you on Sunday."

"Sunday?" Parker came around the corner. "Hey, Kansas. Did you stop by to tell Genna about the big cookout?"

"I did." Kansas smiled. "And I'd heard about everything that's been happening to her, so I wanted to check on her, too."

He met Genna's gaze, his expression serious, before looking back at Kansas. "Be honest. You also heard she is staying with me, and you wanted to check out the situation yourself."

Though Kansas had the grace to look sheepish, she simply shrugged. "Genna was kind enough to humor me."

"Did she set you straight on the situation?" he asked.

"She did." Kansas moved toward the break room door. "And now I have to run. I'll see you both at the cookout."

They followed Kansas into the front office. Side by side, they watched her drive off.

"How's it been going today?" Parker asked. "Any more hang-up calls?"

"All morning," she replied. "I'm even thinking about call-

ing the phone company and having them check to make sure something isn't wrong with our line."

"That's a great idea." He put his arm around her shoulder and pulled her close. She allowed herself to lean into him, enjoying the comfort of his muscular body. But then she remembered Spence and his group were due to return soon and stepped away. The last thing she needed was to give the Colton family anything else to talk about.

She made a call to the phone company. After they promised to check the company phone lines, she hung up. Turning around, she saw Parker had taken the chair in front of the other computer and appeared to be checking the schedule.

"Are you okay?" he asked, glancing at her.

"Yes," she replied. "Why does everyone keep asking me that?"

"Maybe because you seem a little bit jumpy?"

"Do I?" Then, without waiting for an answer, she continued. "You can't blame me, though. I think anyone would be unsettled with all that I've got going on."

"Agreed." His smile crinkled the corners of his eyes. "I have an idea. How would you like to get away for a couple of days? After the cookout, of course."

Intrigued, she nodded. "Tell me more."

"We could take one of my favorite hikes," he said, his smile widening. "Starting on one of the trails I take clients on, but branching off to another where they don't go. It's pretty remote. Perfect for camping out. We could spend a couple days out in the wilderness, just the two of us."

"Isn't that where the Fiancée Killer is finding his victims?" she asked. "On remote hiking trails?"

"On public land," he countered. "This is Colton land. And, also, those women were all hiking alone. You'll be with me. I promise, I'll protect you."

Though she'd never been the hiking or camping type, she really liked the idea. Except for one thing. The gossip their going away together would cause.

"You're worried about my family, aren't you?"

"Honestly, yes. They're already talking about us," she said. "The cookout has the potential to be brutal."

This comment made him laugh out loud. "Not my family. They're nosy. They'll ask a lot of intrusive questions, but all of it will be out of love. Do you really feel you have to worry about what they think?"

"Don't I?" she asked. "I do work for them, after all."

"Come on, just think about it." He got up and stretched, the movement drawing her gaze to the way his shirt stretched across his muscular biceps. "No pressure, but I really think it might do you good to get out of here for a while."

"You might be right about that," she admitted. "But we both have to work. I can't just ask for additional time off when I haven't been working here that long."

"You have two days off already scheduled," he said. "And I've moved mine so we're both off the same time."

Which explained what he'd been doing on the computer.

"I've never been camping," she admitted, bracing herself for his reaction. This was Alaska, after all.

"Never?" he asked, clearly not sure if she was joking.

"I tried once, when I was in high school and a bunch of us partied a bit too hearty up in Crowder's Meadow. They pitched a couple of tents, one for the boys, another for the girls. But Linda Sudan's dad showed up and insisted we all load up in the back of his truck." She shook her head, remembering.

"Several people got sick on the drive down to town. He woke up everyone's parents and told them what we'd been up to."

"Ouch." Parker covered his mouth with one hand, clearly trying not to laugh. "How old were you?"

"Seventeen. I was a senior. I'd lied and told my parents I was staying at my friend's house. They were not happy with me."

"I bet." His shoulders shook but somehow he managed to keep his face expressionless. "Well, at least you no longer have to worry about someone's dad. Or a bunch of drunk teenagers. It'll just be the two of us. We'll unplug and unwind. It'll be fun, I promise."

Seeing the eagerness in his handsome face, her heart squeezed. Though camping had never, not even once, appealed to her, she realized she liked the idea now. With him.

And not just because they were friends, either.

"I'll go," she finally said. "As long as you give me a detailed list of what to bring."

His answering smile felt like the sun coming out at the end of several dull, dreary days. "I'll take care of everything we need. You just pack a change of clothing and whatever toiletries you need. We'll plan on leaving right after the cookout."

And just like that, she realized she was going to go camping.

Chapter Thirteen

Watching Genna struggle to decide whether or not she wanted to go camping, Parker tried to contain his own eagerness. As soon as he'd come up with the idea, he'd realized how much this outing meant to him.

He'd watched Genna's tension and stress spiral, helpless to do anything to make it go away. When the idea of taking her away from it all had first occurred to him, he'd felt a sense of relief.

Except he remembered her saying that hiking wasn't her thing. She'd said something along the lines of never going hiking, so he wasn't sure she'd even go for the idea.

"It's fine if you're not into it," he said. "We can figure out something else we can do."

She locked gazes with him and then slowly nodded. "You know what? I do need to get away. And maybe it's time for me to try something new. So, yes, I'd very much like to go camping with you."

He couldn't help but grin. "Hiking, too?"

"Hiking, too." She smiled back.

"How do you feel about fishing?" he asked. "I know where the best spots are."

Lifting her chin, her smile widened. "I used to be pretty

good at fishing. My dad took me a lot growing up. But it's been a long time."

And then, before he could express his happiness about that revelation, she grabbed him and pulled him to her.

"Kiss me," she ordered.

Needing no second urging, he did exactly that.

They managed to peel themselves off each other and head home. As soon as they took care of feeding the dogs, they kissed again.

They ended up in his bed, their lovemaking as wild and passionate as ever. Later, as she dozed in his arms amid the tangled sheets, he found himself hoping that she might stay the entire night. But sometime later, while he slept, she got up and went to her own room. He'd only realized that when he'd reached for her and come up empty. He managed to fall back asleep, knowing he'd see her again once he woke.

Sunday morning dawned sunny and bright. Humming under his breath, he got up and showered before making coffee. When Genna came out to the kitchen for her own coffee, her lack of a smile and tight expression revealed her nervousness. She made her coffee and carried it over to the table. He'd already taken both dogs out and fed them their breakfast.

Sensing Genna's nervousness, June Bug immediately went to her and demanded petting. Genna's expression softened as she gathered her dog close.

"Are you all right?" he asked.

"I'm not sure about this," she admitted. "I'm all for socializing with my coworkers, it's the rest of your family that worries me. Everyone seems determined to make something out of nothing."

Her words hurt him, though he took care not to show it. "Define 'nothing,'" he said.

She gave him a sheepish look. "You know what I mean."

Since now was not the time to ask her to put labels on their relationship, he let her off the hook. "Just have fun with it. You already know most of them anyway. I've got your back, Spence and Hetty do, too. And you've already talked to Lakin and Kansas and Eli. That leaves my brother Mitchell, if he even shows up."

"And your parents and aunt and uncle," she said. "I guess I'm a little worried about seeing them again, that's all. Do you think they've heard the gossip about me staying with you?"

He couldn't help but chuckle. "Since Aunt Abby is a reporter for the newspaper, I'm sure she has. And since she and Uncle Ryan are super close with my mom and dad, it's likely they've heard the speculation."

"I see." She took another large gulp of her coffee.

"Do you mind if I ask why this bothers you so much?" he asked, even though he wasn't sure he wanted to hear her answer.

When she lifted her gaze to his, the anguish he saw in her eyes made his chest ache.

"I don't want them to think I'm taking advantage of you," she said. "You've been kind enough to let me stay here until I'm ready to go home. If I've overstayed my welcome, I need you to say so. Because I'm still not comfortable with being alone in my parents' house. I won't until whoever has been breaking in is caught."

Reaching across the table, he covered her hand with his. "No one will think that," he said. "They know me. I asked you to stay. I'm enjoying having you here."

A ghost of a smile flitted across her face. "It's the sex, isn't it?"

"That, too," he agreed, smiling just a little. "But it's been awesome getting to know you. I like you, Genna."

Some of the tension seemed to leave her. "I like you, too, Parker. I'm really looking forward to going camping with you." She took a long drink of her coffee. "But first, we've got to get through the cookout. Speaking of that, I'm going to go make sure I look presentable."

After she went back to her bedroom and closed the door, he decided he'd better do the same. A quick shower and a change of clothes later, he figured he was as ready as he was going to be.

When he came out to the living room, he found Genna already there, dressed and pacing.

"There you are!" she exclaimed, coming to a stop. "Are you ready to go?"

Surprised, he checked his fitness watch. "Sure, but we'd be way too early. It doesn't even start for another hour."

"True." She resumed taking laps around the room. "I definitely don't want to be the first ones there. But I don't want to be late, either. That will draw too much attention."

"Genna."

Stopping a few feet away, she looked at him. "What?"

"Come here." He held out his arms.

She walked right into them without hesitation. Wrapping her up and holding her close, he kissed the top of her head. "It's only a cookout. Don't make too much of it."

Face pressed against his chest, she sighed. "I know. I'm not generally so high-strung. Usually, a social get-together like this would be something I'd enjoy. But with the feeling that someone is always watching me and might jump out from the shadows at any moment, it's hard to feel even remotely normal. It feels like anxiety simmers just under the surface in everything I do."

"I get it. If you'd rather we cancel, we don't have to go."

He kissed her again, loving the way she clung to him, and aware in that moment he'd do anything to make her happy.

She shook her head. "No. A cookout will be fun. I'll be fine. I want to see everyone."

Though everything she said sounded like well-rehearsed reasons she'd used to convince herself, he simply nodded. "Up to you," he said. "But I think if we get there a few minutes after the start time, that'll be when everyone else is arriving. Except maybe Lakin. She's been known to be fashionably late."

This made Genna laugh. She moved away from him and went into the kitchen to grab a bottled water. "Thank you," she told him when she returned. "I'm all packed for the camping trip, too."

"Great. After the cookout, we'll come back here, collect the dogs and our stuff, and head out."

She nodded and then frowned thoughtfully. "Are you sure Revis is up for a hike?"

"He'll love it," he assured her. "I've taken him out a couple times and he truly enjoys it. We're not doing anything too strenuous, so he'll be fine."

"Good." Clearly relieved, she picked up her little JB, who'd come running over the moment Genna said Revis's name. "I'll be carrying her. I want to keep her close because I don't want to risk her getting eaten by something."

When the time came to leave for RTA, Genna appeared much calmer, even though she'd changed.

"You look great," he said, admiring her yellow sundress.

"Thanks. I changed four times." Her self-depreciating smile made him want to kiss her.

"I even put on makeup," she continued. "Which means no kisses, or you'll be wearing my red lipstick."

He held out his hand and she took it. They walked out to

his truck together. Genna had been instructed to bring chips, so she carried a cloth tote with four bags of them. "They didn't want me cooking," she said. "Which is fine, since they don't know me yet. There'll surely come a time when they'll be begging me to make my signature cheesecake."

Since the drive to headquarters wasn't long, he took his time. Unusually quiet, Genna kept her head turned so she could watch the landscape out the passenger's-side window.

When they turned onto RTA's long driveway, they could see the parking area already had numerous vehicles. A large sign had been hung from the covered porch: Closed to the Public. Private Party in Progress.

"Just in case," Parker said, finding a spot and pulling into it. "You never know when some customer is going to take it upon themselves to just show up and expect to be included in the festivities."

"Seriously?" She shook her head. "Has that actually happened?"

"More than once," he replied. "We treat our customers like family, so sometimes they actually think they *are*. That's why we've learned to put up a sign to discourage them."

Once he'd killed the engine, he went around to her side to help her out. The sun blazed up above from a blue sky, with little wisps of perfect white clouds dotting it like fat, woolly sheep in a field.

"Do you want to go in together?" he asked, guessing she wouldn't want to hold hands as that would be making too much of a statement. The scent of meat on the grill filled the air.

Glancing sideways at him, she nodded. "Of course."

Relieved, he took her arm. "Then let's do this."

"Okay," she replied.

Though they kept moving forward, he squeezed her arm. "Nervous?"

"Surprisingly, not really."

"Good," he said.

Inside the small office, two older women stood behind the counter, chatting. They fell silent as Parker and Genna moved toward them, though they both smiled. Genna recognized them from when she'd worked at RTA as a teen. The taller, curvy woman with the short brown hair was Abby Colton, Ryan's wife. Though he hadn't been by since she'd started working there, in the past he'd stopped by frequently because he loved to fish.

And the petite woman with the beautiful silver hair in the messy bun was Sasha Colton, Will's wife and Parker, Eli, Mitchell and Lakin's mother.

"Hi, Mom," Parker said, smiling back.

"Come here, you," she said fondly, holding out her arms.

The two hugged and then, to Genna's surprise, Sasha pulled Genna in for a hug, too. Then Abby hugged them both, before dragging them out back to see the rest of the noisy family.

Almost immediately, Parker and Genna got separated. Lakin, Kansas, and Hetty dragged her over to a buffet table where they were setting up a huge charcuterie board. Since Genna appeared to be having a great time, Parker decided not to worry about her and went over to help his dad, uncle and cousin Spence man the grill and smoker.

The next couple of hours flew past, with lots of laughter, good food and great company. Despite Eli's usual focus on work, he didn't once mention the Fiancée Killer. No one did. It was as if everyone needed a respite from the ominous shadow that hung over their town.

As things started to wind down, Spence and Hetty,

holding hands, slipped away. Next, Mitchell and Dove said goodbye. Lakin and Troy claimed they needed to check on something they were doing in their hotel renovations. Parker and Genna glanced at each other. With a slight smile, she gave a tiny nod and they, too, made their excuses and left.

"That was fun," Genna enthused, practically bouncing in her seat. "You're lucky to have such a large family. They're a lot of fun. Growing up, I always wished I had a brother or a sister or both."

"Thanks. I guess your family cookouts are a lot quieter."

"When we had them, yes. Since I'm an only child, I'd often invite one of my friends. But that was a long time ago. Both my parents embraced a vegan lifestyle after they retired, so there hasn't been a lot of grilling out." She shrugged. "When I stayed with them after my divorce, they didn't even allow meat inside the house. If I wanted a burger, I had to eat out."

They turned onto his street. She sat up straight, her expression eager. "I can't wait to see my little June Bug. I almost took her to the cookout today, but wasn't sure how that would go over."

"Same with Revis," he admitted. "Hopefully, they'll both enjoy camping."

As he pulled into his driveway, Genna gasped. "The front door is wide open."

Since he'd locked it, that meant someone had broken in.

Parking, he ran for the house, Genna right on his heels.

"June Bug," she called. "Revis. Where are you?"

Heart sinking, he realized there were no signs of the dogs anywhere. Either whoever had broken in had taken them or they'd escaped out the open door.

"No." Genna stood frozen for a moment. "They have to be here somewhere. Help me search the house."

Quickly and methodically, they conducted a thorough search of every inch of the place. They opened closet doors, checked under beds, and even looked in the fenced backyard in case they'd been locked out. The entire time, Parker found himself praying nothing cruel had been done to the dogs.

"Time to search the neighborhood," he finally announced. "Depending on how long they've been gone, we can only hope they didn't get far."

"Or that someone took them," she responded, her tone as bleak as her expression. "I swear no one had better have harmed a single hair on those dogs."

"I don't think they did," he reassured her, even though he wasn't positive. He kept his worry and anger banked low inside, wanting to offer Genna nothing but hope. "If it's your stalker, their main objective seems to be to make you aware they have access to your life. Harming an innocent pet wouldn't serve any purpose."

"I hope you're right."

Outside, after closing the front door, they faced the street. "You go west, I'll take east," he said. "Call me if you see them."

SPEED WALKING, while searching for any sign of either of the two dogs, Genna felt as if her heart had been pulverized inside her chest. Not only was she terrified, worried about her beloved little dog and Parker's big one, but for the first time since all of this stalking had begun, rage simmered inside her. How dare they—whoever they were—come anywhere near JB and Revis?

She could only hope the two had simply wandered off. Because if someone had picked them up and taken them somewhere, the chance of getting the dogs back would be slim to none.

If they were out here, she'd find them. She had to. Swallowing hard, she kept looking, refusing to cry.

Her phone rang. Parker. "Did you see them?" she asked, breathless with hope.

"Not yet. If I remember right, the shelter microchipped them before we adopted. That's a good thing."

Rubbing her aching temple, she agreed. "Only if they're found."

"They will be." He sounded confident. Clearly, he didn't share her secret fear that whoever had taken them would harm the dogs.

"I've checked all the way to the end of your street," she said. "I'm thinking maybe we should call animal control, but they're probably not open on Sunday."

"I'll call and leave a message. Since they're part of the police department, they'll know Eli. Let me do that now."

After Parker had ended the call, Genna turned north and continued searching. She continually called June Bug's and Revis's names, even though she wasn't confident either dog knew their new names yet. She had no idea what they'd been called before ending up in the shelter.

Each step she took without spotting them felt like another nail driven into her heart.

Finally, she turned around and headed back to the house. If she wanted to cover a greater distance, it would be better to use a vehicle.

She and Parker got there at the same time. "I think we need to drive around and keep looking," he said. "I also left a voicemail for my friend who works for animal control."

Trying not to panic, she agreed. They got into his truck and drove slowly, with the windows down, calling their dogs' names over and over.

"Still no sign of them," she said. "They've got to be

around here somewhere. Unless whoever broke in took them."

"I refuse to consider that possibility," Parker responded. "Whoever broke in, deliberately left the door open, knowing the dogs would run off."

A flash of black in the trees caught her eyes. "Stop," she said. "I think I might have seen Revis." Either that, or some other kind of wildlife. The kind that would make a meal of JB in two bites.

Immediately, he pulled over. "Let's be careful. Just in case."

"Agreed." Cupping her hands to her mouth, she called out June Bug's name. A second later, Parker called for Revis.

If she'd hoped for one or both of the dogs to come running out of the woods, she was sorely disappointed.

Side by side, she and Parker pushed through the tangled undergrowth into the forest. Up above, birdsong continued, but they saw no footprints, no trampled plants, no sign the dogs had been there.

"Maybe you saw a deer," Parker said. He called for Revis once more. Genna joined him, her voice breaking as she said June Bug's name.

"Let's go back." Parker took her arm.

"I'm not giving up."

"We're not," he told her. "Let's keep driving around the neighborhood and hope we spot them."

"Maybe we should make signs and stick them up at every intersection," she said, climbing back up into the truck.

"If we don't have any luck this time, we'll do that," he replied.

Heart in her throat, she nodded.

His phone rang. "It's Spence," he said. "Let me fill him in on what's going on. I'll put the call on speaker."

"Hey, Spence, what's up?"

Spence laughed. "Did you lose something?"

Genna sat up straight, exchanging a look with Parker.

"What do you mean?" Parker asked.

"I had to go back to headquarters to help my mom find something, and those two dogs you and Genna got just showed up."

"What?" Genna squealed. "I can't believe it. We've been searching all over for them."

"We brought them inside and gave them water," Spence said. "They seemed a little thirsty."

"We're on our way," Parker said, starting the truck. "See you in a few."

After ending the call, he leaned over and gave her a jubilant kiss. Unable to contain her relief, she kissed him back. Then he put the truck in gear and they went to collect their dogs.

As they pulled into RTA's lot, Spence came out to meet them. He waited on the covered porch as they hurried over.

"Mind telling me what happened?" he asked, looking from one to the other. "How the heck did your dogs wind up here?"

"Long story," Parker drawled. "Which we'll be happy to tell you after we see Revis and JB."

"Go for it." Spence stepped aside.

Genna rushed past him, pushing open the door. Once inside, she spotted her little dog all curled up in her dog bed. "June Bug," she said, dropping to her knees and holding out her arms. "Baby girl, come here."

JB lifted her head. Then, tail wagging, she trotted over to Genna.

Focused on reuniting with JB, Genna heard Parker calling Revis. A second later, Revis blew past her, barreling to-

ward his owner. He barked twice, ran a quick circle around the room, and then settled on his belly in front of Parker.

"I can't express how glad I am that they're okay," Genna said, looking up at Spence. "Thank you for holding them until we could get here. I had all kinds of awful scenarios going through my head."

Spence nodded. "I still want to know how they got loose."

Fingers still tangled in Revis's fur, Parker told him. As he listened, Spence's expression darkened.

"Did you make a police report?" Spence asked.

"Not yet. We didn't have time to look around and see if anything is missing," Parker replied.

"I bet nothing is." Genna spoke up. She scooped up her dog and got to her feet. "I think this was another attempt by my stalker to mess with me."

Parker nodded. "I agree."

Spence looked from one to the other. "This needs to stop," he said. "Have you talked to Eli?"

"Yes. And to Kansas," Genna said. "But this time, whoever is harassing me went too far. You don't mess with my dogs. I'm pulling out all the stops. I intend to do whatever it takes to catch this person and put a stop to all of this."

"What are you going to do?" Spence asked, crossing his arms.

"I don't know yet," Genna admitted. "But we'll figure something out."

"Let me know if I can help." Spence squeezed Genna's shoulder before clapping Parker on the back. "I've got to run. Will you two lock up?"

"Of course." Parker walked his cousin out, Revis trotting along at his side.

When he returned, Revis rushed over to check on JB.

Genna set her down and the two dogs walked off together, curing up with each other in the larger dog bed.

Parker watched them for a moment and then heaved a sigh.

"Do you still want to go camping?" he asked.

"I don't know. We haven't even had time to see if anything is missing from your place."

"Checking that will only take a few minutes," he said, his unruffled tone matching his expression. "And I vote we go. Now we need to get away even more."

She couldn't help but agree with him. "We're all packed. Let's do it. I'll actually feel safer getting out of town."

"And you could use some time to decompress," he said.

After loading up the dogs, they drove to Parker's place. After he backed his truck up to the garage, she cuddled JB close and sat for a moment before getting out.

Parker and Revis stayed close and they all went inside together. As far as Genna could tell, nothing appeared to have been disturbed.

"I don't think they took anything," Parker said, turning a slow circle so he could view the entire room. "Let me check my bedroom really quickly. You check yours."

Though she already knew she wouldn't find anything missing, she nodded. Still carrying JB, since she didn't want to let her out of her sight, she took a quick look. As far as she could tell, nothing had been disturbed. Still neatly made, her bed hadn't been touched. She opened a few dresser drawers just in case, but everything remained exactly the way she'd left it.

When she returned to the living room, she found Parker waiting for her. "I'm beginning to think I've lost my mind," he said. "Maybe I didn't close the front door all the way and it blew open. Not only has nothing been disturbed, but

I can't even find a point of entry. No broken windows and the back door is still locked with the dead bolt, so I'm beginning to think no one has been in here."

Except Genna felt positive that someone had. The same person who'd broken into her house twice. The one who'd slashed all four of her tires. She just needed to find proof.

But how?

Setting JB down, she went over to the front door and inspected it. As Parker had said, she saw no sign of forced entry.

"I'll be right back," she said and stepped outside. Walking the perimeter of the house, she wasn't entirely sure what she was looking for. She only felt she'd know when she saw it.

Opening the fence gate, she made a mental note to tell Parker it needed to be locked. She stepped into the backyard. On the backside of the house, she finally noticed something. A small bush under one of the windows appeared crushed.

It could have been anything. It could have been nothing. Or it might be the clue she'd been looking for.

She moved closer. There. That impression in the dirt next to the bush could be a footprint.

Curious, she stepped closer and tried to lift the window. To her astonishment, it easily opened.

"The point of entry," she said out loud. She spun around so quickly, she almost lost her footing. To her shock, she realized Parker had followed her and was standing a few feet behind her.

"See?" she asked, gesturing toward the still-open window.

"I do." His furious expression at odds with his calm tone, he moved past her and shoved the window the rest of the way up.

"Should we notify the police?" she asked.

"And tell them what? That nothing was taken? No, if someone broke into my home, didn't touch anything, and left the front door open so the dogs could get out, they only had one intention. To harass us."

She nodded.

"I agree with you a hundred percent," he continued. "Mess with our dogs and you've gone too far. This means war. We're going to find out who is doing this. They need to be stopped."

"And pay for what they've done," she finished. "Now we just need to figure out how."

He touched her shoulder. "Let's get out of here. Camping will help clear our heads. Surely, we can come up with a plan."

Chapter Fourteen

After making sure all the windows in the house were now locked, Parker and Genna loaded up his truck. They'd packed the dogs' blankets to sleep on, as well as their food and bowls. As usual, he'd been able to fit everything in his oversized backpack.

"What about the tent?" she asked, looking around. "Honestly, I don't know how we're going to carry all the stuff we need."

"I've packed it." He patted his gear. "Over the years, I've mastered the art of filling this. I think we've got everything we need."

Her eyes widened but she nodded. "No ice chest?"

"Nope. There's a stream with fresh running water near the campsite," he replied.

"I guess that's good." She didn't sound too certain.

Eyeing his pack, she looked at her significantly smaller one. "How heavy is that?"

"A little heavy," he said. "But not too much for me to carry."

Once they were settled in the truck and had driven off, the righteous indignation that had fueled Genna earlier appeared to dissipate. She put JB in the backseat so the two

dogs could sleep and then heaved a sigh. "I need this more than I realized."

"I know you do," he said, aching to touch her but keeping his hands on the steering wheel. "I do, too."

Her answering smile stole his breath. For a heartbeat, he considered telling her how he felt, but decided not to. Not yet. In case she didn't feel the same way, he didn't want to make things awkward on the camping trip.

"You were pretty impressive back there, figuring out how they got into the house," he said instead.

Just like that, the smile vanished from her face. "If you don't mind, can we not talk about that for a little bit? I'd like to forget, even if just for a few hours."

"You got it," he replied, mentally kicking himself. Fiddling with the radio, he asked her what kind of music she wanted to listen to.

"Hip-hop or rock," she said, surprising him. "Though I usually tend to listen to country music, I need something fierce and loud to go with my mood right now."

This made him laugh. "I do something similar. I don't know why, but it helps."

"It does," she agreed. "Once I get this out of my system, I'll be fine." She glanced back at the dogs, now sleeping. "Unfortunately, we can't blare it. I don't want to hurt their ears."

He found the only station that played what they called "Hit Music and Classic Rock."

"KVAK, 93.3," he said. "Hopefully there's something on their playlist that will hit the spot."

A country song was playing. They exchanged looks. "Hit music," she said. "It's fine. Any music is good."

They drove past RTA headquarters, continuing on for a few miles. The elevation increased as they headed up the

side of the mountain. "This is where we take the hiking expeditions," he said as they pulled into the small parking lot with a sign that marked it as the trailhead.

"Are there going to be other people here?" she asked, not even trying to mask her disappointment. "I'm not sure I'm up for a big crowd."

Unable to resist, he squeezed her arm, battling the urge to let his hand linger. "No. There's a point midway up where the trail splits off. I take the tourists up on the south side. We're heading up the north."

They shouldered their backpacks and set off. He let Revis range ahead of them, but Genna insisted on carrying JB. "She's so small, I'm afraid something will eat her," she explained.

Which made perfect sense.

As they headed up the trail, Genna kept a good pace. Since he didn't want to make her overdo it, he watched her carefully in case she needed to rest.

"I'm not going to topple over," she said dryly, catching him as he sneaked a sideways glance at her. "Despite me telling you that I don't go hiking, I'm still in pretty decent shape physically."

"I'll say," he drawled, earning her laughter.

When they reached the halfway point, marked by a bench and several signs, Parker removed his backpack and plopped down. "Let's take a quick break," he said, whistling for Revis. The dog immediately returned, sitting down at Parker's feet.

With a grateful smile, Genna took off her own pack and sat next to him. "Thanks," she said, grabbing her water bottle from the side of her backpack and drinking deep.

Parker opened a collapsible dog bowl and poured water into it for the dogs. They both drank eagerly.

"Now the fun begins," he said. "The trail is going to get markedly steeper once we make that turn. If you need to stop and rest, just say so, okay?"

"Okay." She grimaced. "So far, this hasn't been too bad. And it's beautiful here."

"Just wait until we get to the meadow where I usually camp," he told her. "And at night, the skies are amazing."

"How often do you camp up here?" she asked, genuinely curious.

He shrugged. "Whenever I feel the need to get away. Most times, I come by myself. But Spence has been here with me a few times. Eli, too. Mitchell has even been a couple of times." He flashed a sheepish grin. "It's a great place to get your mind aligned with your soul."

His poetic choice of phrase made her melt. To be honest, not only did he continually surprise her, but the more she got to know him, the more she realized how unique he was. Looking at him, with his muscular, toned body and outdoorsy appearance, the depths of his personality added to his already compelling sex appeal.

Renewed, they carried on. The exertion felt good, as if the hike brought a rush of endorphins. She felt strong and capable and unbelievably alive. Happy.

"Are you doing okay?" he asked. Then, without waiting for an answer, he asked her if she wanted him to carry JB for a bit.

"Thank you, but I've got her," she replied. "I'm fine and she's not heavy at all."

The trail grew progressively steeper and narrower as it curved up the side of the mountain. Since they could no longer hike side by side, Parker trekked ahead. She found she enjoyed having his backside to look at, especially since the height made her feel a little dizzy.

The drop-off to her right looked treacherous, even though there seemed to be plenty of trees to help break the fall. Luckily, the path they were on seemed solid. Despite that, she kept to her left, just in case her clumsy self were to take an accidental misstep. She wasn't too worried about hurting herself. But she couldn't risk anything happening to JB.

Apparently unconcerned, Parker walked a few feet ahead of her, though he kept close. She realized he'd purposely made his own pace slower to match hers, which she appreciated.

"Where's Revis?" she asked, looking around for the large dog.

Hearing his name, Revis came trotting back to them, panting happily. He made a few loops around both Parker and Genna before settling in to walk in between them.

"He's really enjoying himself," Parker said. "I'm so glad I was able to get him out of the shelter."

"Me, too."

"What about you?" he asked, glancing over his shoulder. "Are you having fun?"

She thought for a moment. "Actually, I am. More than I expected. It's not as physically taxing as I thought it would be."

His grin made her breath catch. "I can think of some other activities we can do later that will definitely be exhausting."

Grinning back, she wondered if he knew her entire body flushed. "You know, I might be able to be convinced to do this again," she mused. "With the right incentive, of course."

His laughter echoed off the rocks. "Look." He pointed. Above them, an eagle wheeled, beautiful against the bright blue sky. She'd grown up seeing the majestic birds, but for some reason out here, the sight hit differently. To her surprise, tears stung her eyes.

Keeping her hold on JB, she quickly wiped them away. Though she'd felt raw ever since realizing she'd simply traded one stalker for another after moving here, the emotion felt like a different kind of vulnerability. Was she ready to take the kind of risk she'd sworn she'd never take again? Did she dare to trust Parker with her heart?

Completely unaware of her thoughts, Parker stopped and turned to face her. "Up ahead, the path looks like it ends at some boulders," he warned. "It's a good place to stop and rest, as long as you watch out for snakes."

She started. He'd said that so casually. "I think I'll pass," she said. "Since I'm not a fan of snakes, I'd rather just get to our camping area."

"I get it." He smiled at her before moving forward. Though he loved his large family, both immediate and extended, being out here with Genna and the dogs felt like another kind of family togetherness. Both wholesome and intimate. He could definitely get used to this. He wondered what Genna thought, but decided it would be better not to ask.

Finally, the incline started to level out. "We're almost there," he told her, glancing over his shoulder.

"Good," she replied, huffing and puffing just a little. She wiped at her forehead with the back of her hand. "I'm getting to the point where I'd been thinking about telling you I need to rest."

"Not too much longer, I promise." Though he wanted to pick up the pace, he stayed steady. "We keep a little storage building up here with supplies like a cook stove and folding chairs. And if whoever camps up here last has firewood left over, it's stored in there, too."

"Interesting." She seemed to be struggling to catch her

breath. "But why not store your tent there, too? Seems like it would be less to carry."

"There's a spare tent in case it's needed. But we all have our own tents, and I prefer to bring mine. You'll like it, I promise."

"I'll like it when we can stop hiking," she grumbled, shifting JB in her arms. "My little dog has gotten heavier."

This made him chuckle. "A few more yards." Unable to contain his eagerness, he moved ahead.

Her pace slightly slower, she followed.

GENNA DIDN'T WANT to be a party pooper, but she clearly wasn't as fit as Parker. He hiked for a living, while her exercise routine consisted of riding her Peloton bike. She'd always considered herself in pretty good shape, but this uphill hiking took things to another level.

"Here we are," he announced, turning a slow circle with his arms outstretched. "My favorite meadow."

More of a clearing than a meadow, the grassy area sat nestled in between a rock wall on one side, forest on two others, and the sloping hill that led to the cliffs on the fourth. There was more than enough area to pitch a tent, build a fire pit and set up some chairs. A small, weathered wooden building had been built near a grove of trees. Close to the place they'd stopped, someone had already made a stone fire pit, the circle large enough for a decent fire.

"I should've brought marshmallows," she impulsively said.

Glancing at her, he grinned. "I did."

Unable to keep from smiling back, she sighed. "What about bears?" she asked, slightly nervous.

He looked up. "As long as we don't keep food out, they

tend to leave us alone. The shed comes in handy for that, too."

"Food." She swallowed. "I didn't even think to pack any of that. What did we bring to eat? And please don't say we're going to forage for berries and mushrooms and edible plants."

"You stole my line," he teased. She loved the way the sun made his blue eyes sparkle. "I thought we'd fish for our dinner and eat from the endless bounty that nature provides."

Dismayed, she stared at him. "You're kidding, right?"

He held her gaze, expression serious. "It's fun and easy, I promise."

Though she had a feeling she'd be going hungry tonight, she reluctantly nodded. "I guess I'll just have to trust you."

"If you weren't carrying JB, I'd hug you right now," he said. Which made her want to set her little dog down, which she wouldn't just yet. She wanted to thoroughly check out the area for snakes and any other kind of menace, before letting JB set her little paws on the ground. On a leash, of course.

"Maybe later," she said. Then, as he tilted his head and drank her in with his eyes, she amended her statement. "Definitely later."

"I'll say." Setting his pack on the ground, he began removing what she guessed must be the tent. "Do you want me to help you set up?" she asked.

"Sure." He continued unpacking. "By the way, I was kidding about foraging for our meals. I brought food. Most of it's in cans, which the bears can't smell. Nothing fancy, but enough to fill our bellies. And if we catch any fish, I can clean them and fry them up."

Thinking of a fish fry, her stomach growled. She'd picked

at the spread at the cookout, too nervous to sit down and do justice to the repast.

"You didn't eat earlier?" he asked, his brows raised.

"I tried." She shrugged. "I actually got kind of busy socializing. I did grab a pulled pork sandwich and some pasta salad, but that was early on. All this exercise has made me work up an appetite."

His smile widened. "Me, too," he said, the husky thrum in his voice making her think he wasn't talking about food. Flushing, she ducked her head, which made him chuckle again.

After getting everything laid out in the spot he'd chosen, Parker showed her what he needed her to do to help.

The tent, once spread out, looked a lot bigger than she'd expected. "This is really nice," she said, finally clipping June Bug's leash on and setting her on the ground. Immediately, Revis ran over and sniffed his friend before bounding off, eager to show her around.

Aware of the leash, JB glanced up at Genna, as if pleading to be set free. Since Genna wasn't willing to do that, she decided she'd take her little dog to follow Revis once they were done.

Her assistance mostly consisted of her standing around and holding poles up while Parker hammered pegs into the ground. June Bug, clearly bored with the entire situation, laid in the grass and watched them. Revis returned and sat down next to his little friend.

Once the tent had been set up, Parker thanked her for helping and immediately got busy doing other things.

"I'm going to take June Bug to go potty," she told him.

"Okay," he replied, looking up from where he'd begun stacking firewood for them to use later. "Don't go too far. And stay close to the path. There are quite a few cliffs up

here and if you wander off the trail, you could easily take a tumble before you realize the danger. Over the years, we've had more than a few hikers take nasty falls."

She nodded, eyeing his growing woodpile. "I'll keep that in mind. Do you want me to bring back any branches or anything if I find some?"

"If you see any good ones in your path, sure. Otherwise, I'll just keep foraging. There seems to be no shortage of them right around us, in the woods close to the camp, so there's no need to go out of your way."

After double checking the leash onto JB's collar, Genna waved at Parker and walked away. Luckily, even out here in the flatter area, the trail looked well defined and she stuck to it. Revis ranged ahead, but little JB trotted a few paces away.

Glad she'd had time to rest from the hike, Genna glanced around. It might only be her imagination, but the air felt clearer, the sky seemed bluer and the sun warmer. She felt… lighter, somehow.

As Parker had promised, out here in the wilderness she felt like she could look at things differently. As if her burdens had fallen away when they'd left civilization behind. When she got back to camp, she'd thank him. Imagining his reaction made her smile.

Despite the beauty and the sense of peace, she stayed alert and continually scanned the woods around them. She kept her bear spray handy, tucked into her pocket. Hopefully, she wouldn't have to use it.

June Bug seemed eager to explore. Genna smiled as she watched the little dog trot ahead of her, pulling slightly on the leash. Revis made joyous circles around them before bounding ahead and disappearing momentarily from view.

As they so often seemed to do these days, her thoughts circled back around to Parker. She'd never felt closer to an-

other human being. Her feelings had slowly blossomed over time. Now she couldn't imagine life without him.

Love. A word that, until recently, had only meant anguish, pain and bitterness. She'd thought she'd never trust her heart again. But Parker, sexy, kind Parker, had showed her there was another way.

Damn it, this had become more than next-level physical attraction. The sparks that blazed between them at even the slightest touch, the way his kiss rocked her all the way to her core. And the lovemaking. Oh, hell. She'd never had lovemaking so intense, so…perfect.

She loved the man. She just hadn't said it out loud. Because she wasn't sure he felt the same way. And if she scared him off…well, she thought losing him might just destroy her.

JB wandered off the trail and Genna followed her, careful to only let her go a few feet as she remembered what Parker had said about the cliffs. Above, in the tree canopy, birds sang and flitted from tree to tree. She'd hoped to see some smaller wildlife, a rabbit or a deer, but figured Revis crashing through the underbrush probably scared them off.

Again, she wondered how Parker would react if she told him how she felt. Just trying to imagine made her stomach ache.

Maybe it would just be better to keep going the way they'd been. Day by day. Hoping that once her stalker was caught and she returned home, she and Parker would continue to see each other.

Behind her, a sound. A twig snapping. Heart skipping a beat, she spun, canvassing the woods for signs of wildlife. JB whined. Quickly, Genna scooped her up, holding her close, ready to run if she needed to.

Revis returned immediately, panting. He came to Genna for a pet, sniffed JB, and then continued his exploration.

Since he didn't seem alarmed, she relaxed slightly. But decided it was time to return to camp.

Turning, she and her two canine companions went back the way they'd came.

At camp, she saw that Parker had up two chairs around the stone fire pit and had piled a neat stack of wood inside for later. The door to the storage building sat open, and he'd pulled out what looked like a small grill or cook stove.

Spotting Parker, Revis gave a happy woof and ran over to him, plumed tail wagging. Parker dropped down to his haunches and gathered his dog close to him. "He's a good boy," he crooned, which made Revis wiggle his entire body with joy.

JB watched all this, tilting her little head. Genna realized, to her little dog, Revis was family. The notion made her chest tight.

Something of her thoughts must have showed on her face.

"What's wrong?" Parker asked, looking up from his dog.

"Nothing," she answered quickly. "I just enjoy how much you love Revis."

Getting to his feet, he shrugged. "About the same as you love your June Bug."

She decided to tell him the truth. "Honestly, I'm having a hard time letting go of what happened earlier. Breaking into my house is one thing, but breaking into yours is another. And messing with our dogs…" Swallowing hard, she tried to tamp down her still-simmering rage.

"I'm going to level with you. I've had enough of this stalking nonsense," she told Parker. "Whoever is trying to terrorize me has finally gone too far. I want them caught."

Watching her, he slowly nodded. "I agree. What are you thinking?"

"Simple. We set a trap. Pretend to be gone but one of

us—likely me—stays hidden in the house. If we can catch them in the act, it'll all be over."

"Maybe so, but that could be incredibly dangerous," he cautioned. "I don't think it'd be safe at all."

"Maybe not, but the thought of losing our dogs made me physically ill. This has gone on far too long. I'm going forward with my plan, with or without your help."

He studied her for a moment. "Then I insist that I be the one who stays behind. Not you."

Instead of arguing, she shrugged.

"Tell me this first…" He asked, "What's the plan once we catch them?"

"Turn them over to the authorities," she answered promptly. "I will definitely be pressing charges."

"Can we let this go for now? It bothers me, too, but the entire reason we came up here was to escape from all the stress of what was going on back in town."

He had a point. "I'll try," she promised. "I actually feel better now that I've let you know how I feel."

"Good." Crossing over to her, he kissed her. Not on the mouth but on the cheek.

Bemused, she considered asking for more, but decided there'd be time enough for that later. After all, they were sharing a tent.

Now that her heartbeat had slowed, she once again looked around them. Surrounded by nature, the sheer beauty of this Alaskan wilderness would be enough to calm even the most stressed-out psyche.

"I'm letting it go," she promised.

"I'll hold you to that." Moving away, he grabbed a battered, plastic tackle box, opened it and looked through it. Then, apparently satisfied with what he'd found, he closed it up and stood.

"This looks great," she said, gesturing at their campsite. "Like something out of a camping magazine. One of the ones we keep in the waiting room at headquarters."

Her comment made him beam. "Thanks. I really think you're going to enjoy this experience."

She almost told him she knew she would. She had everything that she could ever want and need right here.

"What's on the agenda for the rest of today?" she asked, dropping into one of the chairs, still holding JB on her lap.

"There is no agenda," he answered. "That's the entire point in coming up here. Just relax and do whatever feels right." He blinked then grinned at her. "It's all very Zen."

Startled into laughter, she leaned back and closed her eyes. "Maybe I'll just sit here and rest," she said, covering a yawn with one hand. "I also brought along a book I've been dying to read. I can do one or the other."

"Enjoy," Parker said. "Revis and I are going fishing. You're welcome to come if you want."

Shaking her head, she waved him away. "I'm good. I hope you catch something. I'm looking forward to that fish fry you promised earlier."

His short bark of laughter made her smile.

"I'll be back," he said. "The river isn't too far away, but I probably won't hear you if you holler for me. Please call or text if you need anything. But only if it's urgent."

She loved that he tacked that last sentence on. "What could be urgent out here?" she said and then thought of bears and wolves and even an angry moose. Pushing those images out of her head, she watched until he and his dog disappeared from sight.

"You never know," Parker replied. "Just be careful. Cell service is iffy at best."

Once Parker and Revis had left, she glanced all around

the campsite one more time, just in case. All quiet, all calm. And still rustic. One deep breath and then another. She leaned back, exhaled and closed her eyes again. Slowly, she felt all the tension leaving her body.

JB felt it, too. Still curled in Genna's lap, the little dog began to quietly snore.

In the peace and quiet, she must have dozed off. A loud crash from somewhere in the woods startled her awake. JB jumped down and, completely disregarding the leash trailing after her, took off in the direction of the sound, barking urgently.

"June Bug!" Genna jumped to her feet, grabbing for the leash. She missed. Calling for JB, which the dog ignored, she ran after her. Heart pounding, she hoped and prayed the little minx wasn't pursuing something dangerous.

Leaves and twigs cracked under her feet as she ran. JB had crossed the hiking path and run down the first of several inclines. Aware she had to be careful—but also knowing she needed to catch JB before something awful happened—Genna kept going. Holding on to saplings, skidding down the slope and praying she didn't fall as she followed the sound of June Bug's frantic barking.

Whatever this was couldn't be good.

Finally, she caught sight of her dog. JB had stopped in one spot, though she continued barking at something hiding in the brush. As Genna drew closer, a chill raced up her spine. The spot where JB stood appeared to be mere feet away from the edge of a particularly steep drop-off.

"Baby girl, come here," Genna begged. She wished she had some dog treats or something she could use to lure JB to her. Still barking and intent on whatever she'd found, the little dog ignored Genna.

Moving slowly so she didn't startle her pup, Genna crept

closer. All she could do was hope whatever JB had cornered wasn't something big and vicious.

A shape stepped out from behind the tree. Genna gasped. "You!" That was all she got out before they grabbed her and shoved her off the cliff.

Chapter Fifteen

Reeling in a good-sized salmon, the sound of shrill barking broke the quiet of the late afternoon. In the act of tying the fish on a line and placing it into the water, Parker froze and listened. Frantic barking, again and again. Since they were alone in the woods, he could vividly imagine what kind of creature the dog might have discovered. It might be something small. But then again, it might not be.

Revis had also been listening, head cocked. He glanced at Parker, almost as if asking for permission.

"Go," Parker ordered. "Find JB."

The dog took off. Parker briefly debated gathering up his gear, but in the end just left it and ran. Revis had already disappeared from his sight.

And then he heard Genna scream. The shrill sound was abruptly cut off, which seemed even worse. JB however, continued barking.

Heart pounding, Parker increased his speed. He knew this area like the back of his hand. Judging from where the barking seemed to be coming from, he thought he had a good idea of the location. It was where the hiking trail made a sharp turn before continuing to make a zigzag path up the steep face of a rock cliff. The terrain there grew tricky, the path even narrower. Most hikers turned around at that point,

unless they were into rock climbing. Parker had only gone up there once and that had been enough. He sure as hell hoped Genna hadn't tried making it up with her dog in tow.

JB's continued frenetic barking meant at least she was alive.

Still running, Parker reached camp and found it empty. JB continued barking from somewhere in the distance. He realized he couldn't hear Genna calling for help, though he was aware that could be a bad thing, too.

If June Bug had gotten into some sort of trouble, he knew Genna would be there trying to rescue her. "Genna!" he called, stopping to try to catch his breath. "Where are you?"

She didn't respond. But a moment later, Revis reappeared, running a quick circle around Parker before heading back the way he'd come. The big dog slowed and looked over his shoulder, almost as if watching to make sure Parker followed.

"Genna!" Parker called again. "June Bug!"

The little dog had stopped barking. Parker's heart sank, hoping that didn't mean something awful.

Revis appeared, standing on the trail ahead. He woofed once, likely urging Parker to hurry.

Once he'd caught up with his dog, the two of them continued together. The plateau sat ahead, the trail's sharp turn to the left, a staggering cliff face to the right. And no sign of Genna.

Then JB appeared, squeezing out from under a bush. Though she whimpered, she looked unharmed. "Where's Genna?" Parker asked then mentally scolded himself since he knew the dog couldn't answer. "Genna!" he called again.

This time, Genna responded. "Down here. Help me. I hit my head."

Parker started forward.

A figure stepped in front of him, blocking his path. Tall and almost painfully thin, the woman had long blond hair tied up in a high ponytail. She wore black leggings and expensive hiking boots that looked brand-new.

"Back away," she said, raising a pistol. "Or I'll shoot you." Revis growled and she glanced at him. "Maybe I'll shoot your dog, too. Call him off me."

Her wild eyes warred with her serious expression. Not wanting to risk Revis or JB getting hurt, he called them both. Revis came immediately, taking a seat by his side. JB barked once before disappearing into the brush. No doubt going back to Genna.

"Who are you and what do you want?" Parker asked, wondering if she was skilled with the weapon. He judged the distance, figuring if he played his cards right, he might be able to jump the woman and disarm her.

Instead of answering, she continued to stare, her grip on the pistol steady. "You have one option," she said. "Take your dogs and leave. Genna is mine to deal with. You won't be seeing her again."

"Not a chance," he replied, keeping his hands hanging loosely by his sides. "What have you done with her?"

She laughed. "She's hurt. But not hurt enough. Yet. I'm thinking she'll bleed to death. If not, the wolves will get her."

A chill snaked up his spine. "Who *are* you? And why do you want Genna dead?"

"Move," she ordered. "Go back the way you came. Now."

"No."

At his response, she slowly swung the gun away from him, pointing it at Revis. "Then I guess I'll have to shoot your dog."

Now! Parker leapt forward, sweeping his arm up and kicking the pistol from her hand. She let out an unearthly squeal of rage, snarling at him as she staggered backward.

They both dove for the gun at the same time. Since he was bigger and heavier, when they collided, Parker's momentum sent her flying. As he grabbed the pistol, she scrabbled to maintain her balance. Instead, she toppled over the edge of the embankment, screaming as she went.

Revis tried to go after her. Worried his dog would fall, Parker called the Lab to him. Carefully, the two of them walked to the edge of the incline. The woman had grabbed a large branch as she'd fallen and was hanging on for dear life. Since her feet were planted on another branch below her, Parker judged she wasn't in immediate danger of plunging any further down.

"Help me!" she called.

"After I help Genna," he shouted back.

JB barked again then popped up from the underbrush. She eyed Parker and Revis before barking a few more times, clearly trying to direct him toward Genna.

Moving carefully, Parker made his way down the slope after the dog. With all the trees and plant growth, he couldn't see Genna. Using trees and branches and roots as handholds, Parker continued making his way.

Revis remained at the top, watching him, aware this time he couldn't follow.

Finally, Parker spotted Genna. She lay on a ledge. When she saw him, she lifted her head and then winced in pain.

"I'm coming," he promised. "I need to call for help. Don't move just yet."

"Move?" Her voice sounded strangled. "I can't. My arm is broken. Maybe my leg, too. I don't know how I'm going to get out of here."

Hearing Genna's voice, little JB whimpered. She ran back and forth, a few feet from where the ground dramatically dropped off.

"Don't let her fall," Genna cried. "I couldn't live with myself if anything happened to her."

He couldn't get a cell signal, which didn't surprise him. It was one of the reasons he and his family like to unwind up here. No interruptions.

"I'm going to need to climb up higher and see if I can get a signal," he said. "First, I need to check on the woman who attacked you."

Genna didn't answer. When he looked, he realized she'd lost consciousness. Which might mean she'd been badly hurt.

Just the thought made him fight back panic. Forcing himself to move, he went to the place where Genna's assailant had fallen. No longer hanging on to a branch, she'd managed to pull herself up enough to be able to straddle it, using the limb as a kind of a seat.

"Help me," she ordered when she noticed Parker looking down at her. "Throw me a rope or something and pull me out."

"In good time," he told her. Then he turned and walked away without another word. Calling both dogs, he headed for the path that ascended the rock face, hoping once he reached the summit, he could manage to get enough of a cell signal to call for help. Revis walked with him, but JB only lay down and refused to leave Genna. Aware the smaller dog might need protection, Parker made Revis go back to stay with his little friend.

The old dog cocked his head and then trotted over to sit next to JB. "Good boy," Parker called and then continued on.

At the base of the cliff, he stopped and took a deep breath. It had been years since he'd attempted a climb like this. He couldn't fail. If he did, no one would be able to come help him or Genna, not to mention the unnamed woman who'd pushed Genna.

Forcing himself to move slowly and deliberately, he began the climb. Since there was a trail of sorts, it wasn't as if he were trying to pull himself up the rock. While the path turned incredibly narrow and he had to hug the side, technically it was still a hike, though an incredibly arduous and dangerous one.

By the time he made it halfway, Parker had to stop and wipe away perspiration. Though he'd never been afraid of heights, he knew better than to look down.

Once he'd caught his breath, he carried on. He kept seeing Genna lying on that ledge, broken and helpless. Pushing past frustration and rage, he only knew one thing. He had to help her. He couldn't lose her, not now. Not ever. And he hadn't even told her he loved her.

He clenched his jaw. Almost there. One foot over the other, keeping as close as he could to the rock, Parker kept going.

Finally, he reached the summit. Here, he could see the valley below and the other mountains. Carefully digging his phone out from his pocket, he held it up.

Still no bars.

Cursing, he turned in a slow circle and tried again. Even in remote areas, he knew he could call or text 9-1-1. The call would be picked up by the closest cell tower.

He tried dialing first. The call immediately dropped. Since he had nothing to lose, he sent a quick text.

Help. We are camping up on the trail near Crowder's Meadow and need help. Someone has fallen and is injured.

Once he'd sent it, he waited. And waited. Usually, the screen said "Delivered" once a text had been received. It did not this time.

A moment later, he got a red error message, letting him know his phone had been unable to send his text.

Damn it.

He tried several times to make the call. It wouldn't go through.

On the western side of the cleared area, there were several huge boulders, larger than his truck. He'd never tried to climb them and, truthfully, didn't have the equipment. Even if he managed to make it up onto one, he didn't know if doing so would even give him a signal.

Still, he had to try.

Making a quick circle around the nearest rock, he saw no way to scale it. The second one looked better. There were several trees close to it. Some of the branches even brushed against to the stone. Since time was of the essence, he didn't waste it. He climbed up one of the trees; high enough and close enough to the top of the rock. From there, he could see several flat surfaces that he could stand on, if he could just manage to get there.

Now or never.

Hoping that the branch didn't break, he grasped it and swung out over the boulder. As soon as his feet touched stone, he let go.

For a second, he remained crouched, stunned that he'd made it. Then he stood and took out his phone.

This had to work. It had to. Otherwise, he'd have to hike back to his truck at the trailhead parking area. He'd definitely have a signal there.

Lifting his phone, his heart stuttered when he saw two bars. Not a strong signal, but should be enough to call 9-1-1.

Just then, his phone rang. Eli.

Parker answered, talking without giving his brother a chance to speak. "We're at the remote campsite, Genna's

badly hurt. I need you to get some help up here. We'll need a medevac copter to get her down. And her stalker's here also."

"Parker?" Eli asked, his voice fading in and out. "You're breaking up. Did you say Genna's hurt?"

Repeating what he'd just said, Parker asked Eli if he understood. But Eli didn't answer. That's when Parker realized he'd lost the signal.

He tried again and again, but couldn't get his phone to work. Texts weren't delivered and no calls, even to 9-1-1, would go through. He had to hope Eli had understood. But in case he hadn't, Parker knew he'd need to come up with an alternative plan.

WHEN GENNA CAME to for the second time, it took a moment for her to realize what had happened. She managed to sit up, ignoring the searing pain in her arm and leg. If she could get to her feet, she honestly thought she might be able to climb back up to level ground. But when she tried, she realized her leg wouldn't support her weight. Definitely broken. Between that and her arm, going anywhere would be impossible. At least Parker had found her. She had to hope he'd been able to get a cell phone signal and call for help.

If he couldn't, she knew the only other choice would be for him to hike down to his truck and either try to call from there, or drive to town. By then, darkness would have fallen. While her location would likely protect her from predators, she hated the thought of spending an entire night trapped on this ledge and in pain.

But she also knew she'd do whatever she had to, to stay alive. At least she knew Parker would make sure June Bug and Revis were safe.

At that moment she realized she had no idea what had happened to Ann. Seeing her ex-best friend and ex-hus-

band's new wife way out here, she'd finally understood that it had been Ann—and likely with Chad's help—stalking her all along. Why and how, she didn't know, since Shelby was so far away from Anchorage.

Clearly, Ann had decided that simple harassment was no longer enough. She'd decided to push Genna off a cliff and end her life. Even worse, since Ann hadn't succeeded, if she were still out there in the woods somewhere, she might decide to come back and finish the job.

Not knowing made Genna's entire situation worse. Except, as she looked up the steep slope, she knew Ann couldn't get down to her ledge without risking serious injury. For now, she'd be safe. From both Ann and any other predators.

Genna dozed, drifting in and out of consciousness. Her head hurt, which meant she'd likely hit it when she'd fallen. Likely a concussion, she thought.

JB's insistent barking made her open her eyes. She had no idea how much time had passed, if it had been minutes or hours.

"Genna," Parker called. "How are you doing?"

"I'm okay," she managed to respond, though her voice sounded weaker than she would have liked. Clearing her throat, she tried again. "Please make sure my dog doesn't fall down the cliff."

"She won't," he promised. "She and Revis are sticking pretty close to my side. I think I got through to Eli. The call kept breaking up, but I'm hoping he understood enough to realize he needs to send help."

"What about Ann?" she asked. "The woman who pushed me."

"She's still trapped," he replied. "She fell, too, but landed on top of a large tree. She's straddling the branch and as

long as she doesn't move, she'll be safe there until we can pull her out and arrest her."

"Okay." Again she struggled to sit up, wincing at the pain. Not only her arm, leg and head, but her entire body felt bruised and battered. "But what if Eli didn't hear you? How will you know?"

"I thought about that," he said. "That's why I'm hiking down to the parking lot now. I should have signal there and I can find out if help is on the way."

"Sounds good," she rasped. She really wanted to beg him to promise not to leave her alone in the dark. Instead, she swallowed hard and told him to be careful.

Once he'd gone, Genna slowly slid back down to lie flat on her back and close her eyes. She had to believe this would all work out. Luckily, the temperature had stayed mild, even at night. And despite some cuts and scrapes, she wasn't bleeding a lot. She didn't think her other injuries were life threatening, and she would likely survive even an overnight stay.

She just wanted to be somewhere else—anywhere else— other than stuck on a rock on a cliff in the Alaskan wilderness.

Time passed. How long, she had no idea. She slept some, woke in fitful starts, and drifted back off again.

When she finally heard Parker calling her name, for a dazed moment she thought she must be dreaming. But then JB barked and so did Revis.

"A chopper is on the way," Parker told her. "They're sending a team to rescue you. Is there enough room for a stretcher to fit on that ledge?"

Blinking, she looked around her. The stone outcropping that had broken her fall was large. "Easily," she replied. She'd seen enough television shows to realize they'd lower

a couple of EMTs and a stretcher to her and then lift her out via helicopter. While she wasn't really fond of that plan, she also understood she had no choice.

More time passed and she struggled to stay awake. Parker kept up a steady stream of conversation, no doubt trying to cheer her up. She tried to make occasional responses, but the drowsiness dragged her back under.

The whomp-whomp sound of a helicopter roused her. Instinctively she sat up, way too fast, which brought blinding pain. She groaned. Above her, JB started barking again. Parker tried to shush her.

"Help is on the way," he said. "Just stay still and let them rescue you."

"I will," she promised. "But please keep the dogs safe."

"They're with me. And they'll stay with me until the police arrive and take Ann into custody."

Then it would finally be over. Tears stung her eyes. She wiped them away before stealing herself for the ordeal yet to come.

In retrospect, her rescue from the side of the mountain seemed like something out of a movie or a television drama. The chopper, the EMTs landing on the ledge, carefully checking her out—it all seemed to be happening to another person. Later, there were a few times she wondered if she'd dreamt it.

But there were a couple of things she remembered quite well.

The paramedic, or doctor, speaking quietly to her, with a patient smile. She'd found his positivity encouraging, which was exactly what she'd needed. She regretted that she'd never gotten his name. Even as she'd struggled to remain awake, she had felt herself slipping away.

"She's in shock," he'd said, speaking to someone else be-

fore lightly touching her arm. "Genna, I need you to try and focus, just for a little bit longer. We're going to need your help if we're going to get you out of here, okay?"

She'd nodded, immediately wincing at the pain. A stretcher had somehow materialized, no doubt let down by the hovering chopper. Carefully, she'd tried to lift herself up so her rescuer could slide it underneath her. The entire time, she'd had to bite her lip to avoid crying out, mainly because she'd known Parker would hear and she hadn't wanted him to worry.

The EMT had strapped her in. Heart pounding, she'd stared at him with wide eyes, dreading the moment when the chopper lifted her into the air.

"Don't worry, we've got you," her rescuer had told her and then given the signal.

Her stretcher had lifted, sending her airborne. Though she'd known the straps holding her in were secured, she'd gripped the sides so tightly her hands had ached. She'd wished fervently that she could black out, because knowing she was suspended by a rope several hundred feet in the air had terrified her.

At some point, she must have lost consciousness, because the next time she'd opened her eyes, she was in the back of an ambulance and on her way to the ER.

Once there, she'd been poked and prodded. X-rays had been taken, her injuries deemed not life-threatening, and she'd been given a small room. A kind nurse had placed her on an IV. "The fluids will make you feel better," she'd said. "A doctor will be in to see you shortly."

Genna waited, but no one came. She figured all the ER doctors were busy with genuine emergencies and would get to her when they could. Since she no longer had her phone

and had no idea what had happened to it, she closed her eyes and tried to rest.

But with all the sounds and the machines and the way-too-bright lights, she couldn't.

When Parker walked into the room, she let out a glad cry. "You made it back," she said, unable to hide her relief.

"Yes." His smile warmed her to the core. He lifted up a cloth grocery bag. "I brought you some clothes since yours were likely cut off of you. And before you ask, Revis and JB are fine. I took them home and fed them."

She couldn't look away. "What about Ann?"

"They lowered a rope and helped her get up. Once she was out, she was arrested. I told them that you definitely wanted to press charges."

"I do." Swallowing, she reached for her water and took a sip. "And did they also arrest Chad? I'm reasonably sure she didn't travel all this way alone."

"Your ex?" Parker frowned. "I think Eli contacted him to let him know about his wife, but I'll find out."

"Thanks."

He came closer and sat down in a metal chair next to her bed. "What about you? Are they getting you all fixed up so we can get you out of here and back home?"

Home. For no good reason, she once again found herself blinking back tears. "They said I'll get a cast for my arm, a splint or boot for my leg, and they're referring me to an orthopedic specialist. I'm not sure when all that is supposed to happen, but hopefully soon. And they think I have a concussion. They gave me something for my headache and said to follow up with my regular doctor within seventy-two hours."

Taking her hand, he leaned over and kissed her cheek.

"I'm glad you're all right. I have to tell you, there was a moment when I really thought we'd lost you."

Openly crying, she reached for the tissue box with her free hand and blotted at her eyes. "I never even saw her. One minute, I'm walking June Bug, and then Ann came out of nowhere and shoved me off the side of the mountain."

"Your little dog's barking is what alerted me," Parker said. "After this, I'm guessing you'll never want to go hiking or camping again."

Almost against her will, she laughed, even though it made her head hurt. "Not for a long time, that's for sure." She thought about it for a second and then amended her statement. "If ever, that is."

The doctor and a nurse came in then.

Letting go of her hand, Parker got up from the chair and moved out of their way.

Before long, she had a cast on her arm and a clunky walking boot on her leg.

"It looks like just your ankle is broken," the doctor said cheerfully, pushing her glasses up on her nose. "Hopefully, the boot will take care of it and you won't need to have surgery. I'll have my nurse discharge you. Once that's done, someone will bring a wheelchair around to get you out to your car. Then you can go home and get some rest."

Genna thanked her.

Once the doctor left, the nurse went over the discharge instructions. Basically, Genna needed to keep the cast dry. They'd send a referral and an orthopedic specialist's office would be contacting her.

"Here are your discharge papers," the nurse said. "I just need your signature in a few places, and then you'll be free to go."

Accepting the clipboard with her good arm, Genna signed where directed and then passed it back to the nurse.

"These are your copies," the smiling woman said. "You have a nice rest of your day."

After the nurse left, Genna looked up to find Parker watching her. He had a peculiar expression on is handsome face.

Alarmed, she touched his hand. "What is it? What's wrong?"

Leaning in, he brushed her mouth with his. "I'm just awfully glad you weren't seriously hurt," he murmured, lips against hers.

Her heart skipped a beat. Though he clearly was trying to be careful, she kissed him back with all of the pent-up passion she had inside.

For an instant, he allowed the familiar fire to ignite. But then he quickly pulled back. Breathing heavily, he got to his feet and dragged his hand through his hair. "You need to rest and heal," he said, his voice raspy. "We shouldn't be doing that."

"I want to do all that and more," she murmured, watching his gaze darken. Then, just as she opened her mouth to tell Parker how much she loved him, her ex-husband walked into the room.

Chapter Sixteen

When Genna paled, as if all the blood had drained from her face, Parker turned to call for the nurse. Instead, when he saw the tall, broad-shouldered man standing just inside the doorway, he realized that was the cause for Genna's distress.

Short dark hair in a military cut, hard brown eyes and an aggressive stance, the stranger glared at Parker before directing his gaze to Genna.

Acting on instinct, Parker moved to place himself between the intruder and Genna.

"Who are you and what do you want?" Parker demanded.

Jaw tight, the stranger took another step into the room. "I might ask you the same question. Please leave. I need to talk to my wife alone."

"Ex-wife, Chad," Genna corrected. "Parker, please stay. I don't want to be alone with him." She took a deep breath. "In fact, call security."

"No need," Chad quickly responded. "Ann called me and asked me to bail her out. She told me everything she's done, including trying to kill you. I just wanted to let you know that I had nothing to do with her actions. Ever since I left her for Claudia, Ann has been unhinged. Claudia even had to take out a restraining order on her."

"So did I," Genna reminded him, her voice and expression tired. "You've said your piece. Now please leave."

Jaw working, Chad simply stared, unmoving. "You look terrible," he mused. "Small-town life obviously hasn't been good for you."

"She asked you to go," Parker said, keeping his tone level. "It's time for you to do that."

For one split second, he thought the other man would refuse. But then Chad shook his head, muttered something unintelligible under his breath and stalked off.

"Whew," Genna exhaled. "I'm just glad he didn't start any trouble."

"Me, too." Dropping back into the chair next to her bed, Parker glanced at the doorway. "Do you believe him when he says he had nothing to do with Ann harassing you?"

"I'm not sure. I know right after they got together, he was pretty invested in tormenting me. But it's been a year. I had no idea it was her." Genna shifted restlessly. "She traveled all the way to Shelby just to continue hounding me."

"I'm surprised she didn't move on to the new woman," Parker said.

"Me, too. That would make a lot more sense than her continuing to stalk me. I've moved on. I would have thought Ann would, too." She sighed again. "Well, now that I've been discharged, I'd like to get dressed and get out of here."

Parker handed her the bag of her clothes that he'd grabbed at the house. After pulling the curtain around the bed, he stood guard while she dressed.

"All done," she said.

He pulled open the curtain. "Still no wheelchair. Let me go see if I can find one for you."

"I don't really need it," she protested. "A pair of crutches would help just fine."

Just then an orderly arrived, pushing a shiny-black wheel-chair. "Are you ready to go home?" he asked, his cheerful voice matching his smile. He helped Genna into the chair before turning to Parker. "Go ahead and pull your vehicle around to the side entrance and I'll bring her out."

Finally, with Genna buckled carefully into the passenger side, Parker headed home. Since he didn't have a wheelchair, he stopped at a drugstore on the way and purchased an in-expensive portable one. After he'd loaded it into the rear of his truck and got back in, Genna shook her head.

"I plan on using crutches," she said. "I have some in the garage at my parents' house. I think you can return the chair. I don't need it."

"Crutches will be impossible to handle with a broken arm," he pointed out. "You can't hold on."

She stared at him for a few seconds. "I didn't even think about that. I guess I don't have a choice but to use the chair."

Since he was driving, he couldn't give in to impulse and kiss her. He promised himself he'd make up for that once they got home.

After pulling up in front of the house, he asked Genna to wait in the truck while he got her chair. Though she nodded, her grimace told him she was unhappy with the situation. Opening her door, he bowed low.

"Your throne awaits, my lady," he said in his best Brit-ish accent.

Though she shook her head, her frown turned into a smile. When he gently lifted her out of the truck and into the wheelchair, she clung to him a millisecond too long. Which he didn't mind at all.

Then he pushed her through the garage and into the house.

Once inside, both Revis and JB greeted her, tails wag-

ging. She spent time with them both, crooning endearments. JB appeared beside herself and, after Genna invited her, the tiny dog jumped into her lap and snuggled into Genna. "She thought I was going to die," Genna said, her eyes shiny. "She didn't leave my side."

"She's a good girl," Parker replied. "Her barking is what alerted me to the possibility that there was some kind of trouble."

She nodded. "I'm just glad all that's over and Ann is in police custody."

"Me, too." He pushed her over toward the couch. "Do you want to lie here or should I take you into your bedroom?"

"Neither." She hesitated. "I have another favor to ask. I really need to take a shower. I don't feel clean. Will you help me?"

Due to her condition, he tried like hell not to imagine her naked, water sluicing down her body. But the sensual images wouldn't stop and his body immediately reacted.

"I'll help you," he offered. "I know you have to keep that cast dry."

"And my foot, too," she said. "They wrapped my ankle inside this boot. I'll need you to help me wrap both of those in plastic."

"Are you hurting at all?" he asked.

"No." She didn't even have to think about it. "I'm guessing whatever pain medication they gave me at the hospital is still working, because I feel fine."

Luckily, the main shower had a place where she could sit. He pushed her wheelchair inside and carefully helped her to undress.

Then he wrapped her arm, using several plastic bags and a rubber band, hoping like hell he didn't inadvertently hurt

her. Moving on to the foot, he knelt in front of her wheel-chair and carefully undid the Velcro straps.

After he wrapped her foot so the bandage wouldn't get wet, he helped her from the chair to the shower ledge. He then turned on the water, waiting until the temperature seemed perfect before turning the showerhead on her. He placed a couple of towels nearby, within easy reach, and then beat a fast exit.

"Call me if you need anything or when you're done," he said, closing the door behind him.

Though he suspected there was no way she could have missed his arousal, he hoped she understood that he'd never do anything that could hurt her. She'd been through a lot. And he'd do whatever it took to make sure she healed. Including resisting his ever-present desire for her.

Waiting for her to finish her shower, he finally admitted how terrified he'd been at the prospect of losing her. Seeing her lying on that ledge on the side of the mountain, unable to discern the extent of her injuries, the thought of losing her had nearly brought him to his knees.

Even now, with her hurt and needing to heal, he couldn't bear the concept of inadvertently doing something wrong.

He heard the water turn off. Though he tried not to, he pictured her toweling herself off. He kind of wished she'd asked him to help her, even though he knew doing so would only make him rock-hard again.

"Parker?"

Blinking, he shook off his thoughts and went to help her get dressed. She'd asked for a soft T-shirt and a pair of terry-cloth shorts, telling him they were her version of pajamas.

A short time later, Eli arrived at the house, bearing gifts. "A pizza from Pizza World," he said, handing the box to Parker. "And a decent bottle of red wine to go with it."

"Thanks." Ushering his brother in, Parker led the way to the living room, where Genna, JB and Revis were all snuggled on the couch. Though both dogs looked up at the intruder, they must have decided Eli was safe because they laid their heads back down on Genna.

"I brought you food," Eli announced, gesturing toward the pizza box in Parker's arms. "Hopefully, it'll make up for whatever crap they fed you in the hospital."

"Thank you." Genna smiled. "Any news? Did Ann bond out?"

"Not yet. She kept saying her husband would be coming to rescue her, but the dude never showed. Now she's demanding to talk to you."

"Me?" Recoiling, Genna looked at Parker. He shrugged.

"I'm sorry," Eli said. "I have no idea what she wants to say, but apparently there's something she needs to get off of her chest."

"I don't think I care to hear it."

"I don't blame you." Eli looked at Parker. "She tried to kill you after all."

"She probably wants to try and talk you into dropping charges," Parker interjected.

"That's not going to happen." Eyeing the pizza box, which Parker still held, she gestured. "I'd really like to have some of that. Would you mind grabbing some paper plates so we can eat?"

Both dogs perked up at her words.

"Not for you," she scolded, half laughing.

"I brought wine, too," Eli pointed out.

"Thanks, but I'm not sure I can drink with all these pain meds."

Eli shook his head. "Sorry, I didn't think. Well, just save the bottle for later."

Parker went into the kitchen and returned with plates and napkins. Eli set the pizza box down in the middle of the coffee table and opened it. "I just got basic pepperoni," he said. "And a large, in case you both are hungry. I hope that's okay."

Parker's stomach rumbled, reminding him he hadn't eaten in a long while. "That's perfect," he said.

"That smells so good!" Sitting up, Genna shooed the dogs away. Making an appreciative sound, she grabbed a couple of slices, looking up at both men. "Don't be shy. Help yourself," she said, licking her fingers. "Thanks for getting this, Eli."

Parker grabbed a few slices and Eli did the same. They all ate, sitting around the living room, with the two dogs watching intently. Both men took seconds, though Genna declined.

"That was wonderful," Genna said, covering her mouth as she yawned. "And now I'm going to close my eyes for a bit. Please don't mind me. I just really need to rest."

"I'd better be going." Eli stood. He grabbed the empty pizza box while Parker gathered up their plates. Together, they carried everything into the kitchen.

"I'll walk you out." Moving quietly so not to disturb Genna, Parker led the way to the front door.

Outside, Eli stopped on the front porch. "How's she doing mentally?" he asked, his gaze searching Parker's face. "This is a lot for anyone to deal with."

"She still seems to be processing it all," Parker replied. "I've been awfully worried about her." He shook his head. "To think it was Ann all along. Genna really thought moving five hours away had put an end to the harassment."

"Normally, it would, at least under normal circumstances.

However, that woman has been talking up a storm." Eli grimaced. "We're going to have to ask for a psych evaluation."

"I imagine. Her ex, Chad, stopped by at the hospital."

Eli went very still. "How did he know he'd find her there?"

"Good question. I have no idea." Parker thought for a moment. "Are you thinking he was with Ann when all this went down?"

"Now I am. Because otherwise, wouldn't he be back in Anchorage?"

"True. But when he visited Genna, he told her that he'd left Ann for another woman." Parker shook his head. "Which seems about right, considering what Genna has said about him."

"Did he now?" Eli asked. "Because Ann is somehow convinced that Chad and Genna got back together. She claims he told her so. When he left her, she decided to make Genna's life a living hell. In the end, she decided to kill Genna. In Ann's mind, that would make Chad go back to her."

"Wow." Unsure how to react to this, Parker finally shook his head. "Are you going to bring him in for questioning?"

"If we can find him, yes. I've had people looking for him since Ann was arrested."

"He told Genna his new girlfriend's name is Claudia," Parker said. "He claims this Claudia had to take out a restraining order on Ann. Maybe that will help you find him."

"If it's the truth and not some BS he made up, it definitely will help. I'll have Kansas look into it. Since she was very upset when she heard about Genna being attacked, she asked to be assigned to this case in addition to her Search and Rescue work."

"Once again, you two have proved it's good to have fam-

ily in law enforcement," Parker said, his voice breaking. "I appreciate all your help with all of this."

Eli eyed him, expression concerned. "Are you okay?"

"I am," Parker replied. "It's just been a long day. Genna and I went camping to get away from all the stress, and drama still found us. I don't know that she'll ever want to hike or camp again. Which really would be a shame, considering how much I love both of those things."

"And her?" Eli asked quietly. "Do you love her?"

Parker almost didn't answer. How could he confess his feelings to his brother before he'd even discussed them with Genna? But he knew Eli cared, and since Parker planned to talk to Genna as soon as possible, he didn't see any harm.

"I do love her," he admitted. "I have since the moment we first reconnected a year ago."

Eli's eyes widened. "That long?"

"That long."

"Does Genna know?" Eli asked.

"Not yet." Parker took a deep breath, about to admit his greatest fear. "I'm not sure she's ready for any kind of committed relationship, to be honest. I really don't want to screw things up."

"I get that." Eli nodded. "But I think she's more into you than you realize. Haven't you noticed the way she looks at you?"

With that, his brother walked away, climbed into his vehicle and drove off.

Parker stared after him, a hope so strong it hurt blooming inside his chest.

AFTER EATING THE pizza and deciding to take a short nap, Genna slept so deeply that when she woke up in bed, she had no recollection of how she'd gotten there. She still wore

the same T-shirt and shorts that doubled as pajamas. Her new boot had even been removed, though placed within easy reach.

Since her wheelchair had been pushed next to her, turned just the right way to make getting into it easier, she realized Parker had either carried her to her bed or put her in the wheelchair to get her there. What she didn't understand was how he'd done all this without waking her up.

Her ankle throbbed, letting her know she'd need to take something to help with that.

"Are you ready for some coffee?" Parker appeared in her doorway, steaming mug in hand. He set it down on her nightstand and smiled at her. "I hope you feel well rested. You must have really needed your sleep."

"I do." Sitting up, she stretched, wincing slightly. "Let me get this boot back on and then, if you don't mind, I could use some help getting back into my chair."

After she swung her legs over the side of the bed, Parker knelt and helped her guide her foot into the clunky boot. She tried to close it up herself, but like just about everything else, it proved impossible to do with only one hand.

Once Parker had helped her with that, he carefully assisted her shift from the bed into the wheelchair. Handing her the coffee he'd brought, he pushed her into the living room. On the way there, she told him she wanted to use the bathroom, and also wash up and brush her teeth. Despite knowing she'd probably need it, she declined his help and insisted she could do it all herself.

And she did, though none of it was easy. Finally back in her chair, she called for him to open the door.

"You're doing great," he said, pushing her into the living room. "When do you see the specialist?"

"I think they're supposed to call me today."

"As soon as you have an appointment, let me know. I'll get you there. And if I happen to be working, someone else in the family will drive you."

She smiled. "Thanks. I hate to be a bother, but I really appreciate all the help."

Parker got her all set up on the couch with her coffee. He brought her breakfast, sat with her while she ate, and then took the plate away. He made sure she had snacks, some bottled water, the remote, a book, and anything else she could possibly need, before telling her he had to head to work.

"I'd rather go in with you," Genna protested. "I can do my job sitting down."

"Not until you see the specialist and you're cleared," he said, lightly kissing her cheek. There'd been a lot of that cheek kissing lately and she wasn't sure why. She considered turning her head so his mouth connected with hers, but didn't. If he didn't want to give her a real kiss, she wasn't going to force him.

"Hetty is going to fill in for a couple of days," Parker continued. "I've got a couple of tours today, but if you need anything, just call the office. If I'm not in, someone else will make sure to get you taken care of."

With that, he smiled, waved and disappeared out the door. As she listened to the sound of his truck starting and driving away, she tried not to feel depressed. It wasn't easy.

For most of her life, Genna had never been one to sit around and do nothing. But having her ankle in the boot with orders to keep all weight off of it, and her arm in a cast, had severely limited her mobility. She knew she should count her blessings and be glad she had Parker and wasn't dealing with this on her own, but she couldn't seem to get there yet. Maybe she just needed to indulge herself and have a little pity party before she could get back to feeling semi normal.

It didn't help that she kept obsessing about revealing her feelings for Parker to him. She wasn't sure of the timing, or even if she should. Sometimes she thought maybe it was the kind of secret she should keep inside and take with her to her grave.

To occupy and distract herself, she tried watching TV, but found every show she tried annoying. Sitcom, drama, news or documentary—it didn't matter. Finally, she turned it off and decided to try her book.

A few weeks ago, she'd purchased a popular new thriller with every intention of reading it. As of yet, she hadn't even cracked open the cover. Parker had seen it on her nightstand and placed it near her on the coffee table just in case.

She read a few chapters, got sleepy and took another short nap. Her new capacity for sleep amazed her, but she also knew a lot of rest would help her body to heal.

Lakin stopped by shortly before noon. She's knocked a couple times before letting herself in with a key. "Parker gave me his key and asked me to check on you," she said, smiling. "He said you might have difficulty navigating the wheelchair around the kitchen, so I brought you something to eat."

She held up a white paper bag. "Burger and fries," she said. "Not the healthiest thing, I know. I actually almost got you a salad, but then I thought about how much it would suck to have a broken ankle and arm, so I went with this instead."

Accepting the bag gratefully, Genna laughed. "Thank you. I really appreciate this." She peered inside, saw only one wrapped burger and container of fries, and frowned. "Are you not eating?"

"Not that!" Lakin rolled her eyes. "I just had a protein smoothie, so I'm not hungry. But I can keep you company while you eat, if that's okay?"

"I'd like that." She thought for a moment. "Would you also mind letting June Bug out? Parker took Revis to RTA with him, so I just have her."

"I can definitely do that," Lakin said. "I imagine it's a bit difficult navigating things in that wheelchair with only one usable arm." She called the little dog. JB appeared uncertain, but when Genna assured her it was all right, she trotted out after Lakin.

Once she was alone, Genna sagged in her chair, a wave of exhaustion washing over her. Her stomach growled, reminding her she needed to eat to keep her strength up. And the burger smelled mouthwatering. She unwrapped it and took a tiny bite, and then another. She didn't want to eat the entire thing while Lakin was out back.

A moment later, both Lakin and June Bug returned. "She was a good girl," Lakin said, smiling. "What a special little dog you've got there."

This compliment made Genna grin. "Thanks. I love her."

"She loves you, too, I can tell." She gestured at the unwrapped burger. "Does it taste all right? It doesn't look like you've eaten much of it."

"It's delicious," Genna replied. "I've been trying to wait until you came back."

"No need. Go for it."

Lakin chatted about her hotel renovations while Genna practically inhaled her burger. "This is so good," she said, trying not to talk with her mouth full. "Thank you for bringing it. First, Eli got us pizza, and now you…"

"I talked to Eli this morning," Lakin said. "It seems they brought your ex-husband in for questioning. Kansas is handling the case."

Genna went still. "Chad? They think Chad had something to do with this." Then, without waiting for a response, she

shook her head. "I knew it. When he showed up at my hospital room, I wondered how he'd gotten there so quickly. And how he'd known that I'd been injured. He must have been there with Ann in the woods, waiting for me."

Patting Genna's hand, Lakin grimaced. "I'm sorry all that happened to you. What an awful lot to have to go through."

"Thanks. I don't know how I would have made it without Parker's help. He's been amazing."

Lakin's gaze sharpened. "He might be my brother, but I agree. He's pretty special." She gave Genna a thoughtful look. "I take it you two are getting along pretty well?"

"We are." Genna could have elaborated but didn't want to open the door to questions about the two of them and their relationship. Not yet. Especially since Parker had no idea how she felt about him.

Luckily, Lakin didn't press. "I should be going," she said. "But I wanted to make sure you were doing okay. Please, and I mean this, call me if you need anything. Anything at all."

"Thanks." Genna smiled. One thing about the Coltons, once they decided they liked you, they had your back. No matter what.

After Lakin left, Genna stretched out on the couch to nap again. She couldn't seem to get enough sleep. Why not embrace it?

Some time later, her phone rang. Sitting up, she rubbed her eyes and squinted at the screen. Caller ID showed it was Kansas.

"I have news," Kansas declared. "And I wanted you to be the first to know. We've arrested Chad, too. He's being charged as an accessory to murder. Ann admitted he was there with her. She seemed rather proud of that, claiming it proved he loved her the most since he wanted you dead."

Genna shuddered. "But why? That's what I don't under-

stand. I moved away. Got out of their lives. What did I ever do to make them hate me so much?"

"We're trying to get to the bottom of that now and establish motive. Ann claims that Chad never stopped talking about you and comparing Ann to you. Apparently, that was one of the numerous things that sent her over the edge, though between you and me, she was already there."

"I'll say," Genna replied. "Chad was a serial philanderer. He left me for Ann, someone I thought was my best friend. And then he claimed he left her for another woman."

"Claudia. That's the name he keeps saying, but he can't provide any specifics. I'm beginning to wonder if he made her up." Kansas paused. "We'll get this all sorted out. But I thought you'd want to know that they're both in custody."

"For how long?"

"Well, once the judge sets bail, they'll have to stay here until they can make it. Attempted murder usually carries a pretty high dollar amount. And then they need to find someone to pay their bond. Do they have family around here?"

"Ann's family is pretty wealthy," Genna said. "They've been really good about getting her out of trouble in the past. Who knows though? They might have finally reached their limit."

"You never know." After asking Genna if she needed anything, Kansas said she had to go.

Parker swept in around five, bringing takeout. Apparently, the Coltons believed a good meal went a long way to fixing what ailed a person.

"Chinese," he said, holding up a large paper bag. "I got us a little of everything."

Revis pranced over to JB and sniffed her before coming to greet Genna. Parker took the food into the kitchen. When he returned, he leaned against the wall. "How was

your day?" he asked. "Kansas told me both Ann and Chad have been charged."

"Yes and they're in custody. So at least I don't have to worry about them for a while."

"I know." His smile widened. "Kansas thinks their bond will be set really high. At least there's that."

Watching him, for the first time she realized how powerful he appeared. Despite his broad shoulders and muscular arms, he never made a show of his physical strength. This, combined with his chiseled features and bright blue eyes, made him one of the most appealing men she'd ever met.

But she found the tender gentleness with which he treated her sexier.

Before she let desire take hold of her again, she wanted to get everything straight. "We need to talk," she declared. Parker stared at her, the expression on his handsome face going from relaxed to wary.

"I'm not sure I like the sound of that," he said. Then, before she could say another word, he continued. "Listen, I understand how you might feel it's safe for you to go back home now that your stalkers are locked up. I get it and I agree. Except I really think you ought to consider staying here just a little bit longer."

Stung, she swallowed. "Why?"

"Because you need to heal." He came closer. "Let me help you with that. I'd like to take care of you."

She pretended to consider. "But you have to work. What's the difference if I'm alone over here or alone at my parents' house?"

"You don't want to stay?"

Since she couldn't tell if he minded or not, she countered with her own question. "Do you really want me to?"

"Of course," he answered without the slightest hesitation.

"But only because you think I need to be here until I get better?"

"Do you want the truth?" he asked, dropping down on the couch next to her wheelchair.

Though she suspected it might hurt, she turned her chair around to face him and answered in the affirmative.

"I know you've been through a lot," he said. "And I'm aware you're not looking for anything serious. But I kind of like having you around."

She suppressed a smile. "Kind of? I'm touched."

Clearly frustrated, he dragged his hand through his hair. "Damn it, Genna. I don't want to scare you away."

Not sure how to respond to that, she simply waited.

"Do you think you might want to extend this living together thing?" he asked, his casual voice at odds with the intensity in his gaze. "No pressure. Just hanging out with each other and seeing where this might go?"

Looking up at him from her wheelchair, she wasn't sure whether she wanted to laugh or to cry. While she'd been fully prepared to tell him how she felt about him, now she'd begun to realize she might have been premature. Her heart ached and she could barely swallow past the lump in her throat, but she had to know the truth. If he only wanted to continue the "friends with benefits" situation they had going, this would crush her. Because she wanted more.

And if he didn't, it was definitely time to move on.

"Why?" she asked. "I need you to be honest with me."

Instead of answering, he leaned over and kissed her. Not on the cheek this time, but full on the lips. As always, his kiss made her melt.

When he finally stopped, she could easily have dissolved into a puddle.

"Is that enough of a reason?" he asked, smiling slightly.

"No. We have great chemistry together, as you're fully aware." She smiled back, hating that she already felt as if her heart were breaking. Bracing herself, she continued. "But what if I want more?"

"Do you?" His expression sharpened, a warm glow making his eyes appear even more blue. "Want more? Because I do, too. I've been afraid to ask you, thinking I might scare you away."

She lifted her chin. "I'm not afraid. Not of you. Never of you."

Taking a deep breath, she decided the time had come to tell him the truth. "I think I'm falling in love with you, Parker Colton. Actually, I know I am. I love you."

Keeping her gaze locked on his, she wished she could have taken a step forward. "There, I've said it. I love you."

Heart pounding, she waited for him to respond.

He could have done several things. Walked away. Kissed her again. Or returned her declaration of love.

Instead, he only bowed his head and took several deep, shuddering breaths.

She sat frozen, unsure of what to say or what to do next. The urge to flee was strong, but since she couldn't, she stiffened her spine and tried to brace herself for whatever Parker would say. No matter how much it might hurt, she refused to regret giving him her truth.

Finally, he raised his head. Were those *tears* she saw shining in his amazing blue eyes? But then he smiled, his face so full of joy that her heart began to sing.

"I've loved you from the first moment I saw you," he said. "That night a year or so ago when we met in that bar. I kicked myself for losing your number. And then you moved back."

Moving closer, he knelt down beside her chair and cupped

her face with his hands. "And in the time since, working with you, living with you, I've gotten to know you. My feelings have only deepened."

He kissed her, a slow and sensual movement of his lips over hers. Blissful, she let herself lean into the sensations—warmth, desire and love.

When they finally broke apart, he rested his forehead against hers. "I've been wanting to tell you how I felt for a long time. But I wasn't sure you were ready to hear me, especially considering everything you were going through."

"I might not have been," she admitted. "It took me a while to see that you're the best thing that's ever happened to me."

"The best thing?" he asked, one brow arched. "What about June Bug?"

As if on cue, the little dog barked in agreement.

They both laughed.

"We're quite the little family now," Genna mused.

"Yes we are," he agreed.

And then he kissed her again.

* * * * *

COMING SOON!

We really hope you enjoyed reading this book.
If you're looking for more romance
be sure to head to the shops when
new books are available on

Thursday 20th November

To see which titles are coming soon, please visit
millsandboon.co.uk/nextmonth

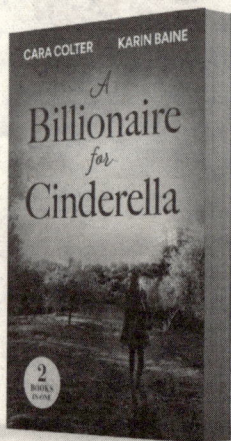

LET'S TALK
Romance

For exclusive extracts, competitions and special offers, find us online:

f MillsandBoon

X @MillsandBoon

◎ @MillsandBoonUK

♪ @MillsandBoonUK

Get in touch on 01413 063 232